Praise for

Portals

4.5 out of 5!...this new Portals series promises to be an exciting one...The plot is very imaginative and well thought out with plenty of twists and action to keep things interesting. Ms Archer's beautifully descriptive writing style makes it easy to imagine... ~ *Blackraven Reviews*

"Ethan's Freedom" is a great start to a new series... The world building is only just starting, I feel, and there will hopefully be much more to discover in the next volumes.
~ *Queer Magazine Online*

The well-written plot "Devon's Revenge" is packed with tension, action, mystery in addition to fantastic intimate scenes. The characters are psychologically true to life... Jade Archer has created an impressively enjoyable saga.
~ *Literary Nymphs Reviews*

...exciting second book "Devon's Revenge" is filled with action, mystery and exceptionally sensual lovemaking... I look forward to the next episode. ~ *Literary Nymphs Reviews*

PORTALS
Volume One

Ethan's Freedom

Devon's Revenge

JADE ARCHER

Portals Volume One
ISBN # 978-0-85715-432-3
©Copyright Jade Archer 2011
Cover Art by Posh Gosh ©Copyright 2011
Interior text design by Claire Siemaszkiewicz
Total-E-Bound Publishing

Published in 2011 by Total-E-Bound Publishing, Think Tank, Ruston Way, Lincoln, LN6 7FL, United Kingdom.

Total-E-Bound Publishing is an imprint of Total-E-Ntwined Limited.

Manufactured in the USA.

ETHAN'S FREEDOM

Dedication

For AC, KD, BG, AK and XR. Because I adore each and every one of you.

Prologue

"Ethan! Ethan, come back you're going to get in trouble."

Ethan could hear his twin's urgent, slightly panicky whisper behind him as he crept forward and scanned the hall, but he chose to ignore it. This was far too good an opportunity to waste listening to his timid, obsessively obedient brother.

All around them the castle was silent and still, everyone having hurried outside to complete the chores that needed doing there before the heat of the day became intolerable. Already the pale, yellow light of Rigial's primary sun, only newly risen over the horizon, was pouring in warm and strong through the windows mounted high on the external walls. But while Ethan knew the foot-thick, strogram-insulated barrier was there to protect them from the harsh, unforgiving climate that was all part of living in a binary system, having spent a lifetime cooped up in a tiny nursery, he was desperate to see what lay beyond them.

Edging forward, he hugged the pale, rendered wall and hoped the shadows created by the overhead light would hide them from any prying eyes that had remained inside. It was fate, he assured himself, that they should find their door unlocked this morning. In just a few days they were scheduled to be moved and start the intensive training that would make them fully fledged pleasure cats. Once that happened and they were inside the harem with its constant demands and endless monitoring, there would be no hope of them ever getting out and exploring the world.

No. This was meant to be, he reassured himself. For this one brief moment, this one tiny window of time, they would be free. They would lose themselves in their exploration and forget all about the heavy, restricting mantel that was about to descend on them. He just wanted to enjoy the moment, to rejoice in a little spontaneous youthful exuberance and freedom before it was all taken away from them.

Pausing to get his bearings, he could hear the sound of his own breathing as it rushed in and out of his lungs in excited pants. It was so loud in his ears, and his lean, lanky, fifteen-year-old body vibrated with anticipation. This was going to be fantastic. The adventure of a lifetime, he promised himself. He was going to see, touch, taste and smell everything there was to discover out here in the big, wide world of the castle. No. Not just the castle, the whole grounds. Now was the moment. Quite possibly their one and only moment of freedom.

Everything looked so much brighter out here, he realised in awe. More vivid. More alive and vital. He gazed around wide-eyed at the high vaulted ceilings and the ornate stonework columns of the massive halls. He wished he could get closer to the tapestries he saw lining the walls. Their stunning colours and interesting depictions drew his eye at every turn, but he didn't quite dare to leave the shadows he was hiding in.

With sheer willpower he managed to rein himself in. But it was hard. He felt like every pore of his body was thirsty for sensation and stimulation. On the other hand, he knew if someone came along and spotted them out here they would stop them from exploring any further. They would take them back to that dreary, boring, all too familiar room he and his brother had spent their whole lives in. And that just wasn't acceptable. Not after he had seen all this. He wanted more. He needed to see everything there was to see. And he was determined that they were going to do it.

Behind him, he could hear Devon scrambling over the slippery marble floor as he struggled to catch up. Ethan smiled wickedly, his bright, emerald green eyes twinkling with mischief. He knew Devon would follow him. His twin would always follow him. He was devoted and loyal to a fault. Of course, he was just as dedicated to his brother, but sometimes Devon needed a little push.

"We are going to get in so much trouble when the Master catches us." Devon gasped as he struggled to catch his breath after his mad dash down the hall. Trepidation danced in his pale blue eyes.

"If we get caught, brother." Ethan emphasised confidently, "*If.* We'll just have to make sure we don't, that's all. Now come on, I want to see outside."

Devon groaned as Ethan moved on down the hall, but he noticed that his brother didn't turn back. Together they cautiously continued on their once in a lifetime escapade.

Thinking back, he couldn't remember ever being allowed out into the castle gardens before. They could see them from their room through the tall, lattice covered arches of their windows, but they'd never been able to truly experience them. The beautiful flowering shrubs and majestic walkways lined with careful clipped trees. The clear, trickling stream that meandered through the grounds. They called to him now, just as they always had. He wanted to climb up into one of the graceful willows that arched over the water and feel the rough bark under his palms and feet. He wanted to scent the cool breeze as it whispered over his face. He wanted to paddle in the little stream and chase the tiny silvery fish that darted through it. Then he…

"I want to go back, Ethan," Devon whined, tugging on his hand imploringly.

Ethan huffed impatiently. Sometimes his brother could be such a pain.

"Look! Go back if you want to, I won't try to stop you, but I'm going outside. If you don't want to come, fine."

He pulled his hand free irritably and quickly moved farther down the corridor, hugging the wall and hunched over to make himself as small and inconspicuous as possible. He didn't want to leave his brother behind, but he would. This adventure was just too important to him. He couldn't stop now. Not now, when he was so close to realising his dream.

At the end of the hall he came to an intersection. He wasn't sure which way would lead him out. He looked left and right uncertainly, then felt Devon slide into place beside him, pressing up against his body nervously. Forcing himself to stand up straight and squaring his shoulders confidently, he chose a direction at random. He didn't want Devon seeing his indecision, so he headed to the left and hoped his natural feline instincts would stand him in good stead.

Slowly, he moved along the corridor, feeling very exposed and vulnerable in the crisp morning light that poured in to greet them. The farther along the corridor they went, the closer Devon shadowed him. Finally, he took pity on his brother and reached back to take his hand. He would never admit, even to himself, that it gave him comfort as well.

He was just starting to relax into the thrill of it all again when he heard loud voices drifting down the corridor towards them. The echoing sound filled the hall, getting closer and closer to them with each passing second. Both of them froze in terror when they recognised their Master voice amongst the cacophony.

Ethan's eyes widened in horror while Devon began to tremble uncontrollably beside him. Ethan couldn't agree more with the sense of terror he felt rolling of his brother in waves. They couldn't be found out here by their Master. Even he had to admit that would be a bad thing. A very, very bad thing.

"Quick! Hide in here," he whispered urgently, reaching for the closest door and pulling Devon in behind him.

Closing the heavy door as quietly as possible, Ethan stared around with growing alarm at the opulent room they found themselves in. He noticed in dismay that it looked like a study.

Please, he prayed silently. *Please don't let this be the room that Master is leading his guests to.*

Bookshelves filled with heavy leather bound tomes lined the wall all the way to the ceiling. Plush carpets covered the floor. A number of very expensive ornaments, heavy wooden furniture and a huge globe of their world filled the space. It was a very impressive room, only the sheer size of it prevented it from feeling claustrophobic, but he really couldn't appreciate any of it. All he was interested in was finding a place for Devon and himself to hide.

In front of a huge bank of windows sat a solid wooden desk with various documents spread out across its surface. The centre of the room was taken up by a circle of six overstuffed wingback chairs in dark leather. None of it looked terribly promising as a hiding place, but as the voices outside got close enough to hear through the thick wooden door, he made a slit second decision and sprinted for the far chair, pulling Devon in behind him just as the door was thrown open and the noisy group entered.

Devon burrowed into his neck in terror, and Ethan felt a cold sense of dread settle in his own belly as he wrapped his arms protectively around his frightened twin.

This was bad. Closing his eyes, he held his breath and prayed to all the gods for a miracle.

"Something has to be done about these rebellions starting to crop up all over the place," their Master bellowed. "This kind of thing starts off as simply annoying, but if it's not crushed soon, word will start getting around, and they'll all start thinking they can break free of our control."

He could hear the barely controlled rage in his Master's voice as the man crossed the floor and sat down in the very chair they were cowering behind.

Ethan stifled a groan of despair. *How much worse was this going to get?* Now, Master Nevin was only inches away from them. If he found them in here, in this mood... *Not good. So not good.*

"I agree, Nevin, but we've seen this kind of thing before. Fellin was lazy. If he'd maintained tighter control of his slaves, this would never have happened. Cat shifters can be a wilful bunch. If you don't constantly let them know who's boss, you're asking for trouble. But none of us here would ever let that happen."

"Exactly, Drellin," a pompous voice added. "Fellin stopped thinking with the head on his shoulders years ago." The mage lower his voice to an excited whisper, obviously tantalised by the prospect of spreading some juicy gossip. "I heard that towards the end he was almost insensible with the madness. You know what happens when a tantric mage gives into his cravings. Apparently he was completely taken over by the need for sex. I even heard he had more than just pleasure cats in his harem to service him."

"Eww," a pinched, high-pitched female voice cried out. "That's just disgusting. I mean using pleasure cats to power our magic is one thing, but lowering yourself to be intimate with other, lesser beings. That's just unnatural."

"I heard he had over twenty-four in his harem before they rebelled and escaped," another female interrupted excitedly.

"Enough!" Master Nevin shouted angrily, quickly silencing the gossiping mages. "This incident has seriously damaged our coven's reputation in the Circle of Mages. Bad enough that they know we rely on pleasure cats to fuel our powers. If we are seen as weak and unable to control our slaves, it could completely undermine our place on the Council. I, for one, know the elemental mages would like nothing better than to take some of our power for themselves. We must be more vigilant."

"I did hear that one of the elemental mages might have lost some cat shifters recently too," the now subdued female mage offered tentatively.

"And I heard that there was a whole shipment of slaves destined for the painmancy labour camps that simply disappeared," the pompous mage supplied.

"Oh, Gods! I hate those pain freaks. They just give me the shivers," the judgmental female mage announced.

"Just think what all those abandoned cat shifters must feel like." The mage they had called Drellin laughed cruelly, and Ethan couldn't help the shiver that worked its way over his thin frame.

Unfortunately, Devon couldn't hold in a soft whimper. And that was all it took.

Instantly, their Master was on his feet and dragging them out from behind the chair. Ethan automatically shifted into his other form—a small, tabby cat, his tiny sharp claws springing defensively from the sheaths in his paws as he yowled in fear.

Master Nevin simply lifted him up by the scruff of his neck and shook him.

Ethan was really too old to be picked up in this way, and it hurt terribly as his almost full grown weight hung from his Master's tight fisted grip. He stilled instantly, instinct telling him to be completely submissive in this position.

At Master Nevin's feet, he could hear Devon whimpering and begging for forgiveness. He felt the Master lash out with his boot and kick his brother aside viciously.

Even though Ethan felt like the flesh might be torn from his stretched face by the fist at his neck, he winced in sympathy. His sweet, gentle, completely loyal brother didn't deserve such treatment. But he was hardly in a position to protest.

"What have you got there, Nevin?" one of the female mages asked with syrupy spitefulness as they gathered round to see what Master Nevin would do. "Looks like you have your own little rebels starting up right under your nose."

Ethan wished the ground would open up and swallow the hateful woman down in a gaping maw of fire and darkness straight to the hell she was surely stoking for Devon and himself. His Master simply growled menacingly as he shook Ethan. When he felt his brain rattle against his skull, he hissed involuntarily.

"Oh! Spirited too," she crooned, licking her lips suggestively. "Maybe I could break them in for you," she offered with a wicked gleam in her eye.

It frightened him even more than the thought of what Master Nevin might do to them. And that was saying something.

"No need, Mirrin. I assure you I can take care of my own," he threatened darkly, looking Ethan straight in the eye. "I think I might particularly enjoy teaching this one his place."

Ethan wanted to throw up, but his current position wouldn't allow it. He thought he might have heard his brother sob as his Master dragged them both from the room.

The day was not turning out to be the adventurous experience he had been looking forward to at all. He vaguely thought he might like to go back to his dreary, dull little nursery now. But it looked like that chapter of his life was well and truly over.

Chapter One

Seven years later

Ethan gazed longingly down through the intricately carved window screen of the harem into the throng of revellers in the courtyard below. From his silk cushioned perch on the window sill, he watched the flickering light of the torches play over the castle servants.

Their eyes gleamed. They laughed and danced with wild abandon. They drank heartily and feasted from the long trestle tables filled with a vast array of festival foods. It all looked so tempting. So alive and exciting.

Ethan stifled a sigh as he watched them all enjoying themselves. He knew that life for most of those below was harsh. The shifters that called Master Nevin's castle home endured long days of repetitive chores, hard physical labour, and the ever present threat of their Master's displeasure. The fickle whims of the elements that often battered their tiny bolt hole in the universe only added to their discomfort. It was good to see them all happy for once. Tonight they were free to make merry and celebrate life to the fullest.

Unlike himself, he thought morosely. He and Devon, along with all the other occupants of the harem, were not permitted to join in the traditional Gifting Day festivities. In fact, they weren't permitted to participate in any of the day to day life of the castle.

He felt a twinge of guilt for feeling so sorry for himself when his own life was one of relative ease and comfort. But how often had he wished he could join the other cats? How often would he much rather have been working in the blistering hot fields or even been sent to scrub his hands raw polishing the acres of marble floors rather than be forced to remain confined in the harem? Some days anything seemed better than that. And yet there was nothing he could do about it. Tonight, like every other night, they would remain, isolated and confined in their gilded cage awaiting their Master's pleasure.

Pampered pets kept exclusively for their Master's amusement, he thought disdainfully as the walls of the beautifully decorated room seemed to press in on him. The heavy weight of his narrow existence hung over him like a shroud and threatened to suffocate him under its restrictions tonight.

Gazing down over the crowd, he snapped out of his maudlin thoughts when he spied Lina making her way through the revellers. She was the newest addition to the household, having been recently gifted to the Master by a fellow mage. Naturally bright and vivacious, she had instantly drawn every eye, and heart, in the castle. Including his, he admitted as he peeked out at the world through his spy holes. But tonight she was simply stunning, and for a moment he was able to forget his self-pity and frustration.

Over the weeks, he had watched her with a strange sort of fascination he couldn't quite explain. Almost as if he recognised something familiar about her. But he knew for a fact he had never met her. He had met very few people outside of his Master and the immediate harem keepers. But he couldn't seem to help watching her for some reason. Perhaps it was as simple as wanting to live vicariously through her.

At first she had struggled to find her place in the huge workings of the castle. But then he had seen her gradually relax as she was quickly accepted by the other cats into their make-shift family pride. And, as the days had gone by, he had gazed on in awe as she blossomed and seemed to fill the castle with her warm presence and infectious laughter.

Everyone seemed to like her. The females mothered her. The young followed her, constantly begging for cuddles or tugging on her skirt for attention. And every male in the place appeared helpless to resist flirting with her. She took all of it with a light-hearted, gracious manner that seemed to come so naturally to her. Ethan had never seen the castle so happily captivated.

Then Marcus had returned from extended patrol and the sweet, innocent look had completely disappeared from her face. Now she was like a lioness stalking her prey – deadly and intent. And he couldn't wait to see what would happen next.

Tonight her bright skirts and the decadent sway of her hips enticed many eyes to follow her as she made her way through the party-goers. But anyone with eyes could see her attention was fixed on Marcus. Around her neck she had dared to thread tiny white flowers into her collar so it looked like a beautiful necklace instead of a symbol of slavery. Her nut brown hair, which had been let out to flow in a long cascade down her back, emphasising her tiny waist and the tempting, rounded swell of her hips as she swayed provocatively to the beat of the music.

She looked incredible, twisting and weaving her way through the crowded courtyard and Ethan watched many of the males try in vain to catch hold of her. But she simply flitted away like a spicy summer breeze until she came to Marcus.

Ethan watched as she favoured Marcus with a coy smile, so at odds with her come-hither eyes beckoning him from under seductively lowered lashes.

Marcus was Captain of the Castle Guard. He was a stunning, dominant male, and stood a good foot taller than the girl's diminutive five foot four or so frame. Thick, muscular arms crossed over his broad chest as his mane of sun-bleached, blond hair fell to his shoulders in tempting waves. But it was his dark eyes, hooded and brooding, that captured so many hearts. Ethan shivered in appreciation of the other male's physical perfection. What he wouldn't give to be in Lina's shoes right now. He could well understand her attraction.

Lina didn't seem to need any encouragement to appreciate Marcus' appeal, however. Ethan watched as she latched onto his arm and dragged him into the centre of the courtyard. His strong, handsome face was serious, but the gleam in his eye, along with the impressive bulge in his pants, told its own tale.

Ethan's heartbeat pounded in anticipation.

Slowly, her hips began an exaggerated sway in perfect time to the music. Provocatively, she wound her way around his much larger frame, bumping against his body with fleeting touches as the beat drove her on. Gradually, the dance intensified. Ethan tensed as the growing rhythmic pulse and tempo of the music made her increasingly bold. She started to slide her body over Marcus' in a series of sensual caresses. Ethan could almost feel his own body kissed by touches and the silky slide of skin on skin.

He marvelled that Marcus somehow managed to hold himself perfectly still, but noticed that as he allowed her movement against him, he watched her with dark, hungry eyes. She undulated and tempted, rolling her hips and seemed to offer herself up as she lifted her arms to wrap around him.

Finally, when the music had reached an almost fevered pitch he seemed to snap. He dragged Lina against his body until they were joined from chest to hip. They moved together in a fluid, primitive dance, as if no one else existed. Faster and faster they writhed, whirling and twisting until the music reached its passionate climax, then suddenly crashed into silence.

The pair came to a halt, panting for breath, their faces wet with perspiration and their hair plastered to their skin. Still glued to each other, their eyes were alive with passion. Around them the crowd went wild with exuberant applause and cat calls.

Tonight the castle would pulse with the beat of many couples joined intimately in their celebration of life. It seemed obvious that these two would be joining them.

Ethan sighed again and looked away. His cock throbbed against his smooth golden belly, hard and aching with a gleaming drop of pre-come balanced delicately at its tip. More than his unfulfilled arousal, however, Ethan felt an ache of longing, deep down in his soul. Just once he wished he could go out and explore the strange and wonderful things he sometimes saw from his window. He wanted to see the world beyond the castle walls. Meet new and interesting people. He wanted to know what it was like to have someone look at him the way he had seen Marcus look at Lina, and he wanted the freedom to return that look. He wanted... He wanted...

"What's the matter, Ethan?" Devon asked from across the room.

Ethan looked over to where his twin lay reclined on a blood red cushioned divan. Naked and completely at ease, Devon rose and stretched languidly before padding over on slim bare feet. His limber body moved with a supple, sultry grace. His pale blue eyes, with their long, coal black lashes looked at him sleepily.

Even Ethan had to admire how sexy his brother was.

Seven years and countless hours of training had certainly changed them from the gangly, naive youths they had been. Gone were the awkward, lanky limbs, the careless, graceless movements. Now they were both seduction in motion without even having to think about it. And he hated it. Yet Devon seemed completely at peace.

As he watched his brother approach, he cocked his head to consider him more closely. He knew their overall size and features were remarkably similar. Both of them were small, and lithe, with long sleek limbs. Their faces were delicate with high cheek bones, and their eyes slanted slightly. But it was as if they had been cast as night and day, and their differences had only become more pronounced as they had grown older.

While Devon's skin was now a smooth, creamy white that seemed to glow like fine silk in the light of the harem lamps, Ethan's was a soft burnished gold colour. Devon's hair was a tousled mop of jet black that framed his delicate face in sultry waves and made him look like he had just gotten out of bed. His own hair was more a wild mane of tawny brown with a multitude of golden streaks running through it from pale gold to dark honey. And unlike Devon's pale blue eyes, he had bright emerald green.

But it was their natures that were the most distinctly different. Devon was quiet, calm and sensual, whereas Ethan was more wild and unmanageable. And while they both might have been considered attractive, he had always thought that Devon had a certain ethereal quality that made him especially beautiful.

Devon was a peaceful soul with a gentle heart, Ethan thought lovingly as he felt his twin rub softly against his bare shoulder in a comforting gesture. He nuzzled the top of Devon's head with his cheek in a reciprocal sign of affection. But, while he was content to enjoy his brother's touch for a moment, it couldn't still the restlessness he felt in his soul.

"Don't you ever wish for something more?" Ethan finally asked, pulling away and eyeing the thin leather collar around his brother's throat. It was identical to his own—a symbol of ownership, of belonging, and supposedly a mark that told the world he was *cared for*. Ethan snorted disdainfully at the mere thought.

"Like what?" Devon asked easily, missing Ethan's rapidly souring mood.

"I don't know. I just wish sometimes that...you know...things could be different."

He knew he wasn't explaining himself well. In truth, he didn't really know what it was he longer for. He had lived almost his entire life in the castle and for all of that time they had been confined, first in the nursery, then in the harem complex. He had only seen glimpses of what it could be like outside the seclusion screens and doors. Brief glimpses through spy holes and one wild adventure that had ended in disaster seven years ago.

"What would you want to be different?" Devon asked curiously as he glanced around their room in confusion, assessing each piece of furniture and decoration as if looking for what could be lacking.

Ethan stared incredulously at his twin brother's total lack of understanding. Devon was far too comfortable in their plush silk prison to be concerned apparently.

"Oh! I don't know," he snapped sarcastically. "Maybe to be able to go outside once in a while. Maybe to meet people, talk to them, even get to know them. Don't you ever wish we could go out and see new and interesting places without having to be hidden away in that tiny carrier that's more like a cage than a conveyance?" He growled in frustration and rising irritation.

Devon merely shrugged dismissively. "What's the point? The Master would never allow that."

Ethan grew angry with his brother. That was the point. They weren't allowed to do anything. How could Devon be so completely unconcerned by that when every day he felt as if he was being suffocated?

"Don't you wish that just once you could have a choice? That you could choose to stay inside or go out into the grounds for a walk? Wouldn't you like to talk to whoever you wanted? Make friends with anyone that took your fancy? Haven't you ever wanted to visit different places? Be alone sometimes, or in a crowd like the one downstairs?" He paced, agitation rolling of him in waves as he tried to work out what it was he wanted. "Haven't you ever wished you could just get away from here? Find your own Master to serve?"

"Ethan, what are you saying?" Devon asked, his voice growing higher and his eyes wider with alarm. He looked appalled at the suggestion.

"I'm saying I want to get out of here. I'm saying I want to leave and meet other people. I want to find a new Master. One that doesn't want to keep me locked up in a cage all the time!"

It was like the clouds had unexpectedly parted and for the first time he could see the sun. If it hadn't been so blinding in its intensity, he might have seen his brother's mounting panic. But it was too glorious. It was true, and honest and enlightening, and it was who and what he wanted, revealed to him for the very first time.

"No!" Devon cried out, breaking into his reverie. "Sshh! Ethan!" he urged desperately, lowering his voice to a whisper and looking around as if someone might jump out at them from behind a curtain and discipline them at any moment. "How can you say that?" he asked in a scandalised tone. "How could you even think that after everything the Master has done for us?"

"What?" Ethan countered boldly. "What has he ever done for us? Locked us up? Controlled our every moment? Taken us out whenever he wanted to power some new spell or simply had an itch he wanted scratching? Then what does he do Devon? He simply dismisses us back to our cell. Don't tell me how much the Master has done for us. I know!"

"Ethan!" Devon reprimanded "The Master cares for us. He protects and loves us."

"That's not love, Devon," he spat out contemptuously. "That's fucking."

"Ethan!" Devon was looking increasingly pale and distressed.

Ethan was sorry he was upsetting his brother, he truly was, but he couldn't stop. He knew what was in his heart now, and it had been slowly eating him alive. He knew he had to tell the truth and let his brother hear it. He hated their Master. Hated being controlled and used and treated like an object created for the sole purpose of pleasuring and powering his spell casting. He wanted more than that. And he was going to get it!

"Stop it, Ethan! Just stop it!" Devon demanded. "The Master saved us. Everything we have we owe to him. We would have died without him. We owe him our loyalty." Devon scolded Ethan like an errant child, but he wasn't a child and he wasn't going to be treated as if what he wanted didn't matter anymore.

"He demands more than our loyalty," he replied darkly. "Much more."

"Enough, Ethan!" Devon's voice was tinged with anger now, something Ethan had very rarely seen in his quiet, softly spoken brother. "He's a mage. He needs the power we give him. I can't believe you would begrudge him that when he uses that same power to keep you and a lot of others safe, with food in their bellies and a roof over their heads. Where would any of us be without the Master?"

"Free?" he hissed sarcastically, unwilling to back down now. "We are slaves, Devon. Don't pretend otherwise. He feeds and shelters us because we provide him with the lifestyle he demands."

"I don't want to hear this anymore." Devon turned away from him and began to stalk across the room to their sleeping chamber.

"You can deny it all you want, Devon, but it's the truth, and I don't think I can live with it anymore."

"You think you could survive out there on your own without the Master?" Devon shot back scathingly.

Ethan knew his brother too well. He could see the fear in his eyes, knew what terror prompted the question. Devon dreaded the thought of being a stray. But Ethan was willing to risk even that now, in order to escape, to finally have choices in his life and how he lived it.

"I'm willing to give it a try if it means leaving this prison behind," he replied bravely.

"You don't mean that." The fear in Devon's eyes intensified to horror as he began to back away, as if he might try to drag them both outside this very minute. "I never want to hear you say that again. If the Master ever heard you…"

Devon couldn't or wouldn't finish the sentence. Instead, he turned and ran this time to their sleeping chamber, slamming the door behind him.

Left standing alone, Ethan sighed and turned back to the window. He knew couldn't take it anymore. It was as if finally saying what was in his heart had broken away the shields he had built around himself and now he felt as if he were burning. His soul yearned to be free. He couldn't stay. He wouldn't stay. He had to get away. He only hoped that one day his brother would forgive him.

* * * *

Hawk leaned his hip against the stone balustrade of the guest suite's private balcony and gazed out over the crowd below. He took another sip from the brandy balloon he cradled tenderly in his hand and tried to forget today had ever happened. It had been long and trying and quite possibly one of the worst of his life. The brandy was actually the best thing that had happened all day and definitely deserved his consideration as he swirled it gently against the glass.

Sighing heavily, he looked across to the building directly opposite his room to see if he could spot the haunted eyes of the pleasure cat sequestered in the harem. Almost completely concealed by the seclusion screens, Hawk had watched him gaze longingly down at the crowd and felt a strange tug of kinship to the unknown cat.

Snorting, he took another sip from the glass in his hand. They didn't call him The Hawk for nothing, he mused sardonically. He could spot a fellow malcontent a mile off these days.

Unfortunately, the cat shifter seemed to have moved away. Hawk didn't blame him. Looking down on the evening festivities from up here without even the faintest hope of being able to join in was hard. He took another, more generous sip of the excellent brandy Nevin served to all his honoured guests. He wondered if any of his slaves ever enjoyed such generosity.

Probably not, Hawk thought with derision, Nevin was a complete and utter bastard.

Even the traditional Gifting Day celebrations he held were little more than an expedient method of boosting slave numbers and morale. Still it was nice to see them all out enjoying themselves, even if it had been difficult to watch Lina forced to work so hard to help set it all up through the blistering heat of the afternoon and join in like a lamb to the slaughter. All he'd wanted to do was go down and drag her away somewhere cool and safe.

At least Marcus had her now, Hawk reminded himself. He could breathe a little easier knowing that it looked like Marcus was going to be taking care of her. Even if his heart did ache a little more with loneliness at the thought.

"Such is life," Hawk murmured stoically, trying to convince himself it was all for the best.

His life didn't lend itself to close relations with anyone, never mind beautiful, young creatures like Lina and Marcus. He had to focus his energies on maintaining the illusion of a bored aristocratic mage and Circle Council lay-about. He should be trying to keep Nevin off-balance and wondering why he had unexpectedly dropped in on him, not mooning over his best friend and lost love. He needed to ruthlessly exploit *every* opportunity to prevent the full scale mage war he knew was brewing just below the surface.

It was important. Essential if any of them were to survive in the long run. But deep in his heart he hated it. He hated having to push others away for their own good. He hated his whole existence actually. All he really wanted was to be free to be with the people he loved. Instead, he found himself once again alone looking on from afar.

Stop it, he reprimanded himself severely. There were plenty of others in much worst situations than he was.

With that thought, he tore his eyes away from the celebration below and looked up again, instantly spotting the cat in the harem.

He was back, looking over the crowd with an expression of soul-deep longing on his face.

A slow trickle of inspiration filtered through Hawk's mind. Maybe he couldn't do anything about his own situation, but perhaps he could do something for this poor soul and his twin.

He knew pleasure cats came as a pair and suddenly losing two of his harem would certainly keep that bastard Nevin occupied and distracted. That actually suited Hawk's plan rather well. The less notice Nevin took of Lina and the other slaves, the safer she would be and the more chance he might have to work out something more permanent to keep her and the others safe and protected.

Yes, he mused, feeling a sense of peace creep over him at being able to do even one small thing to help right the terrible wrongs he saw all around him. Perhaps today wouldn't turn out to be a total loss after all.

A portal marker in the right place should be all it would take. Even a poor, isolated pleasure cat should know what to do with one of those. Especially if Hawk was any judge of the deep desire for freedom he saw in this one's eyes. And by now he thought he should be. He'd been helping cat shifters escape mages for over ten years.

This situation wasn't the most ideal scenario, granted. Without any help or back-up, the little cat shifter would have to manage in a strange, new world all on his own. But it was all that was possible at the moment, and Hawk had learnt a long time ago how resourceful and resilient cat shifters could be. He had every confidence that this pleasure cat, like quite a few before him, would be all right.

Taking another small sip from his brandy balloon, Hawk let a smile tilt the corners of his lips. Yes. It would be his own special Gifting Day offering to that bastard Nevin and a good day's work done in a wicked world. If only he could do more for the poor little cat. Life was sure to get a whole lot harder before it got any easier for him, he thought with pity.

Chapter Two

Michael was utterly exhausted as he stumbled his way up the front steps of his house in the quiet, leafy suburbs of Bayside. Getting out of Sydney and away from the busy inner-city hospital where he worked was always a relief. But today he was especially glad to see the back of both. Last night had been sheer hell in the emergency theatres and the train ride home this morning endless.

While the sun lit the porch with a warm welcoming glow, he was really too tired to stop and appreciate it at the moment. The cute little three bedroom cottage where he had grown up was home, but sometimes he wished it was just a little closer to work. Like when he was coming off his fourth twelve-hour night shift in a row.

Sighing in relief at finally being home, he rummaged around in his pockets for his keys. He knew he would never seriously consider parting with the house. It was his last connection to his family after his parents had been killed in a car accident a little over eighteen months ago.

He'd just have to accept that some things about nursing would always suck, no matter where he lived. Night duty was definitely one of them.

As he continued to work from pocket to pocket trying to locate his keys, he realised that the thing he hated most about night duty was the way his brain seemed to get all clouded and fuzzy. Sometimes he would just find himself drifting off until he was left standing there on the train with a vague look on his face while the other passengers stared at him and shifted away nervously.

He couldn't blame them really. He felt drunk, and he could only imagine what he looked like. It was why he didn't drive while working on night duty, even though it would be quicker and easier. It was also dangerouser.

Dangerouser? Was that even a word? He shook his head. Who cared, he thought tiredly, resetting his satchel over his shoulder as he finally managed to extract his keys. He was finally on leave. Four blissfully free weeks of relaxation. No crazy shifts, no crazy patients and absolutely no crazy co-workers. Ah! Bliss.

It was a pity really that saving his holiday leave over the last year had been more of a necessity than a voluntary decision on his part. He suspected he would probably be feeling a lot less morose right now if it had actually been his choice. But it hadn't been.

His parent's death had hit him hard. He still missed them every day. Growing up he had always known they loved him. When he had told them he was gay at sixteen, they had hardly even blinked an eye. It had just never been an issue for them. He guessed he was just one of those lucky people who grew up to count his parents as his friends.

But their death had left a huge hole in his life. And that had been when he had made the second biggest mistake of his life. Trying to fill the hole and feeling the sudden need for stability and security, he had asked Daniel, his boyfriend at the time, to move in with him.

What the hell had possessed him, he had no idea. He should have known better. Daniel was a party animal, and Michael just wasn't. In fact, Daniel had often complained that he was too serious, too straight-laced and uptight. In retrospect, he wasn't even sure how they had even managed to get together in the first place. What on earth had made him think of trying to form a committed relationship with the man?

He felt like smacking himself upside the head, but he reserved that for the biggest mistake of his life — giving the bastard access to his saving account. He still felt like such an idiot.

For a while things seemed to go well. His grief and work had kept him mostly oblivious to the increasing parties and growing irregularities in Daniel's life. But gradually Daniel's complaints had become more vocal and his behaviour more erratic.

Why can't you be a bit more spontaneous, Michael? Why can't you be a bit more adventurous? Take a few risks, Michael!

Well, it certainly seemed that Daniel had no problems taking risks. Michael had come home early one night, feeling sick and found Daniel high as a kite in their bed with not one, but two strange men.

Needless to say, he no longer had the bed or Daniel in his life.

The bed he had donated to charity. Daniel's lying, cheating ass he had just kicked out. Unfortunately, not before he discovered Daniel had basically cleaned out their savings account in a six months long binge of partying, drugs and gambling. Thank goodness he had never been stupid enough to give him access to the deed to the house!

Blinking to clear his head as he fumbled with the key in the lock, he wondered if he would ever be able to trust anyone like that again. Enough to let them close. Enough to risk his heart.

After he had discovered Daniel had been bleeding him dry, using his house, his money and his affection, Michael had cut himself off completely. He'd severed all ties with his old friends. Most of them had been Daniel's friends anyway, and none of them had even once thought to tell him what Daniel had been up to behind his back. Most of them had been too busy enjoying Daniel's sudden generosity. He didn't miss their worthless asses either.

At least one good thing had come out of it all, he thought wearily as he dumped his bag in the entry way and shucked off his coat, throwing it haphazardly over a peg. After burying himself in his work and accepting every shift he could possibly grab over the last twelve months, his savings account finally looked a little healthier again. Not healthy enough that he could afford to go anywhere on his time off, but enough to be comfortable at least.

Walking down the hall towards the kitchen, he realised it had been twelve months of celibacy too. Over twelve months actually since he had gotten laid, he thought bleakly. Surely, that had to be a record somewhere. A really sad, lonely, horny record.

Maybe he should consider going out again. Get back on the horse, so to speak. Maybe he'd try one of the gay clubs down the coast towards Northpoint while he was on holiday. Of course that meant battling his way across Sydney, but it would be worth it. He had absolutely no desire to risk running into Daniel or one of his cronies.

Still, the whole idea left him rather cold. He was lonely, sure, and certainly horny, but the truth was he liked the idea of some sort of relationship with his sex. He just didn't do casual, no strings attached. Never had really. He preferred the idea of a quiet night snuggled in front of the TV to some noisy nightclub with meaningless hook-ups and overpriced drinks.

Maybe he really was a boring stick-in-the-mud destined to be alone as Daniel had spitefully suggested on his way out the door.

With a resigned sigh, he turned into the kitchen entry way and froze as a small golden brown blur skidded around the countertop that divided the kitchen from the dining room.

What the hell was that?

Michael was wide awake now, adrenaline pounding through his system, his heart rate kicking up to power his sluggish brain. When no answer was forthcoming, however, he cautiously stepped around the counter to take a peek.

Huddled under the far bar stool, a small tabby face peered up at him with wide, fear-filled green eyes. Its body was drawn in tight, almost as if trying to make itself invisible and it looked ready to dart away at any moment.

"Hello there, little one," he crooned softly, hoping to entice the frightened animal to relax by softening his voice and kneeling down. "How'd you manage to get in?"

The cat tilted its head as if listening to him intently, but it didn't move from under the seat. Kneeling down didn't really do much to reduce Michael's intimidating size, especially when you were as small a bundle as the one currently eyeing him warily. He wasn't surprised the cat maintained its distance. It just told him he was a smart cat.

"Hey! Are you hungry?" he asked gently, rising carefully and trying hard not to frighten the little animal.

He crossed to the fridge and retrieved a few slices of leftover chicken he knew he'd stored there before heading out to his shift the night before. Carefully, he extended his hand to hold out the peace offering to his unexpected houseguest. The cat eyed him suspiciously, then stepped forward gingerly, placing one tentative paw in front of the other until it could snatch away the chicken slice and retreat back under the bar stool. It proceeded to gulp down the meat in a few hungry bites.

"Well, aren't you a brave little thing?" He chuckled ironically, then laughed softly when the cat narrowed its eyes at him, as if suspecting his hint of sarcasm.

"Here, you want some more?"

Once again, he held out some chicken, but closer this time, trying to coax the animal to him. He actually was quite impressed with the cat's courage this time when it stepped out slightly more confidently and ate the meat right out of his hand.

"I must really be desperate if I'm trying to bribe a cat to keep me company," he murmured to himself as it finished off the last of the chicken.

Piercing green feline eyes turned up to regard him with a curiously intelligent and expectant gaze.

"More?" he asked with amusement, then shook his head to clear his obviously exhausted brain when he thought he saw the cat nod.

Before long, they had polished off the last of the leftovers together. Still sitting cross legged on the floor, he was stunned and oddly touched when the little cat walked up and rubbed its head against his knee.

"So what are you anyway, a boy or a girl?"

The cat flicked its tail as if in indignation and let out a suspiciously disgruntled mewl as Michael leaned over to take a look. But before it shifted away irritably, he was able to see it was, in fact, a male cat.

Deciding to take a chance, he reached forward and stroked down from its silky tabby head along its smooth tawny back. Instantly, the rumbling sound of purring echoed through the kitchen, leaving him to wonder how such a lot of purr was able to fit into such a little cat. He felt a wave of disappointment, however, when he felt a slim collar under the thick silky ruff at the cat's neck.

The discovery of a collar suggested that the cat was probably lost and already had an owner, one that was, in all likelihood, out there right now looking for him. Sighing in regret, he began to adjust the collar to read the tag. Best to get it over with now before he got any more attached to the idea of keeping the affectionate little thing.

"It figures that a beautiful boy like you would already have a home. Guess we'd better see about getting you back to your owner. Ow!" he cried out as he snatched back his hand from the needle sharp claws that raked across his skin.

Gone was the contented, purring ball of fluff from only moments ago, replaced instead by a hissing, spitting dervish. The cats tail slashing back and forth in agitation as it cowered once more in the shadows under the bar stool, growling softly at him. Michael sucked at his wounded hand as they eyed each other across the kitchen.

"Ooo-kay," he said warily, wondering as he did so why he felt the need to placate the suddenly aggressive cat.

Shaking his head at himself once more, he walked over to wash his abused hand in the sink, aware of the cat's eyes following him the whole time. Dismissing the strange notion that the cat was weighing him up somehow, he assessed the wound. The cuts really weren't very deep, but just to be sure, he dabbed a little iodine over them.

By the time he turned around, the cat sat in the middle of the floor watching him speculatively. It mewed softly, almost as if in apology, and he had the oddest desire to apologise back for upsetting the little creature.

Man, his brain was out to lunch. In fact, he suspected it might have been out for several more meals as well. Being fuzzy and slightly addled from lack of sleep was really messing with him today.

"I'm too tired to deal with this right now," he muttered to himself. "How about some TV and then some sleep?" he asked rhetorically, his hands braced on his hips as he looked down at the now docile cat.

Once more, the cat cocked its head at him as if in question. He just shook his head at himself. At the moment, it was quite possible the cat was the more intelligent of the two of them. Which was kind of sad, he admitted, but at least he was being honest with himself.

The cat followed him through to the living room and leapt up to sit beside him as he began flicking through the channels. Finally, he found an early morning news programme that didn't make him want to hurl the remote through the screen at the perky hosts. Sometimes morning TV was just nauseating. But the cat seemed mesmerised as it watching the screen intently, its wide green eyes fixed firmly on the flickering pictures. He chuckled at his guest's antics.

As he watched the news and the weather report, Michael was shocked to feel the cat jump onto his lap and make itself comfortable. Its eyes were still glued to the flickering screen, but it occasionally paused to lick at a paw or wash behind an ear when a more boring segment aired on the news.

Personally, he found the cat's reactions more appealing than the latest opinion poll results or weather guesstimates. As the picture jumped between segments, the cat seemed to jump too, then stared at the new programme as if taking everything in. But finally, Michael couldn't keep his eyes open any longer and his yawns were threatening to crack his jaw, so he switched off the set.

"Come on. It's time for bed, little one." He realised his thought processes were definitely becoming muddled, and his mind had obviously ceased to function properly when his first thought was how nice it would be not to have to go to bed alone while he invited the strange little cat to bed with him.

With the cat diligently following along behind, he washed up and changed into sweats and a t-shirt for bed. When the cat seemed fascinated by the running water, batting at it playfully, he indulgently put in the plug and watched as its delicate pink tongue lapped at the water.

He chuckled as the cat stared up at him in adoration after it finished.

"Careful," he warned playfully, "I could get use to that. You're certainly good for my ego. I might have to keep you around."

The only answer was a loud, rumbling purr and a soft head butting up against his arm. He ruffled the tabby head of fur playfully, then stroked it smooth again before turning and pulling the thick thermal lined curtains on the bright, sunny morning outside. With another huge yawn, he headed for bed.

Settling in under the blankets, he realised that, despite coming home exhausted and in a bit of a mood after somehow ending up thinking about Daniel again, he had laughed and felt oddly happy more in the last few hours since finding the cat in his house than he had in ages. Perhaps, while he was on holiday, he should get a cat to keep him company. Then again, maybe not, somehow he knew it wouldn't be the same. There was just something about this particular cat that filled a hole in his heart.

It was a pity he couldn't keep him. But the cat was probably someone's beloved pet, and he couldn't live with himself if he tried to steal that away from someone else.

He watched with growing affection as the cat sprang lightly onto the bed. While the curtains made the room dim, it was bright enough to clearly see its supple body as it moved up towards him. Its golden brown striped fur seemed to glow in the filtered light, then, while he watched the cat stalking up his body, it slowly, smoothly began to change right before his eyes into the slim golden skinned figure of a man. A stunningly beautiful man with wildly streaked, tawny brown hair and piercing, eerily familiar green eyes.

"Oh! I have got to get some sleep," he managed to murmur in disbelief. "Or get laid," he added as an afterthought.

"If you keep me, Master, I could probably help you with that," the man now draped across his chest replied.

Ethan couldn't believe his luck. It had been less than twenty-four hours since he had discovered the portal marker mysteriously tucked under his pillow and escaped. It seemed almost impossible to believe he had found a kind and generous Master already. But here he was, looking up at him with his big, beautiful, dark brown eyes as Ethan draped himself across his hard, muscular body. He felt a shiver of desire rush through him.

Mentally, he began to tick off all the important points. There were no harried servants waiting on him hand and foot. No armed warriors carrying out his orders with a heavy hand. No slaves working night and day to maintain his holdings. More importantly, at least to his mind, there were no pleasure cats in residence, forced to re-energise his abilities with their orgasms.

In fact, he hadn't caught the scent of anyone else while he had hidden in this Master's house. Around the strange little flap in the door he had used to sneak in, there had been the faintest trace of strange cat, but it was so ancient he knew it couldn't have been in residence for quite some time. There was just the deep, rich scent of spice and sandal wood and something that was uniquely his new Master. And he so desperately wanted to make this man his Master. There was just something about him that drew him in and made him want to purr and roll around and over him until he was drenched in his scent. He suspected this man would be more addictive than catnip.

Looking around the Spartan bedroom, he realised the man lived quite simply really. Not that he had a problem with that, even though he was used to far more lavish surroundings. He could be content here because, unlike his previous Master, he knew this Master would appreciate and treat him well. The simple pleasure the man had taken in Ethan's company this morning was amazing. There had been no demands for anything else, no salacious comments or rough, groping hands. He had just been…nice.

In fact, he had laughed and smiled freely, which was something Ethan couldn't remember ever seeing his old Master doing. And he had touched Ethan without wanting any sexual release. This Master had fed him, talked to him and just absently stroked his fur in a soft, soothing gesture while he gazed at the world around them in his odd, flat crystal ball. He was incredible!

Rubbing his head under the Master's chin, he waited to hear the man's decision on whether or not he could stay. He desperately hoped this man would want to keep him. He had run away from his previous Master because he was thoughtless and often cruel in his domination. He knew that was not unusual for mages, but he had still hoped to find something different, something better. And he had. This Master was warm and caring, attentive and generous. It almost left him in a daze. This Master was as different from his previous as night from day.

Instantly, he thought of Devon and the small smile of hope and contentment that had started to form, slipped from his lips. He wondered how his brother was faring. It wasn't the first time he'd thought about him, wondered whether he felt the sharp cut of their separation, the aching loneliness and fear of being truly on his own for the first time in their lives. He hoped Devon was okay back at the castle.

Not everything about the past twenty-four hours had been wonderful, he admitted. Settling his head against the Master's chest, he used his rhythmic heart beat to steady himself.

After finally finding the courage to activate the portal marker and make the gut retching decision to leave Devon, he had found himself travelling to this strange and wonderful realm. He knew now, thanks to the Master allowing him to watch while he used his strange, flat scrying device, that this place was called Bayside and was located on a small, blue planet called Earth.

He vaguely recalled hearing about Earth somewhere along the line. He seemed to remember that its people were called humans. Suppressing a shiver, he also recalled that not everything he had heard about them had been favourable. The rumour was that they were a xenophobic, barbaric species with little to no magical ability. The mages were said to have abandoned them and their planet centuries ago. He had to wonder how much of what he had been told was true.

Ethan took the time to consider everything that had happened to him since arriving here. Some of his experiences certainly give him plenty of insight into their harsh ways. Since his arrival, he had been sequentially — chased by a pack of dogs, yelled at, had a smelly old boot thrown at him, narrowly missed being hit by some sort of self-propelled conveyance and had an old lady threaten him with a rather sturdy-looking broom for doing something in her flower beds he would never even consider. He hadn't stopped to find out why they had all been so angry at him. He had been too frightened.

He lifted his head to look down and consider the man looking back at him with a rather stunned expression on his face. Could he be another one of these humans and not a mage as he had first assumed? There was no doubt that he was fabulous, and Ethan definitely wanted to stay with him, but now that he thought about it, he hadn't actually felt him use any magic, even when he was scrying. He was beginning to wonder. And there weren't meant to be any mages left on earth anymore.

Not that it mattered to Ethan. The Master treated him well and seemed to genuinely like him. It didn't matter to him if he couldn't use magic. In fact, maybe it was better that way. But he was obviously going to have to rethink some of his assumptions and take each one of these humans on his or her own merits. Leaping to conclusions in this unfamiliar new world could not only lead to confusion, but it could be dangerous.

He began to smile again. This Master had been so nice to him. Even when Ethan had scratched him in a fit of fear and anger, he hadn't turned on him. Ethan didn't think he would find a better Master anywhere regardless of whether he was or wasn't a mage.

He was kind and attentive and handsome. Ethan couldn't forget handsome. Tall and muscular with beautiful, warm brown eyes and wavy dark brown hair that curled around his ears and just made Ethan long to run his fingers through it, he was just the sort of man Ethan found attractive. Serving this Master would certainly be no hardship at all.

With that thought in mind, he put all his hopes and energy into trying to please. He wiggled and squirmed until he had pushed the blankets aside and could stretch his body out over the top of the gorgeous man beneath him. The lusty groan and the cock he felt swelling and throbbing against his thigh reassured him that he hadn't been to presumptuous, and he grinned from ear to ear.

"Mmmmmm," he echoed appreciatively, licking at the lips that parted invitingly in front of him. "What can I do for you, Master?"

The only answer was his tongue being sucked into the soft, warm cavern of his Master's mouth. Long moments followed as they explored each other. Thrusting and retreating with their tongues as they learnt the taste and texture of each other. He groaned with pleasure at the new and exciting sensation, revelling in the faint hint of mint and warm, spicy male.

Master Nevin might have kissed him once or twice, but it was always spiteful and aggressive. It was nothing like this kiss. This kiss was hard and passionate and demanding and desperate. It reached into his soul and begged for more, more touching, more caressing, more contact and connection. He never dreamed he could nearly come just from kissing alone, but he suddenly found himself so close, teetering on the edge of an orgasmic precipice already.

When they finally parted, panting for breath, the Master gazed into his eyes, stroking soothing hands through his streaked hair.

"I don't know if I ever want to wake up from this dream," the Master breathed softly.

"Then don't, Master," he returned huskily, leaning forward to lick a line up the side of the Master's neck before nibbling gentle on the shell of his ear.

"Let me pleasure you, Master," he pleaded in a sultry, hot whisper.

"Michael." He heard his Master say in a stunned, distracted voice.

Ethan tilted his head in confusion.

"My name is Michael," Master said when the fog of lust cleared slightly from his eyes. "What's yours?"

But before Ethan could answer, or even work out what his Master was saying, his lips were once again sealed in a deep, erotic kiss. Almost as if his Master couldn't wait long enough for an answer before reconnecting with him. He moaned and writhed at the thought.

Gradually, through the haze of passion and lust and desire, he realised what his Master had done. He began to purr into their kiss. He had given Ethan permission to use his name. His heart pounded wildly in his chest with excitement.

The Master pulled back in surprise when Ethan began to purr, but it didn't dim his grin of delight in the slightest.

"Ethan," he offered in reply.

Michael's eyes widened in shock when he heard the man above him begin to purr. "Wow," he whispered in awe.

He ran his hands up and down Ethan's bare back, feeling the vibrations of the purr through the man's rib cage as he ran his palms over it. Ethan smiled serenely, his eyelids lowering with apparent pleasure under his gentle, stroking touch. Slowly, Ethan lent forward and Michael felt a gentle lick at his collar bone just above the rounded collar of his shirt. A shudder passed over him as the hot, roughly textured tongue lapped over his cooler skin.

Apparently reassured by his response, Ethan worked Michael's shirt up over his body.

Lost to the sensation of Ethan touching and caressing him, Michael quickly helped him remove it completely. As soon as he was bare-chested, Ethan kissed his way down to the flat brown disk of one of Michael's nipples. Groaning, Michael worked his fingers through the other man's hair, gently encouraging him to linger. It felt so good to be touched like this after so long.

Taut with arousal, his nipples hardened still further with the languid caress of Ethan's tongue until, taking the hard nub between his teeth, Ethan bit gently on it and Michael bucked wildly up into him in response. But Ethan clung to him determinedly. Apparently mindful of its neglected twin, Ethan then moved to the other side of Michael's chest and began lovingly licking and biting the nipple there with equal attentiveness.

Michael could feel his achingly hard cock pressed into Ethan's firm belly through his sweat pants. It was steadily leaking pre-come and the sensitive head rubbing deliciously against the soft cotton as he thrust helplessly up into the other man. Cat. *Whatever*, he thought fleetingly as a hand eased between them, dipping under the elasticised waist of his pants and firmly encircled his throbbing shaft. He gasped loudly and his head began to thrash uncontrollably from side to side. It just felt so good, he needed...

"More. Please," he begged.

Ethan's head instantly snapped back up from where he had been attending Michael's poor, abused nipples with a soothing tongue. His eyes were wide with surprise and Michael cursed himself for saying or doing the wrong thing just as he was about to have the most explosive orgasm of his life. He prayed the man would forgive him for whatever it was, at least enough to continue.

Suddenly, Ethan was attacking his mouth with a savage, hot kiss. It was filled with need and lust and something else, something Michael was in no condition to figure out. He found he didn't really care. He just wanted to lose himself in the moment.

Fighting furiously with the annoying barrier of his clothes, they both moaned into their fevered kiss when they finally managed to get rid of the sweat pants and their cocks ground together skin to skin for the first time. They thrust and undulated against one another desperately, but soon Ethan seemed to become restless and impatient for more.

He tore his lips away from their kiss and dove down to plunge his mouth over Michael's aching cock in one long swallow straight to the back of his throat.

"Uhhh..." Michael wailed wildly, completely beyond coherent words.

The plea had been like sweet, golden music to Ethan's ears. Never had his previous Master asked. He had only ever demanded and taken. Ordered and directed.

Eagerly, he engulfed Michael's hard, hot cock, thrusting the entire length into the back of his throat and swallowing greedily. Then he eased back to begin licking and sucking the unique flavour of his new Master. Michael, he corrected himself.

He savoured the sharp tang of shared pleasure on his tongue. He couldn't get enough of the man beneath him. Even though he knew it wouldn't take long, he wanted it to last forever. He would make it last forever, he vowed.

His own cock was throbbing insistently and leaking pearly drops of pre-come as he thrust against Michael's lower leg. Wanting to share his pleasure, Ethan slid his hand down to start working on himself as he opened his throat once more and began suckling strongly on Michael's long, thick shaft.

"Oh!" Michael cried out in delight.

If it had been possible he would have grinned, but his lips were stretched tight over Michael's full cock. Instead, he concentrated on holding down Michael's hip with one hand while jerking rapidly on his own hard shaft with the other. His old Master would have demanded Ethan's release. But he wanted to *give* his orgasm to Michael. He wanted to freely offer the power of his release without any need for Michael to ask for it. A gift given without any reservation or begrudging.

Quickly, he brought them both to the very brink of an explosive orgasm, then casually shoved them over the edge into oblivion. Their mutual orgasms continued on for long minutes as he milked the seed from them both.

Crawling back up Michael's body, Ethan finally collapsed beside him. He snuggled in close and waited anxiously to see what the man would do next. He hoped to be able to stay at least a few minutes in the warm, protective lee of the other man's body as they lay spent and limp with exhaustion. But he knew better than to expect it.

Slowly, as if it was almost more effort than Michael could muster, lax fingers began haphazardly combing through Ethan's hair, and he felt the last of his tension drain away. As the minutes ticked by, Ethan smiled and relaxed completely against his new Master's chest

He couldn't believe how incredibly lucky he was. His Master hadn't told him to leave after he had found his pleasure. He hadn't retreated to another chamber and left Ethan to sleep alone. He didn't think he had ever been happier.

Sighing, he nuzzled the warm chest beneath his cheek and let the waves of exhaustion sweep in to claim him. At this precise moment, he couldn't think of anywhere he'd rather be. Life was very good.

Chapter Three

Devon wished he could be anywhere else but where he was right now. His life was suddenly, horribly out of control and spiralling ever downward into his own personal idea of hell. All he wanted to do was go back to the harem where he felt safe and secure. Instead, he found himself in the castle's antechamber where he had been dragged by one of the guards to face their enraged Master.

"Please don't make me leave, Master," he pleaded as he knelt at the mage's feet, desperately trying to rub against him in supplication. "I promise to be good. Please let me stay. Please." He tried to run his hands up the Master's firm thighs. "Let me pleasure you," he offered.

The Master's sharp features twisted in disgust. It was a look Devon was used to seeing on his Master's face when he looked at him, but it still made him cringe. The man had never liked him, and Devon had never understood why. If he knew what the Master wanted, or how to change, he would have done so in a heartbeat, but it was completely beyond his comprehension, and he was far too terrified of the man to ask for direction.

Rough hands shoved him away and sent him sprawling naked across the cold marble floor. Devon curled into himself, fighting the urge to crawl back and cling to his Master. But he didn't like it out here. He felt exposed and vulnerable. He just wanted to go back home, back to the harem. Perhaps if he stayed still and compliant Master Nevin would relent, or forget about him altogether, and he could simply creep back in and disappear.

The Master's long white hair, pulled back in a tight braid and hanging down his back to his waist, seemed to twitch in irritation as the Master mage jerked away from him. Cold blue eyes stared down at Devon like chips of ice, and he felt the slim hope that his Master might show him mercy, die in his chest.

"Don't touch me," Master Nevin snapped angrily. "Without your brother you're completely useless to me. I have no time for your foolishness. Thanks to your ungrateful sibling, not only am I behind in my work, but now I have to stop to find a replacement for you both."

Devon recoiled from the venom in his Master's voice and curled his arms protectively around his body.

"Get out before I call the Council in for you."

Without a second glance, Master Nevin whirled around in an expensive swirl of dark blue velvet and stalked towards the door. Panic began to set in as he watched Rolf, the tall, muscle bound castle guard who had dragged him here, pace menacingly towards him. Without the Master's protection, what would happen to him?

Just the thought of being kicked out to become a stray, living on the streets, without a home or a Master or even a single stitch of clothing to his name, was enough to make him tremble with fear. But if the Circle Council got hold of him, they might decide to put him to work in one of the Council run facilities. Or worse still, they might send him to one of the Pain Mage's labour camps. He had heard terrible rumours about those places. Mostly tales told to frighten young kittens into behaving themselves and doing what they were told, but he knew if only half the tale where true, he would never survive.

"Please, Master. I'll find him. I'll bring him back. Just don't make me go," he called desperately, tears pooled in his eyes as he began to tremble uncontrollably.

Nevin stopped and turned to regard the useless pleasure cat silently. The slim, lithe body before him was so like its twin in form and feature. And yet so utterly different, he thought with disgust. He wanted Ethan's spit and fire—his resistance and the feral light Nevin sometimes caught lurking in those amazing green eyes.

Damn it, he wanted his pleasure cat back. Not this pale reflection of him. *How dare the little ingrate run away?* he fumed.

Then again, he paused to consider, perhaps this pathetic creature was a way to retrieve his errant pet.

Nevin knew he didn't stand a chance of tracking Ethan down himself. The sneaky little beast had somehow managed to use a portal to make it through to Earth, of all places, he thought with repugnance. It was the only way the cat could possibly have escaped the harem. And the last portal from the castle had gone to Earth. He most certainly hadn't opened a portal to Earth, and he was sure none of his guests would have either. Why the hell would they want to?

Earth, he sniffed scornfully, with its almost non-existent magically reception and total lack of refinement. He couldn't think of a place he loathed more. It made him wonder how the pleasure cat, being a magical creature, could even survive there. But, all indications were that he was still alive, and while he might not have any desire to go there, and certainly little hope of tracking him down if he did, perhaps the brother, with his sibling familiarity and his sensitive feline senses, would.

He took a moment to consider his options. He had other pleasure cats, of course. No single set could possibly hope to keep up with the demands of a powerful mage such as himself. But Ethan was his favourite. He was so full of life and his energy was as delightfully vibrant and fiery as it was hard won. Ethan had never given it easily and nothing enticed him more than a challenge. And the mastery of all that wild energy was delicious.

It really was not very surprising that the naughty kitten had tried to escape actually. Only that he had succeeded. He was much more resourceful that Nevin had given him credit for obviously. He wondered how in the world the cat had managed it, and whether he had chosen Earth on purpose as his destination or had it all simply been a lucky happenstance of opportunity. Nevin would have to investigate the situation thoroughly. He couldn't afford to lose any more of his pleasure cats.

Regardless of that, however, perhaps his brother could show a little of that good sense and bring the boy back. In truth, he didn't care one wit for the creature that presently cowered at his feet. But pleasure cats came in pairs and there was nothing he could do about it. If he wanted to siphon off the unique energy they produced during orgasm, both had to be present. It didn't mean he had to like both of them, or that he couldn't enjoy sex with just one for the sheer pleasure of it. But if he wanted to use their sexual energy, they had to orgasm together.

He smiled wickedly as he fondly remembered Ethan and Devon's training. It took time and discipline to train pleasure cats synchronisation, and he had enjoyed ever moment. If this boy could find him, perhaps he could still regain his favourite play thing and forgo the need to obtain and train a whole new pair. He seriously doubted he would find another like Ethan anyway.

It was worth the risk, he decided, particularly since he personally wouldn't be risking anything.

"Very well," he finally announced magnanimously. "You have ten days."

It would take him that long to contact a dealer anyway. If the pitiful wretch managed to return with his brother in that time, all well and good. If not, what had he really lost?

Devon's eyes lit with hope. He bowed low over Nevin's hem and kissed the material in relief.

"Oh! Thank you, Master. Thank you. I won't fail you, I promise."

"Enough!" Nevin snapped, pushing Devon's head roughly to the side. He cupped his hands over the leather collar at the hollow of the cat's throat and began to work at getting Ethan back.

Oh! And when he did…

Devon stayed perfectly still as the area around his collar became uncomfortably warm and a peculiar tingling sensation made the hairs on the back of his neck stand on end as it buzzed through him. He could see a glowing light filling the edges of his vision before it started to fade and the irritating prickle against his skin gradually ebbed away.

Master Nevin tugged on a silver disk now suspended from Devon's collar. "Use this to call me when you have him. Just hold the medallion firmly and call my name."

The weight of the disk settled against his skin, and he felt a renewed sense of hope. Hope that soon he would be returning to his Master's side. Soon he would be home and safe and his brother would be with him once again. It might take some serious grovelling on Ethan's part this time before Master Nevin forgave him this stunt though.

"Rolf!" the Master barked to the still-looming figure behind them, making Devon jump in alarm. "Prepare your brothers for travel. The hand will leave in one hour."

Devon looked anxiously to the tall, broad shouldered warrior cat. Unlike his own slim slave collar, Rolf's was thick, dark brown leather, heavily studded and menacing in its own right. His biceps bulged as he crossed his arms and the leather vest he wore threatened to give out under his massive chest muscles. But it was his penetrating golden brown eyes and the small, evil grin that Rolf turned on him from behind the Master's back that had Devon worrying his bottom lip in apprehension. A hand would mean four more of them too. Four more brothers from the same litter equally ominous and imposing to deal with. He couldn't help but quake with fear.

Seeing his nervousness, Master Nevin smiled, a thin, cruel smile filled with malice. "You didn't think I would trust you to accomplish this alone, did you?" he sneered. "Besides, if I know your little spitfire of a brother, and I think I do, you're going to need their help to drag him back here with you."

With that, Master Nevin swept from the room, dismissing the two of them completely and leaving Devon to wonder what in the world his brother had gotten him into this time.

Chapter Four

Michael fought against consciousness. He had been having such an amazing dream he didn't want to wake up yet. He burrowed further under the blankets and snuggled into the warmth he found there, groggily pulling the incredible source of heat towards him.

It wiggled back against him and moaned in approval.

Instantly, his eyes popped open in surprise and he was fully awake. Unfortunately, the room was completely black, so it didn't make much of a difference.

When the hell had he gotten a bed mate? he wondered in alarm, his thoughts still scattered and fragmented as he tried to get his bearings.

What the hell had he done?

His breath began to heave in and out of him in deep, frantic pants. Calm down, he lectured himself firmly, trying to slow his rapid breathing. Panicking wasn't going to help at all. He just had to sort through everything logically and calmly.

Taking a deep breath, he tried to recall how a very warm, very naked man had ended up in his bed. Trouble was he didn't even have any idea what time it was. It was night obviously, but was it nearly morning or had he slept the day away. Sometimes he slept like the dead and missed a whole day after a long stretch of night duty. Or, ironically enough, the same thing happened after a really big bender. He strained to remember which it was.

Scenarios raced through his mind. Had he gotten drunk somewhere and fallen into bed with some stranger he'd picked up at a bar? He remembered thinking about it recently, but he didn't really believe he would have followed through with it. And his head felt amazingly clear and pain free, so he didn't have a hangover. In fact, he felt oddly energised. But it was painfully obvious he had gotten laid recently given the warm naked body pressed so intimately up against his own, equally naked flesh.

Michael's heart beat a rapid tattoo in his chest as he tried to sort out dream from reality. His eyes struggled to adjust, and he quickly realised with relief that he was at least in his own bedroom. A sudden flash of lightening from a fast approaching storm illuminated the tousled, tawny brown and gold streaked head of hair that was currently snuggled into his shoulder affectionately.

Wow. That was nice.

He took a few more, deep, calming breaths as he tried to think through the sequence of recent events. He clearly remembered making it home. Maybe he'd slipped and hit his head because after that he was sure he'd found a…

The man in his arms began to purr. A very distinctive, rumbling purr, that vibrated against his chest and sent warm waves of memory crashing through him. His heart rate sky rocketed, and he found himself suddenly unable to control his breathing.

Clinically, some part of his brain registered that his body was gearing itself up for flight or fight. Interestingly enough, the presence of the warm welcoming male in his arms didn't make him want to do either. But he was holding a man that had been a cat for goodness sake. Or at least he had been before he had changed into an amazingly beautiful man that had given him the best blow-job of his life.

Just as his cock was beginning to recall the happy moment and fill to a hard, demanding ache between his legs, the man in question began to stir. The tawny, blonde head rubbed against Michael's shoulder in a curiously feline gesture then tilted up to regard him sleepily. Another flash of lightening lit the room and reflected oddly in the bright green eyes now watching him and reminded Michael that the stranger was definitely more than just gorgeous.

"Good-evening, Master," the man whispered huskily. "I opened the curtains and the window. It was getting hot in here and I didn't want you becoming uncomfortable. I hope that was alright."

Michael couldn't seem to get his brain and mouth to coordinate enough to reply. Instead, he watched dumbly as the man began to look uncertain and started nibbling nervously on his lower lip. Evidently, his cock didn't have the same issues, though, because his erection only got harder and throbbed insistently against his belly, eager and ready to go.

How on earth did the man do that? He wondered as he fumbled to turn on the bedside lamp. He was so turned on just from that one look and dozen or so words that he could probably drive nails with his hard-on.

It had been the same this morning, he realised. One minute he had been dazed and confused, not to mention too tired to tie his own shoelaces, never mind maintain a functional erection, the next minute he had abandoned all rational thought and was raring to go, hard, hot and needy as hell.

Right now, he wanted nothing more than to pound into the warm, willing body being offered to him until they were both lying spent and exhausted. He couldn't remember being this easily aroused since he was a teenager. Maybe not even then. It was like the man had a mainline to his libido and could turn him on at the drop of a hat! It was ridiculous.

Fantastic, he conceded, but ridiculous.

As they both blinked to adjust to the sudden flare of bright light from the bedside lamp, the man curled closer into Michael's side and began to gently rub at his flat stomach.

"How can I please you, Master?" he asked seductively.

Michael frowned in confusion. He remembered the man, cat, whatever, asking the same thing last night. Or was that this morning? Oh! For goodness sake! What was going on? he wondered in exasperation.

Was he being set up? Was someone playing a trick on him? Was he losing his mind? If he was he hoped he ended up like crazy old Ed Jenkins from his old neighbourhood. He'd eventually believed he was on a perpetual cruise of the South Pacific Islands. Come to think of it, he wouldn't mind taking someone like this handsome man along with him. He shook his head trying to get his thoughts back on track. He really had to get a grip here.

"Michael," he corrected absently as he scrutinised the man's face more closely.

He didn't look like someone who was playing a practical joke. Something about his eyes was too innocent, too open and honest. Oh! And gorgeous too.

The other man's reaction to his gentle correction was curious; he blushed slightly and lowered his eyes, but a shy smile of pleasure flirted at the edges of his lush, full lips. Michael found himself studying those tempting lips intently and felt himself falling more and more under his enticing spell.

Oh! Dear. He always had been a sucker for the cute, innocent-looking, shy ones.

He tried to hold firm. Daniel had looked sweet and innocent too. Pity, he'd never had a shy bone in his body.

"Michael." He heard the man repeat softly, as if savouring the sound as it rolled off his tongue, slightly accented by his low rumbling purr.

He loved the sound of his name on the man's lips mixed with that sexy purr. He craved more husky words and softly spoken caresses. He began to wonder what he would have to do to get them.

Oh! He was in so much trouble.

"Ummm...hi," he replied awkwardly, still struggling to hold it all together.

Maybe if he just ran with the idea that he wasn't going insane, possibly a bit of a stretch, but still...then he could concentrate on abandoning the idea that it was impossible for a man to turn into a cat and he'd be all set.

Maybe it was time to stop reading all those paranormal romance novels. It was obviously starting to affect his brain, because somewhere deep down, in a secret little part of himself where he kept his love of romance books and his addiction to musicals, he was a little excited to be face to face with the stunning little cat shifter and even more taken with the idea that the man might be interested in him.

Come to think of it, he had always scoffed cheerfully at some of the reactions characters in books had when they discovered their lover was a vampire, werewolf...cat shifter, he though drily. But he was finding it a real challenge to maintain his shock and disbelief as he looked at the man leaning over him.

The saucy smile he gave before dipping his head and beginning to nibble his way down Michael's neck was breathtaking. The soft lips that caressed tender flesh as he inched lower, making his way steadily towards a proud, taut nipple that lay exposed above the covers, made it impossible to think anything but 'yes' and 'thank you' and 'more'.

"Umm...ah!" he groaned desperately. "What...ah! What was your name again?"

"Ethan," the man murmured softly as he finally reached his goal and gave Michael's nipple a seductive lick. "I like the way you smell," he said before he playfully bit down on the nipple in his mouth. "And taste," he added with a wicked grin.

"Oh!" Michael moaned, throwing his head back in mounting pleasure. Everything was moving so fast. He was confused and slightly dazed, but he was rapidly losing control of his ability to think, much less care. His cock was demanding that now was not the time to ask stupid questions. And in its opinion, all questions at this point were stupid. Now was the time to fuck, it stated quite clearly. Still...

"Ummm... I think we should probably... Oh!... I think we should probably slow down a bit," he tried to say.

He really did. He tried to get out a coherent sentence. He tried to slow the whole proceedings down and figure out what was going on. He tried to find out who Ethan was, where he had come from, what he was even. But Ethan was having none of it. All thoughts of awkwardness, of how impossible this all was, in fact any rational thought at all, fled as Ethan began to suckle gently at Michael's nipple.

"Oh!" he groaned in ecstasy.

Ethan suckled softly, gentle but insistent pulls that made Michael buck and squirm with pleasure. He went on and on, varying his speed and interspersing it with slow sweeps of his raspy tongue. He pushed Michael's excitement ever upward until he was mindless with need. Finally, Ethan released his nipple and gave it one last, long lick.

"You like that?" he asked huskily.

Before Michael could answer, however, Ethan was kissing his way over to the other nipple and doing the same thing to it.

Ethan ministered to him like an acolyte at a temple. With exquisite care and attention he worshipped Michael's body, touching, tasting, and teasing. It was as if he had all the time in the world in which to lavish pleasure on him, and Michael was powerless to stop him. Not that he wanted to.

Ethan traced a feather light caress down his torso until he reached his hard throbbing cock resting impatiently between their bodies. But instead of touching it, he skimmed around it, and Michael had to work hard not to moan in frustration. He was slightly mollified when the hand worked lower and began to lovingly caress his balls. They were already drawn tight to his body, full and sensitive, and the delicate touch was exquisite torture as Ethan continued to caress the firm round spheres.

He began to worm his way down Michael's body, stopping intermittently to drop tender, lingering kisses. The moment dragged on forever until he reached Michael's cock and began to inch his mouth over the plump, moist head. Michael watched as his full, hard shaft disappeared completely into the warm cavern of Ethan's mouth before he began a slow, easy rhythm of sucking that drove Michael wild.

After several long, wonderful minutes, Ethan released Michael's cock. Gently, he licked and probed at the slit that oozed glistening drops onto his eager tongue. He bathed the tight, throbbing head, then ran his tongue down the sensitive bobbing shaft, tracing the thick lines of veins he found along the way. By the time he had finished his intimate tongue bath, Michael was moaning and thrashing uncontrollably.

Ethan just grinned wickedly, confident and sure now, as if knowing Michael's every need and reaction. He took the pulsing cock firmly in his hand and enthusiastically began to pump away in a steady rhythm, the motion eased by the slick pre-come and his own saliva. With Michael's cock taken care of, Ethan lowered his head and traced his tongue down below his balls, then between the smooth rounded cheeks of his ass.

Michael cried out wildly, eagerly spreading his legs and tilting his pelvis to give Ethan more room. The tongue caressed over the tight furl of his hole, then began to probe gently but insistently at the eager pucker.

He couldn't hold it in any longer. Within seconds thick, hot spurts of cum shot out from his cock to coat his belly and chest. The orgasm went on and on until he was hoarse from crying out with the pleasure of his release.

So much for not doing one night stands or casual sex, Michael thought wearily as he laid spread out and slightly dazed, slowly coming down from one of the most intense orgasm of his life. Even as he thought it, he felt a dull, heavy ache begin in his chest.

He realised it was probably just his loneliness, and yes, perhaps a little horniness as well, though Ethan had certainly helped in that department, but he didn't want this to be just a one off. He couldn't help wishing that this could be the start of something more. He really wanted to get to know this incredibly man.

Sure, all relationships had to start somewhere, he mused. Why not here with a breaking and entering shape-shifting cat from who knew where, that he knew nothing about other than the fact he had a predilection for calling him Master and was absolutely amazing in bed? *Perfect start*, he thought acerbically.

Closing his eyes, he tried to rein in his sarcasm. It wasn't helping, and though he may not know much about where Ethan was from or who he was, he knew the man was special. Not in 'a man that can turn into a cat' kind of way, though there was that too, of course, but in a fiery, passionate, 'grab the world by the horns and take no prisoners' kind of a way. He really liked that. Actually, he had to admit, it was sexy as hell.

Looking down, he took the time to study the slight figure curled into his side with his head resting over Michael's heart. He was so lovely and a generous and affectionate lover as well.

Michael had to admit he liked that idea too. A considerate, generous lover who wasn't afraid to go after what he wanted. Michael had to suppress a chuckle at himself. He really was a romantic fool.

He knew it was probably an unrealistic fantasy, a projection of what he wanted to find most in the world rather than what he was likely to find. But perhaps it was time to take a chance and see what happened. He was sick of not living. Of simply existing, playing it safe so no one could stab him in the back or heart, again. Why couldn't they take one day at a time and see where it might go?

It was weird, yes. It was impossibly fast, certainly. It was the most bizarre set of circumstances he could possibly imagine, definitely. But there it was. Even the idea of letting the man in his arms get away was too painful to think about. So he wouldn't.

"Ethan?" he said into the quiet tranquillity that filled the room.

"Yes, Mas— I mean, Michael," Ethan responded softly. He seemed just as unwilling to disturb the calm afterglow they were basking in as Michael was.

There were so many questions, so many things to ask, so many things to find out about this man. But not right now. Everything seemed so precious and yet so precariously balanced. He didn't want to upset what he had only just unexpectedly found. What if he started to pry and everything unravelled around him and he was left alone agai—

He cut off his thoughts. He wasn't going there right now.

"Are you hungry?" he asked simply.

It was a little cowardly that he was avoiding things. Important things. But he wasn't ready for anything more deep and meaningful just yet.

Ethan sat up and stared at him, his luminous, emerald green eyes shining with an odd mix of uncertainty and banked passion. Then he smiled, a sweet lovely smile that lit up his whole face, as he began to purr and nod his head eagerly.

Michael felt his heart melt just a little more.

"What would you like?"

"You," Ethan whispered huskily.

Oh!

Okay! He definitely wanted to keep him now. All he had to do was get the man to want to stay.

He suddenly realised he'd been sorely neglecting the man. And after all his thoughts of generous partners and considerate lovers! He felt like kicking himself in the ass for being so preoccupied. Of course, he'd been dealing with some pretty heavy reality checks. Checks he wasn't sure had quite cleared the bank yet. But that was neither here nor there. He had work to do if he was going to convince the gorgeous man beside him to hang around.

He grinned, this was going to be fun. He couldn't wait to give Ethan a taste of the same pleasure he had received. Lots of tastes, in fact, he thought excitedly. But one thing in particular sprang to mind. Or throbbed, he corrected wickedly as he felt Ethan's hard cock pressing insistently against his thigh.

Gently, he tilted Ethan's chin up to meet him in a tender kiss, gradually working his tongue into the other man's mouth until he felt him begin to respond passionately. Ethan enthusiastically straddled his lap as their kiss turned almost feral. Michael would have shouted with joy if his mouth hadn't been busy with more important things.

Even so, his smile eventually broke the connection of their lips as Ethan groaned and moved against him. Oh! This was going to be so much fun.

Using his superior size and strength, he rolled Ethan over onto his back then kissed a line from his mouth to his delicate, pointed ear. He nibbled softly on the flesh there and was rewarded by a groan of pleasure. Encouraged, he sucked gently, but insistently on the lobe, and Ethan went wild, moaning and writhing in ecstasy beneath him.

Well, what do you know, he thought, extraordinarily pleased with himself. Now he knew something else about his passionate, fiery little lover, apart from the fact he could turn into a cat, which was admittedly pretty significant. It seemed that the smaller man had extraordinarily sensitive ears. He would have to store that little bit of information away for later, because he was becoming more and more determined that there would be a later.

After several long moments lavishing attention on Ethan's delicate ears, he gradually worked his way down his neck. He treated both nipples to a similar loving caress before continuing to work his way down to probe gentle at the shallow indent of Ethan's belly button with his tongue. Finally, he found himself staring at Ethan's long, slim cock.

It too was beautiful. Long and slim and gently curved with a wonderfully rounded head that dripped glistening drops of pearly pre-cum onto his smooth belly. Gently, he licked and probed at the slit, savouring its surprisingly spicy flavour. He leisurely lowered his mouth all the way down Ethan's shaft until his nose pressed against the sparse covering of curly golden brown hairs at the base of his cock. Advancing and retreating, he set up a steady pace that had Ethan thrashing and moaning in seconds.

For a few moments, he let a finger ride alongside the cock in his mouth, then used it to gently explore the soft, sensitive tissue behind the balls before circling and probing at the puckered entrance at the back. Ever so slowly and carefully he pushed his finger in and the slight stretch dragged a deep moan from his suddenly writhing lover. Soon one finger was joined by another and Ethan's delicate pink hole was riding the digits in counterpoint to the action of his mouth.

He knew from experience that the combination was delightful. He set up a slow, almost languid rhythm determined to push the man higher and higher before he finally let him climax. When he felt Ethan's muscles begin to tremble with his need, he rotated his hand slightly and pegged his gland, rubbing over the soft, spongy pleasure spot with practiced ease. God bless Anatomy and Physiology 101!

Instantly, Ethan thrust up, bucking his hips wildly and crying out in bliss. A fountain of hot cum was pushed from his pulsing shaft and his hole clenched tight around Michael's fingers in an explosive orgasm. Michael swallowed, desperately trying to control his self-satisfied grin and maintain his seal around the throbbing cock in his mouth. He didn't want to lose a drop of the man's delicious offering.

When he had gently milked every last drop of cum, he tenderly cleaned Ethan's spent cock with his tongue. Ethan had long since collapsed back on the bed with a final moan of relief and now lay sprawled out limply among the rumpled sheets.

Michael rested his head down on Ethan's hip, allowing a small, smug smile to playing across his lips.

"I didn't... I mean I don't... Why did you do that?" Ethan finally managed to ask in a shocked, slightly shaky voice.

Michael started with surprise, jerking up into a sitting position to look down into his lover's eyes in alarm.

"You didn't like it?" he asked, too panicked to stop and think for a moment about the fact that the man had just come. And quite spectacularly too.

When Ethan didn't say anything in reply, Michael got even more worried. He felt himself pale, horrified and self-conscious as terrible possibilities began running through his mind. Was he a bad lover? Was that why he was alone? Had he been too forceful and demanding? He thought Ethan would like him reciprocating. Had he somehow done something wrong without even knowing it? He'd always prided himself on being sensitive and understanding of others. What if...

Ethan picked up on his distress and quickly plastered himself to Michael's chest. He began to rub his head against him in what appeared to be a very catlike attempt at offering comfort and reassure.

"Oh! No, Master. I mean, Michael. I loved it. It's just..." Ethan squirmed, suddenly looking very shy and dipping his head to hide his eyes. "What I mean to say is no one... That is..."

"No one's ever gone down on you before?" Michael asked, his voice rising sharply in surprise and sudden comprehension.

Ethan was now the one looking nervous as he turned troubled, uncertain eyes up to him. Slowly, he shook his head and Michael could only stare at him in disbelief.

Unexpected anger began to build inside him. How was that possible?

Ethan knew his way around the male body too well to have never been intimate with another man before. There was no way he thought Ethan was a virgin, but...then there was the recurring master reference.

His mind was a whirl of chaotic thoughts. He really didn't understand any of this. Then again his lover was a cat, for crying out loud.

No, he corrected himself, he was a man. A man that had very much enjoyed getting a blowjob. He realised now that his insecurities had taken a back seat, and he was thinking clearly again. Ethan was a very attractive, open and giving man, and he was his lover.

Michael squared his shoulders and prepared himself mentally to talk to Ethan. He didn't want there to be any misunderstandings between them. He had the feeling that this was going to be very important conversation if they were to have any chance at a relationship together.

"How many lovers have you had, Ethan?" he asked gently.

"Just one," Ethan answered easily.

"Selfish bastard," he muttered under his breath.

He couldn't help feeling terribly angry on Ethan's behalf. He knew about dominance and submission, and he had absolutely no problem with BDSM. While he wasn't into kink himself, it didn't bother him that someone else might be, as long as it was done sanely between two mutually consenting adults.

Perhaps it was wrong to assume anything about Ethan, but his obvious pleasure in being given Michael's name to use and the ease in which he had given up calling him Master, not to mention having taken the lead and not having once deferred to Michael's authority as they had made love, made Michael fairly sure Ethan wasn't naturally submissive. This suggested that Ethan had either been coerced or forced into BDSM. And that was just wrong as far as he was concerned.

How could anyone do that to the beautiful, generous, giving man that was now his lover?

And regardless of the craziness of the whole situation, he knew that was exactly what he wanted now. For Ethan to be his lover, he thought possessively. He just desperately hoped he wasn't setting himself up for a big fall.

At Michael's vehement utterance, Ethan's eyes had widened until Michael knew exactly what they meant when they said 'eyes as wide as saucers'. He couldn't help himself, he pulled Ethan into his arms and stroked his hands lovingly down the younger man's beautiful body. He wasn't sure how to make things right or what to do to put Ethan at ease, but he knew he had to say something. He finally decided on honesty. It seemed the right place to start, and the situation was so sudden and bizarre he didn't seem to have anything to lose and maybe a whole lot to gain by opening up to Ethan.

"Sex," he began hesitantly, "for me anyway, is about intimacy. It's about sharing. About a giving and taking between two people that care about each other." He was instantly embarrassed to have revealed so much about himself and his heart, and braced himself for Ethan's reaction. For his derision.

But Ethan didn't laugh at him. He just stared as if in awe then smiled his beautiful, sweet smile that made Michael think of the sunshine finally peaking out after an endless week of rain, and purred.

Once again Michael felt his heart give a little more. He felt light. Free. He knew his ideas sounded sappy and would probably never be the most popular amongst some of his peers, especially the party going crowd he had once hung out with when he had been with Daniel. But there it was. It was more than just a bit of fun to Michael. More than just wham bam, thank you, man! If that made him a pussy, so be it.

Michael stared to snigger. A pussy! Oh, man. Sometimes he was such an idiot.

Once he started he couldn't seem to stop. His snigger grew into a chuckle which quickly became a full-bodied laugh. Ethan looked at him in confusion, but a small uncertain smile played at his lips as well. Michael knew he sounded hysterical. Most probably he was hysterical. But at the same time he felt oddly free for the first time in a long, long time. Free to be true to himself. He was going to be honest and live with the consequences.

"Master?" Ethan asked uneasily.

"Do you know how unbelievable you are?" Michael demanded when he finally got himself under control.

"Well, I'm starting to understand that you don't seem to run into too many pleasure cats here," Ethan replied seriously. "I certainly haven't."

"No." Michael chuckled, even though that wasn't exactly what he had meant and wasn't even sure what a pleasure cat was.

There was a long pause as they settled once more into each other's embrace.

"Do you mind?" Ethan finally asked tentatively.

"Mind what?" Michael asked, his mind already drifting sleepily.

"What I am? A pleasure cat?"

"No," Michael replied easily. "I have to admit I'm not exactly sure what that is, but I like you just the way you are."

For a moment Ethan looked up to search his eyes. It was a desperately hopeful look tinged with trepidation.

"You do?" he asked, almost as if pleading for it to be true.

Michael nodded solemnly and found himself with an arm full of ecstatic cat shifter a moment later, as Ethan threw his arms around him and hugged him fiercely.

He soaked in the other man's warmth. Things were a long way from settled but maybe it would all work out in the end. He certainly wanted to believe it would. What he had said to Ethan was true. He did like him just the way he was. And not just because he was fantastic in bed and had the hottest body he'd ever seen outside of those buff calendars he pretended not to ogle.

It was more than that. It was something about the man himself that made him want to get to know him better. To learn more and everything there was to know about him.

Just then, Ethan's stomach voiced a loud rumbling complaint.

"Still hungry, baby?" Michael chuckled.

"Always," Ethan replied saucily, despite another loud protest from his tummy to make with the food.

Slapping playfully at Ethan's bare rump, Michael pushed the man off him reluctantly, but he was determined to look after the man now he had found him.

"Come on. I make a mean omelette. Let's get you fed so we can get back to bed."

"Oh! Yes, please," Ethan crooned as he wiggled his butt and climbed out of bed seductively.

Michael groaned. He might need to start working out more regularly and taking his vitamins.

Chapter Five

A storm had begun to close in on the city. The heavy scent of ozone filled the air and flashes of lightening splinted across the sky, followed rapidly by the deep rumbling sound of thunder. The wind was picking up and had begun whipping through the streets sending stray papers and leaves swirling high into the air. It gusted and battered at the glass of the shop front windows in the nearly deserted downtown shopping precinct.

The few remaining people still out and about were hurrying in the direction of parked cars or warm buildings, too busy trying to beat the rain to notice when a particularly bright flash of lightening seemed to hit the centre of one of the dingy allies leaving six figures in its wake, five tall and bulky men surrounding one small and naked.

The huge, broad shouldered warriors turned around cautiously. Muscles flexed and rippled under skin-tight leather pants and vests. Eyes, a curious golden brown, took everything in. They scanned about with quick, efficient movements, calmly assessing the area for any threat.

In contrast, the slim, dark haired figure huddled in the middle of them looked as if he was trying to sink into the suspiciously stained concrete. Still naked, having had no clothes of his own to put on, Devon gingerly sniffing the air and instantly regretted it as he drew back and wrinkling his nose in disgust. He began to breathe in shallowly through his mouth instead. Now he knew exactly why he had never had a desire to leave the shelter of his Master's castle. This place was strange and terrifying. And it smelt really bad too.

"Pair up and fan out," Rolf barked at the other men. "If you find him, send one to follow and the other return to rendezvous at this location in six hours."

Some of the men shared a hesitant, confused look.

"Shouldn't we stay together, brother?" one of the men standing around Devon asked quietly. "Maybe we should see if the little one can track down his twin first or at least point us in the right direction."

"Are you challenging me, Ryan?" Rolf snapped back, visibly bristling and drawing himself up threateningly. "Do you want to fight me for leadership of the hand?"

"No," Ryan replied.

Devon could almost hear the man's teeth grinding together he looked so frustrated. The other brothers just looked between each other nervously.

"Then go!" Rolf bellowed, throwing his arms up in an aggressive, dismissive gesture.

Two broke off immediately to hurry away and a third tugged on Ryan's arm when he seemed reluctant to back down. Finally, he relented and followed his brother, stalking sullenly off down the alley.

Rolf watched them go, glaring all the while at his rebellious brother's retreating back. But when Devon hesitantly stepped forward to follow them out onto the street, a large, beefy hand closed around his upper arm and jerked him to a stop.

"Where do you think you're going?"

"T-To start tracking down my brother," Devon stuttered nervously. "I know the Master said this was the last portal activated from the castle and must have been the one Ethan used, but I can't pick up his scent, not with all the other smells in here. I thought if I could just get out on the street I could..."

"Oh! You thought, did you?" Rolf sneered. "And while you were thinking did you stop to think what exactly might be in it for me?"

Devon blinked owlishly up into the leering face above him.

"The Master..."he began hesitantly, watching Rolf closely with increasing uneasy. "The Master said you were to help me."

He tried hard not to sound afraid. He tried to keep his voice firm and level, without the telltale quaver of fear, but something in the way Rolf looked at him made him tremble uncontrollable. He really didn't think he was convincing anyone, least of all himself.

"Well, the Master's not here now, is he?" Rolf began slyly as he slowly advanced on Devon, forcing him to step back as he relentlessly invaded his personal space.

"But..." Devon stammered, desperately trying to look around Rolf in the hope that one of his brothers might come back and rescue him. Ryan had seemed almost reasonable, if intensely focused on his duty, when they had left. He was sure he could appeal to the man to call Rolf off. But the rest of the hand was nowhere to be seen.

As Rolf approached, Devon tried side stepping, but Rolf merely followed him until he was pressed back against the rough bricks of the alley.

"Tell you what. How about a little exchange? You help me with my problem and I'll help you with yours."

Devon watched in horror as Rolf started loosening the ties on his leather pants. He tried to pull away, but the wall at his back prevented him from retreating any further.

"But it's…it's forbidden. I belong to the Master. He'll kill you," Devon whispered in disbelief and growing alarm.

"No one here to see us and last I saw, Master Nevin was ready to kick your ass out the door. Don't think he'd care much what I do with you right now. Not unless you find that brother of yours. Then it's just you and me knows, and if I go down, you don't want to know what will happen to you."

Devon shivered. He knew there were always ways of getting to someone if you were as determined and psychotic as Rolf. Even a supposedly protected pleasure cat wouldn't be safe.

As he spoke, Rolf had been releasing his thick, ruddy cock. Its bulbous head bobbed obscenely in front of him, and Devon found that he couldn't take his eyes off it. He watched in horrified fascination as a clear bead of pre-come formed at the slit of the huge cock and oozed down the shaft.

"I think you like the look of my cock," Rolf leered. "I bet you can't wait to get your lips around it and let me fuck your mouth until you can swallow all my hot cum down your throat."

Devon shook his head franticly in denial, but he couldn't drag his eyes away from the throbbing monster. Rolf grabbed at Devon's hand and before Devon could even think of trying to pull it back, Rolf used it to slowly stroke over himself.

"Mmmmm, feels good," Rolf growled, closing his eyes in approval as he masturbated with Devon's hand. "I know you're keen to get back to let the Master fuck your tight ass, but I think that until we find that wayward brother of yours, you can at least show me some appreciation for my help. Keep you in practice, so to speak. Of course if you don't want my help..." Rolf left his statement unfinished. The implication was clear, as was his intent as he continued to enjoy Devon's hand.

In truth, Devon didn't know how he was going to find his brother. The map the Master had shown them of the place he suspected Ethan had come to, was huge. And it was frightening being away from the comfort of the castle walls. The thought of all the strange things and people he was sure to meet here terrified him.

Of course the thought of taking Rolf's cock was nearly as terrifying. But not quite.

But since Rolf had sent the rest of his brothers away, he was all that was left of home and the only world he had ever known. At least if Rolf was with him, he wouldn't be quite so alone. And being so big and aggressive, Rolf could protect him in this scary place if it came down to it.

Hopefully, when they reconnected with the others in the morning, they wouldn't let Rolf send them away again. With any luck, they would keep him too preoccupied and distracted to think about taking anything worse than a little pleasure from his mouth. Ryan certainly seemed to rile his brother. Not that that was necessarily a good thing. This could just be a one off thing, he reassured himself. And it really was a small price to pay for getting home safely.

Reluctantly, Devon lowered himself to his knees. He saw Rolf's cock jerk in anticipation as the rough ground dug painfully into his bare flesh. Gently, he took the tip of his shaft into his mouth and began to caress the sensitive underside with his tongue timidly.

But Rolf was having none of that. He fisted his hand in Devon's messy black locks and thrust hard to the back of his throat. Devon couldn't help the automatic gag that squeezed his throat shut and brought tears to his eyes. His reaction only seemed to spur Rolf on.

Devon concentrated hard on opening his mouth and throat wide to take the thick member in as Rolf ruthlessly fucked his mouth. Over and over he pounded into Devon until finally, with one powerful thrust he pushed to the very back of Devon's throat and came.

Devon felt the heavy pulse of Rolf's shaft in his mouth as seed exploded down his throat in long, powerful waves. He swallowed convulsively, desperately trying to take it all and prevent himself from choking. Rolf's orgasm went on and on until Devon thought he just might pass out from lack of oxygen.

Finally, Rolf sagged over him where Devon still knelt, shocked and sore from the brutal taking. He swallowed several times, trying to get the taste of the man out of the back of his throat, but it didn't really work. Slowly, Rolf removed his obviously sensitive cock from his mouth, a slight gasp escaping him as it slipped over Devon's swollen lips.

"Mmmmm…not bad." Rolf panted with satisfaction, tucking his still half-hard shaft back in and refastening his pants. "We'll just call that a little down payment on what you owe me."

Devon remained on his knees. The bitter taste of Rolf's seed still clung to the back of his throat and tongue as he felt the hot blush of shame and a dawning horror at what his life had become until he could return to his Master. He had to find his brother. And fast.

"Come on," Rolf barked as he stepped back.

Before Devon had a chance to collect himself and move to obey, Rolf grabbed him by the arm and dragged him up to his feet.

"Much as I like you naked and in this form, I think it might be best if you changed. You won't draw anywhere near as much attention, and I know you wouldn't be stupid enough to run away on me. Not that I probably wouldn't enjoy chasing after this cute ass." Rolf slapped Devon hard on the rump and let out a ribald chuckle when he jumped at the unexpected sting.

He quickly changed forms, relieved to be hidden beneath his thick, black fur coat and wishing he had thought to change himself earlier. Maybe if he stayed in his feline form, he could avoid anymore of Rolf's 'payments'. He could only silently hope so anyway as Rolf led the way out of the alley to begin their search for his errant twin brother.

Chapter Six

Michael absently smoothed his hand over the firm, warm chest he was resting his head against. They were both awake, idly stroking and petting each other as the last of the day's light faded away behind the distant mountains. It had been a wonderfully lazy start to his holiday, Michael mused. Loving and eating and playing, energetically and dreamily in turns. Now they were content to just lie together, softly stroking and touching one another.

Michael felt strangely sated. More than having simply taken the edge off his physical desire, he felt content and at peace as he listened to the steady drum of Ethan's heart. It was a good heart, he had decided during the day. Still, he didn't know much about what made the man tick. They had been too busy exploring other, more urgent matters. Suddenly, he found himself wanting to know more about the man in his bed and quite possibly edging his way into his heart as well.

"Ethan, where did you come from?" he asked absently into the peaceful silence.

Ethan tensed then began to struggle beneath him. "I won't go back there. I'll just run away again. You can't make me go back," he said vehemently, a touch of fear hidden in his voice.

"Calm down," Michael soothed as he struggled to sit up, still holding on to Ethan, and looked into his amazing green eyes. At the moment they were filled with agitation and a hint of dread. "No one's going to make you do anything you don't want to do."

Ethan just looked at him.

"Okay. I'm not going to make you do anything you don't want to do," he rephrased.

Ethan still looked slightly suspicious, but he also saw overwhelming relief fill his face as well, and it made Michael's heart ache. As the tension gradually melted away from his lover's slight frame, he felt the need to continue to comfort and reassure him.

"Never, Ethan. I promise. I'll never make you do anything you don't want to do."

It was as if he had handed Ethan the keys to the eternal city. The wonder and awe on his face made Michael uneasy. What on earth had his man been through?

"I don't want to go," Ethan finally blurted out, as if challenging his promise to him.

"I don't want you to go either," Michael replied evenly.

"You want me to stay?" Ethan asked, a hopeful look slowly entering his eyes.

Michael nodded silently. The three little words he heard whispering in his head might be too much right now, but he didn't deny he was starting to feel them, and he didn't want to lose the opportunity to keep this amazing man in his life. Ethan must have understood what he didn't say because he launched himself at Michael, knocking the breath out of him as they tumbled back in the bed. He felt a chuckle, both of relief and amusement at Ethan's antics bubble up inside him, and let it out on a sigh of contentment.

After a long silence of just holding and stoking one another, Michael quietly began to explain. "I just want to know you better."

Instantly, he felt Ethan begin to purr, but he also felt drops of moisture land on his chest and a slight hitch to Ethan's breathing as well.

"Are you alright?" he asked softly, uncomfortable with the idea that he had made the other man cry, but refusing to withhold the opportunity from him to vent his tears. If this was what Ethan needed, Michael would hold him for the rest of his life while he cried.

Ethan simply nodded "Just happy," he croaked out.

Such a simple thing to make someone so overwhelmingly happy, Michael thought. Was it so unusual that someone would want to get to know Ethan? He guessed it must be and that thought made him rather sad, as well. And determined. From now on, he promised himself, he was going to give the little man a chance at a better life. He wanted more than anything to be allowed to do that, to love and care for the man in his arms.

Michael took a deep breath. More and more the word 'love' was filling his head when he thought of Ethan. He had always considered himself fairly level headed, if secretly a bit of a romantic. He was steady and reliable but a bit boring and well, ordinary. It was crazy, but this time he wanted to run with the feelings bubbling up inside him.

Ironically, he wanted to be wild and adventurous and take a risk on this stunning, curiously innocent, generous man. He wondered sardonically whether Daniel would be proud. Because on gut instinct alone, which told him Ethan was not only worth the risk but would never betray him, he wanted to throw caution to the wind and try to keep Ethan. And even more amazingly, he felt not the slightest hesitation, only relief and hope.

"Why did you keep calling me Master?" he finally asked quietly, still holding Ethan against his chest, the tousled head of golden brown hair tucked securely under his chin.

For a while, he thought that Ethan would refuse to answer him. He was disappointed that Ethan wouldn't confide in him, but he wouldn't pry it out. Ethan would open up when he was ready. It just put a little damper on his earlier exuberance.

"It's all I have ever known," Ethan finally began to explain. "I'm a pleasure cat. I was raised to be a courtesan. All cat shifters are property of one sort or another. Used by mage-kind to facilitate their privileged existence. But pleasure cats are very specifically sex slaves to the Tantric Mage Clan. We are locked away from the world and meant to service a Master Mage, or sometimes an entire coven, and provide them with the energy they need to perform their magic through sex, or more specifically by mutual orgasms between the mage and pleasure cat twins."

"Wait," Michael interrupted, his mind reeling with shock. Courtesans? Sex slaves? Mages draining energy from his little cat in some sort of strange ménage sex rite. "You have a twin?" he finally forced out, trying to focus on one of the tamer things that had come out of Ethan's mouth.

"Yes," Ethan answered calmly. "A brother named Devon." Ethan paused as if trying to think how to explain something very important to him. "We're not really allowed to be free. I mean there are strays and ferals of course, but without a Master's protection... Well, we're fair game. We have to fend for ourselves and any mage is allowed to hunt us. They can kill us or capture us, whatever they want really. We have no rights or recourse." Ethan seemed to consider his next words very carefully. "Most realms are pretty harsh, unforgiving places for us but..."

"But you wanted more," Michael finished for him, wanting to end the man's obvious discomfort.

He couldn't blame Ethan for hesitating to talk about it all now. He was finding it hard just listening to what Ethan had been through.

"I just couldn't take it anymore. I didn't want that life and I didn't want it for my twin either. But Devon...Devon would never run away. At least now that I'm not there...well, at least the Master will finally leave him alone. He wouldn't be able to...use him without me. At least he's safe from that, even if he can never be free. I just wish..."

Ethan didn't finish that thought, but Michael's heart bled for the proud, fiery spirit he saw almost crushed before him. To have lost his brother, a brother he obviously loved, to this terrible regime. On top of everything else, to know that he would probably never see his twin again. It was heartbreaking.

Michael had sensed and seen the flickers of passion and lust for life in the other man, but it was almost gone now. Smothered just by talking about his past, until all that was left was smouldering embers, banked and tamped down until they were almost extinguished with the sadness of his twin's loss. His own heart was heavy and ached for him.

But he was also glad Ethan had been brave enough to risk everything and escape. He couldn't even begin to imagine what his poor baby had been through. Having to think of him enduring it for a lifetime was unbearable. How had he even managed to survive that sort of life this long?

In their short acquaintance, he could easily see how intolerable Ethan would have found such an existence. He was far too passionate to live like that. It only made Michael all the more determined to help Ethan find what he was looking for.

"I don't want to be your Master, Ethan," Michael began tentatively, feeling Ethan stiffen in his arms.

But he had already anticipated what Ethan's response would be. He would think he was being rejected. Nothing could be further from the truth. Gently, he tilted Ethan's chin up so they could look into each other's eyes. He didn't want there to be any misunderstandings. "I don't want you to leave," he said firmly.

Ethan looked confused. "But..."

"You wanted something more, Ethan? Something different?" He waited until Ethan gave a bemused, hesitant nod before continuing. "I don't want a courtesan or a slave or whatever else you were to your Master. I want someone I can share my day with. Someone I can talk to. I want someone I can see new and exciting things with or just curl up and watch TV along side of." He paused, searching Ethan's eyes for understanding. "Do you think you might like to try that?" he asked levelly, not wanting to unduly influence the other man's decision, but desperately hoping he would want to try being together as an equal partner. "Would you like to try with me?" he clarified.

The answer to Michael's question was tears that began to slip down Ethan's cheeks and the frantic nodding of his head before he threw his arms around Michael and burrowed into his embrace, clinging to him desperately.

Smiling while he held Ethan in his arms, he looked around his bedroom as if seeing it for the first time. Everything was made new and wonderful by Ethan's presence and acceptance of him, even his dull bedroom.

Their bedroom, he corrected himself. It was their bedroom now, and it was peaceful and quiet except for the occasional hitch in Ethan's breathing.

He'd had the oddest start to his holidays, he acknowledged. And it was the most bizarre start to a relationship he'd ever heard of. Still, he thought while holding the warm, gorgeous man tightly in his arms, it was a good start.

Perhaps he could expand on that good start, he mused as his hands continued to caress Ethan, beginning to make steadily bolder forays downwards to his smooth, round ass. Ethan didn't say anything, but gradually Michael felt his body relax and melt into him. He felt a soft, rough tongue lapped gently at the hinge of his jaw beneath his ear.

He turned his head and touched his own tongue to the tip of one of Ethan's oh, so deliciously sensitive ears. The man in his arms shuddered as he began to squeeze and kneed his firm ass in concert to his exploring tongue.

"Want you," he breathed lustily in the shell of the ear he had been fondling.

"Want you too," Ethan breathed back.

It was such a natural thing to return when two people moved together intimately as they did now. But he knew how special this moment was for Ethan. It would be like a first time really, raw, exciting, just a touch frightening, but exhilarating at the same time. Because this time, unlike every other time, when he would have thought it was expected of him, Ethan would truly choose to participate. It would be a sharing of passion, not a giving or a taking. And Michael was determined to make sure this time, his first time, was everything it could be.

"Roll over," Michael whispered into the spell of passion that wove around them.

Ethan didn't hesitate to roll onto his stomach. For a moment, Michael considered the strong, lean back before him. He would be willing to bet the last dollar Daniel had left in his ravaged bank account that Ethan had never had anyone love on him with a sensual back rub.

He grinned. They were something of a speciality of his, actually. He loved the feeling of connection he made as he moved his hands over a lover's back. Not that there had been terribly many, but his previous boyfriends had never knocked him back when he had offered them a rub down.

He reached for the oil he kept bedside his bed. In the last twelve months, the bottle had certainly gotten a work out. He was rather pleased to realise that, with any luck, from now on he would be using it with Ethan rather than just by himself.

Pouring a little into his hand, he worked his palms together to warm and spread the oil around. When he was satisfied the oil was at just the right temperature and coated his hands liberally, he slowly began to work them over Ethan's back in long, firm strokes. He felt the muscle groups under his hands and savoured every perfect inch of Ethan's back. He concentrated on finding the spots that held tension and needed his special care and attention.

Steadily deepening the massage, he worked over tense shoulders, never hard enough to hurt, but just enough to sooth and relax. He worked down from the shoulders to knead the muscles running away from Ethan's spine then concentrated for several long minutes on his lower back before attending to his temptingly firm, rounded ass.

He could feel the tension draining out of Ethan and slowly brought his hands back to the long slow caresses that he had started with. He lost himself in stroking and touching Ethan's beautiful skin, feeling his own tension fading away as he concentrated on giving pleasure. It was very cathartic actually, this sensual giving. Finally, he brought his hands to rest over the centre of Ethan's back, taking a moment to just breathe in the spicy scent of the warm oil and his lover's own unique fragrance.

When he finally peered into Ethan's averted face, he was stunned to find the man sound asleep, breathing deeply and making the cutest little snuffling noises. Not quite the effect he had been after, he thought dryly as he smiled to himself. But to be honest, he couldn't find it in himself to be truly disappointed.

He had the feeling the man currently sleeping so peacefully beside him had been given very few opportunities in his life to be given something without needing to give exponentially more in return. It pleased him down to his soul that he had been able to do this small thing for Ethan and take nothing in return but the joy of feeling closer to him.

That really was enough. More than enough actually, he realised as he snuggled down, pulling the sleeping man into his arms. Ethan sighed in his sleep and settled more closely against Michael. The soft rumbling purr he was beginning to crave lulled him to into a contented sleep as well.

Chapter Seven

Rolf stalked along yet another street with Devon creeping along timidly beside him still desperately trying to catch a hint of his brother's scent. It was pointless. After the heavy rain yesterday, the city had been washed clean. But he was happy enough to follow along, for the moment.

Actually, he couldn't believe his luck. He had been sent out to help retrieve the Master's favourite pleasure cat in the company of a twin he quite obviously didn't give a toss about. It was a wet dream come true, and he was sure he wouldn't be able to wipe the wicked grin off his face for at least the next week. Possibly longer if he played his cards right.

He had never been allowed anywhere near the coveted and cosseted sex slaves before. He planned on taking full advantage of the opportunity he had been given. He was never likely to get another opportunity to sample their very special delights.

Getting rid of the rest of his brothers again had been too easy. He had sent them all off on another wild goose chase today, dividing them into a hopeless search pattern with no intention of joining up with them again before they were forced to return home. Now that he knew the basic lay of the land, he could avoid them indefinitely if he chose and enjoy his treat all to himself.

Rolf licked his lips in anticipation. It was said they were trained to give the very highest orgasmic pleasure to their Master to enhance the Tantric Mages' magical energies. But apparently it wasn't restricted to just mages.

Rolf felt absolutely fantastic after their little interlude in the alley the previous night. He felt a bit like the time he and his litter mates had stumbled on a patch of cat nip while playing in the herbalist's garden, a little high, a little free and floaty, and definitely like he was ready to take on the universe.

Rolf had no idea why the Master didn't favour this particular courtesan. He didn't really care. He had found this cat's hot, wet mouth exquisite and couldn't wait to sample other hot, sweet holes.

Oh, Yes! The Master had stipulated ten days, and he was going to see that he enjoyed every last one. Ten delicious days with his own personal little sex slave, he thought as he licked his lips again. Delicious! He bounced on the balls of his feet ready to take on this new and exciting world.

Speaking of delicious, he was famished. They had spent the last several hours futilely searching the city and now his stomach was grumbling at him in complaint. It was time to start hunting down some food, rather than wasting their time hunting down a long gone pleasure cat escapee.

He was just about to haul Devon in and demand they find something to eat when a thin, gangly human stepped out from the shadows of a doorway to block their path. He smelled vaguely of ill health and a concoction of chemical stimulants which made Rolf's sensitive nose wrinkle in distaste. But it was the knife blade glistening in the street light that really got his attention.

The bright, metal blade wavered slightly and the youth's jittery movements suggested nervousness to Rolf's trained eye. The stupid human couldn't have advertised his vulnerability and inexperience more if he had shouted it out, he though with disgust.

"Gimme ya cash, man," the youth demanded in an agitated, slightly strained voice. "And any other expensive stuff too," he added quickly as an afterthought.

The man was too anxious for Rolf to consider a serious threat, but even rats, when cornered, could be dangerous he reminded himself. He dropped into a fighting stance, arms held loosely at his side, feet spread wide to provide him with a stable base to launch an attack from.

"Hey! What are you doing, man? Don't be fucking stupid. Just gimme the cash." The youth's voice rose with the scent of his fear. It only goaded Rolf to want to attack him even more.

Slowly, he started to circle his prey. Inch-long claws slipped down to become lethal weapons, huge canines erupted from his gums and flashed wickedly as a low, threatening growl rumbled out of his throat. Only death would stop him now. It was what made his kind so valuable to their Masters, and so very fatal to their enemies. This was what he lived for. The very reason for his existence. And he loved it.

Rolf probably knew the pathetic human was going to strike even before he did. Moving with preternatural speed and agility, he quickly broke the assailant's arm, retrieved his knife and stood above him menacingly as the other man writhed on the ground whimpering.

"What are you?" the man quavered, his voice laced with fear and pain.

"Hungry," Rolf growled back ominously.

The fresh, pungent scent of urine assailed his nose. Fucking dense human, he thought derisively. While he could probably eat off the hoof, so to speak, he much preferred his meals lightly cooked, seasoned and served up to him without the inconvenience of clothing and fur.

"I want a hot meal," he said tersely, hoping for the youth's sake he wouldn't have to explain further.

The human scrabbled with his good arm in his jacket pocket, the pain of his broken wrist apparently inconsequential next to the hope that Rolf wouldn't eat him and might simply leave him alone if he cooperated quickly enough. Rolf allowed the move, confident he could overcome any threat the man might produce from his coat. Quickly, the assailant began to toss crumbled wads of paper on the ground.

"Here. Take it," he yelled. "Take it all. Just...just don't kill me okay."

Rolf sniffed suspiciously at the paper. He certainly couldn't eat this. He scowled down at the man darkly.

"Lucky Jo's. It's just down the block. Take it." The man was panting now, desperately trying to shove the paper at him. "Really, that's all I got."

Rolf regarded him for a moment. Turning, he saw Devon had retreated into a nearby alcove. He was huddled into a small ball of trembling black fur against the far wall trying to disappear into the shadows.

"Come here," he demanded.

Devon looked like he desperately wanted to disobey, but then quickly did as he was told.

Smart cat, Rolf would not have been pleased if he had been forced to chase his ass down right now. Bending down, he scooped Devon up along with the paper the terrified man had thrown at him. Stuffing the crumbled wad into his pocket—just in case it turned out to be something important—he tucked Devon securely under one arm. Then he casually took the time to sink inch-long claws into the pathetic human's throat, waiting until the body had finished convulsing and gurgling before rising and striding off in the direction indicated in search of food.

Never leave an enemy at your back, he thought calmly. Though his companion looked like he wanted to leave his lunch behind, he thought with dark amusement.

Rolf smiled to himself. This new planet was really beginning to grow on him. Readily available sex, an abundance of easy prey, and if his nose didn't deceive him, a delicious meal of fried chicken in his not too distant future. Oh, Yes! He could definitely get use to this.

Chapter Eight

They were going to have to go shopping, Michael thought absently as he reached across the countertop for a tomato to finish off their lunch while watching Ethan. It had been days since they had left the house. Food was running low and as much as he liked seeing Ethan wander around the house in nothing but one of his old shirts, or better yet nothing at all, it was time to venture out and dress his handsome stud in something of his own.

Ethan was sitting in the sunny alcove that was the dining room. It was connected directly to the kitchen, and years ago he had hung a crystal sun-catcher from one of the curtain rails to catch the sunlight. It was a whimsical little fancy someone had given him as a gift, but it was pretty. Ethan apparently found it absolutely fascinating.

A rainbow of colours poured from it as the sun refracted in its clear, faceted depths. They played across the table and Ethan seemed unable to help himself from batting gently at the crystals to watch the colours dance. Michael, on the other hand, found Ethan absolutely fascinating and couldn't help watching his every move.

"You really are a cat, aren't you?" Michael chuckled from the kitchen counter where he stood putting the finishing touches to their sandwiches.

Ethan looked up at him from under his long, dark eyelashes. "I've always found things that dangle attractive," he purred, then abruptly a pout formed on his full, lush lips. "Unfortunately, so often when I start playing, they stop dangling. It's a really *hard* problem, but I've learnt to live with it."

His emphasis left absolutely no doubt at all as to what he was referring to and Michael's cock wasn't slow on the uptake either. It had been hanging lost and drained from their most recent 'play' session, but was once again firming and filling, ready to come out of his sweat pants and go again. His little kitten was going to be the death of him, he thought incredulously, but what a way to go! And anyway, that's what being on holiday was all about, right? No schedules, no rushing, just relaxing and enjoying. And oh, boy, was he enjoying.

But right now he didn't want to get distracted from his earlier mission. Plenty of time to play some more later on.

"How about we quickly eat these then get cleaned up and hit the shops?" he suggested casually, still smirking.

Ethan jerked and sat bolt upright in his chair, staring at him as if in shock. "You want me to go with you?" he asked in disbelief.

Michael suddenly felt the need to tread very carefully. He knew Ethan's experiences, and therefore expectations, were going to be very different from his own. That was just a no-brainer. From what he could piece together, he was a shape-shifting sex slave from an alternate universe or dimension or some such thing. So, duh! But this was their first real clash with the realities of that situation and the outside world so to speak.

"Well, yes! I mean, only if you want to," he replied hesitantly. He didn't want Ethan to feel obligated, just welcome. On the other hand he really did want him to come along.

"You really need some clothes of your own and it's easier if you're there to get the sizes right. Not that you don't look adorable in my shirt, but you need something that fits a little better for everyday wear," he added with a leer, trying to lighten the mood.

"You want to buy me clothes?" Ethan asked in amazement.

"Well, sure! It'll be fun dressing you up. Especially knowing I get to take it all off again when I get you home," he added.

Ethan stared at Michael in disbelief. He had heard all the amazing things Michael had said about wanting to share his day with him, but he still had a hard time really accepting it. He was more use to being hidden away; pleasure cats for most Tantric Mages were a dirty little secret. Most hated to admit they needed something to enhance their powers. He certainly knew his previous Master never wanted to be seen with him. Anytime he had needed to take the two of them anywhere, he and Devon had always travelled in a covered wooden box carried by servants and completely obscured from view. Like luggage, he thought with distain.

He had heard that some mages where not afraid to show affection for their shifter slaves and servants, but they were a rarity. Often they were considered eccentric, a laughing stock or frowned upon by the other mages.

Ethan looked into Michael's eyes. They were warm, kind, gentle eyes that, at the moment held just a hint of uncertainty. Michael had said he didn't want to be his Master from the beginning, and now he was inviting him to join him outside, where others could see them together.

He began to worry his lip between his teeth. He really didn't know anything about this world. Michael had only just recently finished explaining that the device he had originally thought was for scrying was, in fact, a television and that almost everyone had and used every day.

Michael had laughed while he'd tried to show Ethan how to use a thing called a remote. He'd laughed even harder when he'd had to wrestle it away from Ethan because he had apparently become addicted to something called 'channel surfing', though he still wasn't quite sure what that was.

Was he going to be an embarrassment to Michael out there in this big, confusing world? Would it reflect poorly on Michael to be seen in Ethan's company if he made a mistake? Could he risk doing that to such a wonderful man?

On the other hand, was he willing to give up such a fantastic opportunity?

He looked at Michael again. He'd come all this way to explore and experience and...well, live. And he had this wonderful man willing to do it all with him. What was he thinking? This was exactly what he had always wanted and he was going to go for it.

Michael waited breathlessly. He watched the jumbled thoughts reflected in Ethan's eyes and the play of emotions pass over his face. He was so expressive. So open and honest, it was like reading a book as he watched uncertainty, apprehension and confusion flit across his features. In a lot of ways, they were like foreigners to each other. Maybe they didn't have a problem with understanding the others' language, why that was, he wasn't sure, but he could still see so much room for misunderstanding.

He was just beginning to wonder how they could ever make this thing between them work when Ethan smiled. It was slightly tentative, but definitely hopeful, and Michael was lost all over again. He'd walk through hot coals for one of those smiles. If it took a little more time and effort to make things work, with the way Ethan made him feel, he'd was definitely willing to take that time and make that effort.

He smiled back. He was sure it was a goofy smile, but he really didn't care. He was happy and he didn't care how sappy he looked in front of this man.

"I think I have a pair of sweats that we can roll up and draw in tight to get you to the shops. Can't vouch for the shoes. Maybe I have an old pair of sandals kicking around from college."

Chapter Nine

Ethan was so excited. The sights, the smells, the sounds of so many people all moving around him and he was finally allowed to be a part of it all. Free to explore and give free reign to his curiosity. He felt as if his heart would burst right out of his chest; he was so happy. He didn't have to try and sneak peeks at things through chinks in a wooded crate. He didn't have to stay still and silent as if he wasn't there.

He skipped and danced along the pavement energetically, tugging on Michael's arm whenever he spotted something he wanted to take a closer look at or have Michael explain to him.

"Come on," Michael coaxed, dragging him away from a toy shop window with an amazing model of something he called a train. "Maybe one day I'll take you for a ride on a real one," he offered in recompense.

"Really?" he breathed in awe.

"Sure." Michael chuckled kindly. "Come over this way, I want to check out the bus routes. There use to be this fantastic tourist loop you could take around the city heart."

Michael pointed out a strangely coloured board that didn't resemble any map Ethan had ever seen. It was all dots and lines and numbers and colour codes that made his head spin. He eyed it with cautious curiosity. But the thought of getting a chance to ride on one of the huge transports he had seen lumbering around was enough to convince him to follow along obediently.

While Michael studied the completely incomprehensible map, Ethan studied the people. They swarmed around them in an abundance of wonderfully bright colours and a dazzling array of styles. It was endlessly fascinating.

Gazing around, he spotted a young couple all dressed in black standing beside a fountain that sprayed columns of water high into the air. Their clothes were uniformly black, but the choices of materials and mix of styles was incredible. Lace and velvet co-existed with heavy coats and thick-soled boots. And it worked. Ethan couldn't look away.

As he watched, the girl got up on her toes and gently kissed the boy on the lips. It was tender and sweet. The boy bent his tall, lean frame and slowly deepened the kiss. The crowd just continued to move and pass around them, but the two remained completely lost in each other, like a calm island in a sea of hustle and bustle. Ethan was mesmerised.

When the kiss finally ended, they continued to speak quietly together. Their heads tilted in close to one another, sharing an intimate moment while the city continued on around them. He studied their faces closely. They were serene and peaceful as they remained focused on each other.

"What are they?" he finally asked Michael in wonder, pointing to the lovely couple across the way.

"Goths," Michael replied absently when he glanced up distractedly from the sign board and looked in the direction Ethan pointed out.

Whereas Michael showed little interest, Ethan didn't want to look away. They were just so wonderful he thought. "They have beautiful eyes." He realised, still staring.

Michael looked over at the Goths then back down at him. "It's make-up," he said.

Ethan cocked his head in confusion, never having heard the term before.

"What is that? Do you mean they have to cast the spell spontaneously to make their eyes look like that? Can't they research a formulaic spell to produce the same effect?"

Michael just stared at him for a moment then began to laugh. Ethan got the feeling he had said something rather stupid and felt a hot blush of embarrassment starting to tint his cheeks.

"I have absolutely no idea what you just said, but it isn't any kind of spell. They buy it. It's something they apply to their faces to make them look like that."

"Oh," Ethan replied in a subdued voice, determined to stay quiet rather than look stupid in front of Michael again.

"Would you like to try some?" Michael asked calmly.

Ethan was stunned at Michael's easy acceptance of his ignorance of the world around them. And of course his generous offer to let him explore the 'make-up' he had found so fascinating.

"Could I?" he asked, feeling the excitement and thirst for adventure creeping back over him.

"Sure. But let's stop and have a break somewhere now. There isn't another bus that does that loop for an hour and a half, and we've been at it for hours already." Michael lifted up the myriad bags that hung from his hands as if in demonstration. "We can have something to eat, catch a bus ride then do a bit more shopping before we go home if you like."

Ethan couldn't believe how generous Michael was being with him. He felt funny little flutters start up in his belly, all hot and jittery and exciting.

"Are you sure?" he couldn't help asking.

"Absolutely," Michael confirmed decisively.

"Are you sure you don't want me to carry any of those?" he offered, well aware that most, if not all of them were for him.

"No. You just look around. I've got these," Michael answered easily.

Ethan felt the flutter of desire for the big, strong man at his side intensify. He was such a lucky cat. Michael knew how much he wanted to be free to explore, to touch and feel and see, and so he made it possible with so many opportunities at every turn and without weighing him down with concerns about bags and bundles.

"Come on," Michael said, oblivious to Ethan's near worshipful gaze. "There's a great little hole in the wall burger place around the corner. I haven't been there for ages, but they're fantastic, a real ma and pa sort of place."

Ethan followed along happily as Michael enthused over real homemade fries and other things with names Ethan had never heard before. But as they passed by a row of glass-fronted shops, he spotted a girl sitting at a bench making some kind of cone shaped object.

Fascinated, Ethan stopped to watch, his face inches from the glass, as she poured batter into shaped pans then set them aside to cook. While she waited, she began to fold and shape a batch she had made earlier.

"What are they?" he asked in awe.

"Ice cream cones," Michael replied easily.

"You eat them?" Ethan suddenly noticed several people in the shop buying and licking at the filled cones.

"Yep!" Michael chuckled.

He was having nearly as much fun as Ethan appeared to be having. Watching Ethan's excited antics and open curiosity had been wonderful. He felt himself getting caught up in his excitement and towed along for the ride.

"Can we have some?" Ethan pleaded, bouncing up and down, unable to contain his enthusiasm. "Please. Please. Please. Please," he begged.

Michael thought he look absolutely adorable. "Sure," he said as he smiled down into the animated face of his lover.

Juggling the bags of clothing he had already purchased for Ethan, he reached once again for his wallet, but stumbled backwards awkwardly when Ethan launched himself into his arms and began to kiss him passionately on the lips. His long, slender legs, now encased in denim, wrapped confidently around his waist. It was lucky Michael was as big a man as he was and worked out regularly, or they both would have ended up on the footpath. Not that Ethan would have been against that apparently, as he rode against his hard, flat belly and groaned in pleasure.

Michael was too shocked at first to react. Then he felt the blood rush to his face in a blush at Ethan's enthusiastic display. The man they had stumbled into, however, wasn't so stunned and a whole lot less than impressed. He shoved Michael roughly from behind.

"Hey! You dumb faggot!" he yelled obscenely. "Watch where you're going."

Michael dropped the bags he was holding and pried Ethan off, pushing him back against the shop front as he turned to face the rude man behind them. He pulled himself to his full six foot two height and frowned ominously at the bigot. He was relieved to see that he was several inches taller and definitely broader in the shoulder than the other man.

Several people who had seen the incident stopped to watch, avidly waiting for his next move. It was like the scenes you sometimes saw on the news where cars were backed up for miles by an accident, not because the road was blocked but because other drivers couldn't help but slow down to take a look.

And this could get just as ugly, he realised as he watched the other man closely. His puffy face was already reddening, either with rage or embarrassment at drawing so much attention. Neither was good. People did stupid things when they were angry or ashamed. He had to try to defuse the situation quickly.

"Sorry about that," he offered in apology. Not very sorry considering the hateful words that had spewed from the other man's mouth, but he wasn't willing to risk getting into a fight in the middle of a busy city street mall over it. The man just wasn't worth it. Equality and making a stand was all well and good, but he had much better things to do than spend the night in jail. Especially now he had Ethan in his life.

"Yeah! Well, you should keep your boyfriend on a shorter leash," the stranger mumbled, avoiding eye contact and not so brave now that he'd had a chance to take a good looked at the size difference between them.

He looked over Michael's shoulder at the much smaller figure of Ethan huddled behind him and obviously spotted the collar around his neck.

"Try a choker chain and keep it at home next time," he sneered.

Michael's mouth dropped open in shock, and he heard a tormented gasp from behind him. Some people shouldn't be allowed to open their mouths, he thought in rising anger. He was just about to let the stupid bigot have it, night in jail be damned, when he felt Ethan start to push and shove at him from behind. He seemed to become more and more frantic with each passing second as he struggled to get passed him.

Distracted, Michael turned to comfort him. But before he could, Ethan shot passed him and bolted down the street. With shock, he realised he was running away from him. The last thing he had seen was the desolate, hurt look that transformed Ethan's previously animated, lively expression to a mask of pain and sorrow.

"Ethan!" he called out after him. But Ethan ignored him, disappeared around the corner and was gone.

Oh, Fuck, he thought as panic started to set in. Where the hell would he go? Would he go home? Was he ever going to see Ethan again?

He turned back, but the ugly stranger had vanished and the gawkers were beginning to drift away, not wanting to get involved.

Not knowing what else to do, Michael picked up the shopping bags and started down the street in the direction Ethan had taken. He wasn't really sure there was much hope of finding him if he didn't want to be found, but he had to do something, and right now going home seemed the only option. He only hoped Ethan thought the same thing.

Chapter Ten

Michael breathed a huge sigh of relief when he got back home and found Ethan sitting dejectedly on the front steps. He was a far cry from the happy, bubbly, excited man he had been shopping with only an hour ago, but he was safe, and he was home.

Michael stopped a few paces away and just took a moment to soak in Ethan's presence and the overwhelming sense of relief and gratitude he had that he had found his way back. It was a small victory and a huge step forward really in their relationship. All he had to do now was find out what had gone so wrong and convince Ethan to stay anyway.

"You came back," Michael said quietly, afraid the slightest misstep would send the man running away from him again.

Ethan shrugged without looking up at him.

"Please, Ethan," he implored. "Talk to me. We can't get past this if you don't talk to me."

Ethan shot to his feet, his dark green eyes flashed with anger and Michael fought hard against the urge to take a step back.

"You lied to me!" he bellowed, but Michael could hear the pain in his voice. "You said you wanted me to come with you and that you wanted to spend your days with me. You said you wanted me. But you lied. I embarrass you. Just like the Master. You were embarrassed to be seen with me as your lover. You didn't like everyone seeing us together!"

"No!" Michael cried out in denial. "I mean yes, but no." He ran his hand through his hair in agitation and sighed in frustration. "Look Ethan, it's complicated."

"How complicated can it be, Michael?" he shot back sarcastically. "Either you want to be seen with me or you don't."

"I do, Ethan. I really do. But you have to try to understand. I don't know what it's like where you come from, but here, on Earth, relationships between two partners of the same sex are...well, it's not exactly conventional. Hell, more than that, in some countries being gay is still illegal and can get you killed!"

Ethan looked appalled. "They could have killed you?" All the blood drained out of his face, and Michael rushed forward to put his arm around the now trembling man.

"No! No! Not here. Well, I mean, yes, it does happen, even here, but it's not right. Not legal, I mean. I'm not explaining myself very well. Look, even in this country there are a lot of people who hate anyone that's gay."

"But why?" Ethan asked with genuine confusion.

Why indeed, he thought. How did he explain prejudice towards gay people when he didn't really understand it himself? After all, who on earth did he hurt by loving this man?

"We're a minority. Minorities get persecuted." It was a cop out, he knew that, but there were bigger issues at stake to worry about at the moment.

"I had heard that about humans," Ethan replied seriously. "I heard they could be unreasonable, even dangerous about anyone that was…different. I was a little afraid about that when I first realised where I was. But I never thought they would hate someone for who they were attracted to or chose as a mate."

Michael was pulled between the urge to defend the human race and the sudden realisation of just how much trust Ethan had shown in him. How much he had risked just by showing him who he really was. He vowed then and there to be as brave and honest, both with himself and with Ethan, about who he really was.

"I know it's wrong and I wish it didn't happen," Michael said softly, "but you have to be careful. We have to be careful. Sometimes it's safer not to show affection publically."

"But, that's one of the reasons I ran away," Ethan cried out in dismay. "I wasn't allowed out because of who and what I was. I don't want to be hidden away."

Out of the mouths of babes, he thought sardonically. "I know, baby. I'm sorry."

"I'm sorry too, Michael," Ethan said sadly, lowering his head in misery. "I'm sorry I'm so ignorant about the ways of your world." His bottom lip began to tremble. "I'm sorry I embarrassed you and put you in danger."

"No! SShhh. It's okay! It's going to be all right," Michael said, wrapping his arms around Ethan as tears began to fall down his cheeks and wet his new shirt.

"Why would you even want to keep me around? I'm just an ignorant run-away sex slave here. I'm only going to be an embarrassment and a burden."

"Ethan!" Michael snapped harshly, making the man jerk back to look at him. "You are not an embarrassment and you will never be a burden to me," he said firmly.

He couldn't stand to see the uncertainty and heartbreaking insecurity in his lover's eyes. He much preferred the exuberant, mischievous, passionate and kind-hearted soul he was getting to know. Gently, he tilted Ethan's chin up and kissed his trembling lips. It was a tender kiss, a kiss for comfort and reassurance.

"I'm falling in love with you, Ethan," he reassured his fretful lover softly.

Ethan just looked at him, his eyes wide with disbelief. "Really?" he breathed.

Michael nodded, never once taking his eyes of the man he was giving his heart to. "I know it's too soon. I know we've hardly even begun to get to know each other properly, but I can't help it. You're incredible, you know that?"

Ethan just continued to stare at him.

"You're warm and funny, and kind. You're curious and innocent and giving." As Michael stared down into Ethan's eyes now clouded with wonder, he wanted nothing more than to wipe away all the pain of the afternoon. He pecked at Ethan's soft, tempting lips playfully. "You're fishing for compliments," he finished with a smirk.

"Hey!" Ethan cried out in indignation, but Michael was relieved to see a small smile tug at the corners of his mouth and a hint of mischief enter his eyes. Ethan gave him a frown and a mock pout. "I was enjoying that and you had to go and spoil it."

"I could give you something else to enjoy," he countered, wiggling his eyebrows comically. Just as he hoped, Ethan giggled.

"Oh?" Ethan asked coyly when he could finally control his amusement.

"Oh! Yes, indeed," he replied before scooping Ethan up into his arms and carrying him to the door.

Chapter Eleven

"Come on, slow poke." Michael laughed as he called out to hurry Ethan along for the third time that morning. It seemed his vain pussy cat was not going to leave the house until every hair was in exactly the right place and his clothes were just right. He had already changed twice.

Michael rolled his eyes as Ethan appeared in the doorway in yet another outfit. He stepped towards his lover as the man fussed with the hem of his shirt. Gently he ran his hands over his firm shoulders and down his slim back to pull him into a tight hug.

Since nearly losing him, Michael took advantage of every opportunity to hold and shower Ethan with affection. He just couldn't help himself, and he hoped he never had to.

Ethan's white dress shirt was artfully arranged to appear casual. He had left a few buttons open at the collar to display a tempting amount of smooth tanned flesh, and the hem was free to hang over his skin-tight faded denim jeans.

That was a pity really, he thought, because he knew from experience that they cupped his ass lovingly, showing off the tempting curves to perfection.

Even so, Ethan looked absolutely stunning. It seemed his little kitty cat was a quick study. Having worn very few clothes in his life, he had meticulously paid attention to every clothing catalogue, fashion magazine and television programme he could find. He now knew more about men's fashion, and probably women's as well, than Michael considered anyone outside the fashion industry had a right to know. Still he couldn't argue with the results.

In a little over a week, he felt as if he had been with Ethan forever. For the past several days they had explored both each other and the city he had lived in his whole life. It had been absolutely amazing, and all because of Ethan.

He was open and funny and affectionate and his curiosity was infectious. It had made him look at things as if for the first time as well while he had helped Ethan explore and try to understand the world he now found himself in.

Ethan was everything Michael had ever wanted in a partner, and for now at least he seemed content with him as well. Michael felt the familiar cloud of his own insecurities cast a shadow over his mood. He couldn't help but wonder how long he could hope to keep Ethan happy.

At the moment, Ethan needed Michael. He was a stranger not only in a strange city but a strange world. But how long would it be before he had learnt enough to be able to make it on his own? And how long after that before ordinary old Michael Barnes became not nearly enough for the free spirited, adventurous kitty?

Michael forced the thoughts from his head. He wasn't going to spoil what he had with ghosts from his past. He would deal with that day when and if it came. Plastering a smile on his face, he handed Ethan a coat. "Better take this, the wind's picking up out there."

"Are you all right?" Ethan asked, a concerned frown on his face as he looked up at Michael.

It seemed he wasn't the only one getting to know his lover, he realised, feeling an odd mix of pleasure and uneasiness. "I'm fine," he tried to assure Ethan casually.

"Are you sure I look all right? I'm just not use to all this. I wouldn't want to embarrass you."

Perhaps Michael wasn't the only one that needed reassurance. A lifetime of conditioning and training couldn't be broken down in a week, not even by the promise of love. Michael knew Ethan still had trouble believing he was falling in love with him, or even that he wanted to be seen in public with him! He fought down the urge to find his so-called 'Master' and beat the living daylights out of him.

"Babe, you look gorgeous. Good enough to eat. I'll be beating them off with a stick." He squeezed Ethan a little tighter and continued with mock sternness, "Just remember I found you first."

His attempt at humour, however, was completely lost on Ethan.

"I will always be loyal to you, Michael. I promise. I will never run away or betray you."

Sometimes Ethan could be so light-hearted and mischievous, and at other times he was so serious and almost fearful. Michael tried not to get too upset when he saw what growing up under the influence of such a dominating, restrictive regime had done to his beautiful boy.

His eyes were drawn down to the slim leather collar around Ethan's neck. He still wore it, and though nothing had been said, Michael knew it was a slave band, a symbol of ownership. And yet Ethan couldn't seem to bring himself to let it go. It seemed it was easier to hang onto it than to believe in Michael's growing, unconditional love for him.

Michael promised himself that one day he would prove himself worthy of Ethan's ultimate trust. It was still very early days. He only hoped that Ethan's affections would also strengthen with his faith and not wan with a lack of interest.

"I know you would never cheat on me, Ethan," he acknowledged seriously. And he did. Ethan was far too open and honest for that. "It's okay. I was just messing around with you. And ditto, you know." He stared intently into Ethan's brilliant wide green eyes. "I promise to always be here for you too. You know that, right?"

Ethan nodded his head in his shy way, eyes dropping down and a pretty blush of pleasure colouring his cheeks.

"Come on." Michael wanted today to be fun as they toured the local Sunday Arts and Craft Market. Or rather, he wanted to enjoy watching Ethan explore his first local Arts and Craft Market. "Let's get out of here before all the good stuff is gone."

He broke the suddenly depressing mood by smacking Ethan playfully on his tight butt.

"Hey," he cried out, but Michael saw the sudden flare of desire ignite in his sparkling green eyes.

Maybe an hour of watching Ethan at the market would be enough, he thought wickedly.

* * * *

The market was crowded and lively as always. An eclectic mix of people rubbed shoulders as they moved in amongst the brightly coloured stalls. It was a melting pot of multiculturalism and diversity. Everything was available from hand-made soap to a tribal music group set up in the far corner of the lot.

Michael was worried Ethan might break his neck as he tried to see absolutely everything at once. It was lucky he'd taken his vitamins this morning, he thought with amusement as they flitted and wove through the throng from one display to the next.

Somewhere ahead he could smell the rich, pungent aroma of coffee and he gently manoeuvred Ethan in that direction. A strong coffee addiction was definitely an occupational hazard for nurses, he mused; just the smell had him craving a cup.

Soon Ethan was moving in the right direction as the music caught his attention and he began to relax as the prospect of a hot cup of coffee got closer.

The band was actually quite good. A deep, pulsing beat that made even Michael, who had definitely been born with two left feet, want to sway to the rhythm. But Ethan seemed almost transfixed.

"I just want to get a cup of coffee from over there. Will you be all right here for a bit while I go get one?" he asked over the pounding rhythm of the drums. Ethan's absent nod had Michael a little concerned, but it didn't look like Ethan was going anywhere in a hurry and the coffee stand was only a few stalls down.

As Michael hurried to get back a few minutes later, he was alarmed to see a large crowd had formed around the band, but no sign of Ethan. Quite a lot of the crowd were clapping and swaying to the beat, and he prayed he would find Ethan somewhere among them. He pushed through to the last place he had seen Ethan and came to a standstill, shocked when he was finally able to find his lover.

The crowd had formed a wide circle at the front and there was Ethan, but Ethan as he had never seen him before. His eyes appeared shut, his mouth slightly parted as he moved in an incredibly hot, sultry dance, almost as if he was in a trace. His entire body moved with the music in a fluid, undulating rhythm. His hips rolled suggestively, his arms weaved around him almost like a lover's caress. He was absolutely stunning, magnificent in his erotic display.

Michael wanted to push him to the ground and fuck him till he couldn't walk, and he was sure he wasn't the only one. He didn't know how he felt about the idea of others coveting Ethan like that as he tried to casually manipulate his cock to a more comfortable position. But while he may not be entirely happy about the crowd ogling and panting after his man, he freely admitted Ethan was amazing. Sensual, erotic and absolutely beautiful, and he had Michael as hard as a pike.

Finally, the music ended and Ethan seemed to come out of his trace. He stared around as if waking up from a dream. The crowd, on the other hand, was going wild, cheering and clapping and offering whistles of enthusiasm. Many wanted to know where the troop was performing next so that they could tell their friends. But Ethan looked absolutely terrified, his cheeks flushed bright red in embarrassment as if he hadn't realised what he'd been doing. His horrified gaze instantly sought Michael out.

Michael rushed to Ethan's side before the crowd could swamp him and tucked the smaller man into his side protectively. A number of people moved forward to ask questions, but Ethan just burrowed into his shoulder. Determinedly, Michael began to lead Ethan away, tugging him towards the exit.

"I'm sorry," Ethan repeatedly whimpered against him.

Michael stopped when he had cleared the worst of the crowd.

"Why are you sorry?" he asked in confusion.

"I embarrassed you again," Ethan murmured miserably.

"No, baby! You didn't embarrass me," he reassured him. "In fact, I thought that was totally hot."

Ethan's shocked face turned up to Michael's instantly. "Really?"

"Really. And a lot of other people thought so too," he went on to say.

Just then, one of the musicians rushed up to them, panting and out of breath.

"Oh, man! Thank goodness." He breathed heavily. "I thought I'd lost you. That was awesome, man. Where'd you learn to do that?" he asked excitedly.

Ethan simply blushed even more and attempted to burrow into Michael's shoulder again. Michael thought he could guess where Ethan might have learnt to dance so erotically, but there was no way he was letting this stranger upset his baby.

"I'm sorry," he said firmly. "We have to go. If you would excuse us please." He went to move away, but the musician grabbed his arm.

"Look. I'm not trying to get heavy or anything, but if you're ever looking for a gig, you know, a job, give us a call. That was really something back there. The number of people that have come on over and started buying our records is just…wow," he finished enthusiastically. "We're trying to get off the ground. Get into some clubs and stuff. You could really be a draw card. Here, take our number anyway." A hastily scribbled card was thrust into Ethan's hand. "Just think about it, yeah? We'd love to have you with us some time." With that, the stranger turned and walked back to the other band members and the music started up again.

Michael looked down into the head of wild, golden brown hair that burrowed into his chest and refused to look up.

"He's right, you know. That really was amazing." He watched as Ethan lifted unsure eyes up to regard him hesitantly. He bent his head to whisper into his delicate, still red tipped ear. "You know, when I was watching you dance, all I could think about was tackling you to the ground, stripping you bare and riding your tight little ass. I wanted to do you so hard and fast till you came and all your sexy seed exploded out of that beautiful cock of yours while I filled your ass."

If possible Ethan's ears seemed to flame an even brighter red and his breath gave an audible hitch. But Michael could feel the rapidly hardening bulge pressing against his thigh.

"Let's go home," he suggested huskily.

"Hurry," Ethan urged, still desperately clinging to Michael's side.

Chapter Twelve

It had been eight days since his arrival on Earth. Eight long, miserable days. Devon ached. They hadn't met up with the other members of the hand since the first morning and since then Rolf had been uncontrollable.

Every muscle felt bruised. Every bone crushed. And he definitely wasn't going to be sitting down anytime soon. For some reason, over the last twenty-four hours Rolf had been insatiable. He hadn't let Devon stand upright since yesterday, and they hadn't even pretended to look for Ethan in days.

Devon hung his head and fought down the urge to cry. Tears certainly hadn't helped so far; they were unlikely to start doing so now. With a groan, he pushed himself painfully to his feet and stretched out his overworked body.

Rolf finally seemed to have exhausted himself and was now out cold. He lay sprawled insensibly across the lumpy mattress they had commandeered when they had evicted the previous 'tenants' from the warehouse they were currently using as shelter. The vagrants had left without a fuss after taking one look at Rolf's impressive size and obvious strength, not to mention his mean growl.

He remembered with a shiver their horrifying first night on this world. Rolf had killed the young man that had tried to attack them in cold blood. He had done it without a second thought, and it seemed to have inspired the brutal cat shifter to a new vocation of violence, domination and intimidation.

Since the killing, Rolf had abandoned any pretext of looking for Ethan. He had cast aside his brothers and gone on a veritable crime spree. When he wasn't bending Devon over, that was. His newfound life of crime spanned eight days and nights of mugging, bullying, breaking and entering, assault and battery. He hadn't killed again, thank goodness, but Devon wondered if it was only a matter of time. It was as if the acts left Rolf high somehow and only craving more.

He wasn't sure what had happened to the others, but he knew he was utterly alone now and one thing was certain. He hated his brother. If it wasn't for him running away and abandoning him, he would never have gotten caught up in this nightmare. He would never have been forced to leave their Master. He would never have had to come to Earth with the hand, and he would never have had to deal with someone like Rolf.

Ethan had abandoned him, he thought again as his breath hitched and he fought against a sob. The realisation of Ethan's betrayal left a cold, hard lump of pain where he was sure his heart use to be. The one thing he had always thought he could rely on was his brother's love. But in the end Ethan hadn't even been able to muster enough feeling to want to stay with him. Without a second thought, he had simply left him behind.

He knew he had to stop. The pain of losing Ethan was too much to deal with on top of everything else. He also knew he had to get away from Rolf for a while. He didn't think he could take much more. It was ironic really, wasn't that nearly the exact same thing Ethan had said to him shortly before running away?

He snorted disdainfully. Their life had never been this intolerable at the Master's castle. Sure at times the Master could be hurtful and dismissive, even cruel. And yes, they were expected to perform sexually for the Master to earn their keep, but to Devon that was infinitely better than his current situation, being out on the streets, frightened, alone and subject to the whims of an increasingly power-crazed psychopath.

He wondered, not for the first time, whether his brother was finding life here equally intolerable. A bitter, nasty little part of himself, a part he had never even suspected existed, secretly hoped so. In a way, he supposed he wouldn't feel quite so alone if he knew he wasn't the only one suffering.

The wind was chilly in the shadows of the abandoned building. Without the sun to warm him, he found himself shivering uncontrollably. Somewhere along the line, Rolf had broken into a clothing store in order to get a leather coat he had fancied. Devon had felt slightly guilty, but had taken the opportunity to get jeans, a t-shirt and a pair of shoes for himself. Just the essentials, he had reassured his conscious. It was the sort of thing he had seen several other young men wearing as they wandered the city. Now he wished he had taken a coat as well.

He rubbed his hands up and down his arms briskly as he wandered a little further away from the doorway. He didn't want to risk Rolf's anger for wandering off too far, but he desperately needed to get just a little further away from the other cat and feel the sun on his face. He would just walk to the end of the building and back, he promised himself.

As he got closer and closer to the chain link fence that ran around the warehouse he saw that some kind of market carnival had been set up. He could see the previously empty lot bustling with people. Colourful tents flapped in the breeze. Produce and merchandise of every kind, including some he couldn't even identify, was laid out for the passing crowd. Off to one side a band of musicians played a primitive, earthy tune, the heavy beat pulsed through him.

The noise was enough to make him want to step back, even as the delicious smell of food made his belly rumble and enticed him to move forward. Just as he was about to turn around and run back into the warehouse a familiar scent joined the smell of baked goods and spicy meats.

Ethan! His eyes widened in shock as he realised his brother was here somewhere among the crowd. Ethan! Who he hadn't sensed hide nor hair of in over a week. Ethan! Who was his ticket out of this hell. Ethan was close by, he just knew it. Close enough that he could smell him on the breeze. Desperately, he began to scan the area. He could go home. The nightmare would be over.

Every muscle Devon possessed strained in hope and anticipation. Then he saw him. He was dancing! The crowd around the musicians opened up just enough for him to watch Ethan moving with a trance like grace. Every inch of his body swayed with the music, sultry and graceful. The people around him seemed just as transfixed. When the music came to an end, they went wild, clapping and cheering. And they were right, he had been magnificent.

He watched as a tall, good looking man with dark brown hair appeared, and wrapping Ethan up in his arms, began to pull him through the crowd towards the exit. One of the musicians rushed up to them and there was a small exchange before they moved off again through the market, a sudden urgency to their steps.

Quickly, Devon slipped through the small hole in the fence that they had been using to come and go and hurried after them, desperately afraid that he would lose them if he didn't. He couldn't afford to lose them now. He might never see them again if he did, and he just might not survive that.

Chapter Thirteen

As they stumbled up the front steps their lips were permanently fused together, their kisses hot, hard and urgent. By the time Michael was fumbling with the front door Ethan was frantic with need. He was pulling at their clothes, as if he was desperate to feel the touch of skin on skin, and he plunged his tongue into his mouth in feverish demand.

Michael knew exactly how he felt. He struggled to open the door because he couldn't bear to release the small, nubile man in his arms. He cupped the tight ass in his hands and dragged Ethan up against his poor, tortured erection, glorying in the answering hardness he felt through the other man's jeans. He helped Ethan ride his thigh with whimpers of need as he battled desperately with the lock.

Finally, the door gave way and they tumbled into the entryway together. With his foot, Michael managed to slam the door closed, never once losing contact with

Ethan's eager lips or his now bare chest. He tore off his own shirt, the sound of ripping material only just audible over their moans and heavy breathing. But he didn't pause. He didn't care. All he cared about was being as close to the man in his arms as possible.

"Michael," Ethan groaned out in an endless litany.

Gradually, it began to register with his lust fuelled mind that the smaller man he held pressed up against the hallway wall was starting to sound increasingly distressed. Alarmed, he pulled back and looked into green eyes completely lost in passion.

Ethan continued to writhe against him helplessly. "Michael," he pleaded. "Michael, please I need."

"Shhh. It's okay. I've got you, sweetheart. I'll take care of you," he soothed.

Ethan's eyes closed as if he was struggling not to become overwhelmed by the stimulation and sensations bombarding him. His breathing was reduced to short shallow pants and his expression almost looked pained.

"What is it, love? What's wrong?" he asked gently, unable to stop his hands from running over the other man's flushed body, but conscious of wanting to make this time perfect in every way.

"I've never..." Ethan took in one long shuddering gasp of air that transformed into a corresponding shudder through his body. "I've never felt like this before." Finally Ethan's eyes cracked open, showing Michael the most beautiful deep emerald green colour he had ever seen. "I've never wanted so much. I feel like...like I'm too big for my skin. I feel like I might explode if you don't take me soon."

"But I don't want to take you, sweetheart. I want to make love to you."

He smiled as he watched Ethan's eyes slide closed again on a moan that had him pushing his body up again Michael's.

Gently, he began to kiss Ethan's mouth. Sweet, tender, teasing little caresses meant to gentle and calm them both. All the time he steadily led them down the hall to the bedroom, walking backwards and relying on long established familiarity with his childhood home and a fortunate preference for minimalistic furnishing.

When he felt the mattress press into the backs of his knees, he sank down onto it. He pulled Ethan over with him until they both lay sprawled across the bed, Ethan spread over him like a warm, horny blanket. Slowly, he coaxed their kisses to become deeper, more intimate and more passionate again. He slipped his tongue into Ethan's mouth and invited him into an intricate dance of tongues, stolen breaths and shared moist, warm air.

"I want you, love. Want to be inside you. Want to fill you up."

"Yes! Oh! Yes!" Ethan replied eagerly.

Caressing down Ethan's spine to his ass, Michael wasn't surprised to feel Ethan tugging at the stiff confining material of their jeans. Chuckling softly he helped his desperate lover, groaning himself when he felt their bare cocks finally come into contact. He thrust his hips up repeatedly so their shafts rubbed enthusiastically together, until both were anointed with a glistening sheen of pre-cum.

When he literally couldn't take anymore, he surged up and flipped them over so he covered Ethan.

Ethan, in turn, spread his thighs and thrust up against him in a clear invitation to enter him. Now! His body seemed to scream. Now!

Michael swooped down to claim another soul deep kiss. Never had he wanted anyone more. Now it was his turn to be the one panting and pressing his forehead against Ethan's, trying to gather his wits and slow down for a moment.

They had already had the conversation a number of days before about the fact there was no need to use lube or a condom. Not for the first time, Michael found himself praising whoever had created pleasure cats to be completely resistant to sexual disease and capable of producing a natural lubricant which meant he was able to feel his lover's warm, welcoming hole bareback, skin to skin. It was almost enough to have him shooting his load right there and then.

Slowly, he pushed a finger into Ethan's wanton hole. Ethan arched, but he could tell it was in ecstasy, not pain. His lover was already well and truly ready to take him, but he wanted to prolong the pleasure, and he knew if he thrust his eager cock into Ethan's tight body now it would be all over in seconds.

Moving his finger in and out he added a second then felt around inside his lover, searching out that familiar shared anatomical feature that he knew would send his partner into orbit.

When Ethan bowed up on the bed and screamed in pleasure, Michael grinned from ear to ear. God bless whoever had thought to include a prostate in the overall design specifications for cat shifters. He watched in fascination as Ethan's cock pulsed several times and a few thin streams of pre-come surged out to land in a small puddle on the man's tight abs.

Deciding that he had tortured both of them enough, he repositioned himself, placing the shiny tight head of his cock at his lover's fluttering rosy pink entrance.

"Look at me, Ethan. Look at me as I love you."

Stunned green eyes blinked up at him as he slowly pushed his way in to the hilt. Michael wasn't sure who moaned louder, and it didn't matter anyway as both of them started up a rhythm that had their bodies meeting and moving against each other in a perfect, synchronised rhythm.

Finally, cresting the wave of orgasm, they plunged into euphoria together. He felt his hot, silky cum pulse up into Ethan, filling his beautiful body with his seed. At the same time, he felt the corresponding jerks of Ethan's cock spilling shot after shot of his cum up between them. He painted their bellies and chests together in a sticky, intimate mess.

Suddenly, two tiny piercing pains stabbed into his shoulder. Dazzling pinpoints of light washed over his vision, and he felt his cock instantly fill and release more cum up into Ethan's hot body. On and on his seed pulsed up into the other man until, exhausted and spent, he collapsed, hardly having the sense left to wrap his arms around Ethan and roll them over onto their sides to prevent himself from crushing his smaller lover.

His breath was laboured and erratic. He couldn't have moved to withdraw from Ethan if he'd wanted to. And he didn't. In fact, he dearly wanted them to remain locked together forever. But that would hardly have been practical and gradually his cock slipped regretfully from Ethan's snug hole.

They lay together while their breathing gradually returned to normal. Hot wet flesh continued to slide against each other while they stroked and caressed. Soothing and quieting each other. Loving, Michael realised.

He had absolutely no idea what had just happened and he wasn't even sure he cared. Whatever it was, it had been magnificent and he couldn't wait to do it again and again. This was what he had always longed for, this man in his arms, from another world, the man that had just bitten him and sent him into orgasmic nirvana. This was the one man he had waited his entire life to find.

And yet he still couldn't help but worry. Even as he held the man of his dreams in his arms, his earlier fears and demons came back to plague him. He knew in his heart they were only his insecurities left over from Daniel's traumatic betrayal. Just as he knew that if he continued to obsess about Ethan eventually wanting to leave, he was highly likely to bring that prophecy of doom to fruition. It would eventually drive a wedge between them, his doubts and lack of faith. He definitely didn't want that, but how could he stop it?

Looking down at Ethan's sleepy, bliss filled face, he began to wonder. Could he just let go of the pain? Would the lessons so painfully learnt with Daniel haunt him forever or could he simply move on? He had accepted that the man beside him already held his heart. Why couldn't he surrender his doubts and fears as well? He trusted him with his body, even after the bite. Especially after the bite, actually. In fact, he very much hoped to be bitten again, and soon. So why couldn't he surrender and trust Ethan with his soul as well?

His fingers gently traced the collar at Ethan's neck. This. This was the reason, he realised. While Ethan kept the collar, Michael knew he didn't consider himself free of needing a Master. Oh! He was sure Ethan had heard him when they had agreed that he wasn't going to be replacing his Master. Ethan might even believe they could be equal partners and lovers. But the collar, this tiny scrap of leather, sexy as it was, said Ethan was still not free. Not completely anyway. And without freedom there was no real choice. And without Ethan making a free and unencumbered choice to stay with him, out of love and commitment and not necessity or need, he would always feel insecure about their relationship.

"I choose you, Michael. I will always stay with you," Ethan suddenly whispered.

Michael started. Could Ethan hear what he was thinking? He'd never actually said anything about his fears. He was only just working it all out himself.

"Partly," Ethan confirmed without Michael having to ask. "When I bit you, I chose you as my mate. I can't hear all your thoughts, but I can tell you're worried about me not staying with you. But that's exactly what I promised when I bit you. I told you, in a very cat shifter kind of way, that I chose you. We mate for life, Michael. I will always choose you. Mates stay together." Ethan was blushing profusely now and wouldn't meet his eyes. "I know I shouldn't have done it without talking to you first. I know. But...I couldn't help it." Ethan looked embarrassed and a little ashamed by his instinctual claiming, but Michael was thrilled.

"No, it's fine," he rushed to reassure Ethan. "More than fine." He let all the pleasure and amazing euphoria he had experienced when Ethan bit him, flood his mind. Like two wicked boys, they started grinning at each other.

But it wasn't long before he focused once more on the collar around Ethan's neck. The grin gradually faded from his lips, and he felt Ethan go very still against him.

"Does it bother you?" Ethan asked softly.

He knew he had to be very careful with what he said next. This was so very important to both of them and whatever he said would likely stay with them for a long,

long time. While Ethan may sense some of his emotions and thoughts, his thoughts on the collar definitely required deeper explanation. Ultimately, it could decide their fate together as a couple, but he wouldn't lie to his lover.

"Yes," he replied quietly, feeling Ethan tense instantly under his hands. "But not for the reasons you're thinking."

Ethan remained motionless, poised as if to run and hide or turn and fight. Gently, Michael rolled him over onto his back so he could look deep into his troubled eyes.

"I don't care that you were once a pleasure cat, or whatever it is you call it. I don't care that you were once a sex slave. There, I've said it and I mean every word. I only care about the man who found his way out, the man who was brave enough to run away to a strange world, with strange people to find his freedom. The man smart enough to try to hide out in my house," he added with a smile that made Ethan snort in surprise at his little quip.

Slowly, he let the smile fade and his expression turn serious again.

"I want you to stay, but I don't want to be your keeper, Ethan. I want you to be free. And I want you to make a free and conscious choice to stay with me. Not because you might think you couldn't make it out there on your own. Because I know you could, and I'd help you even if we weren't lovers. And I don't want you to stay just because you think you have to belong to someone either, because you don't. You're an independent and intelligent individual. I don't even want you to stay with me because of some sort of instinctual mating urge. Don't get me wrong, I liked it, but what I want is for you to stay with me because you want to. Because you want...me. Do you understand what I'm trying to say to you?"

Ethan's eyes searched his face. He knew what he was asking for was a leap of faith. Without his collar, Ethan would be giving up the final thing that had always linked him to something bigger than himself. Without the collar, he was no longer a pleasure cat, he was just Ethan. That was also why Michael was struggling so hard to include the sudden issue of Ethan choosing him as a mate. While it was amazing and lovely to be wanted so instinctively, he didn't want it to override Ethan's conscious freedom of choice. He didn't want to merely replace master with mate for Ethan.

It probably would have been much better, he thought in hindsight, if they had dealt with this issue before the idea of mating had even come up. But it wasn't as if he even realised it was a possibility until a few minutes ago. Besides, he was only now working up the courage to face it all himself. He prayed he had chosen the right moment for them both. He just knew he couldn't let it go on any longer.

But while he was sure about his own thoughts and feelings, and truly believed that getting all of these issues cleared up and out in the open was a good thing, he was also very conscious that it was not what Ethan had ultimately been looking for when he had run away. He was fairly sure Ethan had simply wanted to be free to find a better, kinder Master, one who would allow him greater freedom to explore and be himself. In his heart, Ethan may have dreamed of being loved and appreciated, but he had still expected to be a slave. A possession.

But instead of a powerful mage and Master, he had found a man. A fairly ordinary man, Michael admitted to himself. And now he was asking Ethan to trust he would be loved just for being himself. Not for what he was, or what he could give, but simply because he was Ethan.

Michael held his breath and hoped. He was asking a lot, he realised.

Hesitantly, Ethan reached around for the buckle that fastened his collar. His hands trembled so badly it didn't look like he would be able to release it at first. But finally it gave way and lay cradled in his unsteady hands. A thin piece of black leather that had defined his life up until this point, now just a tiny, limp fashion accessory.

Ethan turned wide, terrified eyes up to Michael, silently begging to be told what to do next. Ironic really, considering what Ethan had just done. He was now finally and completely free.

Michael gave him a moment to catch his breath and come to terms with all the unexpected responsibilities that entailed. "Now you can choose," Michael reminded him gently.

Ethan still looked a little too bewildered to understand. He clutched the collar to his chest as if it might protect him somehow.

"Will you stay with me?" Michael prompted solemnly, his mind clouded with growing worry. With those few words, he saw the fear and anxiety lift from Ethan's face.

Ethan drew a ragged, shuddering breath, but looked up at him with clear eyes, as if he finally realised that just because he was free didn't mean he was alone. Wrapping his arms around Michael, Ethan began to nod and Michael felt the tears pool in his own eyes.

Ethan might have just taken his last, faltering steps to freedom, but somehow Michael suspected he'd been dragged along at the same time. He felt free as well, freed by the small, golden haired man in his arms, to love and trust again. Daniel's betrayal no longer weighed him down because he had the love and commitment of a good man. Cat. Mate. *Whatever*, he smiled happily.

Chapter Fourteen

Ethan had a new Master, Devon realised in shock. He felt hollow and numb, almost as light as air, as if he would float away at any moment. Ethan had gone and got a new Master without him. It was too impossible to comprehend. They had always served their Master together. How was this possible?

No! Devon cried out forcefully in his mind. This was not happening. They already had a Master waiting for them. He would not let Ethan do this to him. It was just going to be more difficult than he had previously suspected to get Ethan back, that was all.

The frantic way they had touched and moved against each other before they had finally entered the house and slammed the door spoke of an attachment that neither seemed willing to relinquish anytime soon. He was going to need help, he realised. He wanted to go home, and he needed Ethan to do that, but to get Ethan he was going to need…Rolf.

His heart sank down to somewhere about the level of his roughed up sneakers. But there was nothing else for it. He was only delaying, a delay that could cost him his one opportunity to recover his brother, as he lingered here fretting over having to return to the big, brutal warrior cat.

With reluctance, he retraced his steps. Back along the tree shaded streets, with the carefully trimmed lawns and neat, tidy houses. Past the few shops and businesses now closed down and empty. Between the rows of quiet, deserted warehouses, with their scrubby tufts of spiky grass and scraggly bushes scattered about. Until, finally he stood in front of the familiar chain link fence.

He had carefully skirted the market. That had cost him time. But now he found himself hesitant to go any further. He closed his eyes and wove his fingers into the cold metal links as he leaned into the fence and took several deep breaths. He was nearly home, he repeated over and over to himself. Just a little more and he could be back behind the harems sheltering walls. He squared his shoulders and pushed back through the wire, hurrying into the warehouse to find…

"Where the hell have you been?" Rolf shouted harshly as Devon stepped into the dimly lit, cavernous room.

Without waiting for an answer, Rolf grabbed him by the upper arms and thrust him hard against the closest wall. The air rushed out of his lungs, making it impossible even to cry out in pain as Rolf's fingers dug painfully into his biceps and he struggled to catch his breath in wild, shallow pants.

"I was just--" he finally managed to gasp fearfully.

"You were just nothing. You keep your ass where I can see it. And speaking of seeing your ass, strip." Rolf's face was inches from his own and he could see the large man was deadly serious. Not to mention pissed as hell.

"But…" he tried, frantically hoping to slow Rolf's roving hands as they started to work on his pants when he wasn't quick enough to obey.

"No, buts. Not unless it's this one right here." Rolf leered down at him, palming Devon's now bare cheeks.

"No, wait," Devon cried as he tried to wiggle out from between Rolf and the wall.

He knew it wasn't the smartest thing he had ever done when he saw Rolf's face contort with rage. But he was desperate to get him to stop and listen to him.

"You did not just say no to me!" he roared. "You say, yes sir, and more sir, and would you like my ass or my mouth, sir? You do not say no!" he screamed.

Devon was terrified, but just couldn't seem to stop his mouth. "But…"

"I'm in charge here! You do as I say!" Rolf continued as if he hadn't spoken.

"But Ethan…" He felt his breathing start to become shorter and shorter with growing panic and his vision threatened to tunnel in.

"I don't care about your stupid fucking brother. I don't need him and neither do you. We're not going back. I like it here."

Devon felt like he just might just throw up, or pass out. He wasn't quite sure which, as he digested the full meaning of Rolf's words.

Rolf's eye's narrowed on him menacingly. "You don't want to see what I would do if you try and force my hand, little cat. I said I have no need of your wilful brother. You just remember that if you care for him at all. Now, get on your knees."

Devon was sinking to his knees without any conscious thought to do so. His mind racing out into the rapidly empty lot and down the city blocks to where his brother had entered the house in the embrace of his new Master. He may hate his brother at the moment, but he didn't want him dead, and that's just what Rolf would do to him, he realised miserably.

But he had to get out of this. He had to get away. He couldn't take this anymore. He just wanted to go home.

As a scream built in his throat and Rolf reached down to release his cock, they heard the warehouse door burst open.

"Freeze!" a deep, menacing voice demanded.

Rolf jerked around in surprise to confront whoever dared to invade his territory.

Devon, on his knees, hidden by the dim lighting and Rolf's body, took the opportunity to change forms and bolt into the shadows. He would deal with Devon soon enough, he promised himself. Right now he had intruders to run off.

"Hands up where I can see them and turn around slowly," one of the men in blue uniforms commanded as he pointed his weapon straight at Rolf's chest.

Rage consumed him. No one threatened him in his own territory. He would punish his wayward sex toy later. Right now these pathetic humans needed to be taught a lesson about who was top predator. A rumbling growl began in the base of his throat as he prepared himself to attack.

He wondered absently where the stupid little cocksucker thought he was going anyway. Was he really stupid enough to think Rolf couldn't track him down? Well, even if he was that stupid, he had a tight ass and glorious mouth, and Rolf wasn't anywhere near ready to give that up. Devon would just have to be taught his place, that's all. And that place was at the end of his cock, whenever he told him to be there.

"I said, hands up and turn around!" the man screamed again.

Rolf struck, moving with the speed and fluidity that came naturally to his kind. The men never knew what hit them. Within seconds both lay in a cooling pool of their own blood, their last breaths gurgling out of their throats.

Rolf rolled fluidly and stretched. It was only then that he noticed one of the missile weapons, which at some point had discharged, had hit his shoulder and a long streak of dark red blood was flowing down his arm to drip from the long claws that he had purposefully kept unsheathed in case of further challengers.

Casually, he probed the wound. A clean entry and exit, he noted dispassionately. He began ripping strips of cloth to pad the wound and applied a rough bandage while his anger began to bubble up inside him. Oh! When he got his hands on that little slut, he was so going to get it.

Chapter Fifteen

Ethan leaned against the kitchen counter as he finished his glass of milk. His body had a pleasant ache to it that constantly reminded him of Michael. His mate. His chosen. He couldn't help but smile contentedly.

This afternoon had been a wild, almost frantic experience as they used their bodies to try to tell each other just how much they loved one another. It had been much more than just sex, and Ethan finally knew the difference. He sighed with delight. He could definitely take more of this kind of thing in the future. In fact, that sounded like an excellent idea right now.

He quickly rinsed his glass and set in on the sink to dry, just as he had seen Michael do. He turned around and began to hurry back to join the man in the bedroom who had quickly come to mean everything to him. A cheeky grin formed on his lips as he imagined the slow torture he had planned for his lover.

Before he could even make it out of the kitchen, however, someone tackled him from behind, their combined weight sent him crashing to the ground. Ethan struggled desperately. The man on top of him didn't seem that big. Maybe if he could dislodge him and turn to face his attacker he would stand a chance in a one on one fight. He unsheathed his small, sharp little claws and tried to get into a better position to use them.

But just as suddenly as the weight had knocked him to the floor, it was gone. He heard a body begin slammed up against the wall beside him, and he flipped over gracefully to see Michael roughly pinning a much smaller man against the kitchen entryway. One of the man's arms was twisted viciously behind his back and the other was trapped against the wall. It was clear he wasn't going anywhere, but the man continued to struggle frantically against Michael's hold anyway.

Ethan was just about to rush to see what he should do to help, when he heard the smaller man cry out. His messy black hair was just visible over Michael's broad shouldered frame, and Ethan felt himself go cold.

"Michael!" he called hysterically. "No! Michael! Stop! He's my brother."

He would recognise his brother's beautiful mess of glossy black hair anywhere. He should have known him instantly by his scent alone, but for some reason Devon's usual sweet honey fragrance was all messed up. Then again, he should have known there was someone in the house too. The overwhelming scent of musk from their love making had clouded his senses and completely masked Devon's presence apparently.

He pulled desperately at the bulging bicep in Michael's upper arm, but his lover had already let go and backed away as Devon's smaller framed slumped forward to lean against the wall in defeat.

Michael's heart still pounded in his chest. When he had come out of the bedroom looking for Ethan and saw the man pinning him to the floor, he had seen red, thinking that someone had broken into their home and was trying to hurt the man he loved.

"Devon, what are you doing here?" Ethan asked with concern, focusing Michael's attention once more as Ethan stepped up and tried to put his arm around his brother's trembling shoulders.

"I'm trying to get home!" Devon screamed as he spun around, shoving Ethan away forcefully.

Michael went to step between them, but Ethan raised a staying hand. He backed off, but stayed close just in case.

"What do you mean, Dev?" Ethan asked quietly, as if gentling a frightened animal.

And perhaps he was, Michael thought as he looked into the red-rimmed, tear-filled eyes and desperately haunted look on Ethan's brother's face.

"I mean," Devon replied caustically. "I'm trying to drag your sorry ass back to the Master so I can go home."

"What?" Ethan cried out in alarm, quickly backing away a few unsteady steps.

Michael stepped forward and wrapped his arms around his lover from behind. Brother or not, there was no way he was letting him take Ethan away. The man was in for one hell of a fight if he tried.

"Devon, I don't want to go back. I'm happy here."

"And what about me?" Devon screamed in agony, his voice hoarse with emotion as tears finally spilled from his eyes and streamed unchecked down his face. "Did you ever even once stop to think about me, you selfish bastard?"

Ethan didn't seem to know what to say to his brother. Michael wasn't sure Ethan even recognised the man in front of them anymore. Something had happened to Devon, something dark and twisted and painful. It was obvious from Ethan's expression that he had never seen his brother like this before.

Devon lashing out at Ethan was a new and frightening experience for them both apparently. The raw pain in Devon's face tore at Michael's heart too, so he couldn't even imagine what Ethan must be feeling.

"He kicked me out, you son of a bitch. He was going to call in the Council if I didn't leave," Devon said, sobbing openly now. As he paused to get himself under control, Ethan reached out a trembling hand, but Devon ignored it.

"I'm sorry, Dev. I'm so sorry," Ethan whispered, apologising over and over, tears now freely coursing down his own face.

Ethan wanted to go to Devon, but Michael held him back, not trusting the wild, unknown and obviously desperate man in front of them.

"I just wanted to stay with the Master," Devon continued to sob brokenly.

"He never cared for you, Devon. Why can't you see that? He barely tolerated you."

Devon's shoulders sagged and he seemed to crumble in on himself, his eyes dimming with pain as if Ethan had hit him. But Michael noticed he didn't deny it.

The sad truth was, despite Devon's physical perfection and complete devotion to their Master, the Master preferred Ethan. To the point that he was either deliberately cruel to Devon, ignored him all together or treated him with ill-concealed disgust. The irony was Ethan couldn't stand the Master and had longed to be free, while Devon was completely loyal to him.

"Oh, Devon! Why can't you see that you're so much better than that? You deserve someone who will love you just the way you are. Please, Devon, don't. Don't go back to him." Ethan was crying in earnest now too. His poor beautiful, frightened brother. "I couldn't stand it anymore, Devon," he continued, trying to make his brother understand. "I just couldn't take it. Letting him use my body, fuck me in exchange for food and shelter like a whore!"

Devon exploded with anger, his eyes wild with hatred and pain. He launched himself at Ethan, slamming him backwards as he lashed out at him with his claws. "Don't you call me that! You son of a bitch! Don't you ever call me that!"

Tears streamed down Devon's face and the waves of pain, anger and humiliation made Ethan's stomach roll more than any physical abuse Devon could possible rain down on him. What had happened to his poor baby brother? What had they done to him? What had *he* done to him?

The back door to the kitchen suddenly exploded in, and a feral roar filled the room. Michael was unceremoniously hauled away from where he had been trying to get Devon away from him. They froze mid-tussle on the floor, and Ethan was horrified to see Michael pinned to the same wall Devon had been held against only moments before. He dangled by his throat inches from the floor, kicking and choking, held up by a massive cat-shifter with wild, blood shot eyes.

Devon was terrified. How had Rolf managed to find him so quickly? He watched, trembling in fear, as the big, muscular cat showed little reaction to Michael's struggles to free himself.

"Well, this is a touching family reunion," Rolf drawled lazily. "Don't move, either of you, or I'll crush this one's wind pipe before either of you can twitch," he threatened casually, his voice so conversational it was terrifying.

Devon and Ethan both froze, well aware that it wasn't an idle threat.

"It seems my plans have changed, little cat," Rolf continued, addressing him directly this time. "We're going back after all. All of us." He looked pointedly at Ethan as he applied slightly more pressure to his Master's throat.

It had the desired effect as the man let out a strangled gasp and clawed more desperately at the hand around his throat, trying in vain to dislodge it and get breath into his tortured lungs.

"It seems these humans don't like it when you kill the ones in the blue uniforms. They're like ants crawling over a picnic out there now. I could hardly move. It's time to retreat. I doubt they would let me continue to enjoy the treats this place has to offer without constantly trying to interfere anymore. It certainly wasn't easy following you here, let me tell you." His casual inflections while he effortlessly suspended a man by his throat was both frightening and left absolutely no doubt in anyone's mind that he was deadly serious.

Ethan sobbed raggedly. The big cat threatening his Master's life was obviously too much for him. He wondered absently why he could never show so much loyalty to their true Master. Regardless of that, warrior cats like Rolf had a well-deserved reputation for being brutally efficient, and Ethan could obviously see the ice-cold determination in Rolf's eyes.

"Please, I'll do whatever you want, just let Michael go," Ethan pleaded, turning frightened eyes on Devon. "Please,

Devon, I'll go back with you I promise. Just make him put Michael down. Don't let him kill my mate."

"Call the Master," Rolf growled, still holding Ethan's 'Michael' in an iron grip against the wall by his neck, but lowering him so he could once again touch the floor now that he looked to be getting what he wanted. He was beginning to relax, but Devon wasn't fooled into thinking he wasn't still just as deadly.

Despite his weakening struggle, Michael still tried to fight against the hold and prevent Ethan from making his bargain. Rolf simply shook the man slightly in annoyance and ignored him.

How many times had Devon wished the big brute had simply shaken and ignored him?

"Please," Ethan begged "Please just don't hurt him. I-I love him." Once again Ethan turned to Devon, pleading for understanding. "That's all I ever wanted, Devon. To find someone I could love and who might…someone who might love me. Just me. Not what I was born. Not what I could do for them. Just me."

"Hurry up, pet," Rolf drawled at Devon, "or I might just decide to break your fool neck along with this one's and take your pretty brother home instead. I'm sure the Master wouldn't really care all that much."

Devon looked from Ethan to Michael and finally to Rolf. Slowly, he raised his hand to the medallion at his neck— the one the Master had fastened to his collar, the one that would summon Master Nevin to take them all safely back to the castle, back to the familiar comfort of everything he'd even known.

Michael whimpered but the ability to struggle had almost left him now. Ethan hung his head in defeat. Rolf grinned smugly.

That was until Devon yanked viciously at the pedant around his neck, breaking its fragile hold, drew back his arm and hurled it out the broken down back door and out into the garden.

"You want the Master so bad, Rolf? Go ahead and call him yourself," he spat defiantly.

"You stupid slut!" Rolf roared in anger, brutally throwing Michael aside to send him crashing into the opposite wall where he slid down to the floor in a crumbled heap.

Ethan cried out and ran to his side in a wild dash across the kitchen tiles. He was sobbing and calling Michael's name hysterically as he tried to wake him up.

Meanwhile, Rolf lunged at Devon, backhanding him viciously across the face. He immediately curled up on the floor, his arms held protectively over his head waiting for the next blow.

Rolf seemed to briefly consider inflicting more pain on him, but then quickly ran for the open kitchen door instead. The pendant was apparently much more important to him than meting out punishment. At least for the moment. Devon was sure Rolf would get back around to it soon enough.

Devon listened as if from far away as Ethan finally managed to rouse Michael and helped him sit up against the kitchen wall. Outside he could hear a great deal of commotion, but he really couldn't bring himself to care. In fact, he found he didn't really care very much about anything but the cold, hollow feeling deep in his gut and the lightheaded sense of terror that rang in his ears. What had he done?

"Quickly," Michael was saying in a painful, hoarse whisper, "both of you change. The police will want to ask questions."

Devon looked at him with dull, unfocused eyes in incomprehension. What had he done? Now he really was a stray.

"Change!" The man was trying to yell at him, his damaged throat letting little more than a hoarse whisper out.

Then Ethan was at his side, petting his arm gently. "Please, baby. Change. It'll all be okay. I promise. Just change for me."

Devon felt as if Ethan had slapped him. Change for him, he'd demanded. After everything he had been through Ethan still wanted more. He still wanted him to change. All his life he had tried to be what others wanted.

Anger and hatred and shame flowed over him just as he felt the change from human to cat form course through him. He became the small, sleek black cat that was his other half and let it deal with his pain and torment.

Using claws he couldn't ever remember unsheathing before today, he lashed out at Ethan, slashing a set of deep ragged groves into his brother's forearm before racing for the door. He had to get away. Away from Ethan, calling desperately for him to come back, even as he clutched his bleeding arm. Away from Michael, with the love-filled gaze he turned on Ethan, begging him to change. Away from Rolf, with his abuse and his rage, as he bellowed in the garden while the police closed in. Away from his Master, who no longer wanted him.

He was alone. Finally and truly he really was a stray. And he had absolutely no idea what he was going to do.

* * * *

Michael gently stroked Ethan. He was still in his tabby cat form, curled up and trembling in his arms while the last policeman walked down the front steps and out of sight. It had taken several hours to answer all the questions and clear out the kitchen of strangers and confusion.

Thank goodness, he'd had the presence of mind to get Ethan and Devon to change. It had been hard enough trying to explain away Rolf's attack as random and unprovoked while the man ranted about revenge and claiming what was his, without adding two strange, unidentified men into the mix.

He was going to have to work on getting Ethan some identification, he realised. He wondered absently how someone went about getting false papers. It wasn't something he had much knowledge about. He guessed that was just another interesting thing life with Ethan was going to teach him.

He waved to the looky-Lous across the street as he closed the front door and bolted it securely before making his way back to the kitchen. Thank goodness for nosey neighbours, he thought wearily. It seemed that one of them had called the police after hearing a disturbance. They were all nervous with the recent increase in crime around the city apparently.

Just as well. Rolf would have been impossible to handle without the help of the police. It had taken several very muscular, well-armed officers and a dog squad to subdue him in the end.

Michael shivered. It could all have gone so badly so quickly. He could have lost the only thing that mattered to him now. He could have lost Ethan. If Rolf had taken Ethan away, there would have been nothing he could do about it and no way for him to have followed.

Suddenly, he felt Ethan wiggling to be put down. He watched the slow, smooth change come over him before slim, warm arms circled his waist and his lover burrowed into his embrace. He smoothed his hand over Ethan's back and absorbed the warmth of his lover's beautiful body.

"There's a storm building," Ethan finally said, his voice broken and tense with worry.

Michael turned to look out the window to see that clouds were indeed drifting in, dark and threatening from the bay.

"Devon hates storms," Ethan continued, his voice hitching suspiciously as he clung to him.

Michael tightened his arms around the smaller man. He didn't offer any platitudes or reassurance. He couldn't.

Devon had simply disappeared in the commotion and there had been no sign of him since. The pain and despair he had seen in Ethan's eyes when it became apparent Devon was not coming back, made him want to go right out and search the streets for the man. He was more than willing to give Devon a home too. But they couldn't make him stay. That would be wrong and they both knew it. They didn't have to say it.

Devon had to come to the point of accepting his freedom and forgiving his brother himself. But it was hard.

Michael knew it prayed on Ethan's mind, knowing his brother was out there somewhere, without anyone who cared for him, alone and fending for himself for the first time in his life. Gently, he leant down and took Ethan's lips in a tender kiss, offering what comfort he could.

Epilogue

Michael couldn't believe he was sitting at the bar in the city's newest gay club, watching what was essentially erotic dancing. Sure, they didn't take their clothes off, but there really weren't that many to begin with, and you knew exactly what the dancers were saying with their bodies.

It seemed Divine, the band they had met at the market, and their unique accompanying dancers were the latest craze to hit the clubs. Everyone wanted to book them for special events and openings, and they always played to sold out crowds.

Tonight, fittingly both partners were male. Michael watched one particularly closely. He was definitely the more skilled of the two. He was also the most gorgeous man he could ever remember seeing. His body flowed like hot, sweet honey. He just wanted to lick him from head to toe.

"Well, well, well," a silky voice drawled beside him.

Michael turned around, not in the least surprised to see Daniel's smug face grinning down at him. Life, after all was nothing if not ironic.

"Slumming it, are we? Or have you finally decided to crawl out from under that rock you insist on burying yourself under and join the world? I'm sure the gay world at large will be so...apathetic."

Daniel always did have a nasty tongue, Michael realised. The man was spiteful and mean, and he never forgot even the smallest slight against him. Michael wondered, not for the first time, what he had even seen in him in the first place.

"Hello, Daniel," he replied without a hint of emotion whatsoever. Why should he care what the man thought or said? He turned back to watch his dancer finish his number.

Daniel followed his gaze to the stage. "Oh, forget it, Mickey!" He chuckled cruelly. "He's waaaay out of your league. Why not try the classifieds, I'm sure there must be plenty of other desperate and dateless out there that you'd have a better chance with."

Michael ignored him as the dancers finished their number and the room erupted into loud cat calls and applause. He stood and added his own shrill whistle to the accolades for the performers. They really had been magnificent tonight.

"You are so pathetic, you know that?" Daniel sneered. "Look at you." He cast his small, red rimmed eyes up and down Michael's tight leather pants and even tighter black shirt. He had taken off his jacket in the heat of the club, and he knew he looked damn hot. Unlike Daniel who, after years of hard partying, was starting to look a little worse for wear.

"Are you really so hard up and desperate right now you have to come and perv on some exotic dancers to get your rocks off? They don't care how loud you clap, you know, just so long as you pay your money at the door."

Michael continued to ignore the silly little man at his shoulder as he remained standing waiting for the dancers to come out from back stage. Finally, he saw his gorgeous man step out from the wings and cross the club to meet him.

He had thrown on a loose shirt over the top of his tight leather pants but the effect was still breathtaking as his lithe body moved through the crowd. The dark eye make-up outlining his gorgeous green eyes was breathtaking. It made him look even more feline and alluring.

As he saw Michael waiting for him, his face lit up in a huge smile. Michael opened his arms as Ethan stepped up and threw himself into their embrace, his arms snaking around his waist to hold him tight. The smaller man rested his head against Michael's chest and rubbed against him affectionately. Daniel could only gap for air like a landed fish as they both ignored him.

"You made it."

"Wouldn't miss it. You were fantastic. As always."

Ethan blushed as he reached up to drag Michael's head down for a deep, drugging kiss.

"Mmmm. Ready to go home gorgeous?" Michael asked.

"More than. That was the last set and I already said goodbye to the guys so let's get out of here. I suddenly need to get out of these tight pants." He wiggled and leered up at Michael with a saucy grin.

"You need any help with that?" he asked.

"If you play your cards right and treat me nicely when we get home," Ethan quipped back.

"Double choc-chip ice cream already in the freezer awaiting your desire."

"Mmmm, you know the way to my heart, but I don't know if my first desire is going to be for ice cream, even double choc-chip."

Michael felt his cock, straining to escape his tight pants, throb at the heated look in his lover's dark green eyes. "You are so good for my ego. I warned you about that once before. You know you have to stay now, don't you?"

"I'll try to grin and bear it." Ethan chuckled around a huge, happy smile.

It was infectious and Michael just had to reach down and cup his cute, tight little ass through his pants. "I'd rather you bare something else."

"Enough." Ethan giggled, dragging him by the hand towards the exit.

Daniel just stared after them in disbelief.

Michael couldn't wipe the mile-wide smile off his face as he walked out into the night, his arm wrapped around his lover, his mate, his partner and his very best friend. Finding the love of his life and learning to live life to the fullest with him was such sweet revenge.

DEVON'S REVENGE

Dedication

For M.E., because you were always brave and now
you are free.

Prologue

"You stupid slut!" Master Gailin screamed as he slapped Mirra's cheek and sent her sprawling across the cold flagstone floor.

Trembling in shock and fear, Mirra barely resisted the urge to curl into a ball and screw her eyes shut—a futile attempt to make it all go away, but still very tempting nevertheless.

She couldn't believe the Master had found them. She'd thought the disused root cellar would be the perfect hiding spot. So far from the main living area of the castle, it was almost in the catacombs and nearly lost to living memory. It had taken her weeks to find it. Yet somehow they had still been discovered.

Covering the side of her red, throbbing face with a trembling hand, Mirra crawled back to the small wicker basket in the centre of the little stone room she had chosen so carefully. She cowered over the woven rim protectively, but with a deep sense of foreboding.

While she didn't make a sound, the two tiny kittens inside—little more than bundles of black and brindle fur—weren't so circumspect. They mewled pitifully, giving voice to their distress as they huddled together against the side and tried desperately to reach her.

They were so frightened. The Master's anger—something she'd managed to shelter them from since their birth nine days earlier—was overwhelming. And Mirra knew just how they felt. Her own terror clawed at her insides—demanding she get away and hide somewhere dark and safe. She wanted so badly to grab the kittens up and run as far away as possible. But she couldn't. There was no escape. Master Gailin would find her. Master Gailin *always* found her.

She couldn't even risk touching them to offer comfort in case it made the situation worse. But then, as Master Gailin stepped up to tower over them—his dark eyes flashing with rage, his thin face white and drawn tight with anger—Mirra knew it probably couldn't get much worse than it was right now anyway. She stayed still and silent regardless, long years of training and experience locking her in place.

"Did you think you could hide this from me?" Master Gailin roared, his fists clenched tightly by his side as his entire body vibrated with fury. Turning, he paced away furiously.

Mirra simply hunched her shoulders—instinctively trying to make herself as small a target as possible. She knew better than to try to defend herself. All she could do was keep her eyes carefully lowered in submission and hope the Master's tirade would burn off some of his anger.

The hardest part was not to comfort and console the terrified kittens. All she wanted was to pick them up, cuddle them close and gently stroke their soft, new fur.

Tears burned her eyes, the pain of denying her instincts lodging in her throat and making it hard to breathe. But she kept her trembling hands to herself.

This is bad. Oh! This is so bad. She cinched her arms around her thin waist and barely resisted the need to begin rocking herself.

Her mind worked frantically. Had she been careless and betrayed the kittens somehow? Or had she been betrayed by someone in the household? Was it one of the other cat shifters, jealous of her position as current favourite amongst the harem slaves? She would gladly give the 'honoured' position to someone else, she thought miserably. How could someone betray her little family?

Panic hit her hard and fast at the thought. If she *had* been betrayed, what else might they have told the Master? Could her mate be in danger? Through sheer force of will she stopped herself from looking over at the tall, silent warrior by the door, but it was almost painful to deny the impulse—her mounting terror for her lover nearly overpowering her.

Somehow her growing fear must have communicated itself to the kittens, because she suddenly felt two raspy tongues bathing her forearms. Hanging onto the wicker edge precariously they had managed to clamber up the side of the basket and now offered tiny wet kisses—as if trying to ease her worries—before they both tumbled back in.

Oh! My poor babies, she moaned softly to herself, crouching down lower in a desperate attempt to hide them and their innocent antics.

Abruptly, the Master stopped pacing—his long, flowing robes billowing out around him. Arcane symbols of power glowed faintly over the material.

Never a good sign, Mirra fretted.

"Who dared to betray me?" the Master demanded of the warrior — her mate, her lover, her only reason to live before the kittens were born — as he stood guard by the door. "I will have names and heads, Dante. How could you let this happen while the household was under your supervision?"

Mirra suppressed the sob of relief that bubbled up inside her as the potential threat to her mate's life skipped over them — at least for now. Their Master couldn't know, or Dante would be dead already.

Dante simply bowed deeply from the waist, his fist pressed over his heart in the customary symbol of obedience and servitude. "I beg your forgiveness, my Master."

Dante's calm, stoic demeanour made him appear aloof and detached, but Mirra knew better. Even the deep timbre of his voice affected her. What she wouldn't give to be in his arms right now.

The Master continued to fume, too caught up in his own anger to notice either Dante's apology or his continued submission. He began to pace back and forth across the tiny cellar again.

"If I wanted more kittens," he ranted. "I'd have had more kittens bred!" He flung his arm in the kittens' direction with a look of disgust on his face. "Look at the mongrel things. Not a hint of good breeding in them," the Master spat contemptuously, missing the dark flash of anger in Dante's eyes and his jaw clenched in a rage every bit the Master's equal.

Abruptly, Master Gailin stopped and turned on Mirra as she cowered on the floor. "Who was it?"

Mirra curled in on herself, preparing for another blow. The question she had feared the Master asking ever since she had discovered she was pregnant hung in the air between them all as she remained silent and refused to answer.

"How dare you!" Master Gailin bellowed, sending out a wave of energy so strong it slammed Mirra back against the rough stone wall with a bone jarring thump.

Pain radiated out from where she had hit, and now she was pinned by her throat to the cold stone wall. The kaleidoscope of agony blossomed out and fluctuated as muscles tensed and strained to try to absorb the impact. Even having steeled herself for the attack, Mirra couldn't completely stifle her cry. It joined with the kitten's increasingly distressed whimpering.

She saw Dante's fists clenched tight, his knuckles standing out white with strain. Mirra prayed he would have the sense to remain quiet. Nothing could be done. If the Master wanted to kill her, she would die. But someone had to protect the kittens. Keep them safe.

As the Master maintained the pressure against her throat, stars of multicoloured light tunnelled in. Her vision dulled around the edges. A grey fuzz settled in, threatening to darken her sight forever if she continued without air for too much longer.

Unexpectedly, the pressure was released and Mirra gulped oxygen convulsively—coughing and spluttering helplessly as she rubbed at her abused throat. She saw Dante's tense frame relax ever so slightly out of the corner of her eye as she collapsed to the floor—still struggling to breathe, but grateful to be alive.

"If you weren't so valuable I'd make an example of you!" the Master hissed, sounding more like a cat than she was. "As it is, if I ever discover the other's identity…"

And that was exactly why Mirra had remained silent. While the Master left the threat unfinished and hanging ominously in the space between them, there really was no need to elaborate. Mirra knew, as every one of the Master's slaves knew, what would happen if her lover was ever revealed. It would be a slow, torturous death, carried out in full view of the household, probably over many days. She would rather die herself than for that to happen.

"Dante! Take these…" the Master sneered down at the kittens as they continued to cry pitifully, still distressed and now huddled together seeking comfort. "Take these creatures and drown them."

"No!" Mirra screamed. "Please, Master!" She tried to catch hold of his robe, but he whipped the material away with an angry jerk.

"Make her watch," he added spitefully. "She'll think twice before defying me like this again!"

Mirra looked up into Dante's eyes desperately and saw the barely perceivable shake of his head that their Master missed in his malice. Mirra held her tongue, but it was nearly impossible with the threat to the kittens hanging over them all.

"We leave at first light for the Capital. It will be done by then, and you will both be ready to go. From now on, you will be coming with me while I travel, Mirra. I'll not trust you again to remain behind while I attend business. You can keep me company on my trips," Master Gailin leered.

Mirra didn't hear or care—drowning in tears as the Master mage swept from the room.

* * * *

A storm was coming. The trees were tossed about like the rolling, tumbling waves of the ocean. Leaves and loose wood fell all around them as they stepped off the road and into the forest.

Mirra trembled. She could smell the faint trace of ozone in the air. Could see the flashes of lightening and hear the echoing boom of thunder. But the torture of her soul was far more devastating than the approaching storm could ever be.

She clutched the basket with her precious babies tightly to her chest as they came to a stop in a clearing just off the road.

Dante's expression was set in a firm, inflexible mask. "It's the best I can do, Mirra. It was the only house I could find that might take the kittens in on such short notice."

"Dante! I can't! I can't just abandon them. Especially not here," Mirra pleaded. Her eyes misted with tears and her throat was raw and husky. "They're just babies. Our babies, Dante."

"We have no choice," Dante countered tightly. He was trying to appear strong and determined, but Mirra could tell he was hurting. Unfortunately, seeing how distressed her mate was only made Mirra's pain worse. "If we take the kittens. If we run. He'll find us, Mirra. You know he will. And then what? He will definitely kill them. Slowly and painfully, to teach us a lesson." Dante stepped forward and wrapped his arms around her, cradling the basket between them. "We won't have an opportunity like this again, Mirra. This is the only way to save them. We live for today and hope for tomorrow."

"But why this house? Of all the houses—" Mirra's voice, shrill even to her own ears, caught in her throat.

"He will see that they are fed and sheltered. I've spoken to the steward. Master Nevin is hungry for power. Gywen is sure they will be taken in. And what more can we ask for? Come on, sweetheart, the servant will be here any minute." Dante leant forward and kissed her brow tenderly, then quickly lifted his head and stepped back when they heard someone coming towards them through the forest.

What more could we ask for? Mirra wondered silently as her grief slowly turned to a molten rage and hot tears spilt down her cheeks. Was it too much to ask to love and be loved openly? Was the freedom to have children, to laugh and hold each other as a family more than they should ever hope for? Was the chance to grow old and die surrounded by the ones they loved more than they could ever expect?

Mirra looked down at the basket she had hidden the kittens in and gently pulled back the blanket she had wrapped around them. The ginger brown tabby lay curled on his side asleep. His tiny paws twitched occasionally, perhaps in a dream of running wild and free, chasing his brother. He took the storm and the unexpected journey in his stride.

The other kitten, the pure black one, however, stared back at her plaintively. Pale blue eyes peered up out of a tiny, ink black face. Tears pooled in her eyes again as he mewled softly, lifting one paw out to her.

What's wrong? he seemed to say. *Don't be sad.*

Sniffing back the tears, she tried to be strong for him. She reached down and stroked his silky soft head lovingly.

"Stay safe, little one. Be a good boy…" her voice faltered.

Leaning down quickly she kissed the top of the kitten's head, wrapped the blanket back around the basket and placed it gently on the ground before letting Dante drag her away.

She blocked her ears to the kitten's cries of distress as he tried to call them back.

Chapter One

"Don't go!" Devon heard himself calling out in a hoarse, raspy voice as he slowly regained consciousness.

Damn! He'd had the dream again. He couldn't even escape its clutches in unconsciousness.

Moaning softly, he forced himself to roll over onto his side and spat out a mouthful of blood onto the threadbare carpet.

How long have I been out this time? he wondered, carefully wiping the blood away from his mouth with the back of his hand and wincing when he encountered a split in his lower lip.

Heaving himself up into a sitting position, he knew from experience that it was a rhetorical question. There was no real way of knowing how long he'd been out. Unconsciousness was a blissfully empty void—a small reprieve to appreciate while it lasted. It was ironic that in all the years he had spent as a pleasure cat—at his Master's sexual beck and call, and not so tender mercy—

he had never had cause to learn that lesson. Now it had been beaten deep into his psyche. Yet another thing to thank his twin brother, Ethan, for.

Devon groaned as he gingerly felt his bruised ribs. He knew that he couldn't let the situation continue. It was time to go. 'Master Tony', a man he had thought might replace his true Master, was getting worse. One day soon he would go too far. And on that day, Devon knew he wouldn't wake up.

"I don't think so," Devon whispered bitterly to himself. If he wasn't ready to take his own life—and at one stage it had been a serious consideration after everything he had been through—then he certainly wasn't going to let this pretender take it from him.

Taking a few deep, even breaths, Devon resigned himself to the inevitable. He was out of here, which meant returning to the streets as a stray. The mere thought made his stomach roll with nausea, but he needed to get away from the increasingly violent physical abuse. 'Master Tony' could go to hell. The man hadn't turned out to be even close to real master material.

Devon felt an unaccustomed thrill of triumph at the rebellious thoughts. It coursed through him and made him feel bigger, braver and stronger than he had ever felt before in his life. For a moment, he let the new sensations wash over him, buoying his resolve.

It was his first act of defiance, and damn it felt good.

Okay! Maybe it's my second, he revised. It had definitely been defiance when he had thrown away the medallion Master Nevin had given him rather than summon the mage after finally tracking down his errant twin. But he hadn't felt anywhere near as good then as he did now. In fact, that one rash act of insubordination had made him feel physically ill and changed his life forever. He could never go back.

Slowly, the good feeling faded away, until all that was left was a dull ache of shame and loss. Thinking of his life before coming to this place—this Earth, with its confusion and chaos—didn't just remind him he was a stray, which was devastating enough. It forced him to think of Ethan, and that brought out a whole new world of pain and anger.

Walking away from Ethan and refusing to have anything more to do with his twin brother hadn't been defiance. He had never followed Ethan out of a sense of duty. He'd done it for love—true, unconditional devotion and love for his brother. And Ethan had thrown it all back in his face, abandoning him to his fate without a second thought.

He wasn't sure he would ever be able to stand seeing his brother again. To have to watch his twin—so happy, so in love—while he was still so miserable, angry, and alone. To know, deep in his heart, that Ethan didn't really care about him.

With a sudden, bone deep clarity Devon realised it wasn't rebelliousness or defiance that was fuelling his courage at the moment. It was anger. Cold, hard, bitter anger.

He balled his fists, trying to contain the new understanding. He'd never really been angry before. He turned the thought over and over in his mind like a shiny black trinket of grief.

Yes, that's what it was, he acknowledged. He was angry. Angry with Ethan for running away. Angry with Rolf for using and abusing him. Angry with 'Master Tony' for all the physical pain and torture he had inflicted. But most of all, he was angry with himself for never being quite good enough.

Devon spat out another mouthful of blood in disgust as he hauled himself to his feet and began scratching around for his few possessions.

Ethan had thought Devon was completely ignorant of their Master's feelings towards him. But how could he be? He had always known he was inferior to his beautiful, wild brother. Ethan had been the Master's favourite from the very beginning, while he had been the barely tolerated lesser half of their duet.

Still, he'd always tried hard to please—to remain loyal and true regardless. It was his place, his duty and his honour to serve Master Nevin. He'd truly seen the good the Master did for the people under his control. They had food, protection, and a warm, stable place to call home. If he could serve the man who provided all that, in whatever small capacity, then he was happy to do it. At least he had been before his brother had ripped it all away from him.

Devon slung his duffel over his shoulder and cautiously edged open the door. This wasn't the best neighbourhood. Seeing the coast was clear, he slipped out, only to pause as he went to pull the door shut behind him.

A small grin started to form, but his split lip pulled painfully, threatening to open and start bleeding all over again just when it had finally sealed shut. It quickly transformed into a grimace of pain.

While life as a stray was hard, Devon reflected as he let the door swing open once more, a little revenge went a long way towards making him feel better. With any luck, by the time Tony got home his light-fingered, deaf, dumb and blind neighbours would know absolutely nothing about what had happened to all his possessions either.

Keeping to the shadows, Devon crept along the deserted street — with its abandoned refuse and sharp, ominous smells. It had been a little over a month since he had walked away from Ethan and started his life as a stray. And he had very little to show for it other than a few more bruises and a single change of clothes.

Walked away, Devon snorted with self-depreciation, *more like ran for the hills.* Because worse than not being able to stand seeing his brother so in love and loved in return, or even the underlying anger he now recognised in himself, was the sudden, overwhelming desire he had for retribution. He wanted to lash out at someone for all the pain and suffering he had gone through, and that scared him to death. He'd never felt the need to hurt anyone in his life, never mind his beloved brother.

And unfortunately, his feelings hadn't diminished over time either. They'd only swollen and crusted over, like a festering wound — all the twisted rage trapped just below the surface ready to explode.

No, he definitely couldn't handle seeing his brother. Not yet and maybe not ever. There were too many things going on in Devon's head at the moment. Too many things he needed to sort out for himself.

Like how to rectify the little problem of being a stray.

Devon didn't delude himself with thoughts of finding the same commitment and love — whatever that was — that Ethan seemed to have found with his mate, Michael. He'd merely hoped to find someone that might take him in for...

Well, he hadn't actually given much thought to why someone would take him in. How it might all work. 'Master Tony' had definitely been a mistake, Devon admitted to himself. He had lasted exactly five days as a stray before stumbling into Tony at a club he had found that was willing to offer food for work.

The work hadn't been too demanding—just clearing tables and wiping up spills—and the food had been wonderful. He was always hungry lately. His skills as a scavenger were sadly lacking after living the pampered life of a kept pet. The only thing missing had been a safe place to sleep.

Tony had said he wanted to be Devon's new Master. He had offered a warm place to stay and regular meals in exchange for his obedience. It had seemed like a gift from the gods and Devon had readily agreed. Unfortunately, he had soon discovered that Tony knew very little about being a good Master and far too much about using his fists for even the most minor of infractions. And lately, Tony hadn't necessarily even bothered making up an excuse to punish him.

Frustrated, hungry and still hurting from his most recent beating, Devon consoled himself with the fact that he had learnt a lot in the last few weeks about life in this strange world that was apparently to be his home from now on. Armed with his new, if somewhat painful lessons, Devon headed out to start again. This time he would expect *money* for his work. And he would buy his own damn food. Maybe he could even work out how to acquire a safe place to live.

Chapter Two

Trapped...Caged...Controlled...Trapped...Caged...Controlled ... Rolf paced back and forth in the tiny reinforced steel cell.

A constant low, ominous growl rumbled deep in his chest as the collar around his neck threatened to choke him — not because it was cinched too tight, but because it was there at all. A red haze of fury clouded his mind, threatening to swallow him down until all that was left was the animal that raged at being confined. At being controlled again.

Rolf snorted. He knew his brain was beginning to shut down to all but the most primitive of responses and reactions, but right now he really didn't care. In fact, he welcomed it. Basically, they were telling him to kill his captors, escape and find Devon. And that's exactly what he wanted to do even in his lucid moments. He wanted Devon. Badly. So he gave free rein to his base, animal instincts.

His pacing and growling became increasingly agitated the more he thought about the situation. They couldn't keep him here. He refused to be confined. More importantly, he refused to be contained like this while what was his roamed around freely without him. Devon couldn't be trusted for a moment to know his place — which was on his hands and knees taking Rolf's cock into his glorious hot body over and over again.

What is the little slut up to right now anyway? Rolf wondered. *Is he even now offering his ass up to some other male? No one is allowed to plunder that tight, warm hole. No one but me!*

Frustration and rage overwhelmed him, and Rolf threw himself at the steel bars. They gave a dull metallic thud and shuddered slightly, but all he really succeeded in doing was draw his captor's attention.

"Settle down, puss. Those bars aren't going anywhere and neither are you," one of the guards said in a bored tone as he lazed indolently against the far wall bouncing a small rubber ball back and forth against the concrete bunker.

The second guard sniggered as he flipped another card over in the game he had laid out on a small table in front of him.

The constant rhythmic percussion of the ball against the wall ate at Rolf's brain. *Thunk. Bounce. Return. Thunk. Bounce. Return.* Like a spike being driven into his skull over and over again it reverberated in his head until he couldn't take it anymore.

Roaring his rage, Rolf snapped and launched himself at the bars of his cage once more.

Quick as a shot, the guard turned and threw the ball at Rolf's head. But it was no real threat. Rolf's quick reflexes kicked in and he was clear before the small rubber projectile even made it half way across the room.

Crouching low, Rolf waited for the next attack. Or the opportunity to wrench the man's still-beating heart from his chest—which of course would be the preferred option as far as Rolf was concerned.

Oblivious to his own peril, the man exploded, "I said settle the fuck down you stupid moggy, or I'll show you what that collar around your neck can really do!"

Rolf steeled himself, but refused to flinch as the guard reached for the remote control on the table. In the twenty-four hours since being relocated here—to a small cage in an underground bunker in the middle of nowhere—he had become well acquainted with what the collar around his neck was capable of.

This time, however, the pain never came. And that too was part of the game, Rolf acknowledged. Never knowing when the mind numbing electric shock would pulse through his body, exploding through his nervous system and leaving him weak and disorientated.

"Dumb, fuckin' animal," the guard grumbled angrily. "Stupid, fuckin' baby sitting. Why'd we pull cat sitting duty anyway, Lester?" he complained to his companion as he flopped down sullenly into a rickety metal chair next to the table.

Lester opened his mouth to reply, but a disembodied voice from the corridor beat him to it.

"I believe it's called being promoted to your level of competence," a deep, even voice offered in answer to the guard's complaint.

Three men followed the voice around the corner into the room.

Rolf tensed, assessing each of the newcomers carefully for signs of a threat. Preparing, watching and waiting.

He recognised one of the men as Dr. Rialand. The innocuous looking man had been responsible for a surprising amount of pain when Rolf had first arrived in the underground facility. He had poked and prodded, taking blood and tissue samples and had ultimately fitted the hated collar.

Rolf gave a low warning hiss, daring the man to try to get close to him again. But the scientist merely pushed his wire-rimmed glasses farther up his thin nose and continued flipping through his files, as if Rolf didn't exist.

Incensed by the dismissal, Rolf shook off his irritation in favour of turning to study the other men who had entered with Dr. Rialand. The dark haired man standing next to Rialand — the one who had spoken as he entered — was much taller, with a solid frame devoted to firm, smooth muscles. He was well dressed and had the piercing blue-eyed gaze of a fellow predator. His sharp features and rigid posture suggested determination and ambition. Rolf knew he would bear watching.

It was the third member of the group, however, who really drew his attention.

He was a slightly older man, not nearly as tall or muscular as the second, but with a striking physical resemblance to him. Both had sharp features and the same dark hair. And they had a shared familial scent too. But it was the oddly flat, almost black eyes of the last man that was the most noticeable difference between the two, and they held Rolf absolutely transfixed.

They reminded Rolf of a shark's eyes, and the man dominated the room in much the same way — as if you instinctively knew never to turn your back on the man. Rolf felt his hackles rise as he acknowledged that this man was extremely dangerous — easily the biggest threat in the room. In fact, his watchful, ominously quiet demeanour had every hair Rolf possessed standing on end. Even his teeth ached with tension.

The guards' reactions were also telling. Both had instantly leapt to their feet — their bodies tense and alert — and Rolf had heard their heart rates pick up dramatically. They seemed completely focused on Shark-eyes too.

Not as stupid as they looked then, Rolf thought from his crouched position while he continued to assess every nuance of movement in the room for an opportunity to escape. He desperately wanted to kill, rend and destroy before hunting down the man whose incredible scent still haunted his senses. The sudden unstable dynamics in the room might provide an opportunity to do just that. He needed to stay alert.

Devon. Need to get too Devon, his mind reminded him forcefully, focusing and heightening his senses as he watched the scene playing out in front of him.

The first guard's face was flushed red with a mixture of embarrassment and...anger. *Interesting.* Rolf filed the information away for later. He wondered whether they were a cohesive group or a loose pack, still fighting and manoeuvring around each other vying for position. If they were functioning on superior strength, fear and constantly challenging each other for rank there was a possibility he could exploit that weakness to escape.

"Grand-Master Vladimir. Master Talan," the ball-throwing guard finally managed to greet respectfully, marshalling his dignity admirably, Rolf grudgingly admitted.

"Gentleman," Vladimir with the shark-eyes countered, his voice like smoke — soft and insidious but in no way something you could ignore. Everyone in the room stood just a little straighter, as if at attention and listened attentively to his every word.

Yes, very dangerous.

"You have a report for me, Eric?" Vladimir asked mildly.

"Yes, of course," Eric the guard replied eagerly, scrambling for a file and quickly passing it across.

Rolf could taste the slightly bitter hint of fear in the man's reply, but otherwise he appeared the very model of calm efficiency.

Vladimir began flipping idly through the file. He didn't pause to focus on anything, obviously waiting for the guard to offer a verbal report instead.

Eric coughed nervously.

"We...ahh...we had no problem securing the transfer. Our *friends* made sure we were granted permission to remove and secure the prisoner together with any records pertaining to his case. We're still having a few problems with the local authorities on the ground asking questions but..."

"I'll take care of it," the taller, arrogant looking man interrupted — his self-assured tone leaving no room for doubt as to his abilities to deal with the situation.

"Very well, Talan," Vladimir agreed with a magnanimous inclination of his head before turning to the skinny scientist at his shoulder. "Dr. Rialand, what do you have to report?"

Never looking up from his files, the doctor continued to flip back and forth, following and double-checking results.

"Tests we ran suggest a male cat shifter of the warrior caste. So far all indicators are that he is a perfect physical specimen, in peak fighting form. He will make an excellent addition to our stable," the doctor predicted before turning over a few more pages. "His hormone levels were a little abnormal, but that can be attributed to his heightened agitation, slightly higher than normal aggression level and excessive arousal recently. We have, of course, begun behaviour modification training with some limited success..."

"Why would he have been excessively aroused recently?" Vladimir interrupted, his eyebrows raised in query.

Eric the ball-throwing guard spoke up, his tone defensive. "There were reports and some supporting evidence found at a number of crime scenes that suggested a pair were involved. And several eyewitnesses reported seeing him mistreating a small domestic cat. We think it more likely there was another cat shifter involved, possibly an escaped pleasure cat based on these sightings. We have been trying to coordinate a search, but our efforts have been severely hampered by the fact we don't want to alert the pride members in the area to our presence."

"That, of course, must be avoided at all cost," Talan said firmly. "Grand-Master Vladimir has worked too long and hard to get an agent in place in the pride to have the whole operation screwed up trying to bring in a pleasure cat. They're nearly worthless to us anyway, and a single one is completely useless. It probably didn't last five minutes out on the streets on its own."

Rolf leapt to his feet again and began to pace, agitated and concerned by the speculation. Devon was his. He wasn't allowed not to survive. The stupid little cat had to know that.

"Want. Mine," he growled ominously to no one in particular.

Everyone ignored him, except Vladimir whose shark-like eyes turned to focus on him.

"We shouldn't waste our time or resources on trying to find it," Talan continued. "We need to concentrate our efforts on reducing the Tantric Mages power base in the

Circle while we have the opportunity. My sources suggest—"

"Mine!" roared Rolf again, throwing all his weight at the bars of his cage. This time, tiny flurries of powdered cement drifted down from where they were anchored to the roof. "Want mine!" he screeched.

"I said shut up, you stupid moggy," Eric yelled at him, reaching for the collar's remote control as if Rolf's behaviour was a direct reflection on his ability as a guard.

"Mine," Rolf rumbled darkly, staring down the guard before roaring in agony as Eric delivered a crippling shock to his nervous system.

"Wait!" Vladimir commanded never once taking his eyes off Rolf, who now lay quivering on the floor but refused to lower his eyes away.

"Grand-Master?" Eric asked, confusion and respect warred for dominance in his expression.

Vladimir glided across the floor—silent and deadly—he eyed Rolf speculatively.

"You say you suspect this other cat was a pleasure cat," he asked, continuing to watch Rolf with calculating eyes.

"Well, I...that is...I ah..." Eric's nervousness and growing fear filled the room, making Rolf instinctively want to crouch into a stalking posture. But his muscles refused to co-operate.

"Dr. Rialand, does this cat have a mating mark?"

"No." Rialand sounded affronted by the question. "I would have reported such a thing. In my professional opinion, he's unmated."

Rolf rumbled low in his chest. Devon was still his. "Mine."

"Where was the last sighting of this pleasure cat?" Vladimir demanded.

Rolf struggled against the weakness in his limbs, trying to get back up to his feet. The shark-eyed man taking an interest in Devon wasn't something he could tolerate, or ignore.

Eric flipped through another file anxiously. "Ahh…it was…somewhere outside Sydney…I know I saw it… Ah! Here it is. East Bayside."

Rolf growled.

"Find it," Vladimir said firmly.

Eric and Lester looked confused, Talan irritated.

"Why bother?" Talan asked with exasperation. "It's just a worthless *pleasure* cat," he added as if the very word caused him some distaste.

"Want. Mine," Rolf continued to growl softly.

"That's why," Vladimir countered, pointing directly at Rolf. "They aren't mates and yet this one is obsessed with it. He's fixated on claiming it. There's only one other reason I can think why that would happen. Find it." A terrifying gleam of excitement entered Vladimir's eyes.

"But—" Talan argued.

"I said find him," Vladimir snapped sharply. "Bring him to me."

"How?" Lester asked with more bewilderment than thought of self-preservation.

Vladimir turned his cold black eyes on the guard, who stepped back in alarm. "Release him," Vladimir pointed over at Rolf as he lay helplessly on the cold, cement floor of the cell, still growling aggressively.

"*What!?*" The chorus of denials and disbelief echoing around the room, but Vladimir remained cool and completely unconcerned.

"He will find him," he answered, gesturing to Rolf with complete confidence.

Without reaching for the remote control, Vladimir stretched out his hand and a sudden wave of pain cascaded through Rolf's system so overwhelming he knew he was about to die. It was hundreds of times worse than anything the collar had ever inflicted on him. He screamed in agony, and when his lungs and throat would no longer sustain that, he flinched and whimpered uncontrollably.

Needles of pain forced their way directly into Rolf's brain, demanding he submit to the man in front of him without question and follow whatever order he might issue. There was no way for Rolf to escape. All he wanted was for the pain to stop. But even as it ebbed away, the mage remained somehow in a tiny, secret corner of his brain, ready to lash out again. And next time, Rolf knew to his very bones, he wouldn't survive.

Rolf's survival instincts were too strong for him to consider disobeying.

"Just remember who your Master is now, cat," Vladimir explained, gazing unblinkingly into Rolf's eyes with ice-cold psychopathic menace.

Rolf had never been more desperate to be compliant, or more terrified in his life.

Chapter Three

After nearly twenty-four hours drifting from place to place looking for work, Devon was exhausted. He was beginning to appreciate how lucky he had been to get his first job, and how stupid he had been to let 'Master Tony' talk him into giving it up.

With no current address, no real experience in anything and no references — whatever they were — Devon hadn't found anyone willing to take him on. Or even give him a chance at earning a meal.

Devon's shoulders slumped. He felt slightly sick with hunger and the beginnings of desperation. And he needed to pee. Again. Taking a deep fortifying breath, squaring his shoulders and straightening his spine, Devon pushed through the door to yet another dimly lit bar. He mentally prepared himself for one more try at honest work before going dumpster diving with the rest of the strays in the alley.

The bar was rather typical of the dozens of places Devon had tried today. The heavy scent of humans pressed in around him, making him feel slightly skittish and heightening his senses, which wasn't necessarily a good thing. The sounds of a multitude of voices all speaking at once assaulted his ears and made him want to cover his head and hide. The low level light in this particular place was no hindrance to his excellent night vision, but the overwhelming smell of alcohol and various chemicals made his nausea noticeable worse. Only the slightly heavier scent of food kept him in place and urged him on. If he could find a way of getting some of that food, he could put up with just about anything.

First priority, however, was finding the restroom. Devon spotted the symbol he had come to recognise and began to make his way across to it. He felt the fine hairs on the back of his neck stand on end as numerous sets of eyes followed his progress with more than casual interest.

Breathe, Devon, he reminded himself, trying to calm what he was sure was just his over-active imagination. *In and out, slow deep breaths. Why would anyone be taking particular notice of you? Just another guy walking through a club. Breathe.*

To Devon's relief, the bathroom was clean and significantly brighter than the bar, which made him feel slightly better. He had been in a few places where the bathrooms where dingy and smelt strongly of male musk and arousal. Not even desperate need had made him stay in those places. He had always turned around and quickly left. This bathroom, however, was okay, and after attending to his business and washing up in the sink, he made his way back out to the bar without incident.

Seeing the bartenders all busy with the steadily increasing early evening crowd, Devon eased onto a bar stool set in a quiet section and patiently waited for someone to have time to notice him. His aching legs and feet silently thanked him for the welcome relief finally sitting down gave them. He let out a low groan of appreciation.

"Hey, gorgeous," a low, husky voice breathed into his left ear. Startled, Devon jumped in his seat and spun around to face the stranger. "You look a little worn out. Can I get you something?"

Devon had been too distracted—both by the noise of the bar and the welcome relief of finally being able to sit down—he hadn't heard the man approach. He quickly pulled his body back against the bar as far as he could, but the man simply leaned in farther, crowding him with his tall, powerful body. Devon trembled, but was too tired and despondent—not to mention slightly off-kilter at being caught unawares—to mince words.

"Yes. I'm looking for work," Devon replied as evenly as possible. "The kind you get paid money for," he added as an afterthought. He didn't want there to be any misunderstandings.

"I could certainly make the evening worth your while," the man returned, sidling closer.

Devon blinked in surprise. Was he truly being offered a job? His heart rate leapt up in hope.

The man was a lot taller than Devon and had the broad shouldered, heavily muscular build that he found particularly intimidating after his experience with Rolf. But his features were actually rather pleasant to look at— with a rounded face, smooth, tanned skin and a strong, if slightly wide nose. Thick, blond hair curled around his collar making his overall appearance almost angelic.

Devon shook his head to focus his straying thoughts.

A job is a job. Who cares what the man looks like?

Then Devon looked into the other man's eyes. They gleamed with a speculative light. As he watched, the man's full lips pulled into a tight, smug leer. Instantly, Devon felt his own eyes narrowing in suspicion and distrust.

"What would you want me to do?" he asked carefully

"Don't worry, gorgeous. I only do safe sex." The man placed an arm proprietarily around Devon's waist and began to pull him forwards, his self-assured smile widening as he effortlessly forced Devon closer.

Devon felt himself go cold to the core, then numb. The man wanted to pay him for sex? Was that why all the eyes in the bar had followed him to the bathroom? Was that all anyone could see in him? A warm body to fuck and push away? Did everyone think he was a whore?

Ethan's harsh, hurtful words echoed in his head...*fucking in exchange for food and shelter...like a whore!*

Bile crawled up Devon's throat as he realised that's exactly what he was. Maybe what he'd always been. Had he fooled himself into thinking there was some higher purpose in offering himself to Master Nevin? Perhaps Ethan was right. At the end of the day, what was the different? And Rolf...he hadn't wanted to, but ultimately he'd exchanged sex for protection. And Tony...*Oh! Gods! I am a whore.* It had just taken a bar full of horny men for him to see it, that's all.

Then again, at least this is something I know how to do, he thought bitterly.

A key factor in why he seemed to remain without the means to feed himself after traipsing all over the city was his lack of experience. Well, here was something he definitely had experience in. He had been getting fucked over since infancy, he thought savagely.

Devon considered the man in front of him again, looking him over in a dull, detached sort of way. He was certainly handsome, as attractive as Master Nevin in fact. He wondered idly why the man would have to pay for sex, but dismissed the question. What did he care?

The man seemed suitably strong, an adequate protector for whatever brief time Devon was with him. Maybe not as fierce as Rolf—the warrior he had been sent to earth with—but that wasn't necessarily a bad thing. The biggest point in the man's favour was that he didn't have the same cruel air he had come to recognise in 'Master Tony'. That was most definitely a good thing.

But in truth, Devon really didn't care. In fact, he didn't feel much of anything. Too depressed and desperate, he buckled at the knees ready to begin pleasuring the man, heedless of the crowded bar around them, when a set of strong arms gently gripped his shoulders and pulled him firmly back against a hard muscular chest.

"Hello, kitten. Sorry I'm late." Devon felt the gentle touch of lips press against his temple, but was powerless to turn his head to see who the man behind him was, or even what he looked like as he was pinned to the man's body. "Forget it, Duncan. This one belongs to me," the man continued in a low voice gone suddenly icy with disdain.

'Duncan' narrowed his eyes and seemed to silently weigh up his opponent.

"Don't see your name on him," Duncan finally countered belligerently.

"Trust me. You're never going to see where I put my mark," the man with the strong set of arms and warm chest shot back over Devon's head.

Devon gasped in shock at the declaration. As he inhaled, the man's scent seemed to tunnel right into his brain. It was all strong alpha male spiced with the faintest hint of musk. But funnily enough, it didn't actually frighten him. In the back of his mind, it registered that he should be absolutely terrified and struggle like mad to get away — lately, any scent of arousal scared Devon. But this man just smelt warm and safe and made him want to inch closer into his embrace.

While Devon considered his bizarre reaction, a silent battle of wills was in progress above him. Finally, Duncan backed down and turned away, grumbling about the dubious parentage of his adversary. The man in question simply ignored his vanquished opponent — once the man had backed away far enough to no longer pose a threat at least.

"Come on, kitten. Come dance with me," Devon's captor demanded, shepherding him towards a small group of people all moving together to the beat of the music on the other side of the room.

All of them moved with a grace and freedom that made Devon feel distinctly ungainly and outclassed. But the man didn't give Devon an opportunity to escape, or even look at him until they had crossed to the dance floor — he held on gently, but firmly to his shoulders.

When he was spun around to face the man, Devon's breath caught in his throat. He was the most gorgeous, powerful male Devon had ever seen.

Hauled into a close embrace, the man skilfully moved them in a sensual slide of bodies, and all extraneous thoughts fled. Devon's entire focus was reduced down to the stunning man in front of him.

"You want to be careful, kitten. Duncan isn't someone you should go teasing," the man said as he smiled down at Devon.

He was taller than Devon by a good half a head. His broad shoulders blocked out most of the rest of the dance floor and forced him to take in the man's dark caramel coloured eyes and short, thick, medium brown hair that outlined his rugged, masculine face. All in all, he was a supremely attractive male and Devon could see only one reason why he would have picked him out and chased Duncan off.

"Are you going to pay me for sex too?" he asked bluntly, not even a hint of emotion left to colour his voice.

The man froze and looked startled for a moment. His voice took on a serious, deep rumble, tinged with apprehension and perhaps a little disappointment. "Is that what you want?"

Devon shrugged and looked away, unable to hold the man's intense gaze. He didn't like the slightly disapproving look, and he didn't know the answer to the question anyway.

No, that's not true. I do, he realised with sudden clarity and determination.

"What I want is something to eat and a warm, dry place to sleep," he finally managed, not sure why he felt brave and safe enough to answer so honestly and too tired to care anyway.

"You been turning tricks to get that?" the man asked gently, leaning in to whisper the words against Devon's ear before pulling away again.

Devon's confusion at the strange term must have shown, because the stranger's gaze softened as they continued to stare at one another.

"How long have you been on the streets?" The music changed to a more intimate beat, and Devon found himself gathered even closer into the man's arms.

"A while," Devon mumbled evasively, avoiding the sharp, knowing eyes boring into him and barely resisting the urge to burrow into the broad chest in front of him to escape.

The man didn't really need to know he had been a stray for over a month now. Or that he was so desperate he was almost at the point of begging a stranger to hold him and never let him go.

"Who gave you this?" the stranger in question asked, gently touching the corner of one of Devon's bruised eyes and letting his finger trail down to the corner of his swollen lip.

His gentle, kind manner was confusing. No one had ever really treated Devon with any true kindness. Well, except maybe his brother, and look how that had turned out. He couldn't even stand to be in the same room as his twin anymore.

Devon shrugged as if it didn't matter, but in truth it hurt. It all hurt. Not being good enough to prevent Master Nevin throwing him out. Wondering why he hadn't fought harder against Rolf. His dashed hopes of finding a replacement Master in Tony. Even his brother's newfound happiness sliced into his heart, leaving it raw and bleeding.

And what sort of a person does that make me? When my own brother's happiness hurts me.

Unexpectedly, Devon felt tears prick the corners of his eyes. He looked down trying to blink them away as he struggled to break the stranger's hold. It all just hurt.

"Shit," the man swore softly. "Come on, let's get out of here."

Devon was in no condition to argue. One pathetic attempt to shrug off the man's hold coupled with the tight knot of emotion ripping at his chest drained the fight right out of him. He followed along blindly as he was led outside behind broad shoulders and a ground-eating gait into the relative quiet of the street outside.

Nate had never liked Duncan. Something about the man just rubbed his fur the wrong way every damn time. He was far too smooth, smug and self-important in Nate's opinion. And Nate enjoyed nothing better than tweaking the other cat's tail, every chance he got. Which was what had prompted him to approach the little man he'd seen Duncan hitting on.

Once he'd got close enough to realise the man was a cat shifter, however — and not one he recognised — Nate had become even more determined to intervene. Strange cat shifters were dangerous cat shifters.

Looking back over his shoulder at the little cat trailing along behind him, Nate couldn't find it in himself to really believe this one was a threat though. Unfortunately, he couldn't rely solely on instincts this time. There was too much at stake.

Nate took a moment to study the smaller man. As the leader of the warriors responsible for helping rescue cat shifters and slaves through the various dimensional portals in the area, Nate should have known him. Not recognising him meant that the cat had come from outside their network. That made him a potential danger to everything the clan had worked so hard to achieve.

He could be a spy sent to infiltrate their pride, or a stray so desperate to win back his master's favour he'd sell out his own mother. Nate had seen both too many times before. The little cat needed to be closely scrutinised before they decided what to do with him.

In theory, it was a textbook case. Something Nate had done a number of times over the years, whenever strange cats appeared. This time, however, was a little different,

Nate acknowledged. This time he could sense the smaller man's innate vulnerability, and for some reason, it triggered every protective instinct he possessed like no other ever had before him.

Nate found himself wanting to take the man home, feed him, clothe him and keep him safe. He wanted to hold him close and rub himself all over that tight, little body until every square inch was marked as his.

He shook his head to clear the other man's amazing scent from his nostrils.

What the hell is wrong with me? I need to be careful and vigilant here!

A sudden surge in the crowd caused the man to stumble. Nate groaned as he felt the hand in his tighten convulsively and another reach out to clutch his waist for support. Careful and vigilant were looking like being an uphill battle. Distracted and horny...? Piece of cake.

When Nate was finally sure they were clear of the prying eyes and ears of the club, and relatively protected in the shadowy lee of a doorway, he pulled them to a stop. Peering down at the hunched figure that refused to meet his gaze now, Nate paused to study the man. A messy mop of black hair obscured a pale, thin face currently downturned, studying his shoes intensely.

As he watched, a shiver worked its way over the man's slight frame — whether from fear or from the cold breeze, Nate wasn't sure. He noticed the man hadn't pulled his hand free. He still held on, even though they were well away from the boisterous, crowded club. In fact, the smaller cat was clinging to his hand rather intensely. Nate found himself in no rush to point it out to him. He knew where the kitten was this way, he assured himself. It wasn't because it was an oddly pleasant sensation being connected with the man. Not at all.

Ah! Who am I kidding?

The man's suddenly hopeless air was pulling at his heart something fierce, until he just wanted to wrap his arms around the smaller cat and hold him. He pushed down his instincts—barely. Careful. Vigilant. He knew absolutely nothing about the man—other than he was a cat and as cute as hell, of course.

"You hungry?" Nate asked when the silence began to stretch out uncomfortably between them.

The man's stomach chose that moment to give a loud rumbling protest. A faint blush stole across what Nate could see of the man's perfect, high cheekbones.

"I'll take that as a yes," Nate chuckled softly. "Come on. I know a great little all night place just around the corner."

Pulling the trembling man in close, shielding him from the worst of the bitter wind, Nate headed over to Burnie's, hoping all the way that he wouldn't have to turn the man over to the pride's Council of Elders before the night was over.

If they felt he couldn't be trusted, couldn't be integrated into the pride, they would order him taken far away from here and abandoned, never to be seen or heard from again. It wasn't something Nate could even bring himself to consider. But he really didn't want to analyse that reaction too closely either.

Devon shivered again. It was colder than one of Master Nevin's icy stares outside. And the breeze was picking up again. Not a good night to be out on the streets with no safe place to shelter from the wind.

Looking up at the stranger leading him who knew where, Devon wondered if this was a better alternative though. He didn't exactly have a good track record when it came to being around others. But ultimately he wasn't sure he cared.

Sure, he'd started out with vim and vigour, determined to stand on his own two feet and no longer be a punching bag for the world. But he'd long since burned through the anger and defiance. His stock of newfound courage was pretty low now, too. Maybe it was the pounding ache in his head. Or perhaps the gnawing pain in his gut. It might even be the plain old exhaustion turning his limbs to lead that had drained him dry of any enthusiasm to continue. The hollow emptiness in his heart certainly wasn't helping.

I just can't seem to catch a break.

Devon tried to gather his thoughts for a moment. Maybe the secret to making this work was not to expect too much. The thought of exchanging sex for food and protection—again—made him feel sick. Images of Rolf still haunted him. And his mind skipping on to Tony in the very next second wasn't an improvement. But maybe the secret was not to take too much and then he wouldn't be expected to give more than he could stomach.

Looking back up at the handsome man beside him, acting as a very nice windbreak and promising him food, Devon suspected it was at least worth a try. He just needed somewhere to regroup.

* * * *

Nate stared over the rim of his coffee—content enough to simply sip at his drink and watch the man finish off the last of his chicken sandwich. The poor starving thing looked more in need of sustenance than he was, anyway. Still, it had taken repeated assurances that the food would only go to waste for the smaller cat to finally take it. Now that he had started on the food, however, it was disappearing rapidly.

Actually, he wasn't entirely sure where the little cat managed to put it all. So far, he'd made his way through a massive hamburger, a double serving of chips, half of Nate's chicken sandwich and an extremely generous chocolate milkshake. But finally, he seemed to be slowing down.

Nate watched curiously as the man sat back with a contented sigh. Eyes closed in pleasure he looked deeply sated and ready for a long nap. Nate was absurdly proud of being the one to put that amazingly satisfied look on the stranger's face. He could only imagine how he would feel if the man was stretched out beneath him, all languid and exhausted and mellow with afterglow after having been ridden hard into —

Whoa, there! Where had that come from? Nate pulled his mind out of the gutter with a not so subtle shake of his lust-clouded head.

Dangerous territory. And so not the time, he scolded himself.

But it was already too late to stop the growing bulge in the front of his pants from forming. Just the mental image of the younger man naked and well pleasured —

"So, kitten, feeling better?" Nate asked, clearing his throat and shifting uncomfortably in his seat to try to reposition his raging hard-on without drawing too much attention to it.

He regretted opening his mouth almost instantly. Across from him, the man who had been looking all sleepy, satisfied and sexy, jerked upright in alarm and blinked at him as if only just remembering he was not alone.

"Umm...yeah...ah...thanks." He looked suddenly pale and exhausted under the glaring fluorescent lights of the cafe. "So...ah...what do I owe you?" he asked nervously, casting his eyes around as if looking for a way to escape.

"Not what you're thinking, kitten, that's for sure," Nate snapped, his voice harsher that he intended at the implication he might expect something — probably sexual favours — in exchange for the meal he had provided.

A tense, awkward moment lingered between them, threatening to forestall any further conversation and once again, Nate could have kicked himself. He wasn't normally this clumsy and blunt. Something about the man just threw him for a loop.

"Why do you keep calling me that?" the man demanded, looking decidedly skittish — like the true cornered cat he was.

"What? Kitten?" Nate asked, cocking his head curiously as the other man stared down at the chipped laminated table top in front of him.

He watched as the man took a deep breath, then raised his head, fixing him with a piercing, pale blue-eyed stare.

"My name is Devon."

Nate was oddly proud that Devon had found the strength to assert himself like that, even if it was only for a moment. It had been just long enough to look him in the eye, before turning away again to cautiously watch the few diners scattered around. He'd seen plenty of cats, both in his previous job helping to manage an animal rescue shelter and as part of the pride's retrieval team, who would never have had the spine to stand up for themselves, especially not to a bigger, stronger cat.

"It's nice to meet you, Devon. My name's Nathaniel James, but everyone calls me Nate." He paused to let the information sink in. "And I've been calling you kitten because I know you're a cat shifter."

Devon froze, apparently momentarily stunned, then sniffed tentatively in Nate's direction, all the while looking ready to bolt for the door.

Nate lifted the mask he had placed over his scent, allowing Devon to properly identify him — trusting him with that much at least. He was only risking himself and even then he was pretty sure he could contain the little cat if he needed to.

"Don't worry, kitten. I am too," Nate reassured. "You probably just got a bit muddled in the club. It takes practice to sort through that lot in there, what with all the alcohol and chemicals," Nate continued conversationally.

He wanted to relax the tense man in front of him, but he wasn't willing to reveal that all the pride members were taught to hide their scent. It was a necessary survival technique when mages sent out teams to recover the slaves they lost. But it certainly wasn't something they wanted just anyone knowing about.

Devon still looked shocked, but vastly relieved as well now that he could smell Nate was telling the truth. Nate could almost see the hope flare in his beautiful blue eyes. He'd seen it so many times before — the need for belonging, the need for kinship and pride.

But Nate was a long way from introducing Devon to the rest of the cat shifters. They had all worked too hard, first to escape their masters, then to begin rescuing other run away cats and kittens, setting up a safe place for them all to live. He couldn't risk introducing an unknown like Devon into their midst, even if every instinct was screaming at him to trust and protect him.

"You're really a cat? You're really..." Devon's voice trailed off as if in awe or disbelief, possibly both. "I...I really haven't been around too many others like us before. I'm not exactly sure what I'm smelling most of the time. And...and I was trying not to breathe in through my nose," he started to explain, as if he needed to justify himself. "I didn't feel well and the club smells made me feel even worse... You're really a shifter?"

Nate nodded slowly. His little cat hesitated and glanced around nervously.

"Do you...do you have a Master?"

Nate shook his head and watched as the flare of hope literally faded from Devon's eyes. *Not a good sign*, Nate thought, as he tried desperately to steel his heart against the possibility that Devon was the most dangerous kind of shifter of all — one who would do anything to get back to his Master.

"You?"

Devon looked down and away, flushing slightly, shaking his head — as if he was embarrassed by the fact.

A dump and run, Nate thought clinically while his heart wondered how anyone could abandon such a cute kitten. He looked Devon over once again. While he was small and slight, he was definitely sleek and firmly toned as well. Without a doubt, he was a pleasure cat, Nate realised, refusing as he did to let his imagination wander too far into any dangerous visuals. It also explained the ease with which he considered trading himself.

He had probably lost his sibling, and therefore any value he had to his Master. Which is why he would have been dumped on Earth.

Masters are bastards, Nate decided, even as his heart went out to Devon for his loss. At the same time he knew he had to be more careful than ever now. Some cats craved a master, and nothing would change that. They wanted nothing more than to return to their life as a slave. If someone like that ever found out there was a way to go back to the mage controlled realms through the natural portals around the area, they could endanger everyone who had found shelter at The Compound here on Earth.

It made Nate very aware of his responsibility to the pride, despite his personal response to Devon. He couldn't afford to trust Devon too far, at least not yet. Not before he had done some serious investigation into the man, his motivations and situation. Until then, however, he refused to make a call—either to turn him over to the elders for relocation, or to take him to The Compound.

For right now, he needed to get the man somewhere he could rest, he realised as he watched Devon sway slightly in his seat. The poor kitten looked ready to fall asleep where he sat.

"You ready for that warm, dry place to sleep?" Nate asked casually.

Devon hesitated a moment before nodding warily.

"Come on. You can crash at my place," Nate offered as he stood to pay the bill.

Devon continued to study his ragged shoes. The toes were so tattered that he could almost see his feet poking through. It was quite funny actually. Not so long ago he hadn't worn any clothes at all and had never felt uneasy. Now he was self-conscious about the sorry state of his footwear.

With a self-deprecating snort, he dismissed the silly notion. He was cold and more tired than he could ever remember being in his life. Shoes really were the least of his worries.

Devon couldn't stand the thought of another night out on the streets. He had already spent enough cold, lonely nights roaming around in his cat form through the city to last a lifetime.

While he was smaller and quicker on four legs, he found he wasn't necessarily any safer. Many nights he had been screamed at, chased, and harassed.

Devon felt himself sway on his feet as he stood, but instantly Nate reached out to steady him. Devon risked a peek up at the much larger man. He didn't look dangerous. Okay! He looked dangerous, but not mean. Could he trust the instincts that told him he would be safe with this man?

Devon sighed in resignation. Who was he kidding? Why should he start trusting his instincts now? This man was probably going to turn out to be just like everyone else and end up hurting him. Why couldn't he just accept that was what he should expect from others and move on?

There was something wrong with him. He wasn't sure what it was, but those around him seemed to sense it and react accordingly. There really was no point in fighting it. At least this way, if he went with Nate, he would have a dry place to sleep and only have to deal with one person instead of a whole city full. Perhaps he could even scrounge a meal or two before Nate turned on him, or got sick of him and he was forced to move on.

Timidly, Devon nodded his acceptance of Nate's offer. He tensed when a large arm wrapped around him, then gradually settled in closer to the man's warm side. It was an odd feeling, being held almost protectively like this, but not necessarily a *bad* feeling. In fact, he found he quite liked it. He wasn't sure what the bigger man might want from him later, but he was willing to give whatever it took to get somewhere he could rest for a little while and maybe stay in the shelter of this warm body for just a bit longer.

Devon felt himself begin to drift. Already more asleep than awake as he let Nate lead him away.

Drifting is good, he decided. Everything felt a little fuzzy and dull, and he found he really wasn't anywhere near as worried any more with Nate guiding him along and keeping him safe.

The pleasant feeling lasted about three minutes, before he realised Nate was leading them back to the club. Devon tensed. Was this some sort of game? Was Nate teasing him? Getting his hopes up, only to abandon him back at the club, or pass him off to someone else?

Devon's heart thumped against his ribs and he wondered what chance he had of getting away from Nate.

"Hey, what's wrong?" Nate asked, squeezing Devon's shoulders gently.

"We're going back to the club?" Maybe he was wrong.

"That's right."

Devon's breath caught in his throat. "I thought you were taking me somewhere I could sleep."

"I am. I live above the club. Most of the ca…ah…The Cat Club staff do. I've got a spare room you can use."

Devon's footsteps faltered, but Nate simply adjusted to match and supported him while he got his balance back. "Really?"

Nate's chuckle was warm and easy. "Sure thing. It's only going to waste. You're more than welcome to use it."

Chapter Four

Devon reluctantly rose through the dreamy layers to a sleepy kind of wakefulness. He peeled his tired eyes open just enough to see the first rays of sunlight filtering in through a gauzy curtain at the window, but he was far too comfortable and his limbs still too heavy with exhaustion to want to move.

The cold pre-dawn light gradually gave way to a glorious pale yellow morning while he drifted in and out of awareness.

It was quiet and peaceful here, Devon realised drowsily. Even the busy city noise he had found so hard to get used to when he had first arrived seemed muted and far away.

The warm nest of bedding Nate had tucked him into last night was far too cosy to abandon yet, but Devon didn't want his host to think he was lazy. He was quite prepared to work hard if he could stay for a little while in this soothing place.

Groaning as he slowly sat up and stretched, Devon rubbed his gritty eyes, forcing himself to wake up properly. Unfortunately, the more aware he became, the more he began to fret as well.

Nate wasn't anything like what he had expected. He seemed...nice. Last night, at the club he'd actually been saving him from Duncan. And not just so he could take Devon for himself. It was...confusing.

Devon wasn't entirely sure why Nate had bothered. He got the distinct impression Nate didn't like Duncan very much, and perhaps that was all there was to it. But he still felt absurdly grateful.

While Duncan's intentions had been less than honourable, Nate's behaviour had been above reproach. After buying them a fabulous meal, he had escorted Devon back to the club. Admittedly, that had initially had Devon in a panic wondering whether Nate intended to abandon him there. Or worse. But Nate had simply taken the time to patiently explain that he lived in a small apartment above the club. He couldn't remember the last time someone had thought to reassure him like that. To consider what he might be feeling.

And that wasn't the only thing Nate had done that left Devon a little stunned and a lot in awe. When Nate had ushered him into the tiny, masculine space he called home, he hadn't forced or demanded anything of Devon. He had just shown him to a room, tucked him into a soft, clean bed and wished him a good night sleep.

And Devon had done just that. He had slept peacefully and completely undisturbed all night for the first time in weeks. It was a situation that Devon found both reassuring and oddly...disappointing at the same time. Which was ridiculous and completely contrary he knew, but over and over he kept asking himself if it was because

Nate didn't find him attractive enough. Did he think Devon was lacking in some way?

Devon was not in a big hurry to repeat the mistake he had made with Tony, but Nate seemed different. Perhaps, if he approached him just right, Nate would agree to take him in on a more permanent basis. He was pretty sure now that Nate wouldn't beat or humiliate him. Nate seemed like a good man. At least he did at the moment.

At the end of the day, however, it really didn't matter much either way. Devon was desperate. With each passing day, it seemed more imperative than ever that he find somewhere safe and secure to live. Something deep inside him forced him on, no matter how hopeless it appeared. But he needed a place to belong, to call...home. Nearly anyone, who could provide that and wouldn't try to kill him, would do.

But what did he have to offer someone like Nate? He had absolutely no skills. He hadn't needed any in the castle, other than to be naked and available to his Master at all times. But Nate didn't seem to want that from him. He could clean and tidy. But Nate's home already looked pretty well cared for in that regard.

Unfortunately, while he had been with Tony, he had soon learnt that cooking wasn't as simple as it looked. In fact, he was a hopeless cook and had often got himself into trouble in the kitchen. Just as well Tony had preferred to eat away from home and had maintained his routine of take-away food and dinners out most of the time. Although he had rarely considered Devon, at least it had cut down on some of the beatings for ruining things. The only problem being that Tony often forgot to bring food in for him.

Even Master Nevin never starved me, Devon thought bitterly.

He wondered now why he had stayed so long with Tony. But then anything had seemed better than being a stray. Well, at least until Tony had started to beat him unconscious.

Still, being abandoned for a number of days once or twice in a house with at least some basic food stuffs had helped Devon learn how to make simple things like toast and cereal, and even halfway decent pancakes—which he was really quite proud of. He couldn't believe he still remembered how after all these years. The nursery-maid had showed him when he was a kitten. It was one of the few bright memories he had from his childhood and it filled him with a small warm glow as he recalled the sweet-faced woman letting him stir the ingredients to a smooth, pale batter.

He wondered if Nate liked pancakes.

Slipping out of bed, Devon started looking around for his clothes and was slightly disconcerted when he couldn't find them. He didn't have enough to lose or misplace any, and while it was true that in the past he had always been naked, he found he rather liked the protection they provided now.

Devon frowned in irritation and confusion when a thorough search of the room didn't turn up any of his clothes.

Resigned to being naked, Devon padded quietly down the hall, investigating cautiously as he went. It wasn't a large apartment. Just one of a number kept above the club they had met in, Nate had explained. So it didn't take Devon long to find the kitchen.

Having found it, however, he honestly wasn't sure what to do next.

He hadn't found Nate on his trip around the apartment, and he wasn't sure what he was or wasn't allowed to do.

Would Nate mind him trying to find some food on his own? Would he accept Devon poking around in his kitchen or would he be annoyed? Would making the man some pancakes please him or make him angry for using things without asking? Or would he be more put out if Devon did nothing? Was he expected to wait on Nate?

Anxious and confused, Devon finally remembered Nate telling him to 'make himself at home'. He hoped making food was covered under that because he was starving again, and the thought of pancakes was making his mouth water.

Slowly, as if expecting to be chastised at any moment, Devon began to search for the ingredients to make pancakes.

* * * *

When Nate entered his small, upstairs apartment after fixing yet another issue in the club, the last thing he expected was the sweet, doughy smell of pancakes. He'd left Devon sound asleep in the spare bedroom. And having witnessed firsthand how utterly exhausted the little cat had been, he hadn't anticipated seeing him much before the afternoon.

Nate took a deep breath in through his nose. He loved pancakes and his mouth started to water in anticipation. Devon had just inched a little farther into Nate's heart if the man was responsible for that wonderful aroma.

Rounding the corner into the kitchenette, hoping to snag a late breakfast treat, Nate nearly swallowed his tongue when he saw Devon completely naked apart for a 'Kiss the Cook' apron. Someone had given it to Nate as a gag gift one Christmas—a satirical commentary on his non-existent cooking skills. While he usually kept it hanging by the fridge, it was looking far better where it was right now.

Nate marvelled at the transformation in his houseguest as he ogled Devon's perfect, pale round ass. The man was absolutely stunning. In profile, Devon's black silky hair framed his angelic face. A smear of flour smudged one cheek, making him look even more adorable as far as Nate was concerned. There was none of the jerky nervousness from last night. Completely lost in concentration, Devon's movements were smooth and graceful.

Nate watched as slim, nimble fingers manipulated the bowl and ladle to pour batter into the sizzling skillet. One lucky index finger managed to catch a stray drip and was swiped delicately with the tip of a pale pink tongue.

Nate's cock hardened behind his zipper. He had to reach down and adjust himself—easing the sudden discomfort in the front of his pants as Devon repeated the process several more times. Eventually, four even circles of batter were cooking in the pan and Devon set the bowl aside.

Nate felt slightly guilty about rummaging through the man's duffel while he was asleep. But he had washed all the man's dirty clothes—and look at the beautiful picture he had been rewarded with. More importantly, however, he hadn't found anything suspicious to suggest Devon had been deliberately sent to spy on them. Nate was leaning towards accepting that Devon was what he appeared to be—an abandoned pet.

After watching for several moments, he finally decided to get the smaller cat's attention.

"Wow! What a sight for a man to come home to." His voice was a little husky, he couldn't help that—Devon was gorgeous—but he had deliberately kept it soft and gentle with a little humour to lighten the moment. Or so he had thought.

Devon reacted as if he expected to be attacked at any moment. He spun around, knocking the bowl with the last of the batter to the floor as he did so. Nate automatically stepped forward, reaching out to help. But Devon flinched away, ducking his head in anticipation of a blow.

Nate froze, lowering his hand carefully. "I won't hurt you," he promised.

Devon nodded, but wouldn't meet Nate's eyes.

Nate got the distinct impression he hadn't been believed. His heart constricted painfully at the terror obviously gripping the man in front of him. They had a long road ahead of them before Devon would trust him, Nate realised. He refused to believe he couldn't earn the man's trust, even though it didn't look like Devon had many reasons to trust anyone.

In the meantime, Nate thought it might be a good idea to move on to something simpler...and delicious.

"Those smell great. Are there enough to share?" he asked, eyeing the steaming pile of cooked pancakes set beside the stove hungrily.

"Of...of course," Devon stammered, his hands fidgeting nervously with the apron before stilling them with obvious effort.

Nate reached out and grabbed the pancakes, setting them in the middle of his small dining table just off the kitchen. Retrieving two forks and the maple syrup, he decided to enjoy the intimacy of sharing from the same plate rather than getting more out of the cupboard. Hopefully, it would help the two of them get closer if they shared food. It was worth a try anyway, even if Nate found himself wanting to share a lot more than food with the little cat.

Ruthlessly, he pushed the thought away. Now was not the time, he admonished himself silently. He needed to keep his damn libido to himself. Devon looked far too...fragile for that sort of thing right now.

Unfortunately, he didn't seem to be able to help himself around Devon. He found himself drawn to the smaller cat. It was perplexing and a little worrying. He'd never had such a strong reaction to anyone before, and it was the last thing either of them needed right now.

"Won't you join me?" Nate asked politely, ignoring his disconcerting thoughts and indicating the chair across from him.

Devon looked between Nate and the chair. He hesitated a moment, but eventually stepped forward, removed the apron then laid the material across the seat. He sat down gingerly as if he were being forced to face his final meal — eyes wide and searching around for an escape route.

Meanwhile, Nate could hardly breathe. He swallowed several times past his suddenly dry throat and hoped he wasn't making a fool of himself. But it was a rather vain hope, he acknowledged. Desperately, Nate tried to concentrate on the food.

They ate in silence, but Nate was pleased to see Devon gradually relax and begin to make his way steadily through the stack of sweet, sticky pancakes. Nate deliberately held back, watching the man eating like he was starving. Judging by his skinny appearance, he probably was.

When the plate was clean and Devon sat back with a contented sigh, Nate gave him a moment before leaning forward.

"Devon, I know you probably don't want to do this right now, but...I have some questions. Things I need to know. I'm sorry, but... I have...responsibilities I need to consider."

Nate saw Devon stiffen and eye him nervously, but eventually he nodded his agreement. He could quite clearly see that Devon would much rather run, but he didn't. Nate wondered why Devon was prepared to stay and answer questions, even as he admired the man's balls — so to speak — for doing so.

Trying to focus back on the problem at hand, Nate ran his hand through the short strands of his hair and cleared his throat. Where to begin?

Might as well get to the big stuff straight away, he decided.

"Do you want to go back?" Nate asked succinctly, watching the man across from him closely.

He would know if Devon tried to lie to him. It was just something he'd always been able to do. Since he was a kitten, Nate could sense an untruth — it was like the heavy, rancid smell of decay creeping into his mind. In fact, he often wondered why others couldn't — the feeling was so overpowering sometimes it made him nauseous. It was what made him perfect for both his job as manager of The Cat Club and as a rescuer. All he had to do now was make sure he asked the right questions.

Devon hesitated. At one time, not too long ago he would have answered with an unequivocal yes. He had wanted to go home. He'd almost dragged his brother back to Master Nevin just so he could return to the safety of the harem. But now he wasn't so sure. As hurt and angry as he was with his brother, he also knew he envied Ethan. He was jealous of the love and security Ethan had found with Michael.

And while he was being honest with himself and admitting he longed for love and security too, he knew he would never, ever get it with Master Nevin. Master Nevin seemed to resent the very air he breathed, the fact that he even existed.

Devon snorted softly to himself. He wasn't likely to get it with someone like Tony either. A man who thought Devon looked better black and blue.

Somehow, he had always been found lacking. Not good enough for the Master to want to keep. Not good enough for Tony to want to stop hitting. Not even good enough to keep Ethan with him in the end.

Devon took a deep, steadying breath, blinking back the tears that burned the backs of his eyes. If nothing else, he knew he didn't want to go back to being not good enough. He refused to accept that kind of life any more.

Maybe it had taken him longer to see what Ethan had recognised was so wrong with their situation in the harem. Certainly, he hadn't thought enough about what he wanted before hooking up with Tony. And perhaps he'd never be able to gain Ethan's respect. But while he might never be able to find the kind of love his brother had, he had seen firsthand now that there was an alternative. He didn't want to go back to that other life, and not just because he couldn't. It was time to find something different for himself. The trick was working out how to go about doing that and not substituting one whore's purse for another.

It was a truly massive undertaking and Devon wasn't entirely sure he was up to the challenge. He wasn't even sure where he should start. Every time he thought he had found a beginning place and could start to pick away at the tangled mess of his life versus what he wanted, it would just turn out to be another great looping knot of confusion and complication. Like a big ball of string played with and wound back up by a toddler.

"What I want and what I can have are two very different things," Devon observed evenly, forcing all the emotion out of his voice.

"Do you even know what you want?" Nate shot back.

Devon felt an instant and unexpected hot flash of anger overwhelm him. He wanted to lash out at Nate. He wanted to scream a great big 'screw you' to the ceiling in rage. He was struggling with everything he had to stay alive and figure that very thing out.

His claws unsheathed and his eyes darkened with rage. Somewhere in the dim recesses of his brain he registered with grim satisfaction the look of shock on Nate's face as he drew back in surprise.

Devon struck out. His voice growling with ill-concealed temper and his eyes flashed with pure pent up rage, even as they filled with tears.

"I want a home. Somewhere that can't be taken away from me. I want somewhere I don't have to pay with my body to belong. I want—" Devon never finished his tirade. He leapt to his feet—knocking his chair over in his haste— and bolted from the room.

Chapter Five

Nate jumped up in panic. He wasn't quite sure what had just happened, but man, the little cat could move. He'd been taken completely by surprise. It must have been too much for Devon. He'd just frozen mid-sentence, eyes going wide with alarm, before bolting from the room. But he must have got disorientated at the same time, because he'd gone in completely the wrong direction if he was trying to find a way out.

Determined to get to the bottom of what was wrong, Nate hurried after the terrified looking cat. He couldn't believe Devon had managed to start off so spectacularly — with so much passion — only to run away.

Then Nate heard the telltale sounds of retching coming from the bathroom.

Hurrying forward, Nate found Devon hunched over the toilet bowl, vomiting wretchedly between heartbreaking sobs.

"Devon!" Nate ran his hand through Devon's silky black hair, easing it away from his face. "Are you all right?"

Devon shook his head vigorously, still crowding the bowl — hanging on for dear life.

Yeah! That was a pretty stupid question.

Confused and concerned, Nate grabbed a washcloth from the bathroom cabinet and wet it down in the sink. Kneeling behind the distressed man, he gently placed the cloth across the back of Devon's neck and ran his hands soothing up and down the smaller man's back.

What on earth is going on? Nate wondered as he fussed with the cloth. Was Devon sick or was what he had to say so upsetting it made him physically ill? Nate frowned as his worry for the little cat began to escalate rapidly. At the moment he guessed there was nothing he could do except comfort the man and wait. But it was hard not being able to do anything more constructive.

Gradually, the retching and sobs subsided, but it left Devon looking pale and visibly trembling. Nate closed the toilet lid and flushed when it appeared Devon had no more in his stomach to give up. Then he gently ran the cloth across the man's white face. Devon's eyes were closed as he leaned heavily into Nate's arms, almost as if he wasn't capable of holding himself up any more.

Feeling helpless and uncertain — two things he rarely experienced — Nate continued to run his hands comfortingly over the man in his arms.

"Devon?" he asked tentatively, not wanting to upset him, but needing to know he was all right.

"My twin ran away. Our Master was so angry," Devon said softly, his eyes still closed as if talking to himself. "He wanted to kick me out. He was going to call the Council to..."

Nate stiffened as Devon took a shuddering breath, well aware of the terrible facilities set up for abandoned cat shifters. They tried to rescue as many slaves as possible, but they couldn't save them all.

"I begged the Master to let me stay. Finally, he agreed but only if I found Ethan and brought him back. He sent me and...and a group of warriors through the last known portal activated from our castle, which is how he assumed Ethan managed to escape."

Nate nodded. If a pleasure cat somehow got hold of a portal marker, he could have escaped without a mage's help. The pride used something similar when they went on their rescue missions.

Devon was quiet for so long Nate thought he had finished his tale. He was just beginning to wonder how he was going to handle the situation when the little cat in his arms took another long shuddering breath that hitched suspiciously at the end.

"Rolf, the leader of the warriors that were sent through with me to retrieve Ethan... He made me...I had to... He wouldn't help me otherwise. I wanted to go home. But in the end, he didn't help me find Ethan at all. Just fucked me," Devon spat out bitterly. "And when we did eventually catch up with Ethan, I couldn't do it. He had found a mate, and I couldn't take him back, not when he looked so...happy here. I threw away the medallion the Master gave me so I could call him to take us home. Rolf was so angry. He...he'd been doing some really bad things while we were supposed to be searching for Ethan, and the police had tracked him down. They took him away before he could...but..."

"Is that where you got the bruises?" Nate asked, desperately trying to contain his growing rage.

Devon shook his head and seemed to struggle for a moment in silence before continuing softly, "I tried to find a new Master. Things didn't work out."

"Who was it, kitten?" Nate growled—he needed to hunt down Devon's attackers. He needed to—

"Tony," Devon whispered with a shudder.

Nate forced himself to back off. He wanted to rip Rolf and this Tony person apart, but even the mention of the men's names seemed to cause Devon pain. And he was determined that, if nothing else, Devon would never hurt again.

Not while I have breath in my body, Nate vowed. He'd find some other way to avenge Devon.

In the meantime, he continued to stroke and caress Devon's back—as much soothing himself as the man in his arms. He didn't think Devon could stand telling much more of his story right now. And to be honest, Nate wasn't sure he was up to hearing any more at the moment. His heart hurt and his stomach ached with tension and anger at the way his kitten had been treated.

His kitten? Nate froze in astonishment at the thought. Where had that come from?

"I'm tired, Nate. Tired of never being quite good enough. Tired of being pushed around and disregarded. Tired of running and never finding anything better."

Devon's head was resting wearily against Nate's shoulder—eyes closed in exhaustion. Nate chose to push the confusing maelstrom of his emotions aside. He was both curious and scared of his rapidly growing feelings for the little cat in his arms, as well as a healthy dose of plain frustrated and horny. But he ignored it all in favour of looking after Devon. That was the most important thing at the moment. Everything else could wait.

Nate scooped the flagging man up into his arms. He was so light Nate hardly noticed the extra weight at all. He vowed to do something about that too. Devon seemed to have quite an appetite, when he wasn't being sick. Nate promised himself that he would make sure Devon was never hungry again. He would soon have some weight on the skinny man's frame.

Back in the spare bedroom, Nate laid the almost unconscious man on the bed and pulled up the covers. Before he could step away, however, a slim hand caught his wrist in a vice like grip.

"Stay with me?" Devon whispered, his exhausted eyes uncertain but pleading with him anyway.

Nate couldn't resist, even though the thought of lying down beside the gorgeous naked creature, even fully clothed, sounded like torture. *But what sweet suffering,* Nate reflected.

Slipping off his shoes, Nate slid into bed and stretched out on top of the covers.

Tentatively, as if unsure of his reception Devon sidled up to him. When Nate lifted his arm in welcome, he was instantly holding a warm, slim body against his side. A body he was very aware was completely naked beneath the blankets. Devon's head came down to rest against his chest, one pale hand stretching hesitantly across him as he settled in.

It was the most perfect, tense moment of Nate's life. He felt as if he held something precious, and at the same time he knew it could all so easily slip through his fingers. Nate held Devon a little closer. Whatever it took, he would make sure Devon was finally safe. He refused to lose the treasure his heart was telling him he had discovered.

* * * *

Devon woke up suddenly, his heart pounding and his muscles tensed ready to fight his way out of the strong arms he felt wrapped around him. But when a large hand gently stoked over his side and a sleep roughened voice mumbled reassuringly in his ear, he paused.

"Shh," it crooned. "It's okay. I've got you."

Nate's sleepy whisper slowly penetrated and Devon relaxed back into the embrace, though he wasn't exactly sure why. Nate's voice was...soothing. He knew the man was trying to help, not hurt or take advantage of him. But the really surprising thing was the fact he *liked* being in Nate's arms. It...helped, he realised in shock. And he didn't want to analyse that either. He just wanted to accept it. Gratefully. Perhaps that made him desperate, maybe even weak, but he'd take the gentleness and care over the alternative for as long as it was on offer.

After a few minutes, he felt Nate stir behind him.

"Hi," Nate whispered in a deep, husky voice, still drowsy from sleep.

Devon peered over his shoulder and saw Nate's lips tilted up in a soft, slightly dreamy looking smile. His heart did a strange little flip in his chest, even as he saw the fatigue shadowing the other man's eyes and instantly felt guilty for waking him up. Probably not for the first time either.

When Devon didn't say anything, but continued to stare, Nate started to frown.

"Are you okay?" he asked with concern in his eyes.

Devon just nodded—he wasn't sure what to say. Nate, on the other hand, suddenly seemed to realise he held a very naked man in his arms.

Devon vaguely recalled falling asleep with Nate on top of the blankets. But at some point that must have changed.

Now they lay wrapped around each other under the covers.

A deep red flush crept up Nate's neck and into his cheeks. He looked away and cleared his throat nervously as he pulled his arms from around Devon and edged out of bed. Devon instantly felt the loss of his warm embrace like a punch in the gut, but didn't protest or try to hold onto him.

"Well...um...that's good... Great...yeah..." Nate looked slightly desperate as his eyes roamed around the room, landing everywhere but on Devon. "So...ahh...are you hungry again? You pretty much lost everything you ate earlier. We could get up and try again. Let me make you something this time."

As Nate got out of bed, Devon sat up to follow him. Food sounded like a great idea, but as he put his feet on the floor a wave of nausea swept over him unexpectedly. He moaned softly and tried to stay as still as possible, not wanting to jostle his delicate stomach.

Instantly, Nate was at his side, his eyes once more filled with concern.

"Are you okay?" he asked, looking Devon over clinically.

Devon shifted, uncomfortable, trying to hide his naked body from Nate's intense gaze, which he knew was ridiculous after being held so intimately only moments before. But Nate's eyes left a hot trail of something that could only be described as...longing as it travelled over him. Devon had the sudden, overwhelming urge to lean forward and rub himself all over the firm, muscular chest in front of him.

While having Nate looking at him so intensely and his own powerful reaction to the scrutiny distracted him from feeling sick, it also confused and frightened Devon. He had never felt anything like it before in his life, and he wasn't sure what to do with the unfamiliar sensations.

"I can't find my clothes," he blurted, trying to divert Nate's attention away from him and... Oh, Gods...his rapidly filling cock.

Devon quickly looked at Nate to see if he had noticed, but Nate still wasn't looking at him. Instead, he had turned bright red again—looking distinctly guilty.

"Sorry about that," Nate mumbled. "I took all your clothes to wash earlier. The...ah...the ones you had in your pack looked like they needed it too. I'll...ah...I'll just go get them."

Devon wasn't sure what Nate seemed to think he needed to apologise for. The idea of clean clothes sounded wonderful. Only slightly less fabulous than the man he seemed to have fallen in with. So far, Nate had been amazing—gentle, caring, considerate. Devon only wished he could work out what the other man wanted. If he knew, he would make sure to do everything possible to give it to him and hopefully stay a little longer.

Devon watched Nate hurry away, only to return moments later with his thin T-shirt and ragged jeans. At least they were clean now, Devon thought, truly grateful for Nate's thoughtfulness.

"Thank you," he said self-consciously as Nate handed him the clothes.

But Nate was frowning again. Devon wondered if he had done something wrong already.

"You know, it's pretty cold. I think I have something that would probable fit." Without waiting for a response, Nate began rummaging through a set of drawers, lifting out a pale blue hooded jacket. "Here you go. Wow, this colour will look fantastic. Really bring out your eyes," Nate said, then coloured again. "I'll just... Yeah! You go ahead and...I'll just go get things ready in the...ahh...kitchen."

With that, Nate fled the room, leaving Devon—who was feeling more and more confused by the second—to get dressed.

* * * *

He was making an idiot of himself, Nate acknowledged. He was supposed to be observing and investigating the little cat, not flirting and blushing like a teenage girl!

He felt utterly ridiculous and yet completely powerless to stop himself. He was irresistibly drawn to Devon, and it made him feel clumsy and oafish. And unfortunately, it only seemed to be getting worse the more time he spent around the man. Something was going to give. He just knew it. Trouble was he wasn't sure whether it was going to be his self-control or his sanity. Neither seemed like a good option to lose, especially not around the skittish man that was his houseguest.

Nate crashed around the kitchen, viciously chastising himself for thinking with the wrong head as he got things out to make toasted sandwiches. He couldn't remember ever being this bad before—not even when he'd first gained the ability to shift and been as randy as hell.

He felt like one big walking hormone around Devon at the moment. And the worst thing about it all was he knew Devon was in no fit state to deal with a physical relationship. It made Nate feel less like an idiot and more like an asshole. How disgusting was it for him to have a boner that would put steel to shame for a man as recently abused, both mentally and physically, as Devon.

Busy kicking his own ass, Nate didn't notice when Devon stepped gingerly into the small kitchen behind him.

"Can I help?" a soft voice asked, almost making Nate drop the sandwich toaster on his foot.

He wondered how he had managed as a rebel leader and a warrior up until now if one little cat could make him so...vulnerable. He was pleased to see he'd been right about the pale blue pullover though. It did make Devon's eyes look amazing.

Nate realised he was staring when Devon fiddled nervously with the hood. Snapping out of his no doubt vacant-looking gawping, Nate managed to smile and turned back to what he was doing.

"Ah, sure. Could you maybe fix some drinks? There's some water in the refrigerator or...ah...I'm not sure. Milk maybe, if you prefer."

Smooth, Nate. Real smooth. He took a deep breath, trying to regain his rattled composure.

"Water sounds fine," Devon answered quietly.

Damn it, Nate thought harshly, he was stuffing this all up. Some smooth investigator and leader he was turning out to be.

"So..." Nate tried for a light, friendly tone. "What are your plans?"

He watched out of the corner of his eye as Devon visibly stiffened and stood frozen for a moment, before turning to place glasses of cold water on the table with deliberate care. He cursed himself silently.

Way to go, hot-shot! Way to make the man feel welcomed and relaxed.

Devon shrugged and refused to look up when Nate turned around to try to fix up the mess he was making of things. He could see the defeated slump to the man's shoulders. And he couldn't stand it.

Enough pussy footing around, Nate scolded himself, he didn't want the man to leave. He didn't want to think too closely on why that was. He certainly couldn't learn more about Devon if he decided to run though.

"You could stay here," Nate offered, he could hear the slightest hint of vulnerability in his own voice and wouldn't be surprised if Devon could see the same thing in his eyes, but he couldn't do much about either.

Devon glanced up in surprise and Nate tried to meet his gaze with a neutral expression. He didn't think he was terribly successful. He wasn't sure what he would do if Devon knocked him back. He couldn't just let Devon wander around free without being sure the man wasn't a threat to the pride. But worse than that, he wasn't too sure how he would cope on a personal level if Devon rejected his offer.

What a mess!

"Why?" Devon finally asked after staring at Nate for a long time.

This time it was Nate's turn to shrug and look away. He wasn't quite ready to answer that question. Not even to himself. "You need a place to stay and I like having you here."

"You have a whole club full of people downstairs to keep you company," Devon pointed out.

What to say to that? Yes, he had lots of friends and a whole pride he could call family now, but there was still something missing, something he very much suspected Devon could help him with.

Don't screw this up, Nate, he thought to himself firmly. Something told him this was one of the most important conversations of his life.

"I know I have a lot of people I can talk to and hang out with but... Well, none of them are you. I'd like you to stay. I'd like to get to know you. I'd like to think we could become friends. Doesn't have to be anything more." Nate could have kicked himself for adding that last part. Devon wasn't stupid, he reminded himself. He would know from that comment what Nate had been thinking on and off since he met the gorgeous cat. The real question was would the thought of something more send him running for the hills?

Nate held his breath. He needed to know more about Devon to make sure he wasn't a threat to the pride. But more than that, he wanted to know Devon – in all senses of the word.

Please don't run away from me. Please don't run away from me, Nate repeated over and over in his head.

"Would...would you..." Devon's voice faltered and trailed off.

"What?"

"I liked it before. When you were holding me. Would you..."

Nate felt his heart jump in excitement, but it was tinged with sadness for the little cat. And he couldn't stand it anymore. Stepping up to the thin, frightened man, Nate wrapped his arms around him.

"I could do that," Nate said simply, emotion eating away at his self-control. "You're safe with me. For as long as you want."

Nate breathed a sigh of relief he hadn't realised he had been holding when he felt Devon soften against him and wrap tentative arms around his waist. It felt so good to hold and be held like this.

A tiny purr started up in the back of his mind. It might even be the best thing that had ever happened to him.

* * * *

Hawk stretched out his long legs and crossed his booted feet in front of him, utilising the bored, insolent aristocratic airs of a First Born Talented that was his birthright. With the kinds of extracurricular activities he liked to engage in it helped to be dismissed as one of the indolent and idiotic, but it was something he had to work at all the time.

Of course, right now the elders of the Circle Council were giving him a serious run for their money on the too-stupid-to-live front. They were debating whether or not rumours of an underground faction of mages outside the governance of the Council were to be believed. Not one of them thought to investigate the stories.

"I really must disagree with your policy of simply dismissing these rumours, Grand-Mistress Zaphin. Shouldn't we, at least, investigate them?" Barnell, a friend and fellow rebel demanded.

"A complete waste of time and resources, young mage!" a crusty, old elder in ancient, faded maroon robes snapped waspishly, shaking one bony finger in Barnell's direction. "I know your type. You'll have to do better than scare tactics and rabble rousing to work your way up in this hierarchy."

Hawk rolled his eyes. Grand-Master Relin was worried that he was going to be usurped by younger, more powerful mages, when he should be worried about being on the business end of a full-scale attack.

Still, Barnell struggled on, brave soul that he was. "That's not what I was trying to do at all," he pleaded. "I'm merely pointing out—"

"It's strange that only a hand full of you young upstarts seems to know anything about this," another of the elders, this time a pinch-faced older female pointed out superciliously.

"But Blood Mages—"

"Are a completely defunct clan that was erased from our circle centuries ago!"

Hawk looked over at the large bare space in the circular grandstand that everyone avoided, even after all these years. No one dared to sit in the 'cursed ones' position.

Hawk looked away. They were all fools if they thought avoiding the issue and pretending that Blood Mages no longer existed would keep them safe. And he knew for a fact at least one elder was aware they still existed. He wondered what Grand-Mistress Zaphin was playing at.

"They're not extinct," Barnell continued doggedly. "Let me prove—"

"Thousands of mages gave their lives in the Mage Wars. Hundreds of us saw with our own eyes the very last of their vile order wiped out. Are you calling us liars?"

"No! Of course not, but—"

"If you continue with this line, I will hold you in contempt of the circle!"

"Enough!" Grand-Mistress Zaphin interrupted. "This bickering and disagreeing amongst ourselves only serves to destabilise our authority and take our focus away from the fact that more and more cat shifters are defying our natural authority and rebelling every day. I suggest we all focus on that and save these...distractions for another time. Grand-Master Venin, do you have anything to report..."

Hawk had heard enough. Stretching his arms above his head languidly, earning himself a disapproving look from his mother that he was rather proud of, he sauntered out.

A few minutes later, in a private booth at a very discreet club several blocks away, a rumpled and visibly distressed Barnell joined him.

"They wouldn't listen," he raged. "Why can't they get their heads out of their asses long enough to see what's staring them right in the face!"

"We tried, Barnell," Hawk replied, slinging his arm around the other man's shoulders in a gesture of solidarity. "We can't do any more than that. We've risked too much already. We have to move on. There are still things we have to do."

Chapter Six

Devon woke up with a jerk, then forced himself to lie completely still and silent. Slowly, memories of the past week with Nate seeped in, muting the terrifying waking nightmare of the month that had preceded it. He was in the soft, warm bed that he had shared with Nate for the last seven nights. Seven blissful nights of peaceful sleep and security.

The first thing Devon became aware of, however, was that Nate was gone this morning. Devon could still sense him—his warmth and the slightly spicy scent that was uniquely Nate lingering on the pillow next to him. But unlike every other morning he had woken up to in the past week here, today Nate's reassuring presence wasn't there.

Devon sighed. Falling asleep in the man's arms and waking up beside him every morning was a little like how he imagined paradise would be. He had felt safe, cared for and protected. Nate hadn't demanded anything. In fact, it was Devon who always initiated their cuddling up — shyly inviting Nate to stay and lie down with him for a while.

It helped to be in Nate's strong, warm arms. It kept the nightmares, if not completely away, then at least at a tolerable distance.

Devon sighed. It would have been nice if it could have gone on a little longer. The tiny taste he had got seemed almost cruel. Like seeing heaven and having it snatched away. But Nate seemed to be tiring of the routine already. This was the first morning he had woken up alone and Devon couldn't help wondering how much longer it would be before he had to find himself another place to live.

Slowly stretching, he became aware of his hunger at exactly the same time as a wave of nausea passed over him. Great, he was so hungry again he felt sick. It seemed to be a recurring theme at the moment, probably as a result of having little to nothing in the way of good, nourishing food over an extended period and subsequently losing a lot of condition. His body seemed to be not so subtly telling him to build himself up again while he could. Unfortunately, it was going to extremes. It was crazy if it thought making him feel so sick he threw up was the right way to go about it!

Just as he was contemplating getting up and fighting off the nausea to try to find something to soothe his unsettled stomach, Nate walked in with a tray. Devon could smell chicken, fresh bread and the sweet tang of citrus. His stomach growled appreciatively.

"Hello, beautiful," Nate announced as he stepped into the room, his wide smile making his already handsome face almost radiant.

Devon's heart beat out a wild tattoo of greeting he was growing steadily used to whenever he saw the man.

"I noticed you always seem to wake up really hungry, so I heated a tin of soup I found in the cupboard. There's some crusty bread and orange juice to go with it too. It's not fancy or anything, but I thought…you know…it might help settle your stomach." By the time Nate had finished his little soliloquy, he was blushing furiously and sounding more and more uncertain.

Devon, on the other hand, was completely incapable of speech. No one had ever done something like this for him. Not even Ethan. He found himself nodding dumbly as Nate placed the tray of food across his lap, not sure what else he was supposed to do in this situation, and not sure he was capable of anything else anyway.

The food smelt delicious and Devon tentatively tried a spoonful of the soup. It tasted divine — slightly salty with the delicate flavour of chicken settling on his taste buds. He made his way steadily through the food, eating more than he thought his belly would have handled. By the time he had finished, he did feel a lot better. He gave Nate a tentative smile of thanks.

For a moment, Nate just stared at him. Devon tensed, the small smile wilting under Nate's intense scrutiny. He wondered if he had done the wrong thing somehow. Was he supposed to have shared? Just as he started to panic, Nate reached out and took his hand.

"I think that's the first time I've ever seen you smile," Nate explained, gently reaching out with his other hand and running it over Devon's hair and down the side of his face before cupping his cheek.

A long moment passed between them — as if neither dared to breathe in case they broke the spell.

Nate stared into the beautiful, pale blue eyes of the man he had spent nearly every waking moment — and sleeping too, for that matter — observing over the last seven days.

Nate had come to the conclusion that Devon was, quite simply, amazing. Gentle and sweet, with a soft, caring heart, yet at the same time unconsciously sensual and with an inner strength Nate had the distinct impression no one — not even Devon — had ever appreciated.

His slim, graceful body was almost delicate, yet sexy as hell as far as Nate was concerned. But it was the man's inner determination to keep going and survive that impressed Nate the most. So many others might have been tempted to simply curl up and die by now. But not Devon.

At the same time, Nate hated to see the insecurity and fear he sometimes caught in the other man's eyes. It was almost painful to watch him trying so hard to be helpful and ingratiating. But then, he loved the little moments of connection they sometimes made, like this one, even if Devon still seemed a little shy about it.

Nate knew he could fall, and fall hard for this man. Hell, he probably already had.

He hadn't really been forced to spend time with Devon, trying to work out whether he was a threat to the pride or not. He'd *wanted* to spend his time — all his time — with him. He longed for the end of the day now when he could curl up in bed with Devon. Not to do anything — although that was certainly becoming harder and harder to deny — but just to hold him. In fact, he found himself a little tense each night as the evening drew on, waiting to see if Devon would invite him to his bed again.

Nate mentally shook his head at himself. Man, he had it bad.

He thanked his lucky stars that one of the shifter mercenaries, Paul, had recently brought in a human that was slowly taking over the day to day management of the club; otherwise, he might never have had the time to get to know Devon. It had all worked out rather well for everyone actually.

Matt needed a job and Nate didn't want to run the club full-time. He would much rather devote his time to rescuing cat shifters and helping with their rehabilitation. And, of course, spending every moment he could with his new obsession—Devon.

Nate was certain now that Devon was no threat to the pride. The man simply didn't have it in him to betray others. He had sacrificed his own security for his brother's happiness, for goodness sake, at great risk to himself personally. Nate shuddered at the story he'd been able to pin together from talking to Devon over the last seven days. Thinking about everything his kitten had been through made Nate feel physically ill. And yet Devon had survived. More than that, the essence of who he was remained intact.

Nate knew Devon was a good man. Loyal. Caring. He would make an excellent addition to the pride. The trouble was Nate wasn't quite ready to share him with the others yet. Something in him didn't want to risk letting the other pride members meet Devon. Not until things were more…stable between them. Besides, there was plenty of time for all that. The pride could be a boisterous, overwhelming lot and right now he wanted to spend a little more time alone with the sexy, little cat.

"Let's go to the park," Nate suggested impulsively.

Devon looked taken aback by the suggestion, but the more he thought about it, the more excited Nate got. The idea of going out with the gorgeous man in front of him, showing him off to the world, made him feel a little like a kid again—giddy and excited. Nate couldn't remember the last time he had indulged in such a simple pleasure as going to the park. Or when he had last wanted to so badly.

"The park?" Devon asked, a small frown working its way into his expression.

Nate just wanted to kiss it away and take the man into his arms to reassure him, but pushed down the impulse, at least for now.

"Yeah! It's getting a little chilly outside. You should wear the new coat I bought you." Nate had the pleasure of watching a slight blush tint Devon's cheeks.

He had bought the man a mountain of clothes since he had arrived to stay with him. Every time he presented Devon with something new, he would be rewarded by a faint blush, a softly spoken thank you and a tiny kiss on the cheek. Needless to say, it was a great incentive to give the man more and more gifts at every possible opportunity.

"I think I might like that," Devon replied shyly.

"Come on then. The day awaits our pleasure." Nate held out his hand to help Devon up out of bed, then hurried off while he got changed.

No need to test his self-restraint unnecessarily, Nate thought dryly.

* * * *

The air was crisp and cool as they walked aimlessly through the park. Clusters of deciduous trees led the way in a riot of colours — their beautiful gold and russet leaves made even more brilliant by the still lush, dark green grass growing underneath them. Devon thought the whole place looked almost magical. So peaceful. So quiet and serene.

Far away he could hear the tiny tinkling sound of children's laughter, the perfect counterpoint to the occasional bird song. Taking a deep breath, Devon tried to draw the whole day into himself through his lungs. It was such a perfect moment. All the more so because he was sharing it with Nate.

Looking up into the man's happy, smiling face, Devon felt a small answering smile pull at his lips. At first Devon had found it difficult to relax. But gradually the serenity of the place seeped into his bones and Nate's obvious pleasure warmed him from the inside out. Now they walked side-by-side in companionable silence.

Devon hoped they could come back to this place again and again, just like this. He was more relaxed than he could ever remember feeling before. No Master to constantly try to please—and, of course, inevitably fail. No Rolf trying to dominate him. No Tony trying to break him. None of them existed in this place. Just Nate, walking beside him.

Still busy taking everything in, Devon spotted a huge glass pyramid that seemed to rise up out of the grass ahead of them.

"What's that?" Devon asked in amazement as he stared at the gleaming structure. He had never seen anything like it.

"It's a hothouse," Nate replied calmly.

"A...hot house?" Devon repeated uncertainly.

Nate chuckled, but not unkindly. "No. Hothouse. One word. It's for growing and keeping certain plants. Some plants and flowers are too fragile or delicate to survive out here in the park with the rest of the specimens. They have to be kept separate, in a more controlled environment. They just wouldn't survive out here on their own. They're not suited to the conditions."

Devon found himself squirming with each new sentence out of Nate's mouth. He wasn't exactly comfortable with how much he had told Nate about his life over the past week. He was even less comfortable with the parallels he saw between what Nate was describing and his own experience up until very recently.

He'd always been kept separate and confined. In the past he hadn't wanted anything else. In fact, he had often felt he wouldn't survive in the outside world. He wasn't sure how he felt about that now. He did know he didn't like the idea of Nate thinking of him as fragile or incapable. And he certainly didn't like the idea of needing to be kept separate from others any more. He just wasn't sure exactly how to live outside the harem yet. His only experiences before now had been either slavery or an ugliness he had always feared was waiting for him on the other side of the harem screens. But that had all changed since meeting Nate. He just needed a little more time to figure it all out.

Apparently completely oblivious to Devon's sudden discomfort and growing anxiety, Nate led them to the entrance of the huge glass green house. After dropping a few coins into a box marked 'donations', Nate held the door open, ushering Devon inside with a little smile.

Devon expected the inside to look…sad somehow. Instead, he was met with an incredible variety of lush, healthy looking plants and an exotic blend of scents that teased his senses, beckoning him on. A vast array of spectacular flowers all seemed to jostle for position to welcome them. It was incredible and Devon gaped in amazement as he stopped to study a long spray of luminous white flowers.

"What are they?" Devon asked in wonder.

"Orchids," Nate answered quietly beside him, but Devon couldn't take his eyes off the stunning cascade.

"They're beautiful," Devon breathed in awe.

"Yes. Beautiful."

Devon turned his head at the odd, husky note in Nate's voice. He felt his face grow hotter as a blush crept up into his cheeks when he realised Nate was looking straight at him — disregarding the flower entirely. Unable to hold Nate's intense stare, Devon lowered his eyes away uncertainly.

An uncomfortable silence settled in between them. Devon wished they could go back to the peaceful companionship of earlier. But if there was one thing Devon had learnt since arriving on Earth, he knew there was no going back. What to do with that knowledge was another thing entirely.

"I have to go down to the club again tonight," Nate finally announced, breaking the tense silence.

Devon wasn't sure what to say. He wasn't happy with the idea of being left alone — too many bad memories and frightening possibilities presented themselves for inspection when that happened — but he couldn't very well expect Nate to stay by his side forever.

"Come with me," Nate blurted.

Startled, Devon looked up into Nate's chocolate brown eyes to see a hint of vulnerability reflected back at him — as if Nate was worried his invitation might be rejected. Devon had to admit he was uncomfortable with the idea of going back down to the crowded club, but he found himself nodding anyway. He couldn't bring himself to disappoint Nate.

"Why?" he asked before he could stop himself. He had to know. "Why would you want me there? Are you sure you want to be seen with me?"

Devon could hear how insecure he sounded and blushed, lowering his eyes again so he didn't have to see Nate's reaction to it.

"Hey!" Nate said firmly, tilting Devon's chin up so he was forced to look into Nate's stern eyes. "I am not ashamed of being seen with you. You get that thought out of your head right now. I want to go to the club with you because you're a sexy guy, but more than that I like being with you. I don't want to go without you. Is that a good enough reason? At least for now?"

Devon nodded automatically. He couldn't seem to make himself say anything in reply—the words caught in his throat with the lump of emotion Nate's words caused. Nate was looking at him with such intense, serious eyes.

Then Nate very slowly reached out to hold Devon's head between his large, slightly calloused hands. He gently tilted his hold to just the right angle so that when he lowered his lips, their mouths met in the softest, most tender kiss Devon could possibly imagine. And yet it set off a riot of swirling sensations and emotions inside him. First and foremost of which was the desire for more.

Afraid that Nate might end the kiss too soon, Devon pressed himself forward into the other man's body, groaning when he felt Nate's hard body against his own, much smaller frame. Suddenly bold with lust and desperate with need, Devon opened his mouth and very tentatively brushed his tongue along Nate's lower lip, inviting the man... Well, to be honest, he wasn't sure what he wanted Nate to do, but he knew he wanted to taste the other man. And he knew he would welcome Nate tasting him in return.

Nate didn't seem to need to be asked twice. He wrapped his arms around Devon, pulling them together in a fierce hug as he plundered Devon's mouth ruthlessly. It was wild and in complete abandon and left no inch unexplored as Nate's tongue roved, thrust and licked endlessly and thoroughly.

And Devon couldn't get enough of it. He held on tight to Nate and enthusiastically began to learn the intimate dance that mated their mouths together. Following Nate's example, Devon brushed his tongue along Nate's, then licked at his lips.

Finally, the need for air forced them apart. Devon couldn't help but feel slightly stunned as they both stood panting and staring at one another, wide-eyed and shocked.

But shocked in a completely good way, Devon thought to himself. A good, thorough, let's-do-that-some-more way.

But, apparently Nate thought they needed to go slow. He steadied Devon for a moment then stepped away. Perhaps he was right. It was probably a good idea, especially considering they were out in the open with no privacy whatsoever. But Devon didn't have to like it.

"Are you okay?" Nate asked, taking short, ragged breaths.

"Yeah. I...I think I'm very okay," Devon finally managed.

Nate chuckled. It was a happy, relieved, pleased-with-himself sort of chuckle, and Devon felt his lips twitch in a small answering smile. And Nate wasn't the only one that was pleased with himself, even if Devon did suddenly find himself more than a little frustrated and his pants slightly restricting.

Devon was pretty sure it was the first time he'd ever faced the problem. But the more he thought, the more relaxed he felt about it all. It just felt...right with Nate.

"Come on. Let's go get something to eat before we have to head home," Nate said with a happy grin on his face.

Nate held Devon's hand and he led them through the twisting paths and out towards the park entrance—

oblivious to the stares and second looks from others as they passed.

Devon found he didn't care either. He followed along, hoping that food wasn't the only thing on offer to sate his sudden hunger. Devon wanted something more, and he wanted it with Nate. Preferably before he had to beg. Not that he wouldn't if it got him more of those delicious kisses.

* * * *

Fuck! Fuck! Fuckity! Fuck! Hawk fumed in mounting irritation and anxiety as the two cat shifters walked away hand in hand down the street towards The Cat Club. This could fuck everything up. Everything he had worked and manoeuvred and plotted and sacrificed for was about to explode quite spectacularly. And right in his face too.

If he wasn't very careful, he'd end up with a full scale war on his hands. And unfortunately, he was going to be right in the middle of it, with enemies vying for his blood on every side.

Fuck! That's exactly what he had been trying to prevent with this whole charade! Avoid an out and out massacre, find acceptance for his people and free the cat shifter slaves. Was that too much to ask for?

Okay! Yes, it was a lot to ask. But he'd been working extremely hard for a very long time.

Hawk tried taking a deep, steadying breath. Tantrum time was over. It was time to fix things so that the blood of those he'd tried so desperately to save stayed on the inside.

Oh, Gods! Lina and Marcus. Thinking of everyone he was working so desperate to save instantly brought up their images. It had been months since he had seen either of them. If this whole thing did blow up, what would happen to them?

Hawk's heart rate accelerated until it threatened to explode from his chest and cold beads of sweat broke out across his brow. He wiped them away and tried to concentrate.

First things first, he admonished as he began to prioritise. One, try to salvage something from this cluster fuck.

Hawk knew Rolf had been released a few days ago about ten miles outside the Bayside City limits. If what he — and now apparently Vladimir — suspected was true, it wouldn't take Rolf long to track the pleasure cat down.

Devon, he reminded himself sternly. The pleasure cat had a name. He hated when mages referred to cat shifters by their caste designations. Especially when they were dead wrong. Devon wasn't a pleasure cat at all. He was something far rarer and far more dangerous to Hawk's plans.

Rolf tracking Devon down was something Hawk simply could not allow to happen. Bad enough they still had access to Lina. Although he'd done his best to protect her, he couldn't let them have Devon too. The gods only knew what the Clan would do with another one.

It was all getting so complicated, Hawk thought tiredly as he rubbed his temples trying to ease his aching head.

But there was no way he was going to give up on his shifters now. He was so close to finding them a new home. *Damn it all! So close!*

Okay! First — prevent the Clan from taking Devon. He had some phone calls to make to find the young cat presently under Nate's protective gaze somewhere safer to hide.

At least he couldn't be in better hands. The way Nate was watching Devon he'd probably take Rolf on with his bare claws and teeth before letting the man be taken. That was good. Hawk had the feeling Nate and Devon were going to need every protective, fighting instinct they possessed.

Chapter Seven

Nate gazed around the club, automatically scanning for trouble. But his focus was really still on the gorgeous man at his side. He smiled as he looked down at Devon staring—eyes wide as saucers—at the busy Friday night crowd. Unfortunately, since sharing their first kiss in the park there had only been time for a few hot, stolen kisses in the stairwell leading up to the apartment and one or two more while they hurried to get ready to go out. Nate consoled himself with the knowledge that he didn't want to rush things anyway.

He was both pleased and surprised with how responsive Devon had been. He didn't want to push too hard. He wanted to make sure everything was perfect before they took things further. Still, Nate felt incredible—excited and filled to bursting with energy. He wanted to shift and burn it off, preferably with Devon. The thought of running and hunting with Devon in cat form sent a fresh wave of pleasure rushing over his body.

Trying to get his focus off his libido and hopefully deflating his burgeoning cock a little as well, Nate carefully steered the smaller man to a table far enough away from the speakers to be comfortable. Being literally a Cat Club meant the music volume was slightly lower than some clubs Nate had been to, but it still had to be louder than was entirely comfortable for cats, or they would have been out of business with no human patrons to support them.

Devon hopped up onto one of the stools at the tall round table and peered around inquisitively. Nate guessed he hadn't had much of a chance last time he was here to have a good look around, what with one thing and another. He was pleased to see there was more interest in the man's expression than fear.

"So you're really part owner of all this?" Devon asked curiously, gazing around.

"Yep!" Nate grinned proudly as he looked at all the people mixing and mingling—enjoying themselves and the club.

While he may not want to run the place full-time, they had all worked very hard to create an open, accepting atmosphere in the club, and he was proud to have been a part of making that happen. Cat shifters and humans, albeit unawares, mixed freely. And everyone seemed to be having a good time too.

"Does the other owner know? I mean about your…tail?" Nate finished cryptically.

"Yes." Nate laughed back, but refrained from commenting further.

This wasn't the place to explain the situation, even though it was well past time to fill in a few details he had neglected to mention—the pride, their compound, the rescue missions…his growing feelings. But there were too many prying eyes and ears around at the moment.

The Cat Club was actually a business owned and operated by the entire pride. He had simply run the club from day to day while they had got it off the ground. Now that Matt was around, and doing a damned fine job of managing the place, Nate found he was spending less and less time attending to the little details that kept it all running smoothly. He was more than happy to hand it over to the very capable human Paul had found. He wanted to move on to the next challenge, whatever that might be.

The pride had started a number of very successful business ventures in the city now. Not only did they cater to the growing number of cat shifters, but they made good money as well. And that money then went straight back towards supporting their ongoing rescue missions and The Compound they had created as their first home here on Earth about four hours drive away in the Hunter Valley.

It was a system that was working well, helping to gradually blend the shifters into their surroundings while at the same time supporting their growing family. At the moment it was slow going. They all knew it was very important that the humans never found out about them. It hadn't taken long to discover humans could be slightly…unreasonable about differences. Like a group of men and women being able to shift into various species of cats at will. It was taking a while to learn how to not give themselves away in human society. Many of them exhibited very…feline tells without meaning to. But gradually they were making new lives for themselves away from their oppressive masters.

And that was exactly why he hadn't told Devon anything about The Compound or the pride they had built—a refuge and a family for all the cats they had manage to rescue so far. There were too many lives at stake to risk telling a man he had only just met about them, even when his heart told him Devon would never betray them. He only hoped Devon understood.

The trouble was, he just didn't know how Devon would react—one way or the other. And that bothered him because he didn't want anything screwing things up. Whatever was happening between them was growing stronger every day, but it was still so new and fragile.

"Can I get you a drink?" Nate asked, trying to distract Devon from asking too many questions and himself from his own growing anxiety as to what Devon's reaction was going to be to the news.

"Oh! Umm. I've never really drunk alcohol before. Could I just have a drink of water?"

"There's juice if you'd prefer," Nate offered

"Orange juice?" Devon asked hopefully.

"Sure." The orange juice earlier had obviously made an impression. Nate smiled before turning to make his way to the bar. He'd have to remember to stock up on OJ.

The crowd hampered his progress, but it gave him plenty of time to consider what a difference having Devon with him made. He had never had the time or inclination to date before, and to be honest, he guessed what was happening between himself and Devon wasn't really dating either. But it was something. Now, more than the undeniable instant attraction and protective instincts he had felt towards Devon from the very beginning, he felt a strong sense of possessiveness as well. How on earth that had happened he wasn't quite sure, but he didn't necessarily dislike the idea. Thinking of Devon as all his was very appealing.

Lost in thought it took a moment for Nate to realise his second in command, Paul, was signalling him from the other side of the room. The tall, platinum blond cat shifter was part of the rescue team, and by the look on his face something was up.

Instantly, Nate felt his senses go on full alert — even more so than usual knowing that Devon was in the building.

Detouring on his way to the bar, Nate joined Paul in the shadowy alcove the man habitually used to watch what was going on in the club as part of his job on the security team.

Paul was leaning casually against the wall, but there was nothing casual about the man. Nate could feel the tension radiating off him. Casting his eyes around the room, Paul's gaze eventually settled on Devon, and his look was anything but approving.

Nate stiffened. "So, what's up?"

"The Hawk contacted us. He wants your pretty, little playmate taken to The Compound."

Nate bristled at the way the other shifter looked at and spoke about Devon. He knew some of the other cats had a negative opinion of pleasure cats and the intimate relationship they had with their masters. Some saw them as liabilities in the war they found themselves in with the mages. Others would always question their commitment and motivations for freedom. It was well known that they lived privileged and cosseted lives in Tantric Mage's harems.

But Nate had long suspected it wasn't all it was purported to be. Devon's story only confirmed his suspicions. He personally wouldn't wish the life of a pleasure cat on anyone.

Nate stifled the urge to lash out at his second in command. He was, of course, entitled to his own opinion, but while it may be true that pleasure cats didn't usually make good warriors, Nate saw no reason to dismiss them completely. They were just as deserving of a place in the rebellion. In fact, in Nate's opinion, there really wasn't much point to the fight at all without the softer, sweeter element that cats such as Devon brought to the shifter community. Regardless, no one would be mistreating Devon while he was around.

"Do you have a problem with Devon?" Nate asked curtly.

Paul shrugged non-committally and continued to survey the room with a nonchalant attitude.

Nate gritted his teeth. He refused to get into it with Paul here, but he made a mental note to bring it up with the man later. Before Devon felt the animosity.

"Did he say why he wants Devon moved?" Nate asked shortly.

"He didn't say much. You know how Hawk is. He just said that the pleasure cat we had found recently should be taken to The Compound for safe keeping. I assumed he meant your pleasure cat." Paul began to scowl in irritation, letting Nate know he wasn't pleased by not understanding the reason why either.

It soothed a slightly ruffled part of Nate's ego to hear Devon referred to as his. Something primitive in him rumbled approvingly that the other man recognised Devon belonged to him. But Nate was still concerned. What the hell was going on? How had the rebel operative they all knew only as Hawk known about Devon?

Nate mulled over the fact that Hawk had become very elusive recently, keeping more distance between himself and the cat shifters than ever. Almost as if he didn't trust them. But that was ridiculous. Hawk had been either directly or indirectly responsible for freeing almost all of the current pride members, including most of the cats that made up the Council of Elders.

Hawk had never led them astray before. Only a handful had actually seen him. And of those, none had actually seen his face clearly enough to identify him. He always wore a deep, hooded cloak. But many owed him their lives and existence in the safety of The Compound. Including Nate.

He looked over at Devon, who was still sitting at the table not meeting anyone's eyes, where he had left him to get drinks. He looked so sweet and vulnerable. If Hawk said he needed to be in The Compound to be safe then Nate would take him to The Compound. But not tonight. It was getting too late and there was a bad storm coming in. Some of the roads they'd need to use were pretty hairy in good weather during the day.

"We'll leave first thing in the morning," Nate told Paul firmly.

The man merely nodded seriously and continued to scan the room. Even as Nate watched, Paul's eyelids seemed to flicker slightly, then his face changed. It was subtle, but the lines around his eyes softened and the tension around his mouth eased. He looked like an entirely different person.

Suddenly, Paul leaned over and whispered playfully, "Your little kitty is looking jealous."

Nate didn't even blink at the change in Paul—he had always been as changeable as the weather. One minute, the sharp and serious warrior, the next instant, light and playful as a kitten. Paul had once explained that he liked to keep people off balance, saying it made them easier to take down, but Nate wondered if the cat's experiences before his rescue hadn't led to some sort of split personality disorder.

It was sad, but Paul wasn't the first cat he'd seen damaged by a mage's cruelty. And Paul had more reason than most. He'd been young, newly orphaned and terrified when Hawk had rescued him from a painmancy camp. Nate had only been a cub himself, but he could still remember Paul being brought to them — wild, half-starved and a little strange.

The fact remained that Paul was a good man to have in a fight. Skilled and so intuitive it was scary. Literally scary. Sometimes Paul seemed to just know things. He'd got the rescue team out of a nasty situation on more than one occasion. And he'd been a good, if capricious, friend over the years.

Nate decided to cut the man some slack. Maybe he was just having a bad day.

Looking towards Devon he could see his kitten — eyes focused intently on the dancers moving enthusiastically to the energetic beat on the dance floor. There was no jealously as far as Nate could see, only fascination. He felt his heart do a funny little jolt in his chest at the sight. Devon was simply…gorgeous.

"Sorry about the attitude before, man," Paul said, breaking Nate out of his reverie. "But you know, he…ah… I'm right. He is a pretty, little thing." Paul offered an easy, open smile with his regrets.

Nate decided to ignore the slip and played along. It might not have been the smartest thing Paul had ever done — messing with him where Devon was concerned, but if Paul was apologising that went some way to soothing his irritation. Besides, this lighter, more relaxed side of Paul's personality that seemed to be struggling to the surface was always easy to forgive, and usually a lot of fun as well. Nate decided to take a moment to chat and unwind with the man while it lasted.

* * * *

Sitting on a bar stool, fiddling with a drink coaster, Devon tried very hard not to notice how close the man on the far side of the room was standing next to Nate. They leaned together and spoke intimately—their body language suggesting long and close association. Devon knew he had no business feeling betrayed or possessive, but he couldn't deny he felt both, along with a sullen attitude creeping over him to spoil what had promised to be such a good evening.

Devon wasn't at all sure where his feelings were coming from. He'd only just meet Nate, and it wasn't as if Nate had offered anything permanent. But he'd thought...hoped...after their kiss...

As the man leaned in to speak into Nate's ear, Devon couldn't look any more. He turned to watch the bodies moving out on the dance floor instead and tried not to think at all. He was so engrossed in losing himself in the music and the writhing bodies that he didn't notice the large man that sidled up to stand at his elbow, watching the dancers with him.

"Beautiful, aren't they?" Devon jumped and would have fallen off his chair if Duncan hadn't reached out to steady him. "Whoa! Careful there. Wouldn't want you to have a fall. Nate would definitely have my hide for that."

Devon subtly tried to draw away, but Duncan managed to keep hold of his elbow without actually forcing the hold, and the look in the other man's eyes made Devon pause.

"Look, I'm really sorry for the misunderstanding the other day," Duncan offered in a sincere, serious voice — his eyes begging for understanding. "I truly didn't mean any harm. I just...you know." He shrugged and looked away as if embarrassed.

Devon was confused. On the one hand, he didn't trust the man, and yet, he couldn't help feeling slightly sorry for him. He didn't know Duncan's story. Perhaps he was lonely, or maybe he had been hurt one too many times and had decided paying for physical comfort was safer. It could have just been a misunderstanding. Devon certainly didn't want to hurt the man's feelings if he really was trying to apologise.

"It's okay," Devon replied warily.

For a few moments there was silence between them as they both watched the lively crush of bodies on the dance floor. Devon still couldn't help but feel tense with Duncan standing so close to him, but he tried not to be too obvious about it.

"So...you and Nate seem to be getting along well," Duncan observed casually.

Devon nodded nervously, peering over towards the alcove where Nate remained locked in conversation. Nate laughed at something the stranger said, and Devon had to swallow down his hurt at being forgotten.

"Has he mentioned when he might take you up to The Compound to meet the rest of the pride? His folks are lovely people. Maybe he'll introduce you while you're there."

Devon felt like Duncan had pulled the barstool out from under him.

What the — ?

Thoughts and emotions slammed into him one after another. Nate had a family? There was a pride somewhere? And what exactly was this 'Compound' that Duncan had referred to? More importantly, why hadn't Nate mentioned anything about these things before?

Oh gods! Had it all been some sort of game? A ploy? Why? What did Nate want from him?

Devon suddenly felt all the blood rush to his feet and the bottom drop out of his stomach. There was only one thing he could think of — only one thing that everyone seemed to want from him. Had everything that had happened since he'd met Nate just been about getting into his pants?

No! No, Nate wasn't like that. He would never —

Devon took a deep breath and let it out slowly — forcing himself to calm down and think. If that was all Nate wanted, they wouldn't be at the club right now. Not after the kiss they had shared in the park, or the later, heated lip locks in the apartment upstairs. Nate wouldn't have insisted that they come down to the club. Instead, they would have remained upstairs…otherwise occupied.

But it did look like Nate had been building a cage around him, and without him even suspecting a thing. Certainly the man seemed intent on keeping Devon in a special, compartmentalised part of his life — isolated from the rest of his world. It was a terrifyingly familiar scenario.

Okay, sure, they had only known each other a short time, but these where major things Nate had withheld. Major things in his life which he had neglected to tell Devon about. Not even a hint. Whereas Devon felt like he had told Nate his whole life story. He felt like he had taken a knife and dissected himself right in front of Nate over the last week. While Nate, he suddenly realised, hadn't given even the smallest detail about himself and his family away.

Pain blossomed full and raw inside him. It radiated out from his heart and threatened to leave him a bloody, exposed mess on the club floor. But for some reason he found himself unable to move. Unable to turn and walk away and never look back.

Duncan was watching him intently. "Oh! He didn't tell you, huh?" His sorrowful voice contradicted his razor sharp eyes as he watched Devon shake his head. "Wow. Sorry...ah...well that sucks. But I guess since Nate is the head of operations, he's got to be careful."

With that, Duncan turned back to watching the dancers, giving Devon a little space and privacy in the crowded night club. Even if that wasn't the other man's intent, Devon appreciated the gesture as he tried to gather his thoughts and emotions.

At the very least, Nate didn't trust him, he realised. But worse, for whatever reason, it seemed Nate was playing him. Testing him. Assessing him. Watching and waiting to see what and who he was. And perhaps how best to use him.

Oh! That hurt. That hurt right down to his soul. He had thought Nate cared. Had even started to believe that Nate liked him. But really...really Nate had just been pulling him apart the quickest and easiest way possible—through his stupid, desperate heart.

"What are you doing here, Duncan?" an all-too-familiar, and at the moment completely unwelcome, voice demanded behind them.

Devon stiffened but refused to turn around to look at the man. He felt a gentle but firm hand settle on his shoulder before a large glass of orange juice was placed in front of him. But he didn't acknowledge it. He was too busy fighting for control.

He wanted to shake the hand off. He wanted to turn around, throw the glass of orange juice in Nate's deceitful face and storm off. The now familiar claws of hurt and anger dug themselves into Devon's chest as he tried to fight the reaction off. He couldn't draw attention to them. Even if Nate didn't trust him, Devon knew better than to make a scene.

Devon took a small, mechanical sip from the condensation frosted glass in front of him, concentrating on the cool slide of the delicious, sweet juice as it made its way down his throat rather than the ragged hole that had just been carved out of his heart.

Surely there can't be much left of the organ by now.

"I came to offer my apologies," Duncan replied stiffly. "Mother always said manners never cost anybody."

"You never had a mother, Duncan. You were hatched somewhere. Or possibly scraped off of someone's shoe. Now go away," Nate sounded pissed, but Devon couldn't work out why.

He couldn't work anything out at the moment. He took another sip of orange juice and watched the dancers as Duncan walked away with a growl.

"You okay, baby?" Nate asked softly into his ear.

"No, actually I'm not okay." Devon was incredibly proud of himself when he didn't cry or scream. He just used a strong, even voice with perhaps a hint of anger — and he could see it scared the crap out of Nate, which pleased him even more. "You lied to me. You made me think you cared and you lied."

Suddenly, Devon was moving and Nate scrambled to keep up. For such a small man, he was quick as he dodged through the crowd heading, Nate noted with relief, for the door that led back up to their apartment.

Their apartment, damn it. Not Nate's. Theirs.

When Devon pulled the private door open and began to scurry up the stairs, Nate was right on his heels. He grabbed Devon by the upper arms and pinned him against the wall as the door slammed shut with an echoing bang.

Now, Nate could see the tears that pricked Devon's eyes and he wished with all his heart they weren't there, knowing that somehow he was responsible for them. Well, him and Duncan, he thought with a flash of anger. He'd be sorting Duncan out later, but that could wait for another time. Right now his man was hurting. He needed to be reassured and taken care of.

"What did that bastard say to you?" Nate demanded, his voice sounding strained and rough even to his own ears.

But Devon ignored the question completely. "Is this about sex? Is that it? Am I just a warm, tight hole you want to fuck?"

"*What?!* No! Is that what he said to—"

"I told you everything. I bared my soul to you, my most humiliating and painful moments. Why didn't you tell me about the others? About The Compound? About your parents? Who are you anyway?" Devon demanded, his voice rising with his accusations until the pain and emotions echoed off the walls of the stairwell. "Why did you pretend to care?"

"I didn't," Nate denied. He was mortified to see a tear slip down one pale cheek.

Devon began to struggle against his hold, but Nate just wrapped his arms around the smaller man and hung on all the harder. "I mean I didn't pretend. I do care for you. More than I should, probably."

Devon stilled in his arms for a moment before he began to struggle once more.

Hell, Nate wasn't sure he understood it either, but he held on until Devon realised he wasn't going anywhere and settled down enough to listen.

"I know we haven't known each other very long, but I feel drawn to you. I can't explain it. You have no idea how much I wanted to tell you. Everything. But I couldn't. I can't risk everything we've all worked so hard for here." He prayed with every fibre of his being that Devon would give him a chance. Forgive him. "It wasn't just a matter of me accepting the risk and living with the consequences. Can't you see? I have to protect them and keep my head. I have to use my brain even when...even when my heart wants to do something completely different."

Devon stood so perfectly still, watching him for such a long time that Nate began to get nervous, wondering if Devon ever intended to talk to him again.

"You went through my duffel. You weren't just washing my clothes. That's why you looked so guilty that day. You were looking for...for what exactly?"

Fuck. "Devon, please. I have to protect the others. It's—"

Devon held up his hand and Nate broke off the excuses. Devon apparently wasn't interested in hearing them.

"I get protecting. Believe me. I don't like it, but I understand."

Nate wanted to breathe a huge sigh of relief and wrap his arms around Devon in gratitude. But he restrained himself. By the look on Devon's face, he wasn't out of the woods yet.

"Who were you talking to?" Devon finally asked bluntly.

"In the club?" Nate asked, taken aback and more than a little confused by the abrupt change of subject.

Devon just nodded.

"Paul. He's a friend."

"Really? Because he looked like—"

"No!" Nate cried in surprise when he finally understood what Devon was suggesting. "Well, maybe once or twice, but not seriously. Not like—" Nate paused to regroup, treading very gently around the jealous man. "Not for a long time, and not like you," he ventured softly. "Please don't be mad at me."

Nate felt completely vulnerable and unsure of himself—an alien sensation he didn't like at all. Slowly, he reached out to cup Devon's cheek, giving the man plenty of time to pull away if he didn't want to be touched. After a brief hesitation, Devon leaned into the caress. Encouraged by the reaction, Nate bent his head down to gently touch his lips to Devon's soft, pink mouth—begging for forgiveness...and understanding.

He swept his tongue across Devon's lips for a taste and suddenly Devon was opening for him. Nate didn't waste a second of the opportunity. He pushed his tongue smoothly inside for a slow, languid kiss. It was deep and lingering. As it drew sweetly to a close, they ended up foreheads pressed together, eyes closed, lips barely parted, sharing each other's breath.

"I'm sorry," Nate offered simply but sincerely in a low, deep whisper. There really wasn't anything else to say.

"I know." Devon sighed.

Nate dared to believe it sounded like acceptance.

Pulling away, he looked down at the once again relaxed, beautiful man in front of him. When Nate had seen Duncan approach Devon, he had instantly been filled with a need to rip the other cat's throat out. Nate was the official pride representative for checking out new arrivals. Devon had no business being with anyone but Nate!

In retrospect, he realised it had been a completely Saber-Toothed reaction, but he couldn't help it. There was just something about Duncan that made Nate want to keep him as far away from Devon as possible.

Jealous much? Nate wondered to himself sardonically.

But knowing the man had upset Devon to the point of crying and tried to drive a wedge between them added fuel to the fire. Worse still, he had the feeling Duncan had very nearly succeeded. And he knew the other cat had done it on purpose too! He just knew it. But he couldn't prove it.

Bastard!

"Please stay away from Duncan." Nate's voice was harsher than he had intended and he felt Devon stiffen in his arms.

"Why? Because he wanted to tell me the truth about you all," Devon asked, a dangerous edge to his voice Nate knew he would have been a fool to ignore.

"No, baby. I just don't trust him."

"Apparently, you don't trust me either," Devon shot back, pushing Nate away again.

"Please don't do this, Devon. I explained to you why I didn't tell you about the rest of the pride and The Compound. And I was going to tell you all about them. Tonight. But big mouth Duncan beat me to it."

His words were met with silence. He wasn't sure Devon believed him. Nate sighed and held Devon a little closer. He knew Devon had issues with trusting people at the best of times, and now he thought Nate had betrayed him.

It was ironic really, because Nate *did* trust Devon. In fact, he was pretty sure he was trusting Devon with the only thing he truly had to give—his heart.

Nate was trying to protect him again. Devon understood Nate needing to protect the pride. He even understood Nate going through his duffel. He didn't like it, but he understood why Nate had done it. He was still pissed. In fact, in a strange, twisted sort of way it pissed him off even more to think that Nate was trying to protect him.

Not like this, Devon raged inside. *I won't go back to living in a cage.* He didn't want Nate's care to come in the form of stifling and coddling. He wanted Nate to...believe in him, he finally realised, still fumbling his way through his own feelings.

"Were you really about to tell me about the others?" Devon asked suspiciously.

"Yes. I want to take you to meet them," Nate replied.

"Really?" Devon was excited and hopeful despite himself. *Guess there's no help for it. Might as well just admit I'm a fool. A fool for Nate.*

"Yes, really," Nate chuckled, a definite sound of relief coloured his voice now. "I'd love for you to meet my parents. They live at The Compound we built in the country. It's so beautiful out there. Clean, fresh air, plenty of room to run. I think you'd like it." Nate's voice was beginning to sound excited as he talked about his home and family.

Devon felt a twinge of jealousy twist his gut, but quickly pushed it away. "How did you manage that?" he asked, trying to distract himself from his confusing emotions. He cocked his head in curiosity and Nate rewarded him with another soft chuckle.

"It wasn't easy getting it all together. One of the elders fell in love with a farmer with a large parcel of land when we first got here. After that...well we have friends that can work absolute magic with the red tape."

Devon stiffened. He felt his eyes widen in terror. *Magic?*

Nate must have seen and understood. "Not literally," he reassured quickly. "He just has this amazing ability to be in the right place at the right time. He's responsible for starting the whole idea of a sanctuary for escaped slaves. I was just a cub when my family managed to escape. I remember thinking Hawk was some sort of god. He just appeared. He rescued all these cats that were scheduled for the labour camps. And he did it all on his own when he wasn't even as old as you are now." Nate blushed, obviously realising how overexcited he sounded. "At least, that's what they say. My family was rescued pretty early on and helped set up the rescue and rehabilitation teams. It's been a really long, hard journey but we are finally starting to carve out a place for ourselves."

"When can we go see this compound?" Devon asked, suddenly wanting to see what they had done, how they had found a way to survive and thrive in this strange place without masters.

"Not tonight, love." Nate's voice was suddenly serious. "There's a bad storm coming in and we need to get some rest before the drive. Most of the roads are dirt and it can get pretty hairy in places, especially in wild weather. But it helps keep us protected, so it's worth it."

Devon nodded. Although he was disappointed, in a way he was relieved they wouldn't be going anywhere tonight—he was so tired suddenly.

"Come on, let's get you all tucked up. You look dead on your feet."

Devon balked. He really was exhausted. The combination of stress, confrontations and recent illness were all taking their toll. He wanted nothing more than to be tucked up into bed again in the warm little nest of pillows and Nate's solid arms, but he knew he couldn't. Nate needed to start seeing him as strong and capable. An equal. Or whatever there was between them would never even get a chance. It would die a short, horrible death.

Devon stiffened his spine, along with his resolve, to get Nate to see him as something other than a needy, desperate, weakling.

"I think you're right. I am really tired suddenly. I think I'll try to get some sleep. No need for you to finish up your night so early though. I'll just go and curl up in the spare room so that you don't wake me when you come in later on. I'll see you in the morning, Nate." With that he pushed himself away from the bigger man and made his way quickly upstairs, not wanting Nate to see any hint of wavering in his resolve to be more independent.

He didn't see the pain and hurt that filled Nate's expression as he watched Devon disappear up the stairs and out of sight.

Chapter Eight

Outside, the wind and rain lashed at the building, pounding against the apartment like the rolling waves of the ocean. Lightning forked across the sky, briefly illuminating the dark room, then thunder cracked and rumbled it away.

Nate rolled over and burrowed deeper under the covers. He couldn't sleep. He was too used to having Devon beside him, and it bothered him to remember the firm, determined look in the other man's eyes as he had pulled away. The idea of what exactly Devon might be determined to do made him uneasy.

Of course, he couldn't really blame the man for wanting to put some distance between them. It still hurt like a bitch, but...it *was* understandable. The lack of trust, the digging, not sharing. Damn! He'd really hurt Devon.

Nate felt like kicking his own ass, but... Well, he couldn't say he'd do anything differently if he had to do it over. Maybe he would have said something sooner, but protecting the pride was important. It's what he did. There were men, women and children that relied on him.

What a mess! At least I'm warm and comfortable, if not happy and asleep. And tomorrow is another day. A day not to fuck things up. A chance to try to repair the damage that's been done. Hopefully.

Caught up in his own head, it took Nate a second to become aware that he was not alone. He tensed, readying himself for an attack. Then another flash of lightning illuminated the room and Nate clearly saw Devon illuminated in the doorway—eyes wide, hair tousled, smooth bare chest heaving in and out in great gasps for air. With the crack of thunder, Devon ran flat out to the bed and dove under the covers.

Nate fumbled for the bedside light, drawing the quivering bundle huddled against his legs up to lie across his chest.

"Shh," Nate crooned softly. "It's just a storm, nothing to worry about, kitten."

"I hate storms," Devon sobbed as his teeth chattered.

Nate ran his hand up and down the younger man's back until he seemed to relax slightly. Unfortunately, the more Devon relaxed the more aware Nate became of the very naked, very alluring man in his arms.

Nate clenched his teeth, desperate to draw his attention away from the temptation. "Come on, let's turn on a few lights. I'll get you a warm drink of milk or something."

"No!" Devon's lax hold suddenly tightened painfully around his neck and shoulders. "Don't leave me. Please don't leave me, Mamm—"

Devon's sob cut off the end of what he had been about to say—but it was pretty obvious he'd been calling out for his mother. Nate's heart ached for Devon as he gently rocked and crooned to him—simple nonsense words of comfort. He wondered if Devon had even really woken up when he had come desperately seeking comfort from the storm.

Nate knew he had been one of the lucky ones. He'd been quite young when he had been rescued with his parents, and they had been part of a labouring colony. Life had been hard but they'd had very little contact with their mage master. Something he thanked the gods for every day. He'd seen and heard plenty of stories of kittens being removed from their mothers way too young and sent to new houses—to new and strange masters that often treated them as little more than property.

My poor kitten. Nate stroked Devon's soft black hair, wishing he could make it all better for the sweet, little cat. He marvelled at how quickly Devon had burrowed into his heart.

Breathing in deeply, Nate inhaled Devon's distinctive scent—honey and something else, something spicy. He wanted to keep Devon, he realised. He wanted to wake up beside him and breathe in his scent, not just today but every day.

Devon gradually became aware of the strong arms wrapped around him and stiffened, only relaxing a little when he realised the arms that held him were Nate's, and that he was rocking him gently, softly murmuring comforting noises to him.

Slowly, memories and realisation drifted in.

Damn! He'd had the stupid dream again. The one where he thought he saw his mother. A mother he had never known. Or at least couldn't remember. He called out to her, but she always walked away.

Story of my life, thought Devon morosely.

His cheeks flushed in deep humiliation. Nothing like waking up calling for Mummy to make a man want to make a run for it. So much for being independent and strong, he realised with mocking bitterness. He tightened his hold convulsively, waiting anxiously for Nate's reaction.

His old Master had sneered and ridiculed him on the rare occasions he had woken up from the dream like this in his Master's presence. Tony had simply smacked him round the head a few times and called him names. Ethan used to hold him gently, but even he'd run away eventually. But ever since Ethan had run away, the dreams had definitely been getting worse, both in degree and frequency, he realised.

I don't want to be alone and unwanted anymore. I want...I want to be accepted...just the way I am. I want to connect with someone and have him...want me back.

The need was so strong, so overwhelming that it overrode his fear of rejection. He found himself tentatively nuzzling into Nate's neck before he even realised it. When he wasn't pushed away, he gently placed a kiss under Nate's jaw.

Devon heard a faint moan and drew back. Nate had closed his eyes—his face a mask of desire and need. After the initial shock, Devon felt a surge of power swell inside him. He had put that look on Nate's face. The feeling rose and filled him—just as his cock rose and filled between his legs.

Perhaps strong and independent were overrated. Needy and desperate seemed to work for Nate just fine, especially at the moment.

"I'm sorry," Nate whispered on another moan of pleasure. "I should have—"

"Ssh. I know. Not now."

Nate fell silent instantly.

Emboldened, Devon carefully straddled the bigger man's hips, adding his own groan of pleasure when he felt his shaft meet and rub against Nate's hard cock.

Oh! That feels incredible. Devon soaked in the amazing sensation.

He had never felt anything like it. Raw power, lust and longing crowded his senses. All he wanted was to spend the rest of the night — hell, the rest of his life — touching and tasting this incredible man beneath him.

Devon set about exploring — taking in every nuance, each breathless gasp and tantalising caress. This was not the hard, painful taking Rolf had introduced him to, this was something else entirely. This was…glorious.

He leant forward and gently took a kiss, savouring the moment as, for the very first time in his life, he initiated a meeting of his lips with another's. It started out tentative and unsure, but it wasn't long before he was pushing his tongue into Nate's mouth to get a better taste of the man. Best of all, Nate never tried to take control of it — he just let Devon explore and discover at his own pace.

But all too soon, Devon found it wasn't enough. He pulled away, panting for breath, wriggling for something, anything to ease the amazing ache inside him.

"Devon!" Nate said, sounding almost desperate. "Devon, stop. Please. I can't—"

"Please, Nate. I want it. I want you."

"Oh, baby," Nate groaned, sounding pained and on the very edge of control. "Are you sure?"

A spike of anger touched Devon like the pure, wild lightning still flashing around the building. "I'm not stupid! I know what I want. I'm not weak, Nate."

"Okay, sweetheart. Okay," Nate placated, only driving Devon's sudden anger a little higher. "I never thought you were weak, or stupid. I just—"

Smart man that he was, Nate stopped talking and set his lips to the sweet sensitive spot beneath Devon's earlobe.

It took less than a second of Nate's clever lips against his flesh for Devon to groan blissfully. Then yelp in surprise as Nate nipped his earlobe—hard. A rough tongue bathed the abuse flesh, and Devon shivered in delight, caught up in the delicious edge between pleasure and pain, his anger drowning under the sensual assault.

"Nate!" Devon called out as the man beneath him worked down the column of his neck—lips gently nipping then soothing over the sensitised flesh.

"Hush, kitten. I have you. Let me take care of you."

Unexpectedly, Devon thought he might cry, but he swallowed down the tears. He didn't want the tears, but it all felt too much—too overwhelming, too all consuming.

Nate seemed to sense he needed a moment and kept his kisses light, gently caressing his back until Devon calmed. Then Nate wiggled a little, inching his way down the bed a fraction, and moved his lips towards the dusky pink disk of one of Devon's nipples.

The first brush of lips against the hard sensitive nub of flesh at its centre nearly had Devon spending right then and there. The sensation of Nate gently nuzzling and suckling at the taut bud was absolutely mind-blowing. Devon couldn't help himself, he eased his hand into the thick, wavy strands of Nate's hair and cradled the man's head to his chest. He would keep him there forever if he could.

Nate chuckled softly against him, sending waves of delicious pleasure coursing over his body, before moving across to explore the other, neglected nipple.

Desperately, Devon began to rock, grinding his cock across Nate's washboard abs in a delicious slide of friction. He could feel the hard throbbing of Nate's erection running over the crease of his ass. Amazingly, it didn't frighten him. He wanted it. He wanted Nate to push his huge cock into him, to join them so intimately that Devon would always have this moment to hold on to.

"Please, Nate," Devon begged shamelessly.

"What, baby? What do you want?" Nate asked, his voice smooth silk and warm as new wool.

"I want you," Devon panted. "I want you inside me. Please Nate, come inside me," he wailed.

Nate knew pleasure cats were incapable of getting or transmitting disease, so he could dispense with the condom. It was just as well, because Nate had the most overwhelming desire to thrust into the smaller cat and leave his cum buried deep inside. It was a primitive and demanding need—to mark Devon with his scent and his seed so that every cat would know this man was his. He didn't think he would have been capable of the logical thought processes needed to remember safe sex, even if it had been an issue.

He couldn't believe he'd been capable of stopping earlier to make sure this was really what Devon wanted. It had required an amazing amount of willpower. But to hear Devon snap back at him like he had—putting him in his place like that, setting him straight and demanding what he wanted. It had made it all worthwhile.

Nate reached down and ran his hands appreciatively over the twin globes of Devon's small, firm ass, gently kneading and manipulating the flesh until he knew he was driving them both insane with lust.

He carefully parted Devon's cheeks and ran his fingers over the tight pucker. He was shocked to find it moist and pliant beneath his fingertips. He looked up in surprise to see Devon's face turn a deep, dark shade of red as he blushed to the roots of his hair.

"It's a pleasure cat thing," he mumbled in explanation.

"Wow. That's so amazing," Nate replied in awe as he massaged his fingers around the opening of Devon's body before slipping a finger up inside him.

They groaned in unison.

"Really?" Devon asked with surprise.

"Mmmm. Oh yes, I like." Nate grinned wickedly as he leaned up for a deep, tongue-tangling kiss.

He'd never been with a pleasure cat before. He had the feeling he wouldn't want to be with anyone else but Devon again regardless, but feeling how readily Devon's body opened and accepted him, even welcomed him was heady stuff.

When they parted, both breathless and panting, Nate gently pushed Devon up into a sitting position over him. Devon eyed him with uncertainty as he complied.

"I want you to ride me, kitten." Nate helped lift Devon's hips and held his ridged shaft steady in preparation for Devon to slide down over it.

"Please, Devon. Take me inside you. Slide that gorgeous body down over my cock and ride me." Nate sounded almost desperate to be joined with him…and it made all the difference.

Suddenly bold and wanton, Devon reached behind himself and joined Nate in holding the throbbing erection nestled in the dark curls at the junction of Nate's legs. Then he slowly lowered himself over the head of Nate's cock.

For an instant, it burned and a flare of panic shot through him. Devon's eyes opened wide with fear. But looking down into the steady, lust filled gaze of his lover, something settled inside him. He relaxed until he was able to take the thick, rounded head of Nate's cock into his body. Throwing his head back in agonising ecstasy, Devon rocked back and forth, gradually taking more and more of Nate's massive cock until he was finally seated in Nate's lap.

Devon took a moment. He felt so full. So incredibly full and complete for the first time in his life. He wanted to savour the moment. He wanted to hold Nate inside him just like this forever. But he could see the strain holding still was taking on the poor man beneath him.

Gently, Devon began a slow glide up and down Nate's shaft. Little noises escaped them both — grunts and groans of pleasure and anticipation. Nate began to thrust up into him helplessly, and Devon took it all — crying out as the head of Nate's shaft brushed against something deep inside his ass. It sent sparks of electric pleasure through him that left a residual tingle all along his nerves before the spot was caressed again and the rapturous sensation ignited once more.

It was too much. Cum exploded out of his shaft — covering Nate's chest and belly in thick creamy-white jets even as he felt Nate's answering explosion deep inside him. He felt pulse after pulse filling him up with powerful bursts of Nate's seed. That feeling alone had him groaning again in pleasure.

As they descended from their mutual orgasms in shallow thrusts and whimpers, Devon collapsed down over Nate's chest in exhaustion. Nate wrapped him protectively in a warm, welcoming embrace and Devon sighed — completely content and at peace. When a tiny kiss was placed at his temple, Devon was too tired to reply, but he nuzzled against Nate, offering a weak hug of gratitude.

As the storm continued outside, for the first time in his life, Devon drifted off to sleep with the thunder and lightning still raging around them.

Chapter Nine

Devon slowly became aware of a heavy weight pressing him down into the mattress. Memories of the days he had spent with Rolf trying to track down his brother rushed in.

Waking up in the damp warehouse they had used as a base. The hard, uncomfortable mattress they had slept on. The feeling of Rolf pressing him down into the smelly, lumpy bed. Hot breath huffing into his ear while Rolf thrust into him, extracting his vile repayment for help that never eventuated over and over again.

No! Devon tried desperately to break out of the memory's hold. Panting for breath, nausea rolled over him — a wave of misery so strong it threatened to overwhelm him at any moment. He knew it was futile to fight it. The last few weeks he had woken up like this he had always ended up vomiting until it felt like his toenails would come up.

Shoving aside the heavy arm that was draped over him, Devon jumped out of bed and bolted for the bathroom, making it just in time as he began retching. His eyes watered and his nose ran, but he felt so thoroughly wretched he really didn't care what he looked like or who heard him at the moment. All he wanted to do was curl up and die.

Slowly, Devon became aware of Nate pressing a cool damp cloth to the back of his neck and gentle hands stroking soothing patterns over his back. When the last of the retching passed, Nate pulled Devon back against his chest and lowered the toilet lid to flush way the mess.

"Feel better?" Nate asked softly.

Devon nodded weakly, feeling too exhausted to talk.

"You've been sick a lot lately?"

"Bad dreams," Devon mumbled.

Nate watched him silently.

"Not last night though," Devon quickly reassured. "Well, not after...well, you know." Lowering his eyes, Devon felt a hot flush creep up his neck and over his face.

"I know, love," Nate replied gently, leaning in to give a soft kiss to the top of Devon's downturned head. "Me too."

Startled, Devon looked up to see Nate had the strangest expression on his face. He couldn't quite put a name to it, but it almost looked...loving? And he had called him love.

Devon squashed the flare of excitement that the thought created. It was too much to hope for.

Nate stood and offered his hand, but Devon just looked at it for a moment. He felt like he needed to explain himself to Nate. But he wasn't quite sure what to say or where to start. In light of what had transpired last night, his retreat to the spare room seemed...pathetic.

"I wanted you to see me as more than some pitiful charity case you picked up. I know you said you really did want to take me to meet the pride but...I wanted to be brave and strong so you would be...proud of me." Devon knew he sounded stupid, but couldn't seem to stop himself.

"I am proud of you, Devon," Nate said firmly. "You don't have to be anything other than just the way you are for me. You don't have to prove anything. And you shouldn't be afraid to ask for my help, even if that's just holding you during a thunderstorm. I want to do that for you. I want to...be there for you. Please...let me."

Devon didn't know what to do or say to that. What could he say? He stared up at Nate with incomprehension. How could such a powerful, self-reliant and self-assured man want to be with him?

"Come on, let's get some breakfast into you," Nate finally said when it became apparent Devon was speechless.

Devon shook his head. He didn't want to even consider food ever again. Then his stomach gave a loud rumbling growl, and Nate pulled him gently to his feet, leading him to the kitchen.

Obviously, his body had other ideas.

* * * *

The drive to The Compound had been long and tedious. About three hours into their journey, Nate had needed to concentrate on the winding, slippery dirt roads and they had fallen into silence. Somewhere along the way, Devon had settled into a light doze, and he was surprised when Nate woke him as they were pulling up to a large gate with a small guardhouse.

Two guards stopped their vehicle and carefully looked Devon over before allowing them through.

"Welcome to The Compound," Nate said proudly.

Devon looked around at the vast, empty fields. There was nothing but grass and trees for as far as the eye could see. It was beautiful, but somehow not what Devon had expected. Where were the other members of the pride? Surely, they didn't live out in the open without any shelter. He looked over at Nate, wondering if the man was making fun of him.

Nate laughed. "Okay, we're not quite at the main complex yet, but this is still pride land. Home."

Home. Devon took another look. What would it be like to be able to call somewhere home, free and unencumbered? He really had no idea. He wasn't sure he'd ever had one. The harem certainly hadn't been a home. It had taken him a long time, but finally, he could see that it had been a prison, not a home.

After about ten more minutes travelling, while Devon considered the jumble of thoughts and emotions that surrounded the concept of home for him, Nate finally pulled up in front of a large central building. Around the main building was a scattering of dwellings—obviously homes, but with very little in the way of home comforts. The whole place looked like a temporary refuge, somewhere to stop and regroup, but not a home.

It was rather…depressing really, Devon thought.

Nate must have seen his disappointment. "I know it's not much, but it's safe, and we're free. And finally things are starting to get going with the businesses in the city, so we should be able to really make something of the place soon."

"No. I mean yes," Devon stumbled to apologise. "It's fine." He looked out over the mountains, filling his lungs with crisp, clean air. "In fact, it's lovely up here."

As he looked out beyond the buildings, he found it was true. The wild, unspoiled beauty of the place was glorious.

The more he looked out over the trees that covered the deep valley in a carpet of dark green down to a lake a few miles off the more relaxed he began to feel. He suddenly realised how much all the cats here must have gone through, how much work must have been involved for them to get to this point and felt a slight blush of shame colour his cheeks at his initial reaction.

"It's getting there," Nate seemed to relax a little as he looked around. "Now that the club is making money for us we're hoping to put a few more facilities in to make it…homier. It's been a bit of a struggle the last few years, but finally the pride is starting to fit in to their new home. Some of the younger members have even begun going out into the wider world and getting jobs. The extra money we're all bringing in has certainly started to make a difference. And the skills they're bringing back to the community are helping enormously."

Nate seemed to consider something for a moment.

"We have a doctor now," he said casually. "One of our own that trained in a human hospital in the city. Man, it was hard to get him through medical school. It's all so damn expensive, but he made it, and now he's working to set up a clinic here, as well as a private practice in the nearby town." Nate seemed to consider him for several long seconds, obviously debating how best to broach the subject. "I'd really like you to see him, Devon. I'm worried about how sick you've been lately. You're so skinny and…"

Nate was watching him too closely. Devon wanted to pull away and reject the idea, but the concern and worry on the other man's face—his lover's face—stopped him.

"Please. For me. Just come and meet him," Nate pleaded, going in for the kill like any good predator when he saw Devon's resolve falter.

Devon found himself nodding reluctantly without any real desire to do so. The idea of a stranger touching him, examining him, sent chills through his body. But he managed to control it so that Nate wouldn't see.

No need to look like any more of a weakling in front of Nate.

* * * *

The clinic was surprisingly quiet. Nate quickly introduced Devon to the pride doctor before the other man could find a way to back out. He truly was worried about his little kitten. He'd feel a lot better once Peter had taken a good look at him.

"Hi, Devon," Peter greeted in his usual friendly way—extending his hand in a very human handshake. He'd been with them since the beginning, and while he hadn't been a cub when they had arrived, he had quickly adapted to their new environment.

Devon stared at the hand in front of him before careful placing his own in the other man's grasp, where it was shaken firmly.

"It's nice to meet you. Welcome to our little compound."

"Thank you," Devon replied nervously.

"Doc, I was wondering if you had time to give Devon a quick check up. He's been feeling a bit sick lately."

Peter's whole demeanour changed instantly—becoming completely focused and professional in the blink of an eye. "What seems to be the problem?" he asked, studying Devon intensely—his natural curiosity burning brightly in his eyes now.

Devon shrugged. "I'm not sure I'm feeling sick exactly. I mean I have been sick a few times, but I'm eating okay. At least I am now. It's not as bad as it was."

Devon looked over and gave Nate a shy look and a smile that went straight to Nate's heart. He felt his insides warm with pleasure at seeing Devon smile at him like that—all soft and happy.

"I'm just a bit worried, Doc." Peter looked over and Nate felt the need to start shifting self-consciously, but he managed to hold it in until the doctor's shrewd gaze shifted back to Devon.

"Okay, then. Let's take a look," Peter said when he had seen whatever it was he'd been looking for.

"Will you stay with me?" Devon asked Nate nervously.

Nate nodded as Peter handed Devon a gown and directed him to a room to change in.

"We'll give you a few minutes to get undressed and into this before coming in, all right?" Peter said kindly, gently steering Devon in the right direction.

Devon made his way into the small examination room and quietly closed the door with one long, last look.

After Nate watched Devon walk away to change out of his street clothes, he turned back to Peter. "He's been getting really sick, Doc. But he eats like a mountain lion..." Nate's voice trailed away as Peter kept looking at him, studying him intensely.

"Don't worry, Nate. We'll get to the bottom of it." Peter put his hand on Nate's shoulder and squeezed reassuringly. "You like this one, huh?"

"Yeah. I...umm...I really think...I think Devon's the one, Doc. My mate." Nate felt a rush of joy at claiming Devon in front of another pride member for the first time, even as he fretted and worried about the man's health.

* * * *

Doctor Peter Manning stared down at the test results in disbelief, completely stunned by what he was seeing, but unable to deny what was right in front of him. He'd run and re-run the test three times with exactly the same results each time. It was time to face the truth. And the music. He had to go tell Nate and Devon what he'd found. It was likely to be a very interesting conversation.

"You might want to sit down for this," he suggested, shaking his head in amazement as he walked back into the exam room where Devon and Nate were waiting for him anxiously.

"What? What is it?" Nate asked, his voice rising with panic.

"It's okay, Nate," he tried to reassure the man before turning his attention to Devon. "Do you know if either of your parents or even your grandparents were Vess'als?" he asked carefully.

"Vess'als?" Devon asked in confusion, his gaze bouncing back and forth between him and Nate.

"Breeders," he tried using the common vernacular, hoping to trigger the man's understanding.

Devon looked at Nate even more confused now than a few moments ago. "I never knew either of my parents. My brother and I were found abandoned in the woods near the Master's castle. But obviously they were breeders, or Ethan and I wouldn't be here."

Devon looked like he was beginning to doubt Peter's grasp of reproduction. The expression on his face clearly saying, *isn't this man supposed to have gone to some sort of advanced education facility?* Peter couldn't really blame him. The situation was quite incredible.

"No, not breeders as in capable of... Okay..." Frustrated, Peter ran his hand through his hair and took a deep breath as he tried to think of how to proceed. "How to explain this…? Vess'als…well, I guess you could say Vess'als are a caste or subspecies within the cat shifter breed. They are individuals that were designed hundreds of years ago as kind of…advanced incubation units. They were used for breeding but give birth very differently."

The more he thought about it, the more excited Peter became, no matter how hard he tried to contain his enthusiasm, it was simply too fascinating and amazing to hold in. "You see, technically Vess'als don't actually have sperm or ova. They produce a third, completely unique cell from special organs in their rectum and throat that adapts to effectively be whatever is needed to complement their partner. Not only that, but it's actually designed to attract sperm and ova. It's a little tricky when a female wants to impregnate a Vess'al. Timing is critical because the egg actually has to be in the uterus to be drawn into the Vess'al when she comes, but basically the Vess'al takes his partner's cum into his body, either male or female, his partner's sperm or ova fuses with the Vess'al's germ cell and the resulting zygote is then directed to a special pouch that forms in the Vess'al's abdomen. When the young are ready to be born, the pouch opens much like the womb of other species and the young are born. Try to imagine a sea horse, in fact I think I remember that's where the mages got the idea from in the first place."

"Sounds painful," Devon observed, his voice wary, but patient.

"Well, yes. I won't lie to you, apparently it is painful. I watched a seahorse giving birth once. It looked quite…ahh…yes, from all accounts just as painful and traumatic as any birth."

"Okay. But what has that got to do with me?" Devon looked over at Nate as if asking him to please take him away from the nice, mad doctor now.

"What are you getting at, Doc?" Nate asked suspiciously, as if he was slowly getting the idea.

"Devon, you're a Vess'al. You're not sick, you're pregnant."

"*What!?*" Devon jumped up from the examination table he had been sitting on, his voice high and incredulous.

Peter watched the blood rush to the man's face then rapidly drain away to leave him pale and shaking.

Nate seemed just as shocked, but still moved quickly enough to help Devon sit back down, wrapping a comforting arm around his shoulders.

"Doc, are you...I mean..." Nate fumbled.

"Very sure. Devon is definitely pregnant."

"No way!" Devon began to struggle in Nate's embrace. "That's not possible."

"I'm afraid it is very possible," Peter continued calmly, hoping to pass on a don't-freak-out vibe. "The tests are very conclusive." He held up the little stick with two pale pink lines across it. "Cat shifters produce hCG when they're pregnant too. Very handy, quick and quite accurate little test these." He knew there was no use trying to dodge around the facts. The sooner both men got used to the idea the better.

"But...but." Devon looked around wide-eyed and panicky. "But I'm a male."

"Actually Vess'als are asexual. They still have sexual organs, of course, and can have sex, but they are not defined by their sexual characteristics. There are 'female' Vess'als, for want of a better term, as well. But they reproduce with their mates and give birth in exactly the same way as you do—from an abdominal pouch. It's part of their ability, not part of their gender."

"I don't understand." Devon sounded very lost as Nate pulled him closer against his side.

"Well, it all started because mages don't necessarily breed true. You see, the ability to use magic is actually a fairly rare gift, and during the great wars that drove magekind from Earth, hundreds of magic users were lost. It put a huge dent in their gene pool. So they created the Vess'als. It was a way to guarantee magic using offspring, because a Vess'al's offspring will *always* take on the genetic characteristics of whoever they are sired by. Unfortunately, Vess'als were apparently very difficult to create and, as you can imagine, getting Vess'als naturally is nearly impossible. Also, as the mages rebuilt their empire of power, using a lowly cat shifter as a parent for their children fell out of favour. So the techniques for creating Vess'als were mostly lost and natural-born ones are extremely rare—more accident than design. These days Vess'als are almost non-existent. I'd almost say they'd passed into our folklore, with only one or two born in an entire generation these days."

"I remember hearing about them when I was a cub, but I thought..." Nate added in an awed undertone.

Peter noticed Devon had gone extremely pale through the explanation. His eyes were large and terrified. Nate seemed too stunned to notice—caught up in the enormity of the situation.

"But...if what you're saying is true... Devon was a pleasure cat. Why didn't he ever get pregnant before?"

Peter was kind of curious himself. Devon was rather small for his age, but he was definitely a mature adult Vess'al. He should have gone through at least a few cycles by now. Both of them turned to look at Devon at the same time.

"Excuse me," Devon mumbled as he jumped off the examination table and ran for the door.

"Devon!" Nate called out anxiously, jumping up to follow him.

Devon froze at Nate's sharp call, but wouldn't turn back around to face them. Long minutes stretched out.

"Devon?" Nate asked softly as he carefully approached him and wrapped an arm around the man's trembling shoulder.

"My Master found me...undesirable," Devon explained in a small, hurt voice, not looking up — as if his shoes were suddenly fascinating.

"I'm not surprised." Peter rushed to explain himself as he saw the hurt and pain that crossed the smaller man's face. And Nate looked ready to start beating someone for it. "From all reports, Vess'als are very soothing, calming beings to be around. By their very nature they're completely unsuited to being pleasure cats. Tantric Mages, or Sex Mages if you prefer, crave passion and fire, they can become addicted to it in fact. Vess'als can't really give a Tantric Mage what they want."

"Devon can be passionate," Nate defended hotly.

Peter felt himself flush to the tips of his ears and saw Devon do exactly the same thing. "Well! Yes! I...ah...of course...I didn't mean..."

"So how long do Vess'als stay pregnant for?" Nate cut in — apparently completely unrepentant for his rash statement.

"Very good question," Peter replied enthusiastically, glad for the change in subject. "Never actually having cared for a Vess'al pregnancy before I would have to imagine it would be similar to any other cat shifter gestation, which lasts about eleven and a half months."

"Eleven and a half months!" Devon shouted in disbelief, doing some quick calculations and feeling the blood abandon his brain — as if it, too, was terrified of what he was thinking and wasn't going to stick around for any more. If his calculations were correct, that would mean he would be a parent in a little over nine months by his best guess.

"Remember you're growing a being that is bi-corporal, having two forms. That takes time."

The doctor obviously thought Devon wanted the whole pregnancy thing over with. But as far as Devon was concerned, if this was real at all, the baby was a lot safer and easier to care for where it was right now.

"I know this is all a bit of a shock," the doctor continued in the understatement of the century, "but...well, I just want to be the first to say congratulations to you both. This is just...amazing." Doctor Manning's smile was so bright it was almost blinding.

Oh gods! He thinks —

"Could you give us a moment, doc?" Nate asked gently.

"Oh! Yes. Of course." The doctor jumped up and began fussing with his paperwork. "I'll want to see you again in a few weeks, and I want to start you on a vitamin supplement, which I'll go and prepare now. Come to my office when you're ready." With that he hustled out and shut the door behind him.

After a long silence, Nate gently manoeuvred them back to sit side-by-side on the exam table again—his arm still wrapped around Devon's shoulders.

"Devon..."

"If this is real then...then this is Rolf's baby," Devon replied, carefully placing an unsteady hand on his abdomen, so many fears and questions and emotions crowding in on him. "The warrior cat I told you about. The one the Master sent to Earth with me."

"Are you sure?" Nate asked quietly.

"Yeah, I'm sure." He just wasn't sure about anything else. The world seemed to have turned him on his head when he wasn't looking. "I was a virgin before Rolf." Devon explained, dipping his chin to his chest. He wondered what Nate thought now. Before he was just a clingy weakling, now he was a clingy weakling that was about to have a child...by another man.

Devon shook his head in disbelief, trying to clear his muddled brain. *This is just so fucked up,* he thought, still dazed and confused.

He jumped up off the bed again and began pacing. He needed to move. He just felt so—

"When I said my Master found me undesirable, I meant completely repulsive. He couldn't stand me. I was a virgin." Words tumbled out of his mouth—hot and painful and...molten with suppressed rage. "He couldn't stand me, okay! He had me watch. I was allowed to... Once he made me...lick Ethan. My brother was being stubborn one day and... I was made to masturbate to add my energy, and I would be touching them when...when we orgasmed, but never touched. That was it. The sum total of my sexual experience. Before Rolf. So yeah, I'm sure. This is Rolf's."

Devon couldn't seem to hold still, he was distressed and overwhelmed and angry and he needed to shift and run.

Then Nate wrapped his arms around him again. "No, honey. They're yours. Completely yours. Rolf has no claim over you or your babies."

"Babies?"

Nate cursed under his breath, but it was too late now. Devon felt the edges of panic closing in again.

"Cats have litters. We have litters too."

"I think I need to lie down."

Nate took more of his weight, supporting him when he felt like he might lie down right where he was—on the floor, in a rush.

"Come on. I have a room I use when I'm here. I'd love for you to share it with me," Nate suggested, gently guiding them to the door.

Devon merely nodded, not really caring where they went. He was way past overwhelmed now.

* * * *

As Nate held the door open to the small room he called home at The Compound, he could see that Devon was lost and in shock. Nate couldn't blame him. He was feeling a little of both himself.

Ushering Devon to the couch against the far wall, Nate sat them down side-by-side, but he was at a loss as to what to say or do. Finally, he decided to launch right into the only truth that really mattered.

"I think you're very desirable."

"Why would you want me? I'm just a wh…"

Nate tensed. "Don't you ever let me hear you say something like that about yourself again, or I'll have to turn you over my knee and paddle your ass. You're amazing." He fought to relax his body and gentled his expression as he placed his hands over Devon's flat belly. "What's happening inside you *is* amazing."

Suddenly, Devon began to purr. It was the first tentative, uncertain purr Nate had ever heard from the man, and both their eyes widened in surprise and confusion—as if he wasn't sure why or where the sound had come from.

"I don't…I mean…I've never done that before…purred, I mean," Devon said, his tone and expression finally settling on awe.

Nate gently kissed Devon's lips, gradually letting their kiss become heated, until eventually tongues plunged and tangled together. Hands grappled and grasped at hair and clothes.

"Fuck me, Nate. I want it. Please. Make me forget," Devon begged.

"No." For a second Devon looked devastated. "I love you, Devon."

"But—"

"No! No 'buts'. I love you and I want to make love to you," Nate explained. "And I want you to remember that I was your first. No one else has ever made love to you before me. I'll always be your first lover. Your only lover."

Devon's purr this time was stronger and filled the room with its soft rumble.

Nate reached out and pulled Devon towards him, taking his mouth in another deep passionate kiss. "Devon," he moaned desperately. "Devon, I…"

"Yes," Devon breathed, pupils gone wide with passion.

It was all the permission Nate needed as they rubbed against one another furiously, both desperate for release. He stripped Devon's shirt off and worked frantically to unbutton his pants before pushing them aside to reveal his lover's long thin shaft with its glistening tip. Nate urged Devon to stand then he knelt down in front of him, taking the head of Devon's cock into his mouth.

"Nate," Devon cried, his hands instantly grabbing hold of Nate's head.

Nate was pretty sure that, given Devon's past, no one would have done this for him before. He wanted to be the first. He wanted to make it the best blowjob ever, but he knew they were both too much on edge right now. He was pretty sure it wouldn't last very long. All he could do was go for quality versus quantity. Nate set to work eagerly to accomplish just that, and soon Devon was thrusting into his mouth, moaning uncontrollably.

"Nate! Oh, Nate!" It was all the warning he got before Devon thrust hard one last time and came in long, creamy jerks.

And Nate lapped it up. He loved the taste of his lover on his tongue—sliding down his throat, filling his belly. He revelled in the firm hold Devon had on his hair. And hearing Devon's cry of release was incredible.

As Devon's orgasm finally came to an end, Nate eased him down onto the floor, far from finished with the gorgeous man who sprawled across the rug. Deftly, he removed Devon's pants completely and wiggled into position between his legs. He manipulated Devon until his kitten was holding his knees against his chest for him. Then he got to work on pleasuring his lover like no other had before. Like no one except Nate ever would.

He had wanted to do this for so long. Spreading Devon's cheeks, Nate ran his tongue between the two perfectly shaped globes, tasting musk and something uniquely…Devon. He continued his intimate tongue bath, licking at the tiny pink pucker of Devon's hole before plunging his stiffened tongue deep inside.

Devon moaned and wriggled. Nate loved that he was making his lover lose control like that. He rewarded Devon with another deep thrust of his tongue—making the man buck up into his mouth.

After several more licks and thrusts with his tongue, Nate got back up to his knees, then slowly prowled over the top of a limp, compliant Devon—completely covering the man with his body.

"I want you, Devon," he whispered, adding a tiny nip to the delicate shell of his lover's ear for good measure. "I want you to take my cock. I want you to hold me inside you."

"Oh! Yes. Nate. Please."

Slowly, Nate eased his weeping shaft into Devon's tight hole until he was fully seated. For long moments he held there, savouring the deep contact with the man he was coming to love beyond reason.

"You ready for me, love?" Nate asked tenderly.

Devon nodded enthusiastically and moaned as Nate began to thrust into him. Long, slow deep thrusts that gradually worked their way up to a pounding rhythm. Before long Nate felt Devon stiffen beneath him and jets of cum spurt out over their bellies. It pulled Nate's own release out of him as Devon's hole spasmed around his hard shaft.

"My mate!" Nate bellowed. The cry wrenched from him almost brutally.

It was mating instinct at its most primal, pure and simple. Still Nate wouldn't have wanted to call the words back, even if he could. He wanted Devon more than he wanted his next breath.

Slowly, Nate became aware of the golden halo of magic that surrounded them, cocooning them in its warm, soft light. True mating, something in the back of Nate's mind told him, nudging him gently as he felt the irrevocable binding taking place between them. It was more than mating; it was a bonding of souls that could only be accomplished between those partners that accepted each other completely and unconditionally.

Nate's vision began to bleed away to black and white. He knew if he could look into his own eyes right now he would see them shifted into the golden eyed, elongated pupils of his cat form. He wanted this—he wanted Devon as his true, bonded mate.

"Devon!" he pleaded, begging the man under him to complete the ritual. To accept him. He felt his long, sharp canine teeth extend as he waited for Devon to respond. But without Devon's expressed permission this wouldn't go any further—there would be no bond formed. Their fate rested entirely in Devon's small hands.

Devon's arms pulled him in tighter. He let out a low keening sound of want and turned his head, exposing his neck in submission—sweet, beautiful, powerful submission.

Nate struck, sinking his teeth into Devon's vulnerable neck in utter bliss as another orgasm rocked through him. It was pure ecstasy, knowing Devon accepted him.

"Yes," Devon echoed, his voice a rumbling purr. "My mate! True mate."

Then, Nate felt the answering pop of Devon's canines sinking into the flesh of his shoulder. The sudden flare of pain quickly faded to unimaginable pleasure as he felt Devon's cock once more throbbing between them, spilling his seed across his belly as he joined Nate in the sheer joy of their joining.

Mates. True mates, Nate realised in a pleasant haze of contentment as he managed to gently settle over the man under him while he drifted in and out—still buried in Devon's ass. He had never experienced a more perfect moment in his life.

* * * *

Rolf panted, taking the strong, alluring scent of the cat he intended to make his, deep into his lungs. Something had altered slightly, subtly, but it only made Devon even more something he craved to possess. Whatever it was about the other shifter that had changed, Rolf was obsessed with having him now. He was completely consumed with finding the man's tight little ass and fucking it through the floor to re-establish his ownership — his right to possess and to keep.

Looking around the tiny rest area, Rolf considered his next move carefully. He couldn't believe he'd happened upon Devon's scent way out here in the middle of nowhere. He'd been forced to lay low on the outskirts of the city because the local police had spotted him. Apparently still after him. He'd been cursing the arrogant bastard of a mage that had sworn he was going to fix it so they weren't a problem anymore — useless son of a bitch — when he had picked up the distinctive scent of the little shifter male he had to have.

Soon! he promised himself. *Going to have him soon.* And then over and over again until the little bastard couldn't possibly run away from him ever again.

Excited by the idea of getting what was his back where it belonged, Rolf studied the area intensely, only to realise that the human transports on this side of the carriageway were all moving away from the city. *Fucking hell!* If he didn't catch up soon, he could lose Devon forever. Once the little slut left the area, he could end up anywhere.

Slightly panicked, Rolf intensified his search for clues to which way Devon might have gone…and instantly picked up the scent of another cat.

Rolf froze. There was another. His mate was associating with another male cat shifter. Fury and blind rage tore through his system, threatening to overwhelm all reason. Throwing back his head, he roared his outrage, before forcing himself to take deep, calming breaths. To find what was his, he needed to think. Then he could rip the other cat apart and take whatever fury was left out on his mate's ass.

Rolf sniffed around a little more, eyeing the land carefully. The highway stretched out before him hopelessly, but where the scents were most concentrated there were also the fresh tracks of a vehicle clearly imprinted in the sloppy mud created by the rain from the night before. And there was as thin, steep mountain trail breaking off from the car park and winding up into the thick trees of the forest. After standing in the mud for a time, the vehicle had made its way up the track.

It was a hunch. It was a guess made by an experienced tracker. Rolf would bet his right paw that the vehicle belonged to the other cat shifter. That they had made their way into the forest from here. Why they would do that, he had no idea. But he was going to follow the instincts that told him his quarry had gone this way.

And gods help the little shit when I catch up with him.

Chapter Ten

Devon turned his face up to the warm late afternoon sun and closed his eyes briefly. He had been at The Compound nearly a week and he was finally starting to feel settled—both within the small shifter community and within himself. It had taken a few days to meet and become more or less accepted into the pride. Nate's parents' support had gone a long way towards smoothing things over with a lot of the other cats. They really were amazing people as Duncan had said. They'd quickly taken him in and insisted he should think of them as family now—obviously sensing their son's claiming.

Devon sighed. He was even beginning to accept the fact that Nate wanted to be with him. Even though they'd mated—something Devon never thought to experience—in a lot of ways, it was even harder to accept than the fact he was going to be a parent in the not too distant future.

Oh gods! I'm going to be a parent.

Devon took several deep breaths and tried to slow his racing heart. He'd been having these sudden flashes of realisation on and off now for nearly a week. The thought was both terrifying and secretly just a little bit thrilling. He found himself fluctuating between disbelief and a strange kind of...excitement.

He was going to have kittens in about nine months or so. Children of his own to care for and love. It seemed a long time away, but Devon was pretty sure he would need the time to get his head completely wrapped around the idea.

Strangely enough, one thing he wasn't having a problem with was who their father was. After the initial stomach churning realisation that Rolf was the biological sire to his kittens, he had quickly dismissed all thoughts of having any issue with it. Nate's words of wisdom had wormed their way in, and helped enormously. They were Devon's, and he was determined to love and accept them for who they were, not reject and hate them for who their father was.

Devon took a moment to look out over the mountains. The future seemed...maybe not exactly rosy — that was too unrealistic — but bearable. No, more than bearable. Good. Devon tested the idea in his mind, tumbling it around to look at it from all angles. Yes, good.

For the first time in his life, Devon wanted something for himself. He wanted Nate as his mate. He wanted his kittens. He wanted to be free and to be able to raise them here, where there were so many opportunities for them to be more than slaves. More than their caste dictated they should be. He couldn't expect to have or keep any of these things if he ever went back to being under the control of a master.

Devon knew that a few weeks ago, if the Master had come for him, he would have gone down on his knees in gratitude and begged the man to take him home. Now, he knew he would fight tooth and nail to prevent being taken away. The realisation made his head spin. But there was no way he would let his kittens be raised the way he had.

The high-pitched sound of giggling brought Devon's attention back to reality and the field into which he had followed several of the children to enjoy the last of the fading sunshine. Devon watched and smiled as they chased each other, dropping down into stalking postures before leaping onto their playmates and tumbling about in the long grass. Most of them were older, but there were a few kittens of various species still too young to shift into their human forms yet. He wondered what the kittens growing inside him would look like. He couldn't wait to watch them playing like this with Nate at his side.

Looking away, Devon sighed again. He wished Nate could be here right now, but the man had gone back to the city to organise something or other at the club. He had promised to be back as quickly as possible, but the time seemed to be dragging out.

All the previous night, he had tossed and turned restlessly—already too used to being held in his lover's strong, reassuring arms to sleep soundly on his own. He felt off balance and slightly edgy without Nate close by, almost as if he were waiting for something bad to happen.

Yes, he knew how paranoid and pathetic that made him sound, but it was what it was. Something just didn't feel right.

Devon shrugged mentally—he was probably simply more comfortable with Nate around now. Perhaps it was something to do with wanting his mate close by to help protect the kittens, he mused.

"Mate," Devon whispered into the afternoon breeze in awe, still getting used to the idea of being mated to the big warrior cat.

"Hello, Devon."

Devon spun around at the rough, terrifyingly familiar voice behind him. He stumbled away from the towering bulk of Rolf as the warrior cat paced towards him, but the high-pitched squeals of the children brought him up short. He couldn't lead Rolf any closer to the youngsters or their home. He couldn't put his new family in danger. He wouldn't bring this monster to their door.

With painful clarity, Devon realised he already had. Rolf wouldn't be anywhere near them if it wasn't for him. He knew it right down to his bones—Rolf was here for him. And he knew with just as much certainty that Rolf wouldn't stop until he had him.

Devon felt all the blood drain from his face. Nate's worst fears about him had come true. He'd brought this to the pride. He'd endangered them all. He had to go. Now. Before it was too late, he had to lead Rolf away from the pride.

He wasn't sure if Rolf meant to kill him, fuck him or take him away. Or even a combination of all three. It didn't much matter which really. All were equally abhorrent and more than likely fatal to the kittens.

Devon froze. No! Like nothing else could have, the knowledge that Rolf would end up hurting, probably killing the kittens, spurred him on to fight. He wasn't giving them up. He wasn't going to abandon them, or give in.

But first he had to get away from here. He couldn't live with himself if any of the others were hurt or killed— especially the children.

The children.

Devon suddenly realised he couldn't hear the children any more, but he didn't dare turn around to see what had happened to them. He hoped they had run back to the safety of The Compound.

"What do you want, Rolf?" he asked, trying hard to make his voice sound steady, even as his hands shook uncontrollably.

Devon slowly edged around to put himself in the best position to make a run for the tree line. He knew he couldn't hope to beat Rolf in a flat out sprint, but perhaps his smaller size would help him outmanoeuvre the bulkier cat in the cluttered environs of the forest.

"You," Rolf answered succinctly, stalking towards him. "I want you. And I plan to have you. You're mine."

Rolf lunged, but Devon managed to dodge away. With more luck than skill, he sidestepped the larger cat and stumbled a few steps in the direction of the trees. He couldn't risk a flat run for it yet, but edging towards his goal while distracting Rolf might work.

Still desperately trying to think of something to say to divert Rolf's attention, the bigger shifter suddenly stopped in his tracks and took a deep breath in through his nose. Devon watched as fury slowly transformed the other man's face into a contorted mask of rage.

"You smell of strange cat!" Rolf bellowed. "Who have you been fucking, you little slut?"

Devon wasn't surprised he smelt like Nate. They had been going at it like bunnies ever since they'd mated nearly a week ago and had only been apart a day. Certainly not long enough for Nate's scent to have faded.

Rolf lunged for him again, and this time he was too quick. He snagged Devon's upper arm and dragged him in to his chest, leaning down to press his nose into Devon's neck.

Terror rooted Devon to the spot. The neck of his shirt had been inadvertently pulled away, exposing Nate's claiming mark—a bright, livid bruise around the twin puncture marks.

With a roar of fury, Rolf reared back, raising his open hand above his head.

Devon turned away, covering his head and instinctively trying to lessen the impact of the blow about to come down hard across his face. But it never came.

Instead, Devon heard a deafening feline scream as a golden body ploughed into Rolf's side and knocked him flying backwards to land with a hard thump on the grassy slope several feet away. The heavily muscled, bright yellow coat of Nate's mountain lion seemed to glow in the afternoon sunlight as he sprang on top of Rolf, snarling and snapping as Rolf fought desperately to protect his face and throat from being ripped open.

Devon, who had been flung sideways by the impact, rolled gracefully to his feet just in time to see Rolf throw Nate off and surge back up to a standing position. Instinctively, Devon knew he had to stop Rolf from shifting. Rolf was a lion. His superior size and strength in his shifted form would tear Nate apart. And there was no way he was going to let that happen.

He jumped onto Rolf's back as the massive warrior turned to face Nate and hung on. Momentarily surprised, Rolf soon began bucking and cursing, trying to dislodge him. Devon felt the muscles rippling and shifting beneath his hands as Rolf started the change. He quickly went for Rolf's eyes with his sharp little claws extended in an effort to distract the cat from his shift.

Unfortunately, moving to strike Rolf's eyes weakened his hold. Sensing his chance, Rolf reached back, grabbing him with his thick, meaty hands and threw him bodily over his shoulder to land several feet away on the ground, but not before Devon had managed to inflict several deep scratches to his face and neck. Little, pinprick trails of blood scored Rolf's cheeks and one long claw mark ran from under his left eye down under his chin.

Devon was in no position to appreciate the small triumph, however. He'd landed hard and all the air had rushed out of his lungs. Hunched over, presenting as small a target as possible, Devon tried to get his breath back. Above him, he heard Rolf's angry growl and Nate's answering snarl of fury. The sound of heavy blows landing against solid bodies repeated over and over as Devon steeled himself for another attack at any moment, still too winded to do anything about it.

He heard Nate yowl in pain, followed by a solid thump as something heavy landed a short distance away. But just when Devon was prepared for Rolf to start hitting him, he heard a single thunderous roar followed by several bellowing growls and cat screams. Looking up, he watched in amazement as cats of every kind converged on the grassy slope.

Their postures were openly aggressive and confrontational. Warning snarls and rumbling growls filled the air—stiff legged gates and wildly lashing tails making an impressive, intimidating display. Devon could see Rolf had managed to shift somewhere along the line, but he no longer dared to attack. Instead, Devon could see him watching the group warily, gauging his chances and obviously coming up lacking.

Rolf took a step back, and that's all it took. The pride surged forward, sensing their enemy weakening. Rolf had no choice but to turn and run into the thick vegetation or risk being torn apart.

Suddenly, Nate was at Devon's side—fussing over him, touching him all over with gentle hands. "Are you all right? Are you hurt? Are the kittens all right?" he whispered urgently.

Devon took a moment to take stock. Apart from a few bruises and a bit of a sore shoulder where he had hit the ground, he felt fine. But he wasn't sure about the kittens. Fear raced through him.

"I don't know. I think I'm fine," he finally managed to reply softly when he had caught his breath. Then he began to tremble. The slight trembling soon working itself up into full blown, body-racking shaking as the fear and shock of the attack began to overwhelm him.

"Nate," Devon breathed, tears streaming down his face. "What did I do? What did I do?"

Guilt, shock and fear all began to collapse in on him. Not knowing what else to do, he wrapped his arms tightly around himself and began to rock in distress. Then Nate's arms were around him, hugging him fiercely and rubbing a cheek against the top of his head over and over again. It was comforting, but in a distant sort of way that Devon couldn't seem to connect with, no matter how desperately he wanted to.

"You didn't do anything, honey. It's okay," Nate whispered.

"I brought him here. I brought his evil to this place," Devon whimpered back, looking up in time to see the wide-eyed, frightened face of one of the youngsters who had been playing in the field.

She was peering at him fearfully from behind one of the adults and Devon knew his crying was only frightening her more. Using every ounce of strength he possessed, he straightened up and bit into his bottom lip, fighting for control. He didn't want to make things worse by scaring the little ones any more than they already were.

After a few deep breaths, Devon felt calm enough to try speaking again. His voice, while still choppy and quavering slightly, held a determination he was quite proud of.

"I'm going back," he said clearly enough for all to hear.

"What?" Nate cried out in disbelief.

"I want to go back," Devon repeated.

"No! I won't let you go back to that bastard."

Devon stared at Nate for a moment. Obviously, he thought going back meant returning to Master Nevin. But that wasn't ever going to happen, he wouldn't do that to the kittens.

"I mean I want you to take me back to the city. Back to your apartment above the club."

Nate seemed to relax slightly, but he still didn't look unhappy with the idea.

"I'm not asking, Nate." Devon explained, looking briefly back over at the child still clinging to the adult's leg and feeling a steely resolve settle in his gut. "Take me back to the city, or I'll take myself."

Nate looked slightly shocked—as if he'd never seen Devon before. Devon guessed that was fair enough—he'd never seen this side of himself before either.

"We protect our own, son," one of the older pride members interrupted sternly, but Devon refused to be swayed.

"I know that, sir," he returned politely. "That's why I have to go."

For a long time the elder just looked at him, then he began to nod slowly—a expression of respect slowly forming on his handsome, tanned face.

Devon turned his head to look straight at Nate. "I won't put them in danger, Nate. Please understand." He could see the struggle Nate went through, but he finally nodded reluctantly.

Slowly, Devon climbed back to his feet. "I need to see Doctor Manning to make sure..." He couldn't even think about anything being wrong with the kittens after his fall. They were fine. They just had to be. "After that, I want to leave right away. As long as I'm here, Rolf will be a threat. Once I'm gone, he'll leave."

Devon knew it. He'd seen Rolf's reaction to the mating mark on his shoulder and knew now that Rolf had planned to put one of his own there. He also knew that Rolf would be back for him. He'd seen it burning in the other man's brutal eyes.

Devon shuddered. He would never accept Rolf as his mate and there was nothing Rolf could do about that. Mating, true mating, was something that had to be given. It couldn't be taken, no matter how much Rolf tried to force him into it. Unfortunately, that thought didn't comfort Devon very much. He knew Rolf would still try to force a mating and the only way to do that was to get rid of his existing mate.

Devon looked over at Nate. There was no way he would get the man to leave him and run away. It just wasn't who Nate was. But Devon would protect his mate every bit as ferociously as his mate had protected him. It was a new and powerful feeling right down to Devon's soul, and he felt the fierce love for his mate sealing his resolve absolutely.

* * * *

The ride back into the city was tense and quiet. Devon knew Nate didn't like bringing him back to the club. He thought it was safer at The Compound. He didn't approve of Devon's determination to draw Rolf away from the pride. He'd made it clear he thought it was too dangerous. But at the same time he didn't push or try to force Devon to change his mind either.

Devon admitted he was slightly in awe of the man for that. No one had ever given him that sort of respect. He fell just a little more in love with his mate as they drove in silence.

Devon couldn't relax—Rolf was too great a threat—but the farther they got away from The Compound the better he felt about his decision. At least at the club there were no children. And that was a crucial point to him now—he refused to endanger the pride's children. There were, however, trained warriors assigned to assist with the club and guard the random portals that opened around the city.

The portals were another point in the club's favour. In the last week at the pride's compound, he had learnt that there was an extensive network of portals around Bayside. As a last resort, he could access them and run if he needed to draw Rolf away from his new family.

And last, but by no means least, there was always the distinct possibility that Rolf wouldn't be able to track him down in the city. Devon knew how hard it was trying to find a person in the vast smelly, melting pot of humanity. He hoped the artificial scents, sheer number of people and strangeness of it all would help hide him.

"You don't have to do this, you know," Nate finally said tightly as they pulled up outside the club.

"Yes, I do," Devon returned firmly.

"Dev, you're one of us now, we protect our own."

"And that's exactly why I have to stay away from The Compound." Devon wasn't going to back down on this.

"If you won't think of yourself, think of the kittens."

"Don't!" Devon snapped, bristling angrily.

He was surprised that Nate would use such a low blow. But looking at his worried mate, Devon's attitude softened slightly. He realised the man must be going out of his mind if he was willing to try something that underhanded.

"I can't take it anymore, Nate." Devon tried to explain. "I don't want it to be this way anymore. I'm sick of being a pathetic little punching bag that everyone thinks they can lay into whenever they feel like it. I hate it and I can't do it anymore. I won't just sit around and wait for him to come get me. I don't want to put the pride in danger and I want the kittens to be proud of me. I want to be brave and make this right for them. For us." He reached out and squeezed Nate's hand, reassured when Nate squeezed back. "I haven't worked out how I'm going to make all that happen yet, but I'm working on it."

"You've never been pathetic," Nate said firmly. "And I'm proud of you. I'm proud of you for not just surviving this long, but for staying so beautiful—inside and out. I've never met a more beautiful person than you and I am proud of you for trying to do the right thing, even if I don't agree with it. I'm unbelievably proud of you for standing up for yourself. But…you don't always have to be brave. It's okay to be frightened and it's okay to need help. I want you to know I'm always going to be here for you. We're partners."

Devon leaned over and gently placed a kiss on Nate's lips. He looked deep into the other man's serious eyes. He couldn't help himself; he had to ask. He had to know. Had to hear it just once.

"Why me, Nate? You could have almost any cat you wanted, why would you want me with all my hassles?" Was it his looks? Devon wondered silently. His body? He still couldn't get his head around how Nate could possibly love a creature his own Master had never had a kind word for.

Nate cupped the side of his face gently. "I love you," he replied simply.

And those three simple words said nothing and everything all at the same time. He couldn't ask for anything more, because in a way he understood there wasn't any more. He loved Nate too, and that was it. No more or less to tell. He just loved him.

"I missed you last night," Devon breathed, leaning in so their lips were barely separated.

"Oh, yeah?" Nate smirked back.

"Yeah." Devon leaned in and placed another kiss against Nate's lips. "Let's get upstairs."

"Yeah. Good plan." Nate fumbled with his seatbelt.

Devon smiled seductively and reached for his own.

* * * *

Nate cursed at the jingling mess of keys that wouldn't let him into the apartment fast enough. Admittedly, warp speed wouldn't have been fast enough at the moment.

Finally managing to throw open the door, he pushed it in and turned around to grab Devon and drag him inside. Pulling the man hard up against him, Nate felt their cocks meet and move against one another through the layers of their clothes as he took Devon's mouth in a savage kiss.

Without breaking their connection, he kicked closed the door and lifted Devon up into his arms. Long legs wrapped around his waist and he rumbled a growl of approval—now he could carry his mate to the bedroom without losing even a second of the delicious contact between them.

Fierce kisses, thrusting tongues, nipping teeth and the feeling of Devon grinding against his hard belly, bumping into his straining shaft with his tight little ass on every step soon had Nate on the knife's edge of coming. He wanted more. He wanted now. He wanted everything. But most of all he wanted Devon's pleasure.

Arriving at their bedroom with that thought in mind, Nate slowed everything down. He carefully removed his lover's clothes—kneeling down to take Devon's boots off, he had the pleasure of seeing a deep, dark red blush cover the man's high cheekbones. Then he stripped off Devon's pants and tenderly kissed the tip of his leaking cock. It throbbed against Nate's lips in eager anticipation.

Standing back up, Nate took his time undressing, even though every second ticked by like a lifetime of separation between them. The heated look in Devon's eyes and the lust that slowly clouded them was more than enough reward so that he didn't regret a moment of the time he took to slowly strip for his mate.

Gently, he moved Devon back until his knees touched the edge of the bed and guided him down to lie in the middle of the mattress. Then Nate crawled up over the top of Devon's gloriously naked body.

Suddenly, he felt Devon tense beneath him.

"Is this okay?" Nate whispered, sensing the man's fear. Seeing Rolf again had probably awoken terrible memories of his time with the warrior cat. Nate desperately wished he could have ripped the bastard's heart out.

Just when Nate was about to back off, Devon took a deep, shuddering breath and began to nod. "Yeah, just...just take it slow."

Nate watched Devon for a moment, wanting to make sure he really was going to be okay. When Devon gazed up at him — steady and determined — he decided to trust his mate.

"Slow as you need, babe," he reassured.

Nate leant down and trailed his tongue up Devon's neck to the base of his ear. He sucked the small, fleshy lobe into his mouth — delighted when he heard a soft moan escape Devon's lips. Determined to distract the man still further, Nate licked and nipped his way back down, over the soft bump of Devon's collarbone and down to one small, pebbled nipple. He bathed the tiny bud gently with his raspy tongue until Devon was groaning and writhing against him.

Tenderly, he trailed his fingers down Devon's belly. He stopped to lightly caress the long, slim cock and softly fondle the tight balls beneath before moving lower to circle the small puckered entrance. It was wet with Devon's natural lubricant and fluttered slightly under his fingers as he touched and stroked it. With a steady, even pressure, he pushed inside.

Devon moaned and thrust back against his hand, taking him in past the second knuckle with his eager response. Nate slowly introduced another finger, followed by a third, working them in and out and curling them against Devon's prostate when he slipped past the soft, spongy mass.

Devon arched and cried out, a pulse of cum shooting out of the tip of his cock, followed by another and another. Before Devon could come down from his orgasm, Nate removed his fingers and lined up his cock, thrusting into his lover's warm, welcoming hole in one long slide.

Helpless to resist, Nate began pounding away at Devon's ass, cradling his lover's slim hips as he moved in and out of the tight hole. In only a few strokes, he joined Devon — exploding his release inside the other man, thrilling to the feel of his cum erupting from his cock while he was buried balls deep inside the man he loved.

As the last waves of his orgasm faded away, Nate lowered himself down beside Devon and lazily began to trace swirling patterns across his smooth, pale skin in long trails. Devon was so perfect. So beautiful.

After several minutes of petting and stroking his lover, Nate turned his head from where it rested, cradled against Devon's shoulder and looked up into his pale blue eyes.

"I bought you something," he whispered, his voice still husky from passion. "Two somethings actually."

"You bought me a present?" Devon asked, his eyes opening wide in surprise as he struggled to sit up—all the lassitude gone from his expression now.

Nate was sad to see it disappear. But since he had every intention of putting it right back there again—soon and often—he let his disappointment go. "Don't sound so shocked. Did you really think I would forget you?" he teased playfully.

"No! Of course not. I mean...you're already very generous. Too generous. I just..." Devon's brows furrowed thoughtfully. "You were only gone overnight," he pointed out.

"It felt like forever. Now shut up and close your eyes so I can give you your pressies," Nate said in his best, no nonsense voice, but he couldn't hide his mischievous smile.

Studying him carefully for a moment, Devon eventually did as he was asked with the air of a man waiting to see what tricks the other might have up his sleeve.

Nate lay the first, carefully wrapped present down in Devon's lap and waited for him to open his eyes. After looking at it hesitantly for a moment, Devon quickly got the idea and began ripping open the bright paper to reveal a hardcover book Nate had taken a long hour pawing through the local bookshop to choose.

"It's a cookbook," Nate supplied when Devon didn't seem to know what to do with it. He felt his confidence falter a little at the lack of reaction—wondering if he'd done the wrong thing. "I'm not really much of a cook, but you need feeding up and...well, when the little ones arrive I want to be able to make them good food too so...ah...I thought we could learn together, you know."

Tears suddenly welled in Devon's eyes and Nate panicked. *Oh, shit!*

Then Devon threw himself bodily into Nate's arms, whispering his thanks interspersed with little wet kisses. "Thank you so much, Nate. No one's...I can't believe you... Thank you."

Nate felt a blush creep up his neck. "You're welcome. I mean, I love your pancakes, they're fantastic, but...well...I wanted us to be able to feed our babies properly, you know." He finished with a shrug.

Devon sat back suddenly. "You mean that. About the kittens, I mean. You want them...I mean—"

"Of course I do!" Nate cried in shock. "Why wouldn't I want them?"

Devon averted his eyes, but Nate was having none of that. He used the tips of his fingers on the other man's chin to gently turn his head back so they were once again looking at each other.

"I'm going to say this just once so it's perfectly clear to you, Devon. I don't care who sired these kittens. As far as I'm concerned they're yours and you're mine so...I mean...I'd like...if you'll let me...I want..."

"You want to claim the kittens as yours too?"

"Yes. I mean if—"

"Yes! Yes, Nate," Devon interrupted before sealing their lips together in a fierce kiss.

When their mouths finally parted, Nate looked down into the dazed expression on Devon's face and wished he could keep it there for all time. But they needed to talk about how they were going to keep Devon safe now. Rolf was at large and a major threat. Nate needed to do everything he could to make sure Devon was as secure as possible.

"I have something else for you. It's not going to be as much fun, but—"

Nate placed a leather holster and gun on Devon's lap, waiting as the man sat stunned for a moment, looking down at the weapon.

"Is that...?"

"It's a gun. A weapon. I want you to start practicing how to use it properly and carry it with you wherever you go, in case you need to defend yourself." Nate didn't want to frighten the other man, or imply he wouldn't be safe with him at the club, in his home. But he wanted to know Devon would always have some way of protecting himself. A last resort he could always fall back on. "Will you do that? For me?"

Devon looked at him—serious and silent for a long time. Nate held his breath, well aware that things could go either way. He wasn't sure what Devon was thinking or how he felt about the idea of carrying a gun. Hell, he wasn't even sure if the man had seen a gun before. Then the smaller man nodded slowly, and he let out the breath he hadn't realised he'd been holding.

"Thank you, love. We'll start training tomorrow, first thing."

Nate watched as Devon carefully put the book and gun on the bedside table before turning back to him. For a moment they just looked at each other. Then Devon wiggled closer and wrapped his arms around him in a tender embrace, his weight gently taking them back down to the mattress where they could snuggle quietly.

And suddenly all was right with the world. Even if only for a few short hours before reality had to intrude again.

Chapter Eleven

They had been back in the city almost a month and Devon was beginning to wonder if he might actually have escaped Rolf. He wasn't stupid enough to be completely complacent, but he had gradually begun to relax enough to start enjoying his new life. Or more precisely, life with his new mate.

Devon smiled as he thought about Nate. He was an incredibly attentive and passionate lover, but had a definite tender side as well. And he was highly protective of both Devon and the unborn kittens.

He still found it slightly amazing to know that Nate really didn't care who the kittens' biological sire was. Nate seemed to have every intention of raising them as if they were his. And subtle things attested to the fact every day. He'd even started bringing toys home for them.

Just the thought of how lucky they were to have found such a wonderful man made Devon's head spin and his heart swell with love.

And true to his word, Nate had begun intensive lessons training him to use the gun he had presented him with soon after they'd arrived back in the city. They spent hour after hour in a specially constructed, soundproof room beneath the club every day perfecting his technique.

Nate had mentioned that they had built the room originally for the rigourous training the warriors did in both human and cat forms to remain in top condition. Occasionally, the room was also used to contain unstable shifters that came to them. But it worked equally well as an impromptu shooting range. A lifetime of necessity had certainly made these cats resourceful.

Devon almost felt comfortable holding the unexpectedly heavy handgun now, and Nate had praised him just the other day for his accuracy. Devon had blushed furiously then pounced on his surprised mate—taking him down to the training mats before riding him enthusiastically until they were both spent and exhausted.

A hot blush worked its way up his neck and into his cheeks at the memory, even as a secret smile twitched the corner of his mouth up in remembered naughty pleasure.

For the last week, Nate had been helping the new club manager with some sort of annual monetary work they had to do. Something to do with tax and governance and taking stock—though where they were taking the stock to he really wasn't sure. To be honest, Devon didn't really understand any of it, but he was determined to keep up his practice while Nate was busy. He'd started coming down alone a little earlier every day. He was sure Nate would join him, as soon as he could, but he really was competent enough now to manage on his own and he was hoping to surprise his mate with how much he had improved by the time Nate had finished whatever work he was doing for the club.

Devon smiled to himself as he realised what he had been thinking. Even a few short months ago, he never would have thought he could get to the point where he truly felt he could manage something like this on his own. It gave him a warm, confident feeling as he pulled open the heavy door to the secret bunker in the basement.

He was careful to shut the door properly—the way Nate had taught him, so the room was soundproof. Otherwise, the police would likely come charging in to find out what all the shooting was about, Nate had explained.

As Devon slowly walked across the huge, underground room, he thought about his mate. He knew Nate wanted to maintain his involvement with the rescue team—he was very proud of the work Nate and the warriors did to save other cat shifters. But he was also looking forward to whatever work he and Matt were currently doing being finished so they could once again spend more time together. He was beginning to appreciate, or rather not appreciate, how very time consuming running a club and rescuing slaves was.

At least by the time the kittens were born, they would be living away from the city, Devon consoled himself. Being born in cat form and not being able to change for several years was a good survival mechanism for the species, but hard to explain to inquisitive human neighbours when several lion cubs joined the family. Then there was the issue of seeing a pregnant male around when he eventually started to show.

Devon hoped they would be moving to The Compound so that the kittens could grow up with other cats their own age. But they would just have to wait and see how things worked out with their current situation first. It all depended on whether or not they could be satisfied that Rolf was no longer a threat.

Walking across the room, Devon wrinkled his nose as he placed the extra ammunition on the small table Nate had set up for him. Being soundproof also made it hard to get rid of the smell. There was the acrid scent of gunpowder, the heavy musky scent of sweat from the intense physical training and the almost rancid smell of unwashed bodies. One of the guys must have left their gym clothes lying around somewhere.

Devon breathed through his mouth and swore to find out who the pig was that couldn't be bothered cleaning up after himself. *Damn it! They were shifters, not animals!*

Devon checked his weapon then raised it, carefully taking aim at the target at the end of the makeshift range. But just as he was about to squeeze the trigger to fire off his first round, he saw movement out of the corner of his eye. Before he could even react to it, a heavy weight crashed into his arm. The shot went wide as the gun went flying out of his hand and skittered across the floor away from him.

Somehow, incredibly, Devon managed to keep his footing.

He jumped away and spun around to face his attacker, fear driving a sudden spike of adrenaline through his system and giving him the extra speed and agility he needed to escape the hand that reached out to grab hold of him.

Rolf's angry, twisted face snarled down at him, intensifying his fear as he quickly stumbled back even farther away from the man. He knocked into the table in his haste to put some distance between them, sending it crashing to the floor with a loud, echoing clatter.

"You have no idea the trouble you've caused me, little cat," Rolf snarled, his eyes thinning to angry slits. "You're so going to pay for making me track you down."

Devon managed to put several more feet between them without Rolf pinning him down. He guessed Rolf felt secure enough in the enclosed space to let him move away a little. Either that or he wanted to play for a while. It was obvious he didn't feel threatened or challenged.

Devon silently vowed to change that.

"How did you find me?" he asked, trying to buy time as he searched around wildly for options.

He finally spied the gun's butt peeking out from under a chair against the far wall. He knew he couldn't risk shifting forms, even though the urge to run was strong. It would leave him too vulnerable in an enclosed room with no opposable thumbs. His only hope lay about a dozen feet away, partially hidden under a seat. If he could make it to the gun he had a chance against Rolf, if not...well, he was through being a doormat. He was, at least, going to go down fighting. There was no way he was letting Rolf take him away from here.

Rolf growled. "It wasn't easy finding you, that's for sure. And for that, you're going to have to do some serious sucking up, if you know what I mean. Now get over here before I decide your useless hide's not worth the effort."

"Go away, Rolf. I'm not going anywhere with you." Devon tried hard to make his voice sound firm and even and was quite proud of how close he came to pulling it off.

"Go away, Rolf," the hulking warrior parroted. "You belong to me, bitch. You go where I say."

"You have no claim over me. Nate is my mate."

Rolf bared his teeth in a snarl. "Nate won't be a problem for much longer."

Fear like he had never felt before roared to life inside Devon. With the threat to his mate, another huge rush of adrenaline poured into his system, giving him a speed and strength he never knew he had inside him. This time when Rolf lunged it was as if it happened in slow motion. He saw every movement the other cat made. The way he extended, leaving himself vulnerable on one side. The slight overconfident gleam in the other man's eye that suggested he was slightly off peak form.

And Devon didn't hesitate to take advantage. He ducked and pivoted in one smooth movement—whipping around to grab hold of the legs of the overturned work table with both hands and swinging it around in a deadly arc at Rolf's head. It connected with a sickening crunch and Rolf rolled to the side, crying out in pain.

Devon didn't waste a moment. He dived for the handgun, and as soon as he felt its hard, reassuring weight against his palm, spun around to face Rolf.

While he was awkwardly positioned on the floor, Devon still held the gun steady and aimed straight for the man's heart. By then, Rolf had surged to his feet and was heading towards him—murderous rage clearly reflected in his eyes. But he froze when he saw the gun.

Devon remembered that Rolf already had experience with being on the wrong side of a bullet and pointed the gun with more aggression, hoping to get the other cat to back off.

"This is my home. This is my pride," Devon said fiercely, a dangerous resolve in his voice that Rolf would be a fool to ignore. "You can't have them!"

Devon felt like he had finally found himself. He had always felt compelled to care for others—his Master, his former clan mates, even his brother. But they hadn't needed him. All of them had either rejected or been oblivious to it, leaving him feeling abandoned, lost and adrift.

But now he had the kittens and Nate. He had young that were totally dependent on him and a mate that, while he might not need him, wanted him. Devon didn't just feel a need to care, he felt a soul deep need to protect and love the tiny creatures growing inside him, and he knew he wanted to share that with Nate — his soul mate.

"Go away, Rolf. Go back to your Master. I won't be going with you." The gun in Devon's hand didn't waiver a fraction as he pointed it at Rolf now. "And take a bath, you smell like an old jock strap."

Devon would never know later why he had goaded Rolf. Perhaps he *wanted* to shoot him. Perhaps he knew that he would never be safe until Rolf was dead. Either way, he knew he was ultimately responsible for what happened next.

Rolf snapped. A roar escaped his mouth as he lunged for Devon — totally disregarding the gun pointed at his chest. The deafening echo of the gun firing nearly masked the grunt Rolf made as the bullet penetrated his chest, heading straight for his heart. Nearly. Devon watched the look of shock and disbelief freeze on Rolf's face in a death mask as he slowly tumbled to the floor — blood rapidly fanning out to pool around his body.

Nate had warned him that he hadn't been mucking around with the bullets he had chosen. He had explained very clearly that he had gone for maximum damage — one shot, one kill. He hadn't wanted any risk of an attacker struggling on to continue his assault. But it was another thing altogether to see that reality.

Devon lowered the gun in shock. He hadn't consciously made the decision to fire the weapon. It had truly been self-preservation kicking in — a survival instinct that overrode his mental processes.

Devon tucked his knees up to his chest as the blood crept closer. He slowly lowered the gun to the floor beside him but couldn't seem to release it completely. It rested loosely in his grip as his only connection to reality.

He stared into Rolf's now sightless eyes and truly felt nothing. He wasn't sure he would be able to feel anything ever again.

He heard Nate's frightened cry from the door, but it sounded as if it came from far away, down a long tunnel. He looked up to see his mate running towards him — terror clearly showing on his face as he took in Rolf's body, the blood and his hunched form on the floor. He wanted to reassure the man, he really did, but he couldn't seem to form the words.

Suddenly, strong arms were wrapped around him. Hands were gliding over his body, assessing him for damage, he realised vaguely. They were gentle and tender, gradually rubbing some of the warmth and life back into his body.

"I'm all right," Devon finally managed through lips that felt thick and numb. Not really his.

"What happened?" Nate asked.

"He was here. Waiting for me. When I came to practice… Will I get in trouble?"

"No, baby. No," Nate reassured him. "We'll take care of this. No one will worry about this piece of shit."

Nate stared down at Rolf's body with open hostility and Devon suddenly felt the oddest surge of sadness and compassion. He thought of his babies, still safe and protected from the world.

Had life broken Rolf somehow, just as it had nearly broken him? Perhaps if Rolf's life had been different he would never have ended up the cat that he was. And he was the kittens' sire. Never their father — Devon knew that position was well and truly filled by the man currently hovering over him like a worried mother hen—but still their sire nevertheless.

"I want...I want him buried decently, Nate," Devon managed to whisper, still staring at Rolf's lifeless face. "Make sure he has somewhere...peaceful to rest."

One day the kittens might need to see it. He just didn't know. But he wanted to make sure it was somewhere...nice, if only for their sakes.

Nate looked at him with confusion, but made no comment. Long seconds stretched out between them, before Nate simply nodded. "Sure thing," he said quietly before reaching for the phone on his belt to get a team organised to dispose of Rolf's corpse.

Chapter Twelve

Pet stepped back into the shadows as another car rolled slowly past — searching out fresh meat in the dark, dank recesses under the fly-over. He looked around warily, eyeing the whores and derelicts suspiciously. It was dangerous out here. Not because of the circling predators cruising for hook-ups, or even the men and women with desperation and hopelessness in their eyes. No. It was the danger of being seen by a member of the pride while he was meeting with his Master that was the real worry.

At the thought, Pet hated them all a little more. They kept him from his Master. But Master had assigned him to spy on the Bayside pride, and he would do his duty proudly, however hard it was to be away from his Master.

It felt like a lifetime since he had seen the man. But at least the Master had insisted on a face-to-face meeting this time. The Master was becoming more and more paranoid about meeting. Pet was thrilled with the opportunity to see the man again. Of being close enough to be touched, even if he had to endure this damp, smelly place to get it. He could never regret a chance to be with his Master.

Suddenly, he felt the hairs on the back of his neck stand on end and the familiar prickle of his Master's magic work its way up and down his body. He shivered in anticipation and turned around quickly to see the shadows part around the older man, his emotionless black eyes glowing like shiny black beetle carapaces in the low light.

Like any good pet, his breath became faster in fear and excitement as he bowed his head reverently. "Master," he whispered in awe.

"The cat I sent to retrieve the one I want failed," the Master observed, soft accusation and threat lacing his voice.

"Yes, Grand-master Vladimir," he acknowledged solemnly, never once raising his eyes to the other man. He certainly wasn't foolish enough to offer any excuses.

"I want that cat, Pet. Get him for me."

"Of course, Master." Pet paused for a moment as he carefully considered his next words. The Master remained still and silent as if he knew he was about to speak. "My cover could be blown."

"Yes, Pet," the Master replied kindly, making him shiver again in response to the positive attention. "Do it. It's worth the risk."

He briefly considered how callously his Master accepted the risk he was taking. If the pride ever found out about his association with the mage before he could escape...

Pet ruthlessly pushed the thought away. His purpose was to serve and obey, not to question his Master. That was what he found so abhorrent about the rebellious pride he was working hard to bring down in the first place. They dared to question and doubt their Masters! He drew in a short, angry breath, trying to calm himself in his Master's presence.

While he struggled with his emotions, he vibrated in place with the need to serve his Master. The need to be petted and praised and used was overwhelming.

"Come here, Pet." Master Vladimir beckoned seductively.

Excited by the knowledge of what might be to come, Pet moved closer to the man who held him enthralled. Slim, but surprisingly strong arms came around him, and he stepped further into the man's embrace, wantonly tilting his head to expose his neck in blatant invitation. Silently, he begged his Master to take him. When the man made no move, he felt a whimpering plea work its way out of his mouth.

"Have you been a good boy, Pet?" The Master asked, his voice like rich, dark, smoky whisky.

"Yes, Master. Good boy. Good Pet." He bent and rubbed his cheek over the slightly smaller man's shoulder in a very cat like caress.

A firm hand grasped his hair cruelly and stopped his movement. He whimpered again, but went utterly still. After a few moments a warm, wet tongue swept over his neck along his pulsing carotid.

"Good kitty. You want to please your Master?" Despite the fingers clenched in his hair, Pet managed to nod with painful little jerks of his head. "You will please me when you bring me the cat. He's a Vess'al, Pet. A breeder. With him under our control, we will have not one but two Vess'als. We can breed more breeders." Vladimir's voice had become energised with his mounting excitement. "Think of it, Pet. With only a handful of Vess'al, we could breed armies of blood mages. We could eliminate the Circle Council once and for all and never again would our rightful place as the leaders of all magekind be taken from us. They will *all* bow before their Masters."

A fanatical light had come into the Master's strange, flat eyes, and Pet felt the swelling of the mage's erection pressing into him. He groaned and couldn't help the thrust of his pelvis as he tried to rub against the man's hardness. But the Master simply tightened his grip, making him wince and still against him once more.

"You get what you're given, cat."

After long moments of showing his absolute obedience to the man by remaining motionless, a tongue once again bathed his neck. Pet's breath came in shallow pants, but otherwise he remained silent and waited.

Suddenly, he felt the burning pierce of the mage's fangs sink into his throat, and he was helpless to stop the orgasm that rocketed through his body as his Master began to suckle. He felt the long, deep pulls of blood that the mage took from him and it prolonged his orgasmic bliss until flaring spots of light threatened to drag him down into unconsciousness.

He didn't care. He was completely addicted to his Master's kiss of death and would do anything to be in his embrace, even risk death for one more moment of this euphoria.

Capturing the cat his Master wanted so desperately was nothing compared to this. He would make it happen. He would make his Master so happy with him.

Nate was the real obstacle, he realised hazily. His constant hovering and observant, annoying presence was becoming more and more of a problem every day. Perhaps he could kill two birds—or cats as the case may be—with one stone.

It was his last, coherent thought as the edges of his vision began to darken and his mind shut down while his Master continued to suckle at his throat.

* * * *

Devon yawned and stretched as he slowly woke up from his mid-afternoon nap and worked the kinks out of his slightly stiff muscles. Blinking away the last vestiges of sleep, he raised himself up from the lounge and made his way into the kitchen in search of something to drink.

After the incident with Rolf in the workout room, Nate had hovered and fussed incessantly. Devon thought he had probably eaten more food, had more massages and been tucked in for more naps than anyone on the face of the planet. It was sweet, and made Devon feel very loved and protected, but it was starting to suffocate him.

Devon sighed in frustration as he reached up to snag a glass from the cupboard. Even with Rolf dead and buried, Nate was convinced Devon could still be in danger. He insisted that until they could work out how Rolf had escaped the police or why he was so focused on tracking Devon down, he was not to leave the apartment without him.

He wasn't sure how he felt about that. On the one hand, he knew it was Nate's way of showing him how much he loved him, and Devon loved Nate right back. But he was beginning to resent his overbearing attitude.

In the last few months, Devon knew he had changed. A lot. He no longer wanted to be closeted and sheltered. He wanted Nate to see he was a capable, resilient and resourceful mate. He wanted to be a true partner not a liability or, worse still, a kept pet. He wasn't some fragile, delicate ornament that needed to be locked away for his own protection, even if the extra naps were admittedly welcomed.

Reaching down, Devon gently rubbed the small swelling beginning to form over his belly. He had been so tired lately. He guessed the kittens might have something to do with that. But the last few days had been devoted to long naps, and now he wanted to get out again.

A loud banging on the door startled Devon out of his rumination and nearly made him drop the glass in his hand. When the knocking continued—harsh and insistent—Devon quickly put the glass down on the counter and hurried to the door, his heart rate picking up speed. He knew something was wrong. He could almost taste it in the air now.

As he opened the door, a panting Duncan leaned heavily against the frame. Devon felt the first stirrings of panic begin to edge its way into his mind. What on earth had happened to make Duncan look so terrified?

"You have to come with me. Nate's been hurt. They're taking him to Bayside Memorial." Duncan panted breathlessly.

"What happened?" Devon's anxiety morphed into true terror.

Nate was hurt. He had to get to his mate.

"A hit and run. Right outside the club. He only stepped out for a second." Duncan's wide-eyed shock mirrored his own mounting horror. "Come on, I'll take you to him."

Duncan began dragging him down the hall by the wrist and Devon stumbled along behind him, still stunned at thinking of his big, powerful mate lying hurt, or worse, somewhere.

"Is he..." Devon couldn't even say it. "Is he all right?"

"I don't know. He wasn't conscious when the ambulance got here. I came to get you. I knew you'd want to get to him straight away." The grim tone of Duncan's voice only made Devon more desperate to get to his mate, and he hurried his steps to catch up.

Oh, gods! What would he do without Nate? Devon could already feel himself starting to hyperventilate in panic.

When they reached the bottom of the private stairwell, Duncan led him towards the door to the back storage area. He could hear the muted music and general noise from the club but was too focused on getting to his mate to pay much attention.

Letting go of Devon's wrist, Duncan disengaged the locking bar and pushed the heavy fireproof door wide. It was really little more than a cubbyhole flanked on one side by the stairwell and the other by the back wall of the long main bar in the club. Stacked high with boxes and crates, Devon could hardly make out the door that opened behind the serving area on the far side as they hurried through into the dark, faintly dusty smelling storeroom.

The boxes and crates of supplies pressed in all around making the already cramped space feel claustrophobic — the thin aisle through the stock so narrow that they had to move forward single file. Devon found himself following along behind Duncan, who continually looked back to make sure Devon was still behind him.

The first prickle of unease skittered over his skin. He slowed for a moment. Something wasn't right. Why were they going out the back way? It was longer this way. Why didn't Duncan take him out through the front doors to the side parking area where everyone parked their cars?

Devon's mind finally registered the noise he had heard in the club. Why was everyone continuing on as normal? If Nate had been hurt, why was it only Duncan hovering and bustling around him? And why would they send him to a human hospital anyway? Wouldn't they call in Doctor Manning?

Devon stopped. He couldn't ignore the growing feeling of unease creeping up and down his spin. The whole situation felt wrong.

"Where are we going? Where's Nate?"

"Not much farther. Come on," Duncan replied, hurrying forward.

When Devon didn't follow, but remained in the middle of the small room flanked by boxes and beer kegs, Duncan turned around to face him. "Come on, my car's out the back. I'll take you to him," he promised.

Something in Duncan's eyes looked…off. Devon took a hesitant step back and Duncan's entire expression changed. He raised himself up to his full height and Devon felt suddenly threatened. He retreated another step and felt his back connect with a stack of boxes behind him. The distinctive clink of bottles as they jiggled together only highlighted Devon's sense of isolation.

"Come with me, Devon," Duncan commanded in a low menacing tone.

"Where are you taking me? Where's Nate?" Devon asked as he flattened himself back against the boxes behind him.

"You're a very popular cat, Devon," Duncan crooned snidely. "My Master wants you. He wants you badly. And what my Master wants, he gets. Now come along quietly or things are going to go very badly, very quickly for you here."

"Where's Nate?" Devon asked again desperately. It was the only thing he could think to focus on at the moment while he struggled to work out what was going on, and a way to get out of it.

Duncan's lips curled up into a terrifying parody of a smile. "Don't worry, Devon. Nate will be joining us soon enough." Duncan's voice was smooth and confident in his ability to force Devon to do as he demanded and Devon felt his anger slowly building.

"With you as bait he'll be like the proverbial lamb to the slaughter," Duncan laughed harshly.

The threat to Nate galvanised Devon's resolve to stand his ground. There was no way he was going with this hateful cat—especially not if it could in any way endanger Nate. He reached back, grabbing the neck of a random bottle clumsily from the open crate behind him. As Duncan began to stalk towards him, he hurled the bottle, but it was heavier than he had anticipated and the glass smashed against the floor rather than Duncan—spraying shards of glass and alcohol everywhere.

Duncan leapt back with a feral snarl. His eyes were hard and full of hatred as the pungent smell of brandy filled the tiny space.

Man, Nate is going to be pissed, Devon thought absently. Nate loved his brandy.

Duncan stepped around the shattered remains of the bottle growling softly in the back of his throat. Quickly, Devon grabbed another bottle, but before he had a chance to throw it, Duncan lunged at him, grabbing his wrist and pulling him off balance as he snatched the offending bottle away.

Completely unbalanced, Devon was sent crashing into the boxes across from them.

"I told you this would go badly if you didn't come along quietly," Duncan growled.

As Devon tried to get to his feet, Duncan casually pushed him over with an almost gentle push of his boot. Landing in an undignified sprawl on the hard concrete floor, Devon narrowly missed a large piece of the broken bottle as he went down again. Snatching it up and flipping over to defend himself, Devon felt the jagged edges of the glass bite into his hand, but ignored the pain in favour of lashing out at his attacker.

Duncan stumbled back away from the sharp, serrated weapon, and Devon pressed his advantage, brandishing it threateningly as he tried to work out the quickest way to get out of his current situation.

If I can just make it to the door, I might have a chance, Devon thought frantically.

Momentarily distracted, Devon was unprepared when Duncan spun around with a perfectly executed roundhouse kick to disarm him. Acting on instinct, Devon jumped clear but stumbled awkwardly over his own feet, landing heavily on his butt. He screamed in pain as the glass he was holding pierced his palm. He dropped the makeshift weapon and clutched his hand to his chest as hot blood began to run freely down his arm.

"You stupid slut! Why do you have to make this so difficult?" Duncan snarled as he paced forward.

From his position on the floor, Devon could see a small opening between the stacks as he looked around desperately for a way to escape. Whimpering softly as his hand began to throb and burn, he crawled towards it and squeezed inside the tiny hidey-hole.

Duncan let out an angry hiss and grabbed for his leg as it trailed behind. But Devon kicked out frantically, catching Duncan in the jaw and making him screech in protest as he reared back from the attack.

Flipping over, Devon used both his legs to push against the boxes he had just squeezed behind. Heaving with all his might, he managed to topple the heavy load and heard

Duncan let out a terrified cry before the boxes tumbled down on top of him.

When the avalanche of stock had finally settled, Devon could see Duncan had managed to escape most of the falling debris, but one of his legs was trapped under a heavy box. More wonderful than that, however, he heard the noise from the club suddenly fill the tiny space as one of the barmen came to investigate the commotion. Shouts of alarm soon followed and Duncan snarled, frantically struggling to extract himself.

Devon noticed that he was favouring his left ankle as he hobbled to his feet. He saw Duncan look between him and the door, obviously gauging whether he could manage to grab him and still make it out safely. But as more and more angry, battle-ready cat shifters burst through the door Duncan seemed to realise it was futile.

A look of pure hatred crossed Duncan's face as he reached into his pocket and pulled out a lighter. It flared to life with a flick of his thumb before he tossed it in the direction of the broken bottle. The spilt alcohol burst to life in a quick flash of light and a loud rush of air while Devon's would-be rescuers cried out in alarm and anger.

Devon could only watch helplessly as Duncan slipped quickly out the back door in the confusion and mayhem that followed.

Suddenly, Nate's strong arms were scooping him up and hurrying them out of the room. As his hand continued to throb viciously, a combination of shock and pain began to set in, making Devon shake uncontrollably. He buried his head against Nate's broad chest as he was carried through the club to the downstairs office. He knew he should be worried about the other cats as they tried to contain the flames. But all he could seem to focus on was the steady drumming beat of Nate's heart against his ear and how grateful he was to hear it.

* * * *

Nate paced with his hands in his pockets, trying to hide the trembling as Peter finished dressing the sutures he had put into the deep gash in Devon's hand. Nate struggled to stay in the room. He had the overwhelming urge to go out and hurt something—preferably that lying, sneaky, traitorous bastard, Duncan.

He had come so close, he realised. So close to losing the one man he didn't think he could live without any more. And once again he had let his mate down. He hadn't kept him safe.

It's all my fault, Nate acknowledged grimly. He should have been more careful, more alert.

"There you go," Peter announced cheerfully as he finished taping the thick bandage into place. "A few days, a few painkillers and you'll be good as new."

"Thank you, Doctor Manning," Devon replied in a polite, subdued voice that had Nate cursing himself all over again.

Devon had come so far, and yet right now he seemed like the reserved, frightened man Nate had first met in the club so many weeks ago.

As Peter stood up, he turned to Nate. "I want you to take good care of this mate of yours, Nate," he chided gently. "Call me if he shows any signs of infection, pain, fever. You know the drill. I'll take the sutures out later this week. Until then, try to keep them dry and clean."

"Thanks, Doc," Nate mumbled, wondering if Peter was subtly reprimanding him too. It would be no more than he deserved — the guilt was already beginning to eat away at him.

As Peter left, Nate couldn't bring himself to look at Devon.

"Are you mad at me?" Devon's voice was small and insecure.

"What?" Nate looked up in time to see the smaller man flinch at his loud shout of disbelief.

"I'm really sorry about the brandy. And the fire," Devon added carefully.

"I don't give a toss about the brandy and the fire never even got big enough to register with the alarm system," Nate replied, his emotions making his voice tight and slightly harsh.

"Then why won't you look at me?" Devon asked hesitantly. "Why haven't you even touched me since you put me down on the couch?"

Nate breathed out loudly in frustration. "It was my fault. I should have known Duncan was a traitor. I never trusted him," he finally admitted. "I should have protected you better. I shouldn't have been down here fussing with the club while you were left completely vulnerable to an attack."

Nate got down on his knees beside the man he loved with all his heart and took Devon's undamaged hand in his own. "I promise to take better care of you. Please forgive me, baby."

Devon jumped up — pushing him away roughly and Nate felt his heart begin to beat out a panicked rhythm. Devon couldn't forgive him, he realised. Not when he had not only failed to protect him, but had endangered the kittens as well.

"Stop it, Nate!" Devon demanded in a tight, angry voice. "Just stop it."

Nate wanted to sink through the floor in humiliation. He couldn't blame Devon for being angry. He was angry with himself.

"How could you possibly have known Duncan was a traitor?" Devon asked furiously. "I'm not some...some fragile hothouse flower you need to keep sheltered and protected. I can take care of myself. I *have* taken care of myself."

Nate stared, unable to come to grips with the complete deviation from what he had thought Devon would be upset with him for. Or the fact that the outspoken, confrontational man in front of him was his quiet, gentle lover.

Then Devon took a deep breath and reached out to cup Nate's face gently in one small hand, and Nate realised that Devon was indeed both—he was strong and determined, but still the same sweet man he loved. Nate flushed in shame as he realised he had been underestimating Devon terribly.

"I don't want you to think you always have to protect me, I don't want to be locked away any more, Nate. Don't you understand that?"

"Of course, I do," Nate cut in, but Devon ignored him.

"I want you to be proud of me," Devon's continued, his eyes pleading for acceptance and understanding. "I want to be someone you're proud to have by your side not someone you always feel you have to keep behind you. I'm strong, Nate. I've proven that to myself now. Maybe not as physically strong as you, but strong enough to survive."

"I know that, love," Nate whispered. "I just...I need to protect you, Devon. But never think I don't know how strong and capable you are. I will always be proud to call you my mate."

"When Duncan was trying to take me away, the only thing I could think of was that I couldn't let him use me to hurt you. I couldn't stand that, Nate. I fought Duncan to protect you too. It's the only thing I'm not sure I could survive. Though I'm not sure I'd want to if you ever stopped loving me."

"Never going to happen," Nate returned vehemently. "I love you with everything that I am, Devon. I will love you till the day I take my last breath, and even then I'll still be in love with you. For always, mate." He rested his forehead against Devon's, breathing in the soft, sweet scent of his mate.

"Make love to me," Devon whispered urgently.

Nate looked down into his lover's eyes. It was the first time Devon had ever asked to be intimate with him, and he hesitated for a moment, wanting to know it was really what he wanted.

"Are you sure?" Nate asked steadily, giving the man in his arms a chance to reconsider. After everything he had been through over the last few days, Nate wouldn't be surprised. If he wanted to collapse somewhere in a heap and sleep for a week, Nate wouldn't blame him.

But Devon growled low in his chest. Nate took the hint. He leant forward and gently licked at Devon's lips, before pushing his tongue farther inside for a slow, deep, claiming kiss. Devon moaned and thrust up against him desperately. Nate smiled at his hungry kitten—so innocent, so eager, no longer threatening to hand him his balls.

Slowly, Nate kissed his way down his lover's neck, leaving tiny nipping bites and soothing the stings with soft kisses and licks of his tongue. He began working at Devon's pants as he lowered himself to his knees in front of the man he loved, pushing up the hem of his shirt to lay gentle, loving kisses over the slight swell of his belly.

"Nate?" Devon's voice trembled slightly.

"Shh, love. Let me take care of you," Nate breathed, once again pressing kisses into Devon's belly.

"Ohhh!" Devon moaned in reply.

Finally, the fastenings gave way and Nate pushed Devon's pants and boxers down his smooth, firm legs, running a hand up and down before gently cupping the already tight balls between his legs. Devon's cock was long and curved up towards his stomach and Nate used his mouth to trace the network of veins along the shaft until he reached the tip where he leisurely tasted the clear drops of pre cum that had begun to ooze from the tiny slit.

Nate knew this wasn't going to last. His mate was too excited and worked up over recent events. But with excruciating slowness, trying to prolong the moment as much as possible, he slipped the head of Devon's cock between his lips, using his tongue to lick at the sensitive area just below the flared glans before pushing forward to take the whole shaft slowly into his mouth and down his throat.

Devon cried out in surprise, unable to stop the tiny thrusts of his hips as Nate continued to take him deep into his mouth and throat over and over again. Nate used his hands to guide Devon's thrusts into him — revelling in the feeling of his mate fucking his face mindlessly, moaning and writhing helplessly.

More and more pre cum slipped down his throat until Nate wasn't sure there would be anything left for the main event. He slipped a finger carefully into the crevice of Devon's butt cheeks. Working his finger until he found the tiny, puckered hole, finding it wet and ready, Nate gently eased his finger in and that was all it took. Devon exploded in a torrent of hot, creamy cum and a loud cry of ecstasy.

As Devon began to tremble and sag in his arms, Nate lowered him down to curl weakly in his arms. Nate petted and stroked the other man's back and hair as he descended from the heights of his orgasm, murmuring soft, loving sounds to him.

After a long time, Devon began to stir weakly.

"Hush, baby," Nate crooned "Just rest." He didn't want to lose the moment yet.

"But what about you?" Devon asked huskily.

"I have everything I want right now, sweetheart. Just rest." Nate felt a soft, rumbling purr against his palm that slowly faded as his mate drifted off to sleep in his arms. He realised he'd never been so content, so complete in his life. After a few minutes, he joined Devon in a light doze.

* * * *

The heavy blow connected with the side of Pet's head and set him flying back against a low lounge a few feet away. He lay stunned for a moment before carefully crawling back on his hands and knees and gingerly wiping the blood from his mouth. He didn't dare look up into the Master's furious face.

Pet wondered idly if he was going to die. He didn't want to die. He wanted to continue to serve his Master. He wanted to bring the rebel cats to their knees. And he wasn't finished with that pathetic little pleasure cat either. Devon would know his place in the order of things if it were the last thing Pet ever did.

Hopefully, his Master would let him live to fight another day. This wasn't over, Pet vowed, not by a long shot. Still, if his death was what his Master demanded of him, then he would, of course, die.

Suddenly, a hand fisted painfully in his hair and jerked his head back until he was looking straight up in the murderous expression on his beloved Master's face. Shame welled up in Pet's chest at having failed the man. He quickly blinked away the tears that tried to pool in his eyes.

"How could you let this happen, Pet? How dare you fail me?" the Master screamed.

"I'm so sorry, Master," Pet whispered in an agonised voice.

Livid bruises were already forming over his naked and bleeding body, but the pain in his heart at failing his Master was so much worse that he hardly noticed them.

"Such a complete fuck-up! I should have known a stupid, pathetic cat like you couldn't get the job done," Vladimir raged.

"He was warned of the threat, Master. They knew Devon was at risk. That's why they moved him to The Compound. They knew Rolf was coming. They must have known I was coming, too," Pet pleaded, desperate to live long enough that he might redeem himself and serve his Master just a little longer. At least until he could see the rebellion come to an end.

Vladimir froze. "What do you mean they knew Rolf was coming?" he demanded, his voice like cold, dark chips of frozen hell.

Pet shivered involuntarily. "I'm not sure, Master. Someone warned them that Devon was in danger." He licked his bloody lips nervously, sensing a possible reprieve as he tasted the heavy, metallic essence of his own blood. Above him, Master Vladimir remained motionless, his fist still clenching tightly in Pet's hair.

"Only a handful knew I had released Rolf to track down the Vess'al," he murmured quietly to himself, his expression thoughtful and considering.

A speculative light shone in his eyes, then a sudden burst of burning fury before Master Vladimir stomped to the door, throwing it open wide as he screamed for his apprentice.

"Riven!" he bellowed angrily. "Where is my son? Where is Talan?"

Epilogue

Devon clutched Nate's hand as they walked up the path to the front door of a house he barely remembered. It had been three months since he had been here, and everything had changed. Everything except how anxious he was about seeing Ethan again.

It was early evening and the lights were on, so obviously someone was home but that only made Devon even more nervous about ringing the bell and drawing attention to himself. From inside loud, energetic music could be heard and somewhere, in the distance, Devon could hear pots and pans being moved about in the kitchen.

"Nervous?" Nate finally asked softly beside him.

"Do you think he's angry at me?" Devon whispered as he considered the bright red door and pretty, white swing seat gently rocking in the breeze.

"No, baby. I don't think he'll be angry that you needed some time. He's probably been worried, but not angry."

Nate didn't push and Devon was immensely grateful for that. It made him feel better knowing Nate would support him whatever he decided to do. Squaring his shoulders, Devon stepped up onto the landing and pressed the front doorbell—unable to stop the slight tremble in his nerveless fingers.

"I'll get it!" shouted an achingly familiar voice from inside, followed by footsteps that heralded Devon's last chance to make a run for it.

Suddenly, the door flew wide and Devon's last chance disappeared as his brother's beautiful smiling face was revealed. The smile slowly drained from Ethan's face as they stared into one another's eyes in silent shock.

Devon felt his heart beat wildly as he waited for his sibling to react. He wanted to turn and run more than ever as his brother stood frozen to the spot just looking at him. Ethan's rejection was something he wasn't sure he was ready to face yet.

Does he hate me for leaving? Is he disgusted by what happened to me? What Rolf did? And what about when he finds out about the kittens?

A strong hand settled at Devon's waist, soothing and settling his panic. Nate was with him. Everything would be all right.

"Devon?" Ethan said breathlessly, as if not able to believe his eyes. But saying his name seemed to break the spell between them. Devon found himself rocked backwards by the weight of his tearful twin. "Oh! Oh gods! Devon! I can't believe you're here. I was so worried. Where have you been? Oh gods! Devon!"

Tears pricked his eyes, even as Devon felt his heart swell and fill with joy at Ethan's enthusiastic embrace. He was finally reunited with his beloved brother. But more than that, he realised that the pain, anger and misery that had driven him away were simply…gone. Vanished. As if they had never existed. All that remained was the love he had for his sibling. It was as if everything else had been washed away, and he was clean and new again.

"I love you, Ethan. I'm sorry I had to go away to remember that," he sobbed brokenly.

Ethan pulled back just enough to look him in the eye, tears still flowing freely down his cheeks.

"I love you too, baby brother. I'm so sorry. For everything. Oh gods! I'm so sorry, Devon."

Devon placed his fingers gently over his brother's mouth to cut him off. "Don't be. You were right to want more. And the rest… I'm so happy now, Ethan. Truly happy. I never even knew I could be happy like this."

Devon spotted the taller, broad shouldered figure of his brother's mate walking down the hall towards them from the back of the house. He filled up the small space as he stepped up behind Ethan.

"Who is it, babe?" Michael asked curiously as he approached. Once he saw Devon, however, he stopped dead in his tracks, momentarily stunned. "Devon? Is that you?"

Devon nodded nervously. He hadn't really had a chance to get to know Ethan's mate, and what little interaction they'd had mainly consisted of them fighting either each other or for their lives against Rolf.

"Oh! Oh! Wow! Devon!" Michael cried, his face lighting up with a smile of welcome and pleasure as he tugged at Ethan's arm. "Ethan, let your brother come in."

The joy the man apparently had in Ethan finally being reunited with his lost sibling was infectious. As they were all ushered inside, Devon couldn't help the huge smile that threatened to split his face. Impulsively, he reached for Nate to pull him into a grateful hug. Without Nate's support, he might never have found the courage and strength to try to get back together with his brother.

"And who's this?" Ethan asked in a teasing, good-natured tone, his eyes twinkling with mischief as he eyed Nate with obvious approval.

"Behave, kitten," Michael growled, playfully slapping Ethan's butt with obviously more noise than actual sting, because Ethan giggled.

Devon took a deep, steadying breath. "This is my mate," he announced shyly, but with deep pride. "Nate."

"Hello," Nate said, holding his hand out for the traditional human handshake, which Michael grasped and shook happily.

As Nate and Michael politely shook hands, Devon reached for his brother and pulled him into a tight embrace so he could rub his cheek over him. He wanted to put his scent back on his litter mate. He wanted them to be as close as they had been before. When Devon heard and felt Ethan's purr of pleasure, he relaxed into his brother's arms and began to purr himself. Everything really was going to be all right, just as Nate had promised when they had left the club to come here.

"Missed you, brother," Ethan rumbled into his ear as he rubbed back.

"Missed you, too," Devon returned quietly.

"I'm sorry, Devon," Ethan whispered in a tone of deep remorse. "I never meant for you to get hurt."

"I know, Ethan. I was angry," Devon confessed, hanging his head and pulling back slightly. He knew he had to get everything off his chest once and for all, but it was hard. "I was so angry with you, Ethan. I couldn't even think straight. I was hurt and confused. I wanted...I wanted someone to pay, and I wanted to hurt...you. I'm sorry, Ethan." A deep sense of shame washed over him at

Ethan's shocked expression. "I wanted...revenge, I guess, for what happened to me. That's why I had to run away. I couldn't handle all the feelings that were bubbling up inside me."

Tears were once more streaming down Ethan's face. Devon couldn't stand the thought of making his brother cry. He rubbed his cheek against Ethan's shoulder, as he had so many times in the past, trying to soothe and comfort him. It only made his poor brother sob harder and curl around him in a fierce hug.

"I don't want that now. I don't want revenge, at least not against you. And the only revenge I plan on taking out on anyone else is to live and love fully for the first time in my life, despite everything I've had to go through to get here. Without you, I would never have known, Ethan. I would never have known what it was to be loved, truly loved just for myself. I would never have met Nate. I would never..." Devon hesitated, unconsciously placing a protective hand over his belly. He knew there was no easy way to say or explain this.

Taking a deep breath, he felt strong arms wrap around him from behind. He began running his hand over the arm that encircled his waist, loving the feeling of support, love and protection Nate offered silently without him ever needing to ask for it.

"There's no easy way to go about telling you this but... Well, Nate and I are going to have children. Soon. Kittens. Our babies."

Devon ran out of words as he waited anxiously for Ethan's reaction, but the sound of Nate purring loudly in his ear as he nuzzled gently into his neck went a long way to easing his frayed nerves.

Both Ethan and Michael looked stunned, disbelief creeping into their expressions, but Devon knew it would be hard to deny the evidence that was squirming under his hand.

Devon froze.

"Did you feel that?" he asked Nate in wonder.

"Oh, wow!" he replied with awe.

"But…" Michael didn't seem to know how to finish the sentence. "I mean…that's not…how?" he finally managed.

"It's a really long story. But there's something else we have to tell you about, too. You have to be careful." Michael looked slightly panicked for a moment before he rushed to reassure the man. "Not about that. At least, I don't think so." He frowned, wondering if it could be possible, whether Ethan could be a Vess'al too. They were twins.

Oh, well! Only time would tell. Michael and Ethan looked stunned as they both sat down heavily on one of the couches. "No, what I mean is there's something going on. Something to do with the masters. You have to be careful. There are things happening among the mages. Nate's trying to find out what's going on through one of his contacts, but he's suddenly disappeared, and we're not sure why or what's happened to him. Promise me you'll both be careful. Maybe they should go out to The Compound." Devon turned in Nate's arms to look up at him in growing concern.

"Shh, baby. It'll be all right. But I think you're confusing your brother and his mate. Maybe you should start at the beginning," Nate calmly suggested, still holding him gently.

"Okay!" Devon agreed before turning back to the others.

Devon knew this was going to be a long night as Nate steered him to one of the seats to start telling his story from the beginning. Nate settled in beside him protectively. Devon took a moment to enjoy the feel of his mate wrapping his arms around him, and their kittens nestled securely under his palm. And suddenly he realised that everything really was going to be all right. He had finally found a home — Nate.

About the Author

Jade Archer was born in 2010 after a prolonged pregnancy and labour of over 34 years! I've decided she is about 24, enjoys long walks in the country because she does not have five kids and a husband to care for, eats as much chocolate as she wants because she never has to worry about putting on weight (must be all those long walks!) and can often be found planning her next whirlwind world tour or endlessly typing away (without any interruptions) on another hot and steamy erotic romance. It might be space pirates; it might be shifters or a lonely vampire with a hunger for the girl next door, one thing is for sure, she loves variety and cannot wait to meet the next characters destined to fall in love.

Jade Arche loves to hear from readers. You can find her contact information, website details and author profile page at http://www.total-e-bound.com.

Total-E-Bound Publishing

www.total-e-bound.com

Take a look at our exciting range of literagasmic™
erotic romance titles and discover pure quality
at Total-E-Bound.